THE
CALCULATING
STARS

TOR BOOKS BY MARY ROBINETTE KOWAL

THE GLAMOURIST HISTORIES

Shades of Milk and Honey
Glamour in Glass
Without a Summer
Valour and Vanity
Of Noble Family

Ghost Talkers
The Calculating Stars

THE CALCULATING STARS

MARY ROBINETTE KOWAL

TOR

A TOM DOHERTY ASSOCIATES BOOK ✳ NEW YORK

THE CALCULATING STARS

Copyright © 2018 by Mary Robinette Kowal

A Tor Book
Published by Tom Doherty Associates
175 Fifth Avenue
New York, NY 10010

www.tor-forge.com

Tor® is a registered trademark of Macmillan Publishing Group, LLC.

The Library of Congress Cataloging-in-Publication Data
is available upon request.

ISBN 978-0-7653-7838-5 (trade paperback)
ISBN 978-1-4668-6124-4 (ebook)

Our books may be purchased in bulk for promotional,
educational, or business use. Please contact your local bookseller
or the Macmillan Corporate and Premium Sales Department
at 1-800-221-7945, extension 5442, or by email at
MacmillanSpecialMarkets@macmillan.com.

First Edition: July 2018

Printed in the United States of America

0 9 8 7 6 5 4 3 2 1

For my niece, Emily Harrison,
who is in the Mars Generation

'Tis thought the king is dead; we will not stay.
The bay-trees in our country are all wither'd
And meteors fright the fixed stars of heaven;
The pale-faced moon looks bloody on the earth
And lean-look'd prophets whisper fearful change;
Rich men look sad and ruffians dance and leap,
The one in fear to lose what they enjoy,
The other to enjoy by rage and war:
These signs forerun the death or fall of kings.

—*Richard II*, by William Shakespeare

PART I

ONE

**PRESIDENT DEWEY CONGRATULATES
NACA ON SATELLITE LAUNCH**

March 3, 1952—(AP)—The National Advisory
Committee for Aeronautics successfully put its third
satellite into orbit, this one with the capability of sending radio signals down to Earth and taking measure-
ments of the radiation in space. The president denies
that the satellite has any military purpose and says
that its mission is one of scientific exploration.

Do you remember where you were when the Meteor hit?
I've never understood why people phrase it as a question,
because of course you remember. I was in the mountains
with Nathaniel. He had inherited this cabin from his father
and we used to go up there for stargazing. By which I mean:
sex. Oh, don't pretend that you're shocked. Nathaniel and
I were a healthy young married couple, so most of the stars
I saw were painted across the inside of my eyelids.

If I had known how long the stars were going to be hidden, I would have spent a lot more time outside with the
telescope.

We were lying in the bed with the covers in a tangled
mess around us. The morning light filtered through silver
snowfall and did nothing to warm the room. We'd been
awake for hours, but hadn't gotten out of bed yet for obvious

reasons. Nathaniel had his leg thrown over me and was snuggled up against my side, tracing a finger along my collarbone in time with the music on our little battery-powered transistor radio.

I stretched under his ministrations and patted his shoulder. "Well, well . . . my very own 'Sixty Minute Man.'"

He snorted, his warm breath tickling my neck. "Does that mean I get another fifteen minutes of kissing?"

"If you start a fire."

"I thought I already did." But he rolled up onto his elbow and got out of bed.

We were taking a much needed break after a long push to prepare for the National Advisory Committee for Aeronautics's launch. If I hadn't also been at NACA doing computations, I wouldn't have seen Nathaniel awake anytime during the past two months.

I pulled the covers up over myself and turned on my side to watch him. He was lean, and only his time in the Army during World War II kept him from being scrawny. I loved watching the muscles play under his skin as he pulled wood off the pile under the big picture window. The snow framed him beautifully, its silver light just catching in the strands of his blond hair.

And then the world outside lit up.

If you were anywhere within five hundred miles of Washington, D.C., at 9:53 a.m. on March 3rd, 1952, and facing a window, then you remember that light. Briefly red, and then so violently white that it washed out even the shadows. Nathaniel straightened, the log still in his hands.

"Elma! Cover your eyes!"

I did. That light. It must be an A-bomb. The Russians had been none too happy with us since President Dewey took office. God. The blast center must have been D.C. How long until it hit us? We'd both been at Trinity for the atom bomb tests, but all of the numbers had run out of my head. D.C. was far enough away that the heat wouldn't hit us, but it would kick off the war we had all been dreading.

As I sat there with my eyes squeezed shut, the light faded. Nothing happened. The music on the radio continued to play. If the radio was playing, then there wasn't an electromagnetic pulse. I opened my eyes. "Right." I hooked a thumb at the radio. "Clearly not an A-bomb."

Nathaniel had spun away to get clear of the window, but he was still holding the log. He turned it over in his hands and glanced outside. "There hasn't been any sound yet. How long has it been?"

The radio continued to play and it was still "Sixty Minute Man." What had that light been? "I wasn't counting. A little over a minute?" I shivered as I did the speed-of-sound calculations and the seconds ticked by. "Zero point two miles per second. So the center is at least twenty miles away?"

Nathaniel paused in the process of grabbing a sweater and the seconds continued to tick by. Thirty miles. Forty. Fifty. "That's . . . that's a big explosion to have been that bright."

Taking a slow breath, I shook my head, more out of desire for it not to be true than out of conviction. "It wasn't an A-bomb."

"I'm open to other theories." He hauled his sweater on, the wool turning his hair into a haystack of static.

The music changed to "Some Enchanted Evening." I got out of bed and grabbed a bra and the trousers I'd taken off the day before. Outside, snow swirled past the window. "Well . . . they haven't interrupted the broadcast, so it has to be something fairly benign, or at least localized. It could be one of the munitions plants."

"Maybe a meteor."

"Ah!" That idea had some merit and would explain why the broadcast hadn't been interrupted. It was a localized thing. I let out a breath in relief. "And we could have been directly under the flight path. That would explain why there hasn't been an explosion, if what we were seeing was just it burning up. All light and fury, signifying nothing."

Nathaniel's fingers brushed mine and he took the ends of the bra out of my hand. He hooked the strap and then he ran his hands up my shoulder blades to rest on my upper arms. His hands were hot against my skin. I leaned back into his touch, but I couldn't quite stop thinking about that light. It had been *so* bright. He squeezed me a little, before releasing me. "Yes."

"Yes, it was a meteor?"

"Yes, we should go back."

I wanted to believe that it was just a fluke, but I had been able to see the light through my closed eyes. While we got dressed, the radio kept playing one cheerful tune after another. Maybe that was why I pulled on my hiking boots instead of loafers, because some part of my brain kept waiting for things to get worse. Neither of us commented on it, but every time a song ended, I looked at the radio, certain that this time someone would tell us what had happened.

The floor of the cabin shuddered.

At first I thought a heavy truck was rolling past, but we were in the middle of nowhere. The porcelain robin that sat on the bedside table danced along its surface and fell. You would think that, as a physicist, I would recognize an earthquake faster. But we were in the Poconos, which was geologically stable.

Nathaniel didn't worry about that as much and grabbed my hand, pulling me into the doorway. The floor bucked and rolled under us. We clung to each other like in some sort of drunken foxtrot. The walls twisted and then . . . then the whole place came down. I'm pretty sure that I hollered.

When the earth stopped moving, the radio was still playing.

It buzzed as if a speaker were damaged, but somehow the battery kept it going. Nathaniel and I were lying, pressed together, in the remnants of the doorframe. Cold air swirled around us. I brushed the dust from his face.

My hands were shaking. "Okay?"

"Terrified." His blue eyes were wide, but both pupils were the same size, so . . . that was good. "You?"

I paused before answering with the social "fine," took a breath, and did an inventory of my body. I was filled with adrenaline, but I hadn't wet myself. Wanted to, though. "I'll be sore tomorrow, but I don't think there's any damage. To me, I mean."

He nodded and craned his neck around, looking at the little cavity we were buried inside. Sunlight was visible through a gap where one of the plywood ceiling panels had fallen against the remnants of the doorframe. It took some doing, but we were able to push and pry the wreckage to crawl out of that space and clamber across the remains of the cabin.

If I had been alone . . . Well, if I had been alone, I wouldn't have gotten into the doorway in time. I wrapped my arms around myself and shivered despite my sweater.

Nathaniel saw me shiver and squinted at the wreckage. "Might be able to get a blanket out."

"Let's just go to the car." I turned, praying that nothing had fallen on it. Partly because it was the only way to the airfield where our plane was, but also because the car was borrowed. Thank heavens, it was sitting undamaged in the small parking area. "There's no way we'll find my purse in that mess. I can hot-wire it."

"Four minutes?" He stumbled in the snow. "Between the flash and the quake."

"Something like that." I was running numbers and distances in my head, and I'm certain he was, too. My pulse was beating against all of my joints and I grabbed for the smooth certainty of mathematics. "So the explosion center is still in the three-hundred-mile range."

"The airblast will be what . . . half an hour later? Give or take." For all the calm in his words, Nathaniel's hands shook as he opened the passenger door for me. "Which means we have another . . . fifteen minutes before it hits?"

The air burned cold in my lungs. Fifteen minutes. All of those years doing computations for rocket tests came into terrifying clarity. I could calculate the blast radius of a V2 or the potential of rocket propellant. But this . . . this was not numbers on a page. And I didn't have enough information to make a solid calculation. All I knew for certain was that, as long as the radio was playing, it wasn't an A-bomb. But whatever had exploded was huge.

"Let's try to get as far down the mountain as we can before the airblast hits." The light had come from the southeast. Thank God, we were on the western side of the mountain, but southeast of us was D.C. and Philly and Baltimore and hundreds of thousands of people.

Including my family.

I slid onto the cold vinyl seat and leaned across it to pull out wires from under the steering column. It was easier to focus on something concrete like hot-wiring a car than on whatever was happening.

Outside the car, the air hissed and crackled. Nathaniel leaned out the window. "Shit."

"What?" I pulled my head out from under the dashboard

and looked up, through the window, past the trees and the snow, and into the sky. Flame and smoke left contrails in the air. A meteor would have done some damage, exploding over the Earth's surface. A meteorite, though? It had actually *hit* the Earth and ejected material through the hole it had torn in the atmosphere. Ejecta. We were seeing pieces of the planet raining back down on us as fire. My voice quavered, but I tried for a jaunty tone anyway. "Well . . . at least you were wrong about it being a *meteor*."

I got the car running, and Nathaniel pulled out and headed down the mountain. There was no way we would make it to our plane before the airblast hit, but I had to hope that it would be protected enough in the barn. As for us . . . the more of the mountain we had between us and the airblast, the better. An explosion that bright, from three hundred miles away . . . the blast was not going to be gentle when it hit.

I turned on the radio, half-expecting it to be nothing but silence, but music came on immediately. I scrolled through the dial looking for something, anything that would tell us what was happening. There was just relentless music. As we drove, the car warmed up, but I couldn't stop shaking.

Sliding across the seat, I snuggled up against Nathaniel. "I think I'm in shock."

"Will you be able to fly?"

"Depends on how much ejecta there is when we get to the airfield." I had flown under fairly strenuous conditions during the war, even though, officially, I had never flown combat. But that was only a technical specification to make the American public feel more secure about women in the military. Still, if I thought of ejecta as anti-aircraft fire, I at least had a frame of reference for what lay ahead of us. "I just need to keep my body temperature from dropping any more."

He wrapped one arm around me, pulled the car over to the wrong side of the road, and tucked it into the lee of a craggy overhang. Between it and the mountain, we'd be shielded from the worst of the airblast. "This is probably the best shelter we can hope for until the blast hits."

"Good thinking." It was hard not to tense, waiting for the airblast. I rested my head against the scratchy wool of Nathaniel's jacket. Panicking would do neither of us any good, and we might well be wrong about what was happening.

A song cut off abruptly. I don't remember what it was; I just remember the sudden silence and then, finally, the announcer. Why had it taken them nearly half an hour to report on what was happening?

I had never heard Edward R. Murrow sound so shaken. "Ladies and gentlemen . . . Ladies and gentlemen, we interrupt this program to bring you some grave news. Shortly before ten this morning, what appears to have been a meteor entered the Earth's atmosphere. The meteor has struck the ocean just off the coast of Maryland, causing a massive ball of fire, earthquakes, and other devastation. Coastal residents along the entire Eastern Seaboard are advised to evacuate inland because additional tidal waves are expected. All other citizens are asked to remain inside, to allow emergency responders to work without interruption." He paused, and the static hiss of the radio seemed to reflect the collective nation holding our breath. "We go now to our correspondent Phillip Williams from our affiliate WCBO of Philadelphia, who is at the scene."

Why would they have gone to a Philadelphia affiliate, instead of someone at the scene in D.C.? Or Baltimore?

At first, I thought the static had gotten worse, and then I realized that it was the sound of a massive fire. It took me a moment longer to understand. It had taken them this long to find a reporter who was still alive, and the closest one had been in Philadelphia.

"I am standing on the US-1, some seventy miles north of where the meteor struck. This is as close as we were able to get, even by plane, due to the tremendous heat. What lay under me as we flew was a scene of horrifying devastation. It is as if a hand had scooped away the capital and taken with it all of the men and women who resided there. As of yet, the condition of the president is unknown, but—" My heart clenched when his voice broke. I had listened to Williams report the Second World War without breaking stride. Later, when I saw where he had been standing, I was amazed that he was able to speak at all. "But of Washington itself, nothing remains."

TWO

ANNOUNCER: This is the BBC World News for March 3, 1952. Here is the news and this is Robert Robinson. In the early hours of the morning a meteorite struck just outside the capital of the United States of America with a force greater than the bombs at Hiroshima and Nagasaki. The resulting firestorm has swept out from Washington, D.C. for hundreds of miles.

I kept running the numbers in my head after the radio finally, finally reported the news. It was easier than thinking about the big picture. About the fact that we lived in D.C. That we knew people there. That my parents were—

From D.C., it would take a little over twenty-four minutes for the airblast to hit. I tapped the dashboard clock. "It should hit soon."

"Yeah." My husband covered his face with his hands and leaned forward against the steering wheel. "Were your parents . . . ?"

"Home. Yes." I could not stop shaking. The only breaths I could draw were too fast and too shallow. I clenched my jaw and held my breath for a moment, with my eyes squeezed shut.

The seat shifted as Nathaniel wrapped his arms around me and pulled me close. He bowed his head over me so that I was sealed in a little cocoon of tweed and wool. His parents had been older than mine and had passed away some years ago, so he knew what I needed, and just held me.

"I just thought . . . I mean, Grandma is a hundred and three. I thought Daddy was going to go forever."

He made a sharp inhalation, as if he'd been stabbed.

"What?"

Nathaniel sighed and pulled me closer. "There were tidal wave warnings."

"Oh God." Grandma lived in Charleston. She wasn't in a beach house, but still, the entire city was low-lying and right on the coast. And then there were my aunts and uncles and cousins and Margaret, who'd just had a baby. I tried to sit up, but Nathaniel's arms were too tight around me. "When will it hit? The meteor struck a little before ten. But how big was it? And the water depth . . . I need a map and—"

"Elma." Nathaniel squeezed me tighter. "Elma. Sh . . . You can't solve for this."

"But Grandma—"

"I know, sweetie. I know. When we get to the plane, we can radi—"

The shock of the explosion shattered the car windows. It roared on and on, vibrating through my chest like a rocket leaving a launchpad. The oscillations pressed against my skin, filling every part of my consciousness with roaring waves and then secondary and tertiary explosions. I clung to Nathaniel, and he clung to the steering wheel, as the car bucked and slid across the road.

The world groaned and roared and wind howled through the empty window frames.

When the sound died away, the car had moved halfway across the road. Around us, trees lay on the ground in tidy rows, as if some giant had arranged them. Not all of them were down, but the ones that remained standing had been stripped of snow and whatever leaves they had left.

The windshield was just gone. The driver's side window lay on top of us in a laminated sheet of spiderwebbed safety glass. I pushed it up, and Nathaniel helped shove it out the door. Blood trickled from little scrapes on his face and hands.

He lifted a hand to my face. "You're bleeding." His voice sounded like he was underwater, and he frowned as he spoke.

"You too." My own voice was muffled. "Ear damage?"

He nodded and rubbed his face, smearing the blood into a scarlet film. "At least we can't hear the news."

I laughed, because sometimes you have to, even when things aren't funny. I reached over to turn the radio off and stopped with my hand on the dial.

There was no sound. This wasn't a matter of being deafened by the blast; the radio was silent. "They must have lost their broadcast tower."

"See if there's another station." He put the car into gear and we crept forward a few feet. "No. Wait. Sorry. We're going to have to walk."

Even if the car had been in pristine condition, there were too many trees down across the road to drive it very far. But it was only two miles to the airfield, and we hiked it in the summer sometimes. Maybe—maybe we could still make it to Charleston before the tidal wave hit. If the plane was okay. If the air was clear. If we had enough time. The odds were against all of those, but what else could I do except hope?

We got out of the car and started to walk.

Nathaniel helped me scramble over a tree trunk. I slipped in the slush as I stepped down, and if he hadn't had my arm, I would have landed on my rump. I kept trying to hurry, but it wouldn't do anyone any good if I broke my neck or even just an arm.

He grimaced at the melting snow. "Temperature is rising."

"Maybe I should have packed a swimsuit." I patted his arm as we kept going. I was being flippant in an effort to keep up a brave front, which would help Nathaniel worry less about me. In theory.

At least the exertion meant that I had stopped shaking. I hadn't been hearing any birdsong, but I wasn't sure if that was due to the hearing damage or because they weren't singing. The road was blocked in most places, but it was easier to orient ourselves if we stayed along it than if we tried to go cross-country, and we couldn't afford to get lost. It was slow going, and even with the warm air from the blast, we weren't dressed for an extended stay outside.

"You don't really think the plane will still be there?" The cuts on Nathaniel's face had stopped bleeding, but the blood and dirt gave him an almost piratical appearance. If pirates wore tweed.

I picked my way around the crown of a tree. "All other factors being equal, the airfield is closer than town, and—"

There was an arm on the road. No body. Just a bare arm. It ended at a rough and bloody shoulder. The specimen had probably been an adult Caucasian male in his thirties. The fingers were curled delicately up to the sky.

"God." Nathaniel stopped next to me.

Neither of us were squeamish, and the successive shocks had created a sort of numb haze. I stepped closer to the arm, and then looked up the hill. Only a few trees were standing, but their crowns, even denuded of leaves, masked the landscape in a tracery of branches. "Hello?"

Nathaniel cupped his hands around his mouth and hollered, "Hello! Is anyone there?"

Except for the wind rustling the branches, the hill was silent.

I'd seen worse things than a severed limb at the front when ducking in to pick up a plane and transport it. This wasn't a war, but there would be that many deaths. Burying the arm seemed fruitless. Still, leaving it seemed . . . wrong.

I sought Nathaniel's hand. "Baruch dayan ha'emet."

His rough baritone joined mine. Our prayer was less for this unknown man, who probably wasn't Jewish, and more for all the people he embodied. For my parents and all the thousands—the hundreds of thousands—of people who had died today.

That was when I finally began to weep.

It took us another four hours to make it to the airstrip. Understand that in the summer we often hiked that route in about an hour. The gentle Pennsylvania mountains were little more than hills.

This trip was . . . difficult.

The arm was not the worst thing we saw. We encountered no one living on our way down to the airfield. More trees were standing here, although anything with shallow roots was down. But I felt the first hope since the light of the blast, because we heard a car.

The purr of an automobile idling crept through the trees to meet us. Nathaniel met my gaze, and we started to run down the road, scrambling over trunks and fallen branches, skirting debris and dead animals, skidding in the slush and ash. All the while, the car got louder.

When we burst free of the last obstruction, we were across from the airstrip. It was really just a field, but Mr. Goldman had known Nathaniel since he was a kid, and kept a strip mowed for us. The barn was twisted at a weird angle, but standing. We'd gotten incredibly lucky.

The airstrip was just mowed grass, set between the trees on a gentle plateau. It ran roughly east to west and was enough in the direction of the airblast that most of the trees had been pushed down parallel to it, leaving it clear.

The road ran along the east end of the airstrip and then curved to follow it on the north side. There, partially obscured by the remaining trees, was the vehicle that we'd been hearing.

It was the red Ford pickup that Mr. Goldman drove. Nathaniel and I hurried down the road, and around the bend. The road was blocked by a tree here, and the truck was pressed up against it as if Mr. Goldman were trying to push it out of the way.

"Mr. Goldman!" Nathaniel hollered and waved his arms.

The windows of the truck were all gone and Mr. Goldman was slumped against the side of the door. I ran toward the car, hoping he was just unconscious. Nathaniel and I had at least had the benefit of expecting the airblast and had been braced and relatively sheltered when it hit.

But Mr. Goldman . . .

I slowed as I reached the truck. Nathaniel used to tell me stories about his childhood trips to the cabin and how Mr. Goldman had always had peppermint stick candy for him.

He was dead. I did not need to touch him or feel for a pulse. The tree branch that had been driven through his neck answered that question.

THREE

ANNOUNCER: This is the BBC World News for March 3, 1952. Here is the news and I'm Raymond Baxter. As fires continue to rage on the east coast of the United States, other countries are beginning to see the first effects of this morning's meteorite strike. Tidal waves are reported in Morocco, Portugal, and Ireland.

As a Women Airforce Service Pilot during the Second World War, I often flew transport missions with planes that were barely airworthy. My little Cessna was more flyable than some of the planes I'd gotten off the ground as a WASP. Dusty and scuffed, yes, but after the most careful preflight check in the history of aviation, I got her airborne.

As soon as we were up, I made a left bank to turn us south toward Charleston. We both knew it was probably futile, but I had to try. As the plane swung around, what remained of my irrational hope died. The sky to the east was a long dark wall of dust and smoke, lit from beneath by an inferno. If you've seen forest fires, you know a little of what this was like. The current fire stretched to the curvature of the Earth, as if someone had peeled back the mantle and opened a gateway into Hell itself. Streaks of fire lit the sky as ejecta continued to fall to the Earth. Flying into that would be madness.

Everything to the east of the mountains had been flattened. The airblast had laid the trees out in weirdly neat

THE CALCULATING STARS ✳ 27

rows. In the seat beside me, just audible over the roar of the engine, Nathaniel moaned.

I swallowed and swung the plane back around to the west. "We have about two hours of fuel. Suggestions?"

Like me, he tended to do better if he had something to focus on. When his mother died, he built a deck in our backyard, and my husband is not terribly handy with a hammer.

Nathaniel scrubbed his face and straightened. "Let's see who's out there?" He reached for the radio, which was still tuned to the Langley Tower. "Langley Tower, Cessna Four One Six Baker request VFR traffic advisories. Over."

Static answered him.

"Any radio, Cessna Four One Six Baker request VFR traffic advisories. Over."

He dialed through the entire radio frequency, listening for someone broadcasting. He repeated his call on each while I flew. "Try the UHF." As a civilian pilot, I should have just had a VHF radio, but because Nathaniel worked with the NACA we had a UHF installed as well so he could listen directly to pilots who were on test flights. We never cluttered the military channels by broadcasting, but today . . . ? Today I just wanted anyone to answer. As we made our way west, the devastation lessened, but only in comparison to what lay behind us. Trees and buildings had been knocked down by the blast. Some were on fire, with no one to put them out. What had it been like, to not understand what was coming?

"Unidentified Cessna, Sabre Two One, all nonessential air traffic is grounded."

At the sound of a living human, I started to weep again, but this was not a time to indulge in compromised vision. I blinked my eyes to clear them and focused on the horizon.

"Roger, Sabre Two One, Cessna Four One Six Baker, request advice on clear landing areas. Heading two seven zero."

"One Six Baker, copy that. I'm right above you. Where the hell are you coming from?" His voice had the telltale hiss and rattle of an oxygen mask, and behind that was the thin whine of a jet engine. Looking back and up, I could just make out the F-86, and his wingman farther back, gaining on us. They would have to circle, because their stall speed was faster than my little Cessna could fly.

"Hell seems pretty accurate." Nathaniel rubbed his forehead with his free hand. "We were in the Poconos when the meteorite hit."

"Jesus, One Six Baker. I just flew over that. How are you alive?"

"I've got no idea. So . . . where should we set down?"

"Give me a sec. I'll check to see if I can escort you to Wright-Patterson."

"Roger. Would it help to mention that I'm a retired Army captain and still work with the government?"

"With the government? Please tell me you're a senator."

Nathaniel laughed. "No. A rocket scientist with the NACA. Nathaniel York."

"The satellites! That's why you sounded familiar. I heard you on the radio. Major Eugene Lindholm, at your service." The man on the other end of the line was silent for a couple of minutes. When it crackled back to life again, he said, "Got enough fuel to reach Wright-Patterson?"

I'd flown into that airbase multiple times, moving planes during the war. It was approximately one hundred and fifty miles from where we were. I nodded as I adjusted course to head us there.

Nathaniel nodded in acknowledgment and lifted the mic again. "We do."

"Great. You'll be there in time for dinner. Not that it's much to look forward to."

My stomach growled at the mention of food. We hadn't

eaten since dinner the night before, and I was suddenly ravenously hungry. Even water would be welcome.

When Nathaniel signed off, he leaned back in his seat with a sigh.

"Looks like you have a fan."

He snorted. "We should have seen it."

"What?"

"The meteorite. We should have seen it coming."

"It wasn't your job."

"But we were looking for things that would interfere with the satellites. You'd think we'd spot a goddamn asteroid that was this close."

"Low albedo. Trajectory that put it in line with the sun. Small—"

"We should have seen it!"

"And if you had, what could we have done?"

The sound of the engine vibrated the seat beneath me and underscored the hiss of air slicing past. One of Nathaniel's knees bounced up and down with nervous energy. He sat forward and grabbed the charts. "Looks like you'll need to lay a course southwest."

I'd already done that, and we had an escort, but if giving me directions made Nathaniel feel useful, then by God he could guide me all the way there. Every streaking flare of ejecta in the sky just drove home how helpless we were. I could see them, but not in time to do anything about them, so I kept my hands on the yoke and flew.

The good thing about the constant pinch of hunger was that it countered the soothing drone of the airplane and kept me awake. Well, that and Nathaniel's terrible baritone. My husband was many things, but a singer was not one of them. Oh, he could carry a tune—in a bucket filled with gravel.

Fortunately, he knew that, and leaned toward a comedic

repertoire in his efforts to keep me awake. Bellowing with a vibrato like an amorous goat, Nathaniel stomped his foot on the floorboards of the airplane.

> *"Oh, do you remember Grandma's Lye Soap?*
> *Good for everything, everything in the place.*
> *The pots and kettles, and for your hands, and for*
>   *your face?"*

Below us, the glorious sight of the Wright-Patterson air-field finally scrolled into view. Its identification light flashed green, then the double-white of a military field.

> *"Mrs. O'Malley, down in the valley*
> *Suffered from ulcers, I understand—"*

"Saved!" I adjusted altitude. "Let 'em know we're com-ing in?"

Nathaniel grinned and grabbed the mic. "Sabre Two One, One Six Baker. So how's the food on the base?"

The radio crackled and Major Lindholm laughed. "It's everything you would expect. And more."

"That bad, eh?"

"I did not say that, sir. But if you're real nice, I might share my wife's care package."

I laughed along with Nathaniel, far more than the joke deserved.

Nathaniel switched the radio to the tower frequency, but before he could get the mic to his lips, another voice crack-led out. "Aircraft on heading two six zero, eight thousand five hundred feet, this is Wright-Patterson Tower. Identify yourself."

"Wright-Patterson Tower, this is Cessna Four One Six Baker at eight thousand five hundred, direct to the field."

Nathaniel had flown with me often enough that he had the routine down. He lowered the mic for a moment, then grinned and raised it again. "And Tower, we have Sabre Two One flight in tow."

"Tower, Sabre Two One. We are *escorting* One Six Baker, request direct to the field."

I snorted. It had to irk a fighter pilot to be trailing a scrubby little plane like my Cessna.

"One Six Baker and Sabre Two One, Tower copies. Approved direct to the field. Remain clear of One Six Baker. Be advised, we have reports of—"

Light streaked past the nose of the plane. A crack like a bomb going off. The entire plane bucked. I wrestled it level again—

And suddenly, I could see the propeller. The nearly invisible blur had become a stuttering, uneven bar. Part of it was just gone. It took me a moment to grasp what had happened. That streak of light had been a chunk of ejecta slamming into the nose of the plane, and it had taken part of my propeller with it.

The engine vibrations shook the yoke in my hand and slammed the seat against the base of my spine. This was only going to get worse. It could shake the engine right out of the plane. I slammed it into idle and began the sequence to secure the engine—by which I mean, shut it down.

Damn it. I wasn't going to make the base. "I need a landing field. Now."

At least we were in farm country, although the snow was going to mask the actual terrain. I pulled the throttle knob all the way out to idle and the engine shut off, leaving only the hiss of wind around us. What was left of the propeller windmilled as air rushed over it.

"What . . . ?"

"Gliding." If the ejecta had hit a wing, we'd be in much

worse trouble, but the Cessna was a darn good glider. I just wouldn't get a second chance at landing.

There was a road cutting between the fields, which might be a good bet, if it weren't for the fences bordering it. Field it was. I banked to line up the approach.

In the corner of my eye, Nathaniel still clutched the microphone. As a WASP, I'd had engines cut out on me far too often. This was his first time. He brought the radio to his mouth and I was so proud of how steady his voice was. "Wright Tower, this is Cessna Four One Six Baker declaring an emergency. We've had an engine failure and are making a forced landing on a field . . . um . . ." He fumbled for the map.

"Cessna Four One Six Baker, Wright Tower. We have eyes on you. You just concentrate on landing. Sabre Two One, Wright Tower. Orbit to assist and pinpoint where they land."

"Wright Tower, Sabre Two One. Already on it." The roar of the jet passed overhead as Major Lindholm and his wingman did a wide sweep past us.

My pulse thrummed through my veins, taking the place of the engine noise. This was not my first unpowered landing, but it was the first time with my husband aboard. After everything else that had happened today, I would *not* be the cause of his death. I refused. "Buckled up?"

"Um. Yeah." But he was fastening his seat belt as he spoke, so it was a good thing that I had asked. "Can I do . . . anything?"

"Brace." I tucked in my chin and watched the altimeter.

"Anything else—"

"Don't talk." He just wanted to help, but I didn't have time for that. I had to slow the plane down as much as possible before I touched down, but not so much that we landed short of the field. The ground rose up to meet us, changing from a smooth white expanse to a model train set of a snowy field, and then—without transition—full size and beneath us. I kept the nose up so that the tail wheel touched down first.

The snow grabbed at the wheel, slowing us further. As long as I could, I kept the nose tipped up. When the wing wheels finally touched, one of them snagged on the uneven rows beneath the snow. The plane jolted. I clutched the yoke to keep the wings level and worked the rudder pedals, trying to turn in the direction of the wind.

Our turn continued until we were facing the direction that we'd come. The plane stopped. Around us, the world was silent and still.

All the air in my lungs hissed out at once. I sagged against the seat.

A jet engine roared overhead and the radio crackled. Major Lindholm's voice filled the cabin. "One Six Baker, nicely done! Are you two okay?"

Nathaniel sat up and reached for the mic. His hand was shaking. "We aren't dead. So, yes."

The congealed mass of kidney beans and utterly questionable meatloaf may have been the best things I had ever tasted. The beans had a sweet tang to them, and puckered the inside of my mouth with too much salt, but I closed my eyes and relaxed against the hard bench in the Air Force canteen. It was weirdly empty, since much of the base had been deployed to deal with relief efforts. Some crockery rattled against the table and brought with it the glorious scent of chocolate.

When I opened my eyes, Major Lindholm settled onto the bench across from us. The picture I'd built of him in my head had no bearing on reality. I'd expected an older man, Nordic blond and stocky.

The real Major Lindholm was black, and younger than I'd expected from his voice. He was a hale man in his late thirties, with dark hair still mashed down from his helmet. The red line of his face mask traced a triangle around his chin and nose. And he brought hot chocolate.

Nathaniel lowered his fork and eyed the three steaming mugs on the table. He swallowed. "Is that hot cocoa?"

"Yeah, but don't thank me. It's a bribe, so I can ask you questions about rockets." Lindholm pushed two of the mugs across the table. "From the stash my wife sends to work with me, not the Air Force stuff."

"If you weren't already married . . ." My hand had closed around the warm mug before I realized what I'd said. I hoped he wasn't offended.

He laughed, thank God. "I've got a brother . . ."

My heart clenched hard. I'd managed to put my family out of my mind in order to keep going, but my brother lived in California. Hershel must think I was dead. My breath shuddered as I inhaled, but I managed to find a smile somewhere and looked up. "Is there a phone I can use? Long distance?"

Nathaniel rested his palm against my back. "Her family was in D.C."

"Oh, geez, ma'am. I'm so sorry."

"But my brother—he's in California."

"You come with me, ma'am." He glanced at Nathaniel. "Is there anyone you need to call, sir?"

Nathaniel shook his head. "Not urgently."

I followed Major Lindholm, with Nathaniel at my back, through corridors that barely registered. What an inconsiderate brat I'd been. I'd taken comfort that Hershel and his family lived in California, but hadn't once thought about the fact that to him, I was as good as dead. He had no reason to think that I wasn't in D.C. when the meteorite struck.

The office Major Lindholm showed me to was small and military tidy. The only thing that marred the right angles was a framed photo of twin boys and a crayon-drawn map of the U.S. pinned to the wall. Nathaniel shut the door and stood outside with Lindholm.

A utilitarian black phone sat on the desk, but at least it had a rotary dial, so I wouldn't have to speak with an operator. The receiver was warm and heavy. I dialed Hershel's home, listening to the rattle of the rotary as it swept through the numbers. Each signal sent a pulse through the lines and gave me time to retreat into a mechanical calm.

All I got was the high, frantic hum of a busy circuit. It was hardly surprising that all the circuits would be busy, but I hung up and tried again immediately. My urgency beat in time with the busy signal.

I had barely hung up again when Nathaniel opened the door. "Company. You okay?"

"Circuit's busy." I wiped at my face, probably just smearing the dirt more. I would ask to send a telegram, but the military signalers would be tied up. "I'll try later."

There was a lot to be said for being alive and upright. I was a greasy, smoky, bleeding mess, but I was alive. My husband was alive. My brother and his family were alive. And if I needed a reminder that this was a blessing, all I had to do was remember how many people had died today.

Still, when an Air Force colonel strode into the room, I caught myself trying to brush my hair into place as I stood, as if it would make a difference. Then, I saw past the insignia to the man. Stetson Parker. Thank heavens I had enough dirt on my face that I didn't have to worry about guarding my expression.

The jerk had been promoted. This was not remotely surprising, since he was a charmer to anyone who outranked him, or who he needed . . . as he proceeded to demonstrate now, with an outstretched hand toward Nathaniel. "Dr. York. I can't tell you what a relief it is to know you're safe."

Even with Lindholm's earlier enthusiasm about rockets, it was easy to forget that Nathaniel had become a celebrity because of the satellite launch. We'd managed to beat the Russians to getting a satellite into orbit not once, but with three different launches. My husband, being unreasonably attractive and charming—a fact about which I am not biased—had become the face of the NACA space program.

"Well, Major Lindholm has been taking good care of us. We appreciate the welcome, Colonel . . . ?" The man had a name tag on, but still . . . an introduction was appropriate.

"Where are my manners? I'm just so awestruck to have you here." Parker gave a shit-eating grin. "Colonel Stetson Parker, Base Commander. Although . . . with affairs being what they are, I appear to be in charge of more than just this base."

Of course he would get that in, to make it clear how important he was. I stepped forward and stuck out my hand. "Good to see you again, Colonel Parker."

He raised his eyebrows in surprise. "I'm sorry, ma'am, you have the better of me."

"Oh, when you knew me, I was still Elma Wexler. One of the WASP pilots."

His face stiffened a little. "Ah. The general's daughter. Yes, I remember you."

"Congratulations on your promotion." I smiled the best "bless your heart" smile I could. "You must have worked very hard for it."

"Thank you, ma'am." He grinned again, clapping Nathaniel on the shoulder. "And I guess the little lady got a promotion, eh, becoming Mrs. York?"

My teeth hurt from grinding, but I kept smiling. "You mentioned not knowing who your superior is. What can you tell us about the current situation?"

"Ah . . ." He sobered, and the mood change might even

have been real. He gestured to the seats on the other side of the desk. "Sit down, please."

Parker took the chair behind the desk, and only now did I notice his nameplate set front and center. I was surprised he had twins. I wonder who'd married him. He steepled his fingers together and sighed again. "An explosion—"

"A meteorite."

"That's what the news reported. But given that Washington was wiped out? I place my money on the Russians."

Nathaniel cocked his head. "Is there radioactivity?"

"We haven't gotten anyone close enough to the blast area to check."

Idiot. I spelled things out for him. "There's ejecta falling all around, which, first of all, you could just test for radioactivity. Second, that's not something that happens with an A-bomb. It occurs when a meteorite punches a hole in the atmosphere and the blast material is sucked into space, then falls back to Earth."

His eyes narrowed. "Then know this. The United States Congress was in session, both the House and the Senate. Our federal government was nearly entirely wiped out. The Pentagon, Langley . . . So even if this was an act of God, do you honestly think the Russians won't try to take advantage of it?"

That . . . that was a terrifyingly good point. I leaned back in my chair and crossed my arms over my chest to ward off the sudden chill in the air.

Nathaniel filled in the gap. "So, the military is planning a defense?"

He didn't quite emphasize "military," but did make it clear enough that whatever happened, a colonel was not going to be running the show.

"It's the prudent thing to do. Dr. York . . ." He paused, but the hesitation was so blatantly calculated that you could almost see him counting the seconds. "You worked on the Manhattan Project, am I correct?"

Nathaniel stiffened next to me. The Manhattan Project had been exciting from a scientific standpoint, but horrific in every other respect. "I did, but I'm focused on space exploration these days."

Parker waved that away. "I hate to do this to you after your arduous morning, but may I pull you into a meeting?"

"I'm not sure that I really have anything to offer."

"You're the top scientist in rocketry right now."

Neither of us needed a reminder of how many people at the NACA were likely dead. I rested my hand on Nathaniel's knee, to steady him as he had steadied me. The NACA, however, was not the only rocketry program. "Not to undervalue my husband's work, but Wernher von Braun is at the Sunflower Project in Kansas."

Parker snorted and gave me a pained smile. He'd hated being polite to me during the war, when he had to because of my father; and now he hated being polite to Dr. York's wife. "Ma'am, it's nice that you want to help, but I hope you understand that I can't involve a former Nazi like von Braun in questions of national security." And then he was looking at Nathaniel again, ignoring me completely. "What do you say, Dr. York? We just want to understand what our options are for keeping America safe."

Nathaniel sighed and picked at a loose thread on his trousers. "All right. But I'm not promising to be bright today."

As he stood, I straightened my legs to join him. Parker held his hand up and shook his head. "No need, ma'am. You can just rest here in my office, while Major Lindholm arranges quarters for you."

The major said, "We have some empty rooms at our place—if you want to avoid the TLFs?"

I was flattered—not that he'd offered a place to stay, but that he used the acronym for temporary living facilities instead of translating for a civilian. "That's very kind. If your wife doesn't mind, Major."

"I'm sure she won't, ma'am."

Parker's smile was unexpectedly warm. "You're in good hands. His wife makes darn fine pie."

I'll admit that I was surprised to see what appeared to be genuine camaraderie between the two men. My own experiences with Parker had been less than ideal. I hoped that didn't mean that Major Lindholm would turn out to be charming but unpleasant too. "Thank you. Now that that's sorted, we can go on to the meeting." Not that I had any desire to go to a meeting, but I would give a lot to feel like I could be of some use.

"Ah . . . I'm sorry, ma'am." Parker tugged at his tie. "What I should have said was that Dr. York already has the necessary clearance levels from the Manhattan Project. You understand."

Clearance, my ass. From what he was saying, there was no hierarchy at all, much less clearance. But if I voiced any of that, nothing useful would follow, so I settled back in my chair. "Well, bless your heart. Of course I understand. I'll just sit here and wait."

Nathaniel raised his brows at that. He knew me well enough to know I was good and angry, if not exactly why. I shook my head at him, reassuring him that I was fine. I smiled, folded my hands demurely in my lap, and settled back. Like a good little girl, I would sit and wait, let my husband do the work, and pray to God that this mishegas wasn't going to start a nuclear war.

FOUR

90 DIE IN IRAN EARTHQUAKE

TEHERAN, Iran, March 3, 1952—(Reuters)—
Ninety persons were killed and 180 injured in earthquakes in LaRistan and Bastak in southern Iran.
Teheran Radio announced today that the earthquakes
are believed to have been triggered by the Meteor
impact in North America.

The sun had set in a vivid vermilion, with copper and
streaks of dark gold. We might well have been transported
to Mars based on the red sky arching over us. The ruddy
light stained everything, so that even the white picket fence
of Major Lindholm's house looked as if it had been dipped
in blood.

Normally, I'd hate to impose on anyone, but Parker had
irked me. And, truly, I was too tired to think, and grateful
to have someone tell me where to go. Besides, they'd be
needing the TLFs for refugee housing.

Nathaniel was still tied up with his meeting. He'd come
out long enough to encourage me to go, and I really didn't
have any excuse for staying on base—aside from the abso-
lute certainty that if I left, I would never see him again.
These are not things that one voices aloud. Not on a day
like today.

As I got out of the jeep, the stains on my clothes seemed

to deepen. I could almost hear my mother saying, "Elma! What will people think?"

I clutched the door of the jeep and bit down on the grief. At least I'd washed my face. Straightening, I followed Major Lindholm through the fence and up the tidy walk to the front porch. The door opened as we were climbing the steps, and a plump woman in a powder-blue dress stepped out.

Her skin was no darker than Nathaniel gets in the summer, and her features were soft and rounded. I realized, with a little bit of a shock, that I'd never been to the home of a black person before. Mrs. Lindholm's curls had been teased into a bouffant hairdo that framed the curve of her light brown cheeks. Behind her glasses, her eyes were rimmed red and tight with worry.

She pulled the door open wider, and pressed a hand to her bosom. "Oh my poor dear. You come right in."

"Thank you, ma'am." The floor inside was a pristine faux brick linoleum. My shoes were so dirty that the original color was gone. "Just let me take my boots off."

"Don't you worry about that."

I sat on the steps to pull them off. Mama would have been ashamed of me if I had carried this much grime into anyone's home. "My husband will track in enough dirt for both us when he arrives."

She laughed. "Aren't husbands just all alike?"

"I'm right here." Major Lindholm paused on the steps next to me. "But you let us know if you need anything. Anything at all. And I'll make sure Dr. York gets back here safe and sound."

"Thank you." If I had to see another look of kindness, I would come completely apart. I concentrated on the other boot. Even my stockings were filthy, and my feet weren't much better.

Mrs. Lindholm took a few steps out onto the porch. "I raised three sons. Believe me, a little dirt is not a problem."

No tears. Not yet. A shallow breath kept the worst of it from flooding out. I swallowed the salt. Grabbing the railing, I pulled myself up to my bare feet. "I really can't thank you enough."

"Oh, I haven't done anything yet." She put her hand near my back, not quite touching me, and guided me into her home. "Now . . . I suspect that the first thing you'll want is a nice hot bath."

"I would take a cold shower at this point."

The front door had opened directly into her living room. All the furniture sat at neat right angles, and even the tchotchkes had been squared with the edges of their shelves and tables. The air smelled of lemon furniture cleaner and cinnamon.

"For a cold shower, you could have stayed in the barracks." Mrs. Lindholm bustled down the hall off the living room and opened the first door on the right. Most of the floor in the bathroom was given over to a claw-foot tub. "I have bubble bath. Lavender and rose."

"I should probably shower first."

She adjusted her glasses, taking in the dirt that caked my clothing and visible skin. "Hm . . . all right. But after that, you soak, you hear me? Else you'll be all over aches and pains tomorrow."

"Yes, ma'am." She wasn't wrong. Given everything, I'd be surprised if I could even get out of bed tomorrow.

"Now. Here are your towels, and a set of my oldest son's pj's." She put her hand on a set of red flannel pajamas. "My nightgowns would just fall off you. Just set your clothes on the counter, and I'll get them washed."

As she bustled out of the room I nodded, hoping she would take it as thanks.

She had to wash my clothes, because otherwise I would have nothing to wear. Not in the despairing debutante way, but a literal fact. We were refugees. Our home. Our jobs. Our bank. Our friends. Everything had been destroyed when the meteorite hit.

And if Nathaniel had not been a rocket scientist—if Parker hadn't needed him—where would we be? I had thought about people like Mr. Goldman, but not about the people who lived. What were all the other hundreds and thousands of people who were on the edges of the destruction to do?

A cloud of steam preceded me out of the bathroom. I crept down the hall in my borrowed flannel pajamas. The trousers were fine, since I have long legs, but the sleeves hung down to my fingers. I rolled them up as I walked, and the myriad nicks on my fingers snagged against the soft fabric. My mind seemed empty of thought.

I think I was still in shock, which was to be expected, I suppose, but at least it wasn't manifesting with tremors anymore. It just seemed as if everything had been swathed in cotton.

In the living room, the television was on but turned down low. Mrs. Lindholm had pulled her chair close to the screen. She hunched forward, staring at the news, with her hands balled in fists around a handkerchief.

Rendered in flickering black and white, Edward R. Murrow sat at his news desk with his cigarette, and spoke about the events of the day.

". . . The latest total of known dead in the wake of the Meteor that struck today was seventy thousand, although that estimate is expected to rise. Five hundred thousand persons have been reported homeless in the states of Maryland, Delaware, Pennsylvania, New York, New Jersey,

Virginia, and into Canada, and as far down the Eastern Seaboard as Florida. These images were taken by airplane some five hours after the disaster. What you are looking at, ladies and gentlemen, was formerly the site of our nation's capital."

The screen showed a pool of water, bubbling like a geyser. I inhaled sharply as the camera panned to show the horizon, and the scale became clear. The border of dark soil was a ring of scorched earth hundreds of miles in diameter. At the coast, the Chesapeake Bay had not simply flooded its banks. The banks had ceased to exist. I was looking at the sea.

And it was steaming.

I sucked in breath as if someone had punched me in the gut.

Mrs. Lindholm turned in her chair, and I could almost see her folding her own shock and grief away into neat squares so she could be a good hostess. "Oh! You look like you're feeling a little better."

"I—yes . . ." I took a step closer to the television, horrified and fascinated in equal measure.

"A state of emergency has been declared across the Eastern Seaboard. The Army, Navy, Air Force, and Red Cross have mobilized, and are providing aid to refugees in need."

The camera cut to footage from the ground of aid workers gathering refugees. In the background, a little girl with burns on her arms toddled next to her mother. Another cut to what had been an elementary school. The children's bodies . . . it must have been morning recess when the meteorite struck. I had thought that anything I could imagine would be worse than the reality. I was wrong.

Mrs. Lindholm turned off the television. "There now. You don't need to be watching that. What you need is some dinner."

"Oh, I don't want to be a bother."

"Nonsense. I wouldn't have told Eugene to bring you if you were going to be a bother." She tucked her handkerchief into the waistband of her skirt as she stood. "Come into the kitchen and let me get a little food into you."

"I—thank you." My etiquette instincts about being an unplanned-for guest warred with the simple reality that I should eat, even if I wasn't hungry. Plus, if she was anything like my mother—I brushed the back of my hand over my eyes—if she was anything like my mother, then turning down food would be inhospitable.

Under my bare feet, the kitchen's linoleum floor was cool. The walls had been painted mint green, and there were crisp white cabinets above pristine counters. Had she cleaned when they said I was coming, or was her house always this tidy? As she opened the refrigerator, I suspected the latter.

She must have a friend that sold Tupperware, or maybe she did. The food was all in matching pastel containers. If I hadn't seen that moment of shock and grief as she watched the television, she might have stepped out of an advertisement for GE. "Now . . . how about a ham and cheese sandwich?"

"Oh . . . maybe just cheese?"

"After the day you've had? You need to have some protein."

Mama said it was always better to get the conversation over with. "We're Jewish."

She straightened, brows rising. "Are you really? Well . . . I'd never have known to look at you."

It was kindly meant. I know it was. I had to believe it was, because I was a guest in her home and had nowhere else to go. I swallowed and smiled. "So, just cheese would be fine."

"What about tuna fish?"

"That sounds lovely, if it's not too much trouble." Neither of us came from families that had kept kosher, but after the war began, I'd stopped eating pork and shellfish. The discipline, if nothing else, helped me remember who I was, and why that was important.

"Not a bit." She pulled a pale pink container from the fridge. "Eugene always has tuna fish for lunch, so I keep some made up for him."

"Is there anything I can do to help?"

"Just sit down." Another container, this one green, followed the first. "It would be harder to explain where everything was than to just do it."

On the wall by the refrigerator hung a dull brown wall phone. Somehow, the sight of it hit me with guilt like a brick. "May I . . . I hate to impose, but may I borrow your phone? It would be a long-distance call, but . . ." I trailed off, uncertain of when I could repay her.

"Of course. You want me to step out?"

"No. It's fine." That was a lie. I desperately wanted the privacy, but I didn't want to impose on her any more than I already had. "Thank you."

She slid the sandwich fixings over on the counter and gestured to the phone. "It's not a party line, so you shouldn't have to worry about anyone listening in. One of the benefits of staying in a major's house, hm?"

I crossed to the phone, wishing it was in another room in the house, or that I had the guts to tell her the truth. After I dialed, I got that damnable circuit busy sound. I managed not to curse. Well . . . not aloud, at any rate.

I tried again, and the phone rang.

The relief sapped my strength and left me leaning against the wall. With each ring of the phone, I prayed: *Please let them be home. Please let them be home. Please—*

"Hello? Wexler residence." My brother's voice was calm and professional.

Mine cracked. "Hershel? It's Elma."

A ragged gasp, and then just the crackle of a long-distance line.

"Hershel?"

I have never heard my brother sob before. Not even when he split his knee open to the bone.

In the background, I could hear Doris, his wife, asking a question—probably "What's wrong?"

"Elma. No—no. She's alive. Oh, praise God. She's alive." His voice came back to the microphone. "We saw the news. What . . . what about Mom and Pops?"

"No." I pressed my hand over my eyes and leaned my forehead against the wall. Behind me, Mrs. Lindholm made the sandwich with unnatural quiet. I had to press the words out of my throat. "Nathaniel and I were out of town. Mama and Daddy were home."

His breath shuddered in my ear. "But you and Nathaniel are alive."

"Do you know . . . how did Charleston fare?"

"The city was hit by tidal waves, but a lot of people were able to evacuate." Then he answered the question I was actually asking. "We haven't heard from Grandma, or any of the aunts."

"Well . . . I had a time getting a clear circuit through."

Doris said something, and Hershel's voice muffled for a moment. "What? Yes . . . yes, I'll ask."

His wife had always been the more organized of the two, even while they were courting. I smiled, picturing the list that she was probably making right now.

"Where are you? What do you need? Are you hurt?"

"We're at the Wright-Patterson base in Ohio. Well, actually, we're at the home of the Lindholms, who have taken us in tonight. So, don't worry. I'm well taken care of." I glanced over my shoulder. Mrs. Lindholm had cut the sandwich into neat quarters and trimmed the crust off. "In fact, I should probably go, since I'm calling on her phone."

"Next time, call me collect."

"I'll call tomorrow, if the circuits aren't busy. Give my love to Doris and the children."

When I hung up, I stood with my head against the wall, as if the mint green paint could cool my forehead. I think it was only a moment.

One of the chairs creaked as if Mrs. Lindholm had sat down, so I gathered myself and straightened. Daddy had always said that deportment was important for an officer and a lady. "Thank you. My brother has been very worried."

"I'm sure I would be too." She had set the sandwich on a bright teal plate and then centered it in the middle of a placemat. Next to the plate stood a glass of water with beads of condensation on its side.

The mundanity of the kitchen, the ticking clock on the wall, the hum of the refrigerator, and this kind woman with her sandwiches, placemats, and flannel pajamas seemed completely separate from the world I had been in all day. The images of the burned children on the television might as well have been on Mars for all the connection they had to here.

The chair creaked as I sat, and my joints ached with frustration. As I'd been taught, I put the napkin in my lap, and picked up the first quarter of the sandwich. I was lucky. We had owned a plane and a way to get out.

"Is the sandwich all right?"

I had eaten a quarter of it and not noticed. My mouth tasted of dying fish and rotting pickles. I smiled for my hostess. "Delicious."

FIVE

TIDAL WAVE STRIKES VENEZUELA

CARACAS, Venezuela, March 4, 1952—(AP)—A tidal wave, believed to be caused by the meteorite which struck off the coast of North America, hit the port of Vela de Coro, inflicting heavy damages, reports to the Government said today. Ships anchored in the western Venezuela port were destroyed, and many houses along the waterfront were flattened, the reports said. The extent of the casualties is not yet known.

At some point, I must have fallen asleep on the couch. I woke up to Nathaniel's touch on my forehead. The light from the kitchen streamed into the dark living room and caught on the white dress shirt he wore. He was clean and had showered, and for a disorienting moment, I thought that I had dreamed it all.

"Hey . . ." He smiled and brushed the hair back from my forehead again. "Do you want to sleep out here, or go to the bedroom?"

"When did you get ho—back?" I sat up, stretching the crick out of my neck. One of Mrs. Lindholm's afghans had been pulled up over my shoulder, and the television was a dark ghost in the corner.

"Just now. Major Lindholm brought me." He nodded toward the kitchen. "He's making a sandwich."

"Did you get something to eat?"

He nodded. "They fed us in the meeting."

Nathaniel offered his hand and helped me to my feet. All of the cuts and aches and bruises that I had acquired during the day found me in the dark. The backs of my calves burned with each step. Even my arms protested, as I folded the afghan. Was it too soon to take another aspirin? "What time is it?"

"Nearly midnight."

If he was only just now getting back, the situation was not good. In the dim light his features were too blurred to read. In the kitchen, Major Lindholm scraped his knife across a plate. I set the afghan down. "Let's go back to the bedroom."

He followed me down the dimly lit hall to the room that Mrs. Lindholm had put us in. It had belonged to her eldest son, Alfred, who was off at Caltech getting a degree in engineering. While there was a "Leopards" pennant from his high school, the partially assembled Erector set and the Jules Verne collection might have come out of my childhood room. Everything else was plaid or red, which I suspected was his mother's touch.

When the door was closed, Nathaniel reached for the light, but I stopped him. For a little while longer, I wanted to be in the safety of the night. Here, with just the two of us, and no radio to remind us, we might just be visiting someone. My husband pulled me into his arms and I leaned against him, nestling my cheek into the contour of his chest.

Nathaniel rested his chin against my head and ran his hands through my still-damp hair. He smelled of an unfamiliar minty soap.

I nestled against him. "You showered on base?"

His chin rubbed the back of my head as he nodded. "I

fell asleep at the table, so they took a break. I showered to wake up."

Pulling back, I looked up at him. The shadows seemed deeper around his eyes. Those bastards. After everything he'd been through today, they kept him awake? "They didn't just send you home?"

"They offered." He squeezed my shoulders before releasing me. Unbuttoning his shirt, he meandered toward the bed. "I was afraid that, if I left, Colonel Parker would do something stupid. He still might."

"He's a schmuck."

Nathaniel stopped undressing with his shirt halfway down his arms. "You mentioned knowing him."

"He was a pilot in the war. Commanded a squadron, and haaaaaated having women fly his planes. Hated it. And he was grabby."

In hindsight, I should not have mentioned that last bit to my husband. Not when he was exhausted. He straightened so fast, I thought he was going to rip his shirt. "What."

Trying to soothe him, I held up my hands. "Not with me. And not with any of the women in my squad." Well, not after I had a talk with Daddy. I shrugged. "Benefits of being a general's daughter."

He snorted and went back to sliding his shirt off. "That explains a lot." Scrapes and bruises mottled his back. "I think I have him convinced that it wasn't an A-bomb, but he's certain that the Russians aimed the meteor."

"They haven't even gotten off the planet yet."

"I pointed that out." He sighed. "The good news is that the chain of command is not as broken as he would like us to believe. General Eisenhower is flying back from Europe. Should be here tomorrow morning, in fact."

I took Nathaniel's shirt from him and hung it on the back of a chair. "Here? As in Wright-Patterson, or as in America?"

"Here. It's the closest intact base."

The numbers sat quietly between us. We were more than five hundred miles from the impact site.

In the morning, I had my first glimpse of what we would be like as old people. Nathaniel could barely get out of bed on his own. During the earthquake, most of the debris had hit him. His back was a collection of hematomas and contusions that would have been better suited to one of Mama's medical textbooks than a living man.

I was not much better. The only time I recalled feeling worse was the summer I'd had influenza. Still, I could get up, and I was fairly certain that once I was moving around, I'd be in better shape.

Nathaniel took two tries to push himself into a sitting position on the edge of the bed.

"You should rest."

He shook his head. "Can't. Don't want General Eisenhower to be swayed by Parker."

My foolish husband held out a hand, and I pulled him to his feet. "General Eisenhower does not strike me as the sort of man to be swayed by an idiot."

"Even geniuses can be stupid when they're scared." He grunted as he stood, which did not fill me with anything like confidence. But I know my husband, and he's the sort of man who will work until his death. He reached for his shirt and winced.

I picked up the bathrobe he'd been loaned and held it out. "Do you want to shower first? Might loosen you up."

He nodded and let me help him into the bathrobe, then shuffled down the hall. I went to the kitchen to find Mrs. Lindholm. The unmistakable aroma of bacon met me before I was through the door.

I braced myself to have *that* conversation with every meal. They were kind people, and we'd be sleeping in a field if not for them. Well . . . maybe that was a little melodramatic. We would have slept in the plane, but still. And then I heard what they were talking about, and the bacon became insignificant.

". . . keep thinking about the girls I went to school with. Pearl was in Baltimore." Mrs. Lindholm's voice broke.

"There now . . ."

"Sorry—I'm being such a goose. You want raspberry or strawberry jam with your toast?"

I rounded the corner while the topic was innocuous. Mrs. Lindholm bustled at the counter, with her back to me. She wiped a hand under her eyes.

Major Lindholm sat at the kitchen table. Coffee steamed in a cup held loosely in his right hand. He had a newspaper in the left, but was frowning over it at his wife.

As I entered, he looked around and put a smile on like a mask. "Hope we didn't wake you last night."

"Nathaniel did, which was just as well, or I would have woken with the worst crick in my neck." We went through the requisite pleasantries while he supplied me with a cup of coffee.

Do I have to explain the glories of a fresh cup of coffee? The deep redolent steam rising from the cup woke me before the first gloriously bitter drop even touched my lips. Not just bitter, but caressing waves of dark alertness. I sighed and relaxed into my chair. "Thank you."

"What about breakfast? Eggs? Bacon? Toast?" Mrs. Lindholm pulled a plate out of the cupboard. Her eyes were only a little red. "I have some grapefruit."

How far inland had Florida's citrus groves been? "Eggs and toast would be lovely, thank you."

Major Lindholm folded his paper and pushed it away from him. "That's right. Myrtle mentioned that you were Jews. Come over during the war?"

"No, sir. Oh—" I looked up as Mrs. Lindholm set a plate with eggs and toast in front of me. The eggs had been fried in the bacon grease. They smelled very good. Damn it. I used the act of buttering my toast to collect my thoughts. "My family came over in the 1700s and settled in Charleston."

"Is that so?" He sipped his coffee. "I never met a Jew before the war."

"Oh, you probably did, but they had their horns hidden."

"Ha!" He slapped his knee. "Fair point."

"Actually, my grandmother . . ." The toast and butter required all of my attention. "My grandmother and her sisters still spoke Yiddish in the home."

Mrs. Lindholm settled in the chair next to me and watched, as if I were an exhibition at the museum. "Well, I never." A little frown deepened the creases in her forehead. "And did they . . . well, you said Charleston, did they have Southern accents?"

I turned up the accent, which I'd learned to tone down in Washington. "Y'all want to come over for Rosh Hashanah? Well, mazel tov, y'all!"

They laughed until tears streamed down their faces as I went through the Yiddish I knew, with the Charleston accent turned on high. It hadn't sounded strange when I was growing up. I'd just thought that was the way Yiddish was pronounced, until we started going to synagogue in D.C.

Nathaniel appeared in the doorway, moving with a little more ease. "Something smells good."

Mrs. Lindholm jumped up and fixed a plate for him. The major talked genially about nothing. We were all pretending so desperately that nothing was out of place. But the newspaper lying on the table showed a picture of New York City, transformed into a misshapen Venice, where the streets were watery canals framed by windowless skyscrapers.

Finally, Major Lindholm looked at the wall clock, which read ten till nine. He pushed back from the table. "Well. We should be getting on."

Nathaniel jumped to his feet. "Thank you for breakfast, Mrs. Lindholm."

"My pleasure." She kissed her husband on the cheek. "It's nice to have someone to talk to instead of the back side of a newspaper."

He laughed, and it was easy to see why she'd fallen in love with him. "What do you ladies have planned for the day?"

"Well . . ." She picked up his plate and Nathaniel's. "I thought I'd take Mrs. York in town to go shopping."

"Shopping?" I picked up the other plates, following her to the counter. "I'd been planning on going in with Nathaniel."

She tilted her head and stared at me as if I'd suddenly spoken Greek. "But you both need new clothes. I washed yours, but they really can't be salvaged for anything, except maybe yard work."

Nathaniel must have seen my stricken look, but didn't understand it. I wasn't worried about money. The world had just ended and I was being sent *shopping*. "It's all right, Elma. Colonel Parker gave us a clothing allowance until we get my employment status sorted. So take the day and go shopping. There's nothing you can do at the base, anyway."

And that was the problem. There was nothing I could do.

Mrs. Lindholm pulled her Oldsmobile to a stop in front of a store in downtown Dayton. The awning over the storefront had a rip in it, and the windows of the shop had a thin grit coating them. They framed a display of smart dresses in vivid jewel tones. I got out of the car and looked down the street at the people going about their lives, as if nothing had happened yesterday.

No—that wasn't quite true. The little clusters of people in conversation seemed to stand closer to each other than might be normal. The flag over the barbershop next door stood at half-mast. And the same grit that clung to the store window dusted everything. I shivered and looked up at the odd ochre haze in the sky.

Mrs. Lindholm saw my shiver and misinterpreted it. "Let's get inside before you catch your death."

"Oh, I'm getting good at outrunning death."

Mrs. Lindholm's face blanched. "I'm so sorry! I forgot about what you went through."

Sometimes my humor doesn't work to diffuse a situation. This was one of those cases. "No, really. It's fine. It's just . . . I'm the one who should apologize. That joke was in poor taste."

"No, it's my fault."

"Really—no. You have nothing to apologize for."

"I was being thoughtless."

"I—" I stopped and narrowed my gaze. "I should remind you that I'm Southern, and you'll never win a politeness battle with me."

She laughed, and people down the sidewalk turned to glare as if she had begun cursing in public. "Truce?"

"Absolutely." I gestured to the door. "Shall we go in?"

Still laughing, she pushed the door open and set the shop bells to tinkling. The saleslady, a black woman in her late sixties with pristine white hair, stood next to a radio, listening intently. At the sound of the bells, she looked around, though her gaze lingered on the radio.

". . . the fires from the Meteor strike yesterday have spread to cover three hundred and fifty square miles . . ."

She smiled, as if she'd just remembered how to do it. "May I help you?" Then her gaze rested on me. Her frown was not obvious—just a tensing of her smile.

All the ground-in dirt that no amount of washing could remove from my sweater grew to cover me. I must look homeless. Mama would be ashamed of me. I swallowed. I wanted to go back out to the car, but that would inconvenience Mrs. Lindholm, so I just stood, paralyzed, by the door.

Mrs. Lindholm gestured to me. "My friend was in the East yesterday."

In the East. At the euphemism, the saleslady's eyes widened and her brows peaked with pity. "Oh—you poor dear." And then curiosity followed, like a predator drawn to blood. "Where were you?"

"The Poconos."

Mrs. Lindholm pulled out a navy blue dress from the rack and held it up. "She doesn't have anything except the clothes on her back."

A middle-aged white woman appeared from between the racks of clothing. "You were really there? You saw the meteor?"

"Meteorite. A meteor breaks up before impact." As if anyone cared about scientific accuracy. I think this might have been the last time I corrected someone. "Meteorite," for whatever quirk of the English language, sounded almost cute. "But no, we were three hundred miles away."

She stared at my face as if the cuts and bruises would give her a map to my specific location. "I have family back east."

"So did I." I snatched a dress from the rack and fled to the changing room. The louvered door shut behind me, shielding me from their view, but not from their hearing. I sank onto the little padded bench and pressed both hands over my mouth. Every breath hurt, fighting to be given sound. *3.14159265 . . .*

"She and her husband flew in last night. Lost everyone except a brother, I understand."

"That's horrible."

. . . 35897932384 . . . Everyone would know someone "back east." I was not the only person who had lost family.

The saleslady said, "I heard on the news that we should expect a lot more meteor refugees, on account of Wright-Patterson."

Meteor refugee. That's what I was. It's just that I was the first refugee that anyone had seen here. Of all the times for the tears to finally hit, it had to happen in a dress store?

"That's what my husband was saying." Mrs. Lindholm seemed to be just outside the door to my dressing room. "I'm going to go by the base hospital to volunteer later today."

"That's so good of you."

Volunteer. I could do that. I could volunteer to fly refugees back from the East, or wrap bandages, or something. I'd done it during the war, and there was no reason not to pull myself together and do it again.

"Is that the CBS you've got on the radio now?"

I wiped my eyes and stood, reaching for the dress I'd snatched. It was a polka-dot number in a size better suited for a pencil than for me.

"Mm-hm . . . They were just saying that they'd found a surviving cabinet member. Let me turn it up, if you ladies don't mind."

In the mirror, it looked as though a ghoul had come to shop. I'd thought I looked homeless, but really, I looked as if I hadn't truly survived the impact. Both of my eyes were blackened. I had tiny cuts all over my face and arms. Something had hit me, right below my hairline, and left a scrape. But I was alive.

"... and those tidal waves have also swamped the Caribbean, leaving many nations there without water or electricity. The devastation is said to number in the hundreds of thousands ..."

I opened the door of the dressing room and tried to tune out the radio. "Silly me. It's the wrong size."

The saleslady came over to help me and we consulted on sizes and current fashion while the news continued in the background. It was like playing the fiddle while Rome burned around us.

SIX

INDIANS OFFER AID TO MRS. ROOSEVELT

Questions by Press Underscore the
Growing Friendship for U.S.

The Times.

NEW DELHI, India, 4 March 1952—Questions
put to Mrs. Franklin D. Roosevelt by Indian news-
papermen at a Delhi press association luncheon for the
former president's widow today underscored the sig-
nificant wide and growing devastation in the United
States after a meteorite struck earlier this week. Initially intended as a hospitality meeting, talks focused
on offers of aid for the United States.

The sky was a high, silver overcast, as Mrs. Lindholm
dropped me off at HQ. "Are you sure you don't want to
go home and rest, dear?"

"Thank you, but I really do feel better when I'm active."

Her mouth turned down in disappointment, but, to her
credit, she didn't argue with me anymore. "Well, I'll be over
at the base hospital, if you need me. Don't forget to eat
something."

"Yes, ma'am." I waved as she drove off. Shopping was all
well and good—and, yes, I'll grant that I felt better with
clean clothes and makeup to hide the worst of the bruis-

ing, but I'd spent the entire time we were out feeling like I was playing make-believe. In every store, a radio or television had been tuned to the news. Delaware basically didn't exist anymore, and the only surviving cabinet member they'd found so far was the secretary of agriculture.

But there were still refugees that needed to be transported. I knew how to fly. So, I brushed off my new polka-dotted navy blue dress, straightened its bright red belt, and headed inside to find Colonel Parker. He would not have been my first choice, mind you, but at least he knew my record of flying.

I knocked on his door, which stood open. He sat at his desk, head bent over a memo. I swear his lips moved as he read. He'd developed a bald spot at the back of his head about the size of a half-dollar. Wonder if he knew about it yet.

He looked up, but didn't stand. "Mrs. York?"

"I saw on the news that the Air Force was mobilizing to deal with refugees." I came in and sat down without being asked. I mean, I didn't want to make him look bad about leaving a lady standing.

"That's right. But don't worry, your husband won't be sent out."

"Since he's not active service and was never Air Force, this does not surprise me." I breathed out, trying to let my irritation go with it. "But I was wondering if *I* might help. With so many of our men still in Korea, I thought having an extra pilot might be useful."

"Well, now. . . . that's very kind of you, but this really isn't the place for a lady."

"There are plenty of women among the refugees. And since I have firsthand experience—"

He held up his hand to stop me. "I appreciate your zeal, but it isn't necessary. General Eisenhower is recalling our troops, and there's an influx of UN aide."

"What about Korea?"

"Cease-fire." He shuffled the papers on his desk. "Now, if you'll excuse me."

"Still, until they are home, you'll have a shortage of pilots."

"Are you proposing to join the Air Force? Because, if not, I can't let you fly one of our planes." He made a mockery of regret. "And since your plane was damaged . . . I'm afraid there's really nothing for you to do here."

"Well." I stood. He did not. "Thank you for your time."

"Of course." He looked back down at the memo. "You might try nursing. I understand that's a good occupation for women."

"Aren't you just so clever. Thank you ever so much, Colonel Parker." What truly aggravated me was that he was right. I wanted to help, but the skills I had were largely useless. Without a plane, what was I supposed to do? Math the problem to death?

My timing, when I arrived at the base hospital, couldn't have been worse—or better, depending on how you looked at it. A plane of refugees had just landed and swamped the hospital. Tents had been set up as a waiting area, filled with people who had been outside for the last two days. Burns, dehydration, lacerations, broken bones, and simple shock.

I was handed a tray of paper cups filled with electrolytes and told to distribute them. It wasn't much, but it was something useful.

"Thank you, ma'am." The blond woman took a paper cup and looked down the rows of chairs to the doctors. "Do you know what's going to happen to us next?"

The elderly man next to her shifted in his seat. His blackened eye was swollen nearly shut, and the blood crusted around his nose made it clear that he'd had a doozy of a nosebleed at some point. "Send us to camps, I reckon. I would've been better off staying where I was than sitting here."

Camps had a grisly connotation, and that sort of talk was not going to help anyone. I held my tray of paper cups out to the old man. "Drink, sir? It will help restore some strength." God. That was my mother's doctor voice. Kind and brisk.

He snorted and crossed his arms, but he winced when he did. "You're not a nurse. Not in that getup."

He had a point. Still, I smiled at him. "You're right. I'm just helping out."

He snorted, and blood bubbled in one nostril. Then a gusher started. "Oh, hell."

"Tilt your head back." I looked around for something to use to stop the blood. The young woman took the tray of water. "Pinch the bridge of you—"

"I know. Ain't my first one." But he still did as I said.

A pasty man across the aisle, in tattered business attire, pulled his tie off and handed it to me. The lens of his glasses was cracked, and his eyes were more than a little glazed.

"Thank you." I pressed the silk against the old man's nose. "This is the finest bandage I've ever had the pleasure of using."

The old man took it from me and glared at the ceiling. "You're trying to distract me."

"That I am." I leaned forward to examine his eyes. "What would you like to talk about?"

He pursed his lips. "You been here . . . so you must know things. How bad is it?"

"I think . . ." I looked around at the battered people surrounding us. "I think that this is perhaps not the best time for that discussion. I'll just say that you are in a better position than many. Another topic?"

"All right." He grinned a little, and I got the sense that

he was enjoying his cantankerous role. "What do you think of Charles F. Brannan?"

"Who?"

"Secretary of agriculture." He turned the tie to a clean spot. "Way I hear it, he was in Kansas on a farm tour when the Meteor hit. Unless they find someone else in the line of succession, looks like he's the new president."

The businessman who'd given us the tie said, "Acting president."

"Well, now that's a subject for debate, isn't it." The old man was still glaring at the ceiling. "Constitutional scholars spend a whole heckuva lot of time talking about what exactly that means."

Under all of that grime, the old man was wearing a tweed jacket, complete with bona fide leather patches at the elbows. "Where did you teach?"

"The Citadel."

"Charleston?" My voice was too loud. People had turned to stare. I swallowed and tried again. "You were in Charleston?"

The old man lowered his head a little and studied me out of his good eye. "You got people there?"

"Hometown."

"I'm sorry . . ." He shook his head. "I was out on a hike with cadets. Way inland. When we got back . . . well. I'm real sorry."

I nodded, clenching my jaw against the truth of what I already knew. The blast radius of the meteorite, followed by the tidal waves, meant there'd been little chance. But if I didn't know, then I could still hope. And hope would kill me.

It took walking up the stairs of the synagogue to realize that entering that door meant admitting that my family was dead.

The thought stopped me on the stairs, and I gripped the dusty metal railing. My family was dead. I had come to the synagogue because I needed to begin the mourning rites.

Daddy was never going to pick up his trumpet again. Mama's giant cross-stitched bedspread would never be finished, and was so much ash.

My eyes closed of their own volition, blocking out the brick exterior and the scrubby little yew trees that flanked the stairs. Beneath the dark shield of my lids, my eyes burned. The grit under my hands was the same ash that drifted through most of the town. Ejecta from D.C.

"Are you all right?" An older man's voice, with a hint of German to it, came from slightly behind me.

I opened my eyes and turned with a smile, even though my eyes must be red. "Sorry. I didn't mean to block the way."

The man, who stood a step down, was not older than I was, or if he was, it wasn't by much. His face, though, had a remnant of gauntness to it that I recognized. A Holocaust survivor.

"You . . . had family?"

God. Spare me from the kindness of strangers. I stared at the horizon, an amber haze over the Ohio plains. "Yes. So—I need to go in to talk to the rabbi."

He nodded and slipped past me to hold the door. "I, myself, am here for the same reason."

"Oh—oh. I am so sorry." I was such a self-centered schlub. I was hardly the only one with Jewish family in Charleston. And the damage to New York sounded extensive, and then D.C., and . . . How many of us had died leaving no one behind to light the yahrzeit candles and recite the Kaddish prayer?

His shrug was small and sad as he gestured me through the door. I stepped into the foyer. Through the open doors

I could just make out the comforting light of the eternal flame hanging in front of the ark as a reminder.

This man . . . he must have escaped Germany, only to have this happen when he thought he was safe. And yet, he had survived. As had I.

That's what we did. We survived.

And we remembered.

It is hard to sit shiva in a gentile's home. I compromised with myself and called our bedroom "home" because I did not feel up to explaining to Mrs. Lindholm why I wanted to sit on low stools, or cover the mirrors.

Nathaniel walked in to find me sitting on the floor of our bedroom, pinning a torn ribbon to my shirt. I hadn't been able to bring myself to tear the shirt itself, not because the grief wasn't there, but to avoid the conversation about why I'd torn something we had just bought.

He stopped, and his gaze went to the jagged tear in the ribbon. His shoulders sagged, as if the fact that I had performed kriah alone let all the grief back in.

My husband came over to sit on the floor beside me, pulling me into an embrace. The custom against speaking to someone in mourning until they spoke first had never made so much sense. I could not have spoken if I had tried. And, I suspect, neither could he.

When the week of shiva passed, I called every mechanic in the phone book. None of them had the parts or time to repair my plane. But I had to do something.

I had survived, and there must be some reason for that. Some purpose or meaning or . . . something. I took to going to the hospital with Mrs. Lindholm every day to roll bandages, clean bed pans, and serve soup to plane after plane after plane of refugees.

They kept coming. I called the mechanics again. And then again.

One of them made vague promises about maybe looking into ordering a propeller, if he had time. If Nathaniel were home during the day, I would have asked him to make the call for me.

But each night he came home even later than I did. Friday night, two weeks after the Meteor, he came home well after sundown. Mind you, we had never been terribly religious about keeping the Sabbath before the meteorite, but somehow after it . . . I needed something. Some continuity.

I met Nathaniel at the door and took his coat from him. Major Lindholm—Eugene—and Myrtle had gone to a prayer meeting at their church, so we had the house to ourselves. "You aren't supposed to work after sundown."

"I'm a terrible Jew." He leaned down to kiss me. "But I was occupied with convincing generals that no, the Russians could not have dropped the Meteor on us."

"Still?" I hung his coat on a peg by the door.

"The problem is that Parker had mentioned it to . . . someone . . . probably several someones . . . and now it's spread through the military as, 'I heard there was a possibility that this was an offensive action by the Russians.'"

"Ugh." I gestured toward the kitchen, where the Lindholms had left the lights on. "There's some chicken and potatoes, if you haven't eaten."

"You are a goddess."

"You really *are* a terrible Jew." I laughed and pulled him into the kitchen.

He dropped into one of the chairs with a groan, sliding forward to rest his head on the table. "Elma, I don't know how much longer I can survive these meetings. I keep saying the same thing over and over. Thank God that the UN's been called in, or there's no telling where we would be now."

"Is there anything I can do to help?" I pulled the refrigerator door open and found the plate I'd prepared for him.

He straightened. "Actually . . . yes. If you have time."

"In abundance."

"Do you think you could calculate the size of the meteorite?" His voice broke a little as he asked, and he had to pause to stare at the table.

Normally, a question like this would have gone to his colleagues at Langley. I pretended to busy myself with the plate to give him time to recover. We both tended to break at odd moments, and the tears were exhausting. Sometimes the best course was to pretend it wasn't happening.

Nathaniel pressed his lips together in a dry grimace that tried to masquerade as a smile, and cleared his throat. "I figure if I know that, I can show that there's no possible way the Russians could have moved it."

I put the plate in front of him and kissed the back of his neck. "Yes. I'm presuming you can get me government charts."

"Just tell me what you need."

It's funny. I'd been helping Myrtle with refugees all week, but since they kept coming, and each group was in worse shape than the last, it had felt like nothing had changed—like I made no difference in the world. I kept wondering why I had survived. Why me? Why not someone more useful?

I know. I know that's not logical or reasonable, and clearly I *was* helping people, but . . . but the jobs I was doing could have belonged to anyone. I was an interchangeable cog.

Calculations? This pure abstraction of numbers *belonged* to me. This, I could do.

SEVEN

CIVIL DEFENSE TO USE "HAM" RADIOS

PHILADELPHIA, PA, March 17, 1952—To coordinate relief efforts after the Meteor strike, civil defense agencies are using various types of emergency communications equipment to transmit messages in the disaster area. In addition to the customary telephone, officials are employing portable radio transmitting sets, "walkie-talkies," Army field telephone equipment, and amateur "ham" radio sets. These will be carried in cars manned by volunteer operators who will set up a secondary means of communication.

I worked on Nathaniel's calculations in the evenings. It helped to have the solace of numbers to retreat to after helping with the refugees during the day. Today I had served soup to a group of Girl Scouts and their scout masters. They had been on a camping trip when the Meteor hit, and by sheer luck had been spelunking in the Crystal Caves. They'd felt the earthquake and thought it was disaster enough. Then they'd come up and everything was just gone.

So, numbers. Numbers were a solace. There was logic and order in the calculations. I could take disparate events and wring sense from them.

The other place where I found order amid the chaos was

in the kitchen. It had taken a week before Myrtle would trust me in the kitchen, and another couple of days before I convinced her to let me make dinner. Now we took turns.

Was the kitchen kosher? Not even a little. Ask me if I cared. I opened the drawer next to the sink and rummaged through it until I found the measuring cups. Tonight I was making chicken potpie.

The filling simmered on the stove, scenting the air with the savory aroma of butter and thyme. In some ways, making pastry was like mathematics. Everything needed to be in proportion in order for the mass to come together.

I walked over to the refrigerator, glancing into the living room. Myrtle sat on the couch with her feet up on Eugene's lap. He was rubbing them while she sipped from a glass of wine.

". . . nothing you can do?"

"I'm sorry, baby. I've tried." He grimaced and bent his head as he rubbed a thumb into the ball of her foot. "But I can't go where they don't send me."

"It's just . . . plane after plane of white folks. Where are our people? Who's rescuing them?"

How had I not noticed that? I stopped with a hand on the refrigerator and ran through the refugees in my head, willing myself to see one spot of color amid the masses.

"You know what would happen, even if the brass were to send us to our peoples' neighborhoods. Say we pick them up, and then what? Our people would be put in different camps."

She sighed. "I know . . . I know. I'll bring it up in church. See if we can get a relief effort going ourselves."

Measuring cup still in my hand, I walked over to the kitchen door. "Excuse me."

Myrtle looked around, and as she did, it was like a mask

had slipped over her features. She smiled. "Do you need help finding something?"

"Oh—no. I just . . . I couldn't help overhearing. Do you—do you want Nathaniel to talk to someone?"

Eugene and Myrtle exchanged a glance that I couldn't begin to understand, and then he shook his head. "Thank you, ma'am. I think we've got this."

After dinner, I retreated to the Lindholms' study. I had strewn papers all over the desk as I tried to pull the data points together into the order I needed. Opening the drawer, I pulled out the little notepad we were using as a log book and jotted down the time so I could pay them back for the long-distance call. Then I picked up the receiver and dialed my brother's work number.

"United States Weather Bureau, Hershel Wexler speaking."

"Hey, it's Elma. Got a minute for a weather question?"

"That is the literal definition of my job. What's up?" Paper rustled on the other end of the line. "Planning a picnic?"

"Heh. No." I pulled the equations I'd been working on closer. "I'm helping Nathaniel figure out how big the meteorite was, and composition and . . . The Chesapeake was steaming for three days. I could sort it out on my own, but . . . I thought there might be an existing equation for figuring out what temperature it would take to make a body of water that big steam."

"Interesting . . . Give me a sec." Beyond him, I could hear the Teletype bringing in reports from weather stations around the world. "You've got the depth and volume of water, I assume?"

"Average depth twenty-one feet. Eighteen trillion gallons."

"Okay. So . . . during March, the Chesapeake Bay is around forty-four degrees. So we'd need a temperature change of 199.4 . . ." A drawer opened, and the timbre of his voice changed. I could picture him with the phone pressed between cheek and shoulder, brows creased as he worked the slide rule. His crutches would be leaning against the edge of his desk. His glasses would be down at the tip of his nose to help him focus better, and he'd have the corner of his lower lip tucked between his teeth, humming between muttered phrases. ". . . divided by water's molar mass . . . and that gives me 1.54E20 J of energy . . . hm-hmmm . . . Adding the two energies together . . . hmmm . . . 1.84E20 J of energy. You'd need . . . It would need to be approximately 518 degrees."

"Thanks." I swallowed at the number and tried not to betray how much it frightened me. "You could've just given me the formula."

"What? And admit that my kid sister is better at math than I am?" He snorted. "Please. I have an ego."

I could now plug the temperature into an equation that took the approximate angle of entry into account, and that *should* tell me generally what sort of composition we were looking at, based on what would heat to 518 degrees during passage through the air. It wouldn't be precise, but it would be good enough for Nathaniel's purposes.

"You said you were figuring out what the Meteor was?" The timbre changed again as he brought the receiver closer to his mouth.

"Yeah. Based on the size of the crater—eighteen miles— and the initial water displacement, I have a pretty good estimate of the meteor*ite*'s size." I started noodling with the numbers that he'd given me. "At some point, they'll get divers down to find out its actual composition, but everyone is focused on the refugee and recovery efforts . . ." And that made me think of Eugene and Myrtle.

"Maybe you can answer a question for me."

"I'm not doing your math homework."

He snorted. "How's Nathaniel doing?"

"Oh . . ." I sighed and checked the door to make sure it was shut. "He's exhausted and frustrated and a bunch of it is classified, so . . . I keep thinking it'll be better when everything is over, but . . ."

"But it's not going to be over."

"No." I rubbed my forehead. "How is it out there?"

"We're just starting to see refugees, but mostly it's business as usual." He sighed. "That's going to change when the weather patterns start to shift."

"Shift how?"

"I'm not sure exactly, but that's what I'm working on. That much sediment and smoke in the air?" I could imagine him pulling his glasses off as he sighed. "Maybe you can answer another question for me."

"I'm still not doing your math homework for you."

"Yes, you are, actually. What was the water displacement?"

"I'll be able to give you an approximate value once I know how big the thing was. Why?"

"Because you kick that much water up into the air, and it's going to have an impact on the weather. I want to see if we can predict what the hurricane season is going to be like because of this."

I smiled at the wall, as if Hershel were sitting opposite me. "Okay. Fine. I'll do your math homework, but you know the deal."

"Yes." He laughed. "You can read my comic books, but that is going to require coming to visit."

"As soon as we're finished here." Once Nathaniel was finished with his meetings, I'd talk to him about maybe moving to California.

I shoved the calculations away from me and rested my head on my hands. Crap. It had taken me two evenings to get all the variables lined up. And now? I'd gone through the numbers three times, and if there was a mistake, I wasn't finding it. I had called Hershel, but it was after work hours, and they were out for the evening. Goodness knows what their babysitter made of my message.

Pushing back from the desk, I stood and paced around the study. A casserole sat congealing on the table next to me. Myrtle had brought it in at some point. Part of it was gone and the fork was dirty, but I had no memory of eating anything.

An ache ran from my right eye and over the top of my head. I needed Nathaniel. I gathered the pages together, both my original calculations about the meteorite impact, and the tidier sheets where I'd reworked them. He would still be at HQ. I could . . . what? Pull him out of a meeting? Nothing on these pages would change if I waited for him to come home.

But I needed my husband, and I needed him now. Rubbing the ache above my eye eased it a little. If my math wasn't wrong, then some of the original data must be. One of the reports probably exaggerated numbers. I must be wrong.

I snatched the plate off the table and carried it into the kitchen. The house was dark, except for the light over the stove. Nathaniel needed to come home. And he would, probably in not too much longer. I could be patient.

I scraped the rest of the casserole into the garbage then stood at the kitchen sink to wash the dish. The Lindholms had a shiny new dishwasher, but the water running over my hands calmed me. After I put the dish in the rack, I stood for a moment and let the water trickle through my fingers.

The front door opened. Thank God. I wiped my hands on the dish towel and ran to meet Nathaniel. He smiled when he saw me, and leaned in for a kiss. "Hello, beautiful."

"I need to show you something." I winced. "Sorry. I mean, how was your day? Convince them that the Russians aren't after us yet?"

"Not quite. And now President Brannan wants to restart NACA and have us look for other asteroids." He loosened his tie. "What did you want to show me?"

"It can wait until morning." This was me trying to be a good wife despite my anxiety, because, truly, showing him tonight would accomplish nothing beyond making him as sleepless as me.

"Elma. No. I don't want to be kicked all night."

"Kicked?"

"Yeah. When you're this worked up, you toss and kick in your sleep."

"I—" How do you argue about what you do when you're asleep? "Do I hurt you?"

"Let's just say that I'd like to see whatever it is."

Really, I needed no convincing at all. I grabbed his hand and pulled him into the study. "I was trying to calculate how much energy it would take to move the Meteor to prove that there was no way the Russians could have done it."

He stopped in the doorway. "Please don't tell me that they could have done it."

"No." In a way, that would have been better. I stood next to the desk and looked at the pages covered with calculations. "No, but I think this could be an extinction event."

EIGHT

FEED GRAINS PRICES CRASH

CHICAGO, March 26, 1952—(AP)—Feed grains dropped significantly on the Board of Trade today in a continuation of the preceding session's crash. Brokers thought the downturn, both today and yesterday, was based largely on the fact that export of corn and oats were blocked due to harbor damage on the East Coast ports.

God help me, I wanted to be wrong. Nathaniel sat at the desk in the Lindholms' study and worked his slide rule, double-checking my calculations. The desk was scattered with encyclopedias, almanacs, atlases, and newspapers from the last week with reports of where damage was showing.

I leaned against the wall next to the window, chewing on the inside of my lip. The night outside had started to turn silver, and if I had any more coffee, I would vibrate through the ceiling.

He hadn't asked me any questions for the last hour. Every time his pencil scratched against the paper, I hoped it was an error, that I'd forgotten to invert a differential or square a root or something. Anything.

Finally, he set the slide rule on the desk and rested his head on his fingertips. He stared at the last page. "We have to get off this fucking planet."

"Nathaniel!" Why I was chiding him about language, I couldn't tell you.

"Sorry." He sighed, sliding his hands over his head until his face was hidden between his arms. His voice was muffled against the table. "I really wanted you to be wrong."

"My starting numbers might be off."

"If they're that far off, someone at *Encyclopedia Americana* should be fired." He sat up, still scrubbing his face and squinting. "I thought we had gotten lucky that the meteorite was a water strike."

"It's the steam that's the problem." I crossed the room to sit on the desk, but Nathaniel caught my wrist and pulled me down onto his lap. I leaned against him and rested my head on his. "Things are going to get cold for a bit, and then all that water vapor in the air . . ."

He nodded. "I'll see if I can get you a meeting with the president."

"The president?" Heart kicking sideways, I straightened a bit. "It's just . . . I mean, a lot of this involves stuff that's not in my field of study and . . . maybe we should talk to other scientists."

"Sure. But . . . right now, they've got me and Wernher von Braun working on a program to spot other potential asteroids and blow them up with rockets." He leaned back in the chair and scratched one of the scabs on his chin. "You know military bureaucracy as well as I do."

"Once a program starts, it's hard to stop."

He nodded. "And we're working on the wrong damn problem."

I stood in front of the closet, staring at my meager wardrobe. Every time I reached for a dress, my stomach knotted itself. Everyone would be staring at me. What if I picked the wrong dress? What if my calculations were wrong? It would be better, for Nathaniel, if I stayed home instead of going with him to meet the general.

"Elma? Which tie should I—you're not dressed?" Nathaniel stopped just inside the door to our room. "We're supposed to meet General Eisenhower in thirty minutes." He had a borrowed tie in each hand.

"The blue one. It brings out your eyes." I shut the door to the closet, and the knot in my stomach immediately loosened.

"Are you okay?" He lowered the ties and came over to feel my forehead.

"Just a little under the weather." I was having my period, but that wasn't the problem. I would milk it, though, for all it was worth, if it meant I could avoid this meeting. "But I've got the report typed up for you, and you understand the equations as well as I do."

"That is a serious exaggeration." He set the green tie down on the desk. "If they have any questions, I'm not sure I'm equipped to answer them."

They. Of course it would be a crowd. It was one thing to follow Nathaniel into a meeting as support, or to argue with Parker, but get more than six men in a room, and . . . all the old memories came back. I wiped my palms on my dressing gown, still nervous even though I wouldn't be going. "The general likely won't be able to follow the equations anyway. So all you have to do is talk about the conclusions."

He sighed and looped the tie around the back of his neck. "That's what I was planning on doing. I wanted you there for the things I couldn't answer. Like the correlation between steam in the air and increased global temperatures."

I grabbed one of the reports I'd typed up and flipped through the pages. "That's on page four, and there's a graph at the back that shows the rise in temperature over the next fifty years. So—"

"I know."

"They'll believe it coming from you. They won't if I explain it."

"Please." He turned from the mirror. "Which of us was a math tutor in college? You're brilliant at explaining things."

My husband was a good man. He believed in me. And he also had a huge blind spot, because he didn't see how people would ignore what I said until he repeated it. "It doesn't matter. I just don't feel well. Okay?"

Nathaniel wrapped the tie into a Windsor and snugged the sharp knot up against his collar. "Sorry. I'd just been planning on having you there. But if you don't feel well, you don't feel well."

I shrank a little into my bathrobe. "I just . . . today's not a good day."

"When is? We haven't had a good day since the meteorite struck."

"I'm—it's a feminine—"

"Got it." He frowned and rubbed his brow. Shaking his head, he grabbed his jacket from the back of the chair. "Well. This is just a precursor to meeting the president. You'll be better for that one."

The problem was that I wouldn't be better. Meeting the president would be infinitely worse . . . but at least it wasn't happening today. And maybe I wouldn't be needed, or maybe my security clearance wouldn't be high enough, or something would save me from having to stand in front of a roomful of men.

I'm an intelligent woman. I understood that there was absolutely no danger. I really, truly did.

And yet . . . and yet, going to high school when you are eleven years old. Being the only girl in a mathematics class. Repeatedly. Going to college at fourteen. Having everyone stare at you because you can do math in your head. Having boys hate you, *hate* you, because you never get questions wrong in class. Being used as a tool by professor after professor. "Look! Even this little girl knows the answer."

By the time I left college, I would do anything to avoid speaking in front of a group. I cleared my throat. "Have you met him before?"

"The president, or Eisenhower? I mean, yes, either way, but only briefly."

"General Eisenhower and Daddy used to golf together."

"See! This is why I want you there."

"Because of who my dad is—was? Whatever." I slapped the report back down on the desk. "I can't go."

He sighed again and stared at the floor. "I'm sorry. I'm being selfish, because I'm nervous." Nathaniel walked over and wrapped his arms around me. "Is there anything you need today? Hot water bottle? Chocolate?"

"Empty promises. Where do you think you'll get chocolate?" With the ports on the East Coast still closed, the grocery store shelves were already getting thin.

"I'll requisition it from General Eisenhower."

"On what grounds?"

"That the fate of the world depends on keeping my wife healthy and happy." He kissed my forehead. "I'm not even sure it's an exaggeration."

There's a cascading effect that happens when you lie about not feeling well. I was supposed to go volunteer at the hospital after the meeting with Eisenhower. After Nathaniel left, Myrtle knocked on my door.

I buttoned the last button on my blouse. "Come in?"

Using her foot, Myrtle pushed the door open. She had a tray with some saltines and a glass of ginger ale. "Nathaniel said you weren't feeling well."

"Oh . . . it's just, you know, feminine complaints." I

tucked in my shirt so I wouldn't have to face her. "The worst seems to have passed, actually."

"I know every woman is different, but mine lays me out for an entire day." She set the tray down on the little desk in our room. "So I've brought you some things to settle your stomach. Do you need a hot water bottle? Or . . . I have some bourbon, if that will help."

How had we gotten so lucky as to land with these people? My eyes watered, which was a sign that my period was, in fact, affecting me. "You are kindness embodied." I wiped my fingers under my eyes. "Honestly, I am much better. It usually doesn't hit me very hard at all. I guess I just . . ." I waved my hand, hoping she would create her own story from the ambiguity.

"All the stress of—well, everything you've gone through in the past couple of weeks." She held out the glass of ginger ale. "No wonder you're wrung out."

"I'm fine." But I took the ginger ale, and even the icy chill of the glass was soothing. "Really. What about you? Any progress with your church on the refugee front?"

Myrtle hesitated, then wet her lips. "Actually . . . yes. Maybe. We have an idea, but it involves asking you a favor."

Oh God. A chance to be useful? "Yes. Anything. After everything y'all have done for us, anything I can do is already done."

"Don't worry—this won't require you to do a thing." She straightened the tray on the desk so it was square with the edges. "Eugene says you have a plane?"

"It's damaged, but yes."

She nodded as if she already knew this. "If he could get it fixed up, can he borrow it?"

"Of course." It was small and petty of me, but I was disappointed that there was nothing more. "But I called all the mechanics and none of them could help."

She gave a little smile. "You called all the *white* mechanics. Not everyone who knows planes is in the phone book. Eugene can get it fixed."

Had she known that there were other mechanics all along and not told me, or was it something that hadn't come up until just now? Either way, resentment was a completely inappropriate response. I owed her. She owed me nothing. "It can only hold four. You won't be able to get a lot of refugees in there."

"Oh . . . I know. We've got a different plan." She straightened and clapped her hands together. "Listen to me, running my mouth off when you don't feel well. Now, you just take it easy for the rest of the day, even if you do feel better. I'll leave some chicken broth—no bacon—simmering on the stove for later."

"Thank you, but really—"

"You're fine. I know. You're as bad as Eugene. If I didn't know better, I'd think you were a man."

"It's a pilot thing, I guess." I shrugged. "They ground you if you're sick."

"Well . . . I don't have daughters, but you're grounded, young lady. I think that's the only way to get you to slow down and take care of yourself."

Slow down? I'd done *nothing* since the meteorite. I should have gone with Nathaniel. I might have been a tiny bit useful there.

"What are you doing in the kitchen?" Myrtle stood in the living room with her hat and gloves still on.

With a handful of lettuce poised over a bowl, I somehow suddenly felt guilty. "Making dinner?"

"Girl, you're supposed to be resting." Sometimes her mid-Atlantic housewife diction disappeared, mostly when she was irritated. I got a sense I was hearing a more honest version of herself. Myrtle set her things down on one of the side tables and came in, making shooing gestures. "Go on. Back to bed."

"I'm fine. There was a little cramping, but really . . ." I put the rest of the lettuce in the bowl and shredded it with, perhaps, a little more force than was strictly necessary. I should have just buckled up and gone with Nathaniel. "I was restless, and you worked all day."

Outside, the rumble of Major Lindholm's jeep gave notice that at least one of the men was home. Glancing out the window, I couldn't quite make out the vehicle. Had Nathaniel been kept in meetings? Again? I should have gone. I was an idiot.

She pulled open the pantry door and reached inside for an apron. "Well, tell me what I can do."

"Um . . . Check the tagliarini to see if the foil needs to come off?"

The front door opened and brought with it the sound of Eugene and Nathaniel talking. It seemed like every time he got a chance, Eugene would pump Nathaniel for information about rockets. ". . . out at Edwards Air Force Base."

"Oh Lord . . . not this again." Myrtle strode toward the living room. "You are not going to be a test pilot. Fighter was bad enough, but at least there was a war on then."

"Baby . . . we're just talking about the rocket work they're doing."

Nathaniel laughed uncomfortably. "We're comparing the facilities at Sunflower in Kansas to Edwards. That's all . . . Um. I should go check on Elma."

"She's in the kitchen."

Nathaniel appeared in the door as I picked up a carrot to grate into the salad. He set his folder of papers down on the kitchen table. "Hey. Feeling better?"

"Yes, thank you." We needed to get him a new briefcase,

but it seemed low on the list of priorities. I picked up the grater and ran the carrot over the rough surface with quick downstrokes. "How did it go?"

"Good. Thank God." He loosened his tie and leaned against the counter. "Anything I can do?"

"Um . . . make a cocktail?"

"Gladly." We had added to the Lindholms' liquor cabinet as soon as Nathaniel had received his first paycheck from the military. And, yes, we stockpiled some under the bed in our room—currency. In case things really collapsed. "Martini okay?"

"Perfect." I set the grater aside and scraped the carrots into the bowl with the lettuce. Every time I'd handled food since doing the calculations, I wondered if this was the last year I'd be eating it. But carrots and lettuce . . . they'd both survive the meteorite winter years. I think. "So what did Eisenhower say? Tell me about your brilliance."

Nathaniel snorted as he pulled the gin out of the freezer. "Well . . . your brilliant, brilliant husband—hang on." He wandered over to the door to the living room, and I wanted to scream at him. Such a tease. "Do you all want martinis?"

Their hushed conversation broke off and Eugene said, "God yes. If my wife allows—oof."

"Thank you, Nathaniel. That would be very much appreciated. Might I have a double?" You could have caught flies with the honey in Myrtle's voice.

Chuckling, I rinsed the grater in the kitchen sink. At least there were no issues with clean water here. Some of the refugees had been without it for days by the time they got to us. Of course, the acid rains hadn't reached the Midwest yet. "A double sounds like an excellent idea."

Nathaniel turned back from the doorway with his brows raised. "And *I'm* the one who had the meeting."

"Medicinal. And you should have a double too." The

dressing was already made, but I wouldn't add it until we were ready to eat. That left . . . checking the tagliarini. "You were telling me about Eisenhower and your brilliance."

"Ah. Right." He grabbed a pitcher from the cabinet. "Well . . . after I dazzled them with my rhetoric and awe-inspiring elocution, I stunned Eisenhower into silence by handing him your brilliant, in-depth report. Not that he could follow the calculations, but—"

"See, I didn't need to be there." As I opened the oven door, the heat from it rushed up into my face. Four hundred and fifty degrees. That was cooler than the air that would have hit Washington from the airblast.

"Well, I did have to bluff my way past some of his questions." Nathaniel measured gin into the pitcher. "But he has enough understanding of rocketry, from a military perspective, to understand that moving the asteroid would have been impossible given the Soviet's current level of technology."

"Thank God." I teased the foil off the tagliarini so the cheese could brown, then shut the oven door. "What about the weather?"

"The weather today was lovely."

"You know what I mean."

"I do. And it's relevant. It's hard to convince people that catastrophic weather changes are coming on a nice day." The bottle of vermouth was standing on the counter next to him. "Besides, it doesn't have 'military significance,' so he didn't feel the urgency of it."

"The bulk of the report was about that!" I should have gone with him. Next time. Next time, I would have to go. "So . . . do you get to see the president? Is that what happens next?"

He shrugged and grabbed the ice from the freezer. "I'm trying. Eisenhower said he would attempt to expedite it, but without the Soviet threat, the urgency isn't there. Acting President Brannan is, understandably, busy with restoring the U.S. government."

"Ugh." I stood with my hands on my hips and hated myself even more for this morning's lie. If I had been there—what? Would General Eisenhower really have listened to a girl talk about math and weather? Maybe, for the sake of my father, he might have given me time, but I doubt I could have changed his mind. "I'm glad I already asked for a double, because if they don't make plans . . ."

"I know." He lifted the lever to crack the ice in the tray with such force that a piece hopped out and skittered across the floor. "But one step at a time. They aren't going to attack the Soviets, and that would have been far worse."

It wouldn't have been. Just more immediate.

NINE

POLLUTION DEFIES EUROPE'S BORDERS

Norway Finds Air Waste From
Abroad a Problem

By **JOHN M. LEE**

OSLO, Norway, April 3, 1952—Rising European
concern about air pollution deriving from last month's
Meteor strike found expression in Norway this week
when a leading scientist declared, "Our freshwater fish
and our forests will be destroyed if these develop-
ments continue uncontrolled."

After that glorious week of calculations, my life returned
to volunteering at the hospital while we waited to hear from
the president. April 3rd. One month, to the day, after the
Meteor struck, one of the daily refugee planes landed. You
would think they would stop coming at a certain point, but
there were always more. The people who had survived the
initial devastation had held out until it became clear that
the infrastructure wouldn't recover any time soon.

I waited in the shade of one of our canvas triage tents as
the plane taxied to a stop. Uniformed men ran the stairs out
to the plane, and the doctors and nurses waited at the ready.
We had a good system down now.

The door opened and the first of the refugees stepped

out, gaunt as a rake. And black. I inhaled and turned, automatically, to look for Myrtle. In the entire month, this was the first black man who had gotten off one of the refugee planes.

She had her back to the plane, squaring bandages on a table.

"Myrtle?" Behind me, a murmur of surprise came from the doctors and nurses.

"Hm?" She looked over her shoulder. Her knees buckled, but she caught herself on the table. "Oh God. Praise God, it worked. Thank you, God, for your mercy."

When I turned back, there was a line of black men, women, and children coming down the stairs. There were white people mixed in, and we saw more as the refugees kept deplaning. First in, last out. The black people had been the last ones they'd let on the plane.

As they came closer, their features were easier to make out. Thin, yes. But also pocked with tiny pink sores. Someone moaned—it might have been me. We'd seen the sores from acid rain before, but the damage was so much more apparent on darker skin.

I shook myself and picked up my tray of paper cups of electrolytes. Hydration. Someone else would be standing by with sandwiches. Glancing back at Myrtle, I said, "So I guess Eugene finally talked someone into changing the location of the rescue missions, huh?"

"No." The smile on her face died away. "No. We used your plane to drop fliers on the black neighborhoods, telling them where to go to be picked up by the refugee planes. But they're here now, and there will be more, and we'll thank God for that."

She picked up a packet of swabs and prepared to meet the incoming wave.

✳　✳　✳

Two weeks later, I'd had ample opportunity to feel guilty for ditching the first meeting about the climate problem like it was a plane on fire. So, feeling the total lack of a parachute, I followed Nathaniel into the meeting with the president, his staff, some cabinet members, and half a dozen other men who served goodness knows what function.

I tried to focus on the mundane details to get past the fear. For instance, whoever had decorated this conference room had gone to great lengths to mask the fact that it was an underground bunker. The wood-paneled walls and green carpet evoked a forest glade. Curtains hung over faux windows, which were lit from the back with a warm golden light.

I clutched my portfolio of papers against my chest and followed Nathaniel into the room. Men in ties and dark suits sat or stood around the room in little knots of conversation. Some stood in front of a chalkboard, where my calculations had been transferred. They stopped talking and turned to stare when Acting President Brannan stood to greet us.

He was sunburnt, and had wrinkles at the corners of his eyes, as though he usually smiled a lot. Not today, though. Lines of strain turned his mouth down, and his hoary gray eyebrows were drawn together with concern.

"Dr. York. Mrs. York." He gestured to the man next to him, who was rotund and balding, but had a splendidly tailored suit. "This is M. Scherzinger from the United Nations. I've asked him to sit in on our conversation."

"Charmed." He bent over my hand with a click of his heels, but his eyes strayed to the small scar my hairline.

Or, at least, I thought they did. I might have been a little paranoid about my appearance. I had tried to find the line between professional and dowdy, but it likely didn't matter. I was the only woman in the room.

Another man, with red hair and no chin, approached and said, "Should we get started, Mr. President? We don't want to waste Dr. York's time." By which he meant that the president was very busy.

"Of course. Thank you, Mr. O'Neill." President Brannan gestured to the front of the conference room.

I kept my gaze fixed upon the chalkboards, scanning the numbers to see if everything had been transferred accurately. It was easier than thinking about the fact that we were about to give a presentation to the president. Or, at least, the acting president.

Around us, the men took their seats and stared at the front of the room expectantly. My heart was racing, and my palms stuck to the portfolio with sweat. To look at me, you wouldn't think that it was snowing outside.

At least I was only there as backup, in case Nathaniel needed additional calculations to explain the situation. Give me an unpowered landing and I was fine. Addressing a roomful of people? Thank you, but no.

At the moment, all I wanted to do was get through the afternoon without vomiting. Besides, there was a disturbing consistency to how data presented by pretty young women was treated. It was better all around if it was Nathaniel doing the talking.

I set my portfolio down on a little table between the chalkboards. One of them was blank and there was plenty of chalk, in a variety of colors, waiting for me. I picked up a piece so I'd have something to do with my hands. The cool white cylinder soaked up the sweat from my skin.

My husband faced the room and waited until he had everyone's attention. "Gentlemen. In the weeks since the Meteor, we have been focused on recovery efforts. Hundreds of thousands of people in countries around the Atlantic have been rendered homeless. In some places, the social order has collapsed, leading to rioting, looting, and other atrocities as people compete for scarce resources. My duty today is to tell you that this is not the worst of our problems."

Listening to the rolling, authoritative tone of his speech, it became much easier to remember why he had become something of a celebrity after we launched the satellites.

"Many people fear that another meteor will strike. It's a natural fear, and why we're buried in this bunker. But . . . but the chances of another strike occurring are astronomically small. The danger represented by this equation is not only much greater, but certain." He gave a rueful smile and shrugged. "For decades, scientists have wondered what happened to the dinosaurs. Why they all died off. This . . . this might explain it."

He walked to the chalkboard with my equations on it. "I won't expect you to follow the math here, but I will say that it has been checked by top people in geology, climatology, and mathematics."

That last one was only me, but I didn't interrupt him. Nathaniel paused and surveyed the room, gathering their attention. The golden light from the faux window brushed his cheeks, picking out the small scars. Under his dark gray suit, his bruises had faded, and he stood with easy confidence, as if he had never been injured.

Taking a breath, Nathaniel tapped the board. "The problem is, gentlemen, that the Earth is going to get warmer. The dust that the Meteor kicked up will clear from our skies. The water vapor . . . that's the problem. It will trap heat, which will cause evaporation, which will put more water vapor into the air, which will, in turn, make the Earth hotter, and kick off a vicious cycle that will eventually make the planet unfit for human habitation."

A plump, sallow man on the right side of the table snorted. "It's snowing today in Los Angeles."

Nathaniel nodded and pointed to him. "Exactly. That snow is directly linked to the Meteor. The dust and smoke that got kicked into the atmosphere are going to cool the Earth for the next several years. We'll probably lose crops this year, not just in the United States, but globally."

President Brannan, bless him, raised his hand before speaking. "How much will the temperature drop?"

"Elma?" Nathaniel half-turned toward me.

My stomach lurched into my throat, and I flipped through the papers in my portfolio to find the one I wanted. "Seventy to one hundred degrees globally."

Toward the back of the room, someone said, "Couldn't hear."

Swallowing, I lifted my head from the papers and faced the room. This was no different from shouting over the engine of an airplane. "Seventy to one hundred degrees."

"That doesn't seem possible." The man at the back crossed his arms over his chest.

"That's just for the first few months." They were focusing on the wrong thing. The temperature drop would be unpleasant, but was short-term. "Then we'll have three to four years of a global climate that's 2.2 degrees cooler than average, before the temperature begins to rise."

"2.2? Huh. So what's the big tizzy over?"

President Brannan said, "That's more than enough to severely affect crops. Growing seasons will shorten by ten to thirty days, so we'll have to convince farmers to plant different crops and at different times of year. That's not going to be easy."

As the former secretary of agriculture, it wasn't surprising that he intuitively understood the trouble with a change in climate. But he was still focused on the wrong thing. Yes, we had a mini–Ice Age to get through, but none of them were considering the eventual rise in temperature.

"Farm subsidies." Another man, maybe the one who'd said he couldn't hear, leaned across the table. "It got farmers to change their crops during the Great Depression."

"All of our resources are going to be tied up in rebuilding."

As they argued, Nathaniel stepped back to me and murmured, "Will you chart the temperature rise?"

I nodded and turned to the board, grateful to have something concrete to do. The chalk slid across the surface, shedding shivers of dust with my upstrokes. The notes in my portfolio were there, in case I lost my place, but I'd stared at this chart so much over the past couple of weeks that it was etched on the inside of my eyelids.

Unseasonable cold for the next several years, then a return to "normal" and then . . . then the temperature kept rising. The line was slow at first, until it reached the tipping point, and suddenly spiked upward.

When I hit that on the board, Nathaniel stepped forward, to the end of the conference table, and stood with his hands clasped in front of him. The conversation quieted.

"In 1824, Joseph Fourier described an effect that Alexander Bell later called 'the greenhouse effect.' In it, particles in the air cause the atmosphere to retain heat. If the Meteor had struck land, the winter would have been longer. The fireball would have been larger. We thought it was fortunate that it struck water, but it's worse. The Earth is going to come out of winter and get hotter. In fifty years, there will be no snow in North America."

The pudgy man who had complained about snow in California laughed. "Coming from Chicago, I gotta say this doesn't strike me as a problem."

"How do you feel about one hundred percent humidity

and summers with a low of one hundred and twenty degrees?"

"Still. Weathermen can't predict if it's going to rain tomorrow. Fifty years is a long time out."

President Brannan raised his hand again. He was staring at me. No. At the board. I stepped to the side so he could see it better. "Dr. York. What does the upturn on that chart represent?"

"That . . . that is when the oceans begin to boil."

It was as if a jet engine had sucked the air out of the room. Someone said, "You can't be serious. That's—"

President Brannan slapped his hand on the table. "I hope you'll grant that I know something about the planet and how it behaves. We're having this meeting because I've already looked over Dr. York's figures and consider the problem serious. We're not here, gentlemen, to debate the matter. We're here to decide what to do about it."

Thank God. Brannan was only the acting president, until Congress could confirm him, which required a Congress, which required elections. But still . . . all the powers of the president were currently invested in him.

He surveyed the room and then gestured to M. Scherzinger. "Will you take the floor?"

"Certainly." He stood and came to stand by Nathaniel. "Gentlemen. Mrs. York. There is a saying in Switzerland, '*Ne pas mettre tous ses œufs dans le même panier,*' which you will know in English as, 'Do not put all your eggs in one basket.' The United Nations feels that, in addition to reducing the damage here on Earth, we must also look beyond our planet. It is time, gentlemen, to colonize outer space."

PART II

TEN

UN URGED TO AID THE UKRAINE

Special to The National Times.

ROME, Feb. 20, 1956—The United Nations Food and Agriculture Organization today urged all member governments to consider immediately what assistance they could give to the Ukraine, part of the former Soviet Union, which is threatened with famine after the failure of its crops during the Meteor winters. The UN instructed its director general to continue to give, upon request of the Ukrainian Government, all appropriate assistance, technical or other, that lies within his authority and competence.

Do you remember where you were when we put a man into space? I was one of two computer girls sitting in the International Aerospace Coalition's "dark room" at Sunflower Mission Control in Kansas, with graph paper and my mechanical pencils. We used to launch from Florida, but that was before the Meteor, and before the NACA became part of the IAC. Sunflower already had a rocket facility from the war, so it made sense to relocate inland, away from the wrecked coast. Three miles away, the fruit of our labor sat on the launchpad: a Jupiter rocket with Stetson Parker strapped into a tiny pod atop 113 metric tons of propellant.

Charming when he wanted to be, even I had to admit

that he was a damn fine pilot. Unless we had really screwed up, he was going to be the first human into space. And if we screwed up, he'd be dead. Of the Artemis Seven astronauts, he was my least favorite, but I wanted him to survive this.

The banks of instrument panels gave a soft glow to the room, and the sound-dampening panels they'd added to the walls kept voices low. Or as low as possible, given a room filled with 123 technicians. The air crackled with electricity. Men paced at the edges of the room. As lead engineer, poor Nathaniel was stuck in the New White House, waiting with President Brannan to talk to the press. They had two speeches written. Just in case.

Across the small light-table from me, Huilang "Helen" Liu played chess with Reynard Carmouche, one of the French engineers, while we waited. Helen, the other computer girl, had joined the International Aerospace Coalition as part of the Taiwanese contingent. Apparently, she'd been a chess champion back home, which Mr. Carmouche hadn't quite grasped yet.

After liftoff, she'd be in charge of extracting the numbers from the Teletype and feeding them to me while I did the calculations to confirm that orbit had been attained. We'd been awake for sixteen hours, but I couldn't have slept if you paid me. I really did need something to do with my hands. Myrtle had been trying to teach me to knit, but it hadn't taken.

From the small raised platform at the end of the room, the launch director said, "All positions are Go for launch commit."

I breathed out. The launch sequence was familiar and terrifying by this point. But no matter how many things we'd launched, this was the first one carrying a human life. You couldn't help but think about the rockets that had exploded on the pad, or the ones that had made it into space carrying a monkey only to return a dead creature to the ground. I didn't like Parker, but by God, he was brave.

And I was deeply, intensely jealous of him.

The mission director replied, "Roger, launch team. We are Go for launch."

Helen turned from the chess game and slid her chair closer to the Teletype. I straightened the graph paper in front of me.

"Stand by for terminal countdown. We are T-minus ten . . . nine . . . eight . . . seven . . . six . . . five . . . four . . . ignition."

Parker's voice crackled over the speaker with the roar of the rocket surrounding him. "Confirm ignition."

". . . two . . . one . . . and LIFTOFF! We have liftoff."

Moments later, the thundering roar of the rocket ignition hit the room in a wave. It pulsed through my chest, even three miles away. Even in a concrete bunker. Even with sound dampening on the walls.

I broke into a sweat. The only thing louder was a meteorite impact. If you were too close to the rocket during liftoff, the sound waves would literally shred you.

"Confirm liftoff. Manual clock is started."

I picked up my pencil and poised it over the graph paper.

"This is *Hercules 7*. The fuel is go. 1.2g. Cabin pressure at 14 psi. Oxygen is go."

As the rocket roared into the air, the Teletype sprang to life with information from tracking stations across the world. Helen started circling numbers as the text came off the machine. She tore the first piece of paper free and slid it across the table.

I sank into the calculations. Raw numbers told the story of position and bearing, and it was my job to use those to reveal the rocket's velocity as it left the Earth. I could see the rocket's smooth, graceful rise in my mind, but plotted the ascent on a piece of graph paper for the men standing behind me.

"Some vibrations. Sky is getting dark now."

That meant Parker was starting to exit the atmosphere. With each piece of paper Helen handed me, the line of the arc I traced continued upward within mission parameters. The roar of the rocket had faded, leaving an eerie silence. Around us, the male voices of engineers at work murmured in a quiet, intense call-and-response.

"Guidance, your report?"

Helen read the numbers from my page, her faint Taiwanese accent coming out with her excitement. "Velocity: 2,350 meters per second. Angle of elevation: four minutes of arc. Altitude: 101.98 kilometers." Her voice was shockingly high amid the tenors and baritones of Mission Control.

Eugene Lindholm, on comm, repeated the numbers to Parker. In response, he said, "Roger. It's a lot smoother now."

The Teletype rattled constantly, and Helen slid another page over to me. I held my lower lip between my teeth as my pencil flew across the page. 6,420 meters per second. The first-stage engine cutoff should be soon.

On the radio, "Cutoff."

"Confirm engine cutoff."

"I can see the booster falling away."

I glanced at the clock, counting the seconds along with everyone else. Half a minute after the booster dropped away, the escape tower should jettison. He'd be well and truly on his own, then.

"Tower jettison is green."

"Confirm tower jettison."

Momentum carried Parker higher, and with the next

page Helen handed me, I started to smile. 8,260 meters per second. Hellooooo orbital velocity. But I did the calculations on the page anyway, to show my work.

"Periscope is coming out. Turnaround started."

"Confirm turnaround."

Behind me, Mr. Carmouche asked, "Why are you smiling?"

I shook my head and drew one more dot on the graph at 280 kilometers above the surface. Getting Parker into space was the first step. Achieving orbit required altering his trajectory, and that was all on him.

"Switching to manual." The radio continued to crackle as he left the channel open. "The view is . . . wish you all could see this."

"Roger, wish for seeing view confirmed."

Didn't we all wish for that? If he orbited successfully, that got us one step closer to a space station, which got us a step closer to the moon base. And then Mars, Venus, and the rest of the solar system.

Helen gave me another sheet from the Teletype. I tracked Parker's position by shifts in Doppler frequency. The frequency of those waves showed the rocket's path over the Earth. I plugged the numbers into the string of calculations and then ran through it again, just to be sure.

Turning in my seat, I lifted the page over my head. "He made it! He's in orbit."

Grown men jumped from their seats, shouting like kids at a ball game. One fellow threw paper into the air, and it fluttered down around us. Someone clapped me on the shoulder, and there was a sudden warm wet pressure on my cheek. I pulled back, glaring at Mr. Carmouche, whose lips were still puckered from the kiss.

"We still have to get him home." I wiped my cheek off and set my pencil on the page again. Across the table, Helen met my gaze and nodded. Then she handed me the next sheet of paper.

The light from the hall outside our rented apartment fell across the bed. I rolled over as Nathaniel's silhouette entered, muffled by his overcoat. The light from the bathroom reflected only on his shoes, and the snow still caught in his trouser cuffs.

"I'm not asleep." That was mostly true. I'd left the Murphy bed down before I went to Mission Control that morning because I knew we'd both be too tired to deal with it after the launch. "Congratulations."

"To you as well." He took off his overcoat and hung it on the peg by the front door. Housing prices in Kansas City had skyrocketed after President Brannan relocated the capital to the center of the country. Between that and all the refugees who needed homes, the only place we could afford, even with a government salary, was a studio apartment. Frankly, I was happy not to have much house to keep up with.

I turned on the bedside lamp and sat up. "You were wonderful in the press conference."

"If by 'wonderful' you mean that I deflected the idiot reporter who thinks the whole program is pointless, then yes. Yes, I was." He shrugged, pulling on his tie. "I'd rather have been at Mission Control. I could hear you over the radio when they retrieved Parker after splashdown. And here I thought you didn't like the fellow."

"How do you know it was me?"

"First, we've been married for five years. Second . . ." He kicked his shoes off. "You were one of two women in the room, and I don't think you were the one speaking Taiwanese."

"*Li ki si.*" Helen had taught me to swear, which came

in handy with some of the engineers. And occasionally my husband. "Anyway. I'm allowed to be excited that the mission was a success, and I'm not evil. Or at least not enough to wish him dead for real. Mostly."

"Hm." He crossed the room and bent down to kiss me, tasting of good scotch. "Mostly evil? Yes, I can agree with—ow! My point's proven."

Reaching up, I undid the top button of his collar. "I think . . ." The next button followed, exposing his clavicle and the top of his undershirt. ". . . it depends on how one defines evil."

Nathaniel traced a finger along the neckline of my nightgown. "I am happy to entertain your definition."

"Well . . ." I reached the last button and tugged his shirt free of his trousers. "For instance. Let's say that one learns something during a press conference that her husband really should have told her."

Nathaniel's hand paused at the strap of my nightgown. "Interesting example." He slid the strap off and bent down to kiss my exposed shoulder. "I might need more specifics."

I inhaled, breathing in muskiness from his aftershave, and the sweet earthiness of a fine cigar. "For instance, the fact that they are expanding the astronaut corps and removing the test pilot requirement." With my face pressed into his hair, I found his belt by touch. The fabric beneath it was already strained out of shape.

My God, I loved a successful rocket launch. Nathaniel nibbled a path from my shoulder to the base of my neck, sending warm currents down to my toes. "Let's say that expanding the astronaut corps was contingent on completion of a mission. Would withholding information about the expansion be considered evil, if the motivation was to keep someone's hopes from rising?"

"Mm . . . rising hopes." I released the zipper on his trousers, and Nathaniel's hands tightened on my upper arms.

"And would that be further mitigated if, for instance, a certain briefcase contained an application? For someone who was, say, a World War II pilot, had logged the requisite flight time, and fit the right height and weight requirements? Ah—oh . . . oh God." He cleared his throat, and his breath was hot against my neck. "I'll take that as a yes."

"Confirmed: evilness mitigated. But . . ." I slid back on the bed, pulling my nightgown off as I did. With my arms over my head and the cool night air bringing my breasts to full attention, I also commanded my husband's . . . full attention. "It's the action one would take to protect a child. Am I a child?"

"God. No." He shrugged out of his dress shirt and peeled his undershirt off. The bedside lamp caressed the curve and flex of his abdomen. After the Meteor, Nathaniel had begun working out. He was not alone in that drive to be more prepared for "what if" scenarios, but, my heavens . . . did I ever appreciate the result.

I threw my nightgown to the side. His gaze stayed fixed on me, and his mouth hung a little open, as if his brain were trying to acquire extra oxygen to compensate for a redirected blood flow.

"So, I have to ask, why wouldn't one tell an adult?" I regretted the question almost immediately, because this one made him pause. On the other hand, he paused in the act of sliding his trousers and underwear off in one motion, so I could appreciate the V of his abdomen as it joined his pelvis, and the dark hair at the base.

"Because they were going to cancel the entire program. If the launch had failed." By "fail," he meant: if Parker had died. Nathaniel slid his trousers the rest of the way off.

"The snow. People think that the warming isn't coming. So . . ."

I reached for him and he slid between my legs, pushing me back to lie on the bed with his warmth pressed against my full length. Wrapping one thigh around his leg, I pressed up into Nathaniel and his eyes fluttered closed. "Warming is definitely coming."

"Yes." He shifted so he could reach between us. His fingers found the bright bundle of delight between my legs and . . . sparked my ignition sequence. Everything else could wait.

"Oh . . . oh God. We are Go for launch."

ELEVEN

IAC IS SPURRING ROCKET PROGRAM

*75 to 105 Vehicles Will Be Fired in
3-Year Schedule, Chief Says*

By BILL BECKER

Special to The National Times.

KANSAS CITY, KS, March 3, 1956—The International Aerospace Coalition plans to launch 75 to 105 major rockets in the next three years, thereby expecting to have a colony on the moon by 1960.

"Do you remember where you were when the Meteor struck?" At the front of the synagogue, our rabbi looked over the congregation.

I don't know about anyone else, but my eyes instantly burned with the threat of tears. Of course I remembered.

Behind me, I heard another woman sniffle. I wondered where she had been four years ago on March 3rd, 1952. Had she been in bed with her husband? Had she been preparing breakfast for her children? Or had she been one of the millions of people who didn't hear about it until later?

"I was counseling a young couple, newly engaged, who were facing all the joys of their upcoming marriage. My secretary knocked on the door—she never does this. She opened the door and she was weeping. You all know

Mrs. Schwab. Have you ever seen her even without a smile? 'The radio,' she said."

Rabbi Neuberger shrugged, but somehow still conveyed all the grief that followed. "I will always think about that moment as the threshold between Before and After." He held up a finger. "If that young couple had not been in my office, I would have given way to grief. But they asked me if they should still get married. It seemed as if the world were ending. Should they marry?"

He leaned forward, and you could hear the held breath of every person in the tense silence around us.

"Yes. Marriage, too, is a threshold between Before and After. We have many of these, every day, which we do not recognize. The threshold is not the question. There will always be Befores and Afters. The question is: what do you do after you cross that threshold?"

I wiped under my eyes with the thumb of my glove, and it came away dark with mascara.

"You live. You remember. This is what our people have always done."

Outside the synagogue, bells began to sound across the city. Probably across the country, and maybe across the planet. I didn't have to look at my watch. 9:53 a.m.

I closed my eyes, and even in the darkness, even four year later, I could still see the light. Yes. I remembered where I was when the Meteor struck.

I did not even make the first cut.

I was consoling myself with a piece of carrot cake at the IAC cafeteria—and, as a sidenote, let me say that the best thing about the *International* part of the International Aerospace Coalition was that it meant the cafeteria had a French pastry chef. But I digress. So the carrot cake and I were sitting at a table with Helen, Basira, and Myrtle. When we'd been living with Myrtle, I'd had no idea she had worked as a computer during the war until she signed on with the IAC two years ago.

Basira, who had come to us from Algiers, made a face. "So, then he tried to show me how to use a slide rule!"

"No—for a differential equation?" Myrtle, the only other American in our group, covered her mouth and laughed until her cheeks turned red. "What a buffoon."

"I know!" Basira put on a terrible American accent. "Weyaaaaahll, liddle lady, this here iz ah mighdy fine instrumen."

Helen had her hands clapped over her mouth and was cackling like a Taiwanese banshee—if there were such a thing. "Tell them where he hold it!"

With a snort, Basira glanced around the cafeteria, but it was the end of the day shift, so it was largely empty. I lowered my fork, making a guess and—yep. She placed her hand in her lap, as if the slide rule were . . . well. Prepared for liftoff. "I ken show ya how ta uze it."

I laughed, picturing Leroy Pluckett, with his wispy sideburns and loud ties, trying to come on to Basira. With her height and dark, smooth complexion, she had easily won Miss Outer Space at the company holiday party last winter. Plus, her accent was to die for.

The company of these women was a newfound joy to me. The NACA computing department had been all women, yes, but due to segregation laws in D.C., they had all been white women. If you told me four years ago that I was going to be one of only two white women in my group of closest friends, I would have laughed. I'm ashamed of that now.

The International Aerospace Coalition, which President Brannan had convinced the UN to form, changed everything. Well . . . the Meteor had changed everything. But

THE CALCULATING STARS * 109

having a Quaker for president did a lot to alter hiring practices all the way down the line. And I couldn't be luckier to have these friends as a result.

Helen wiped her eyes and looked over my shoulder. "Hello, Dr. York."

"Good evening, ladies." He rested his hand on my shoulder briefly, in lieu of a public kiss. "What are you laughing about?"

"Slide rules." Helen folded her hands demurely in her lap. "And their uses."

Which set us off again. Poor Nathaniel just watched the laughter, smiling with us, but otherwise clueless. Which reminded me that I would have to talk to him about Leroy Pluckett. It made for a funny story, but I didn't like him coming into our department and disrupting it. Technically, personnel issues were Mrs. Rogers's job, but I was the one who was sleeping with the lead engineer, so I was in a better position to fix it than the other women.

Wiping my eyes and still chuckling, I slid my chair back. "Looks like my ride is here."

"Are you not going to finish that cake?" Myrtle reached across the table.

"It's all yours."

Nathaniel picked up my coat from the back of my chair and held it up for me. This July was almost warm enough to not need it, but not quite yet. Summer was coming, sooner than we liked. I waved goodbye to the women. "See y'all tomorrow."

A chorus of goodbyes followed us across the cafeteria amid bubbles of laughter. Nathaniel took my hand. "You seem to be in a better mood."

"Well, cake helps. And getting a rose from you."

"I'm glad you liked it." He waved to one of the other engineers as we walked down the hall toward the front doors of the IAC. "I learned something today that might also cheer you up."

"Oh?" I stopped by the door to let him open it for me. "Do tell?"

The late-evening sun cut across the parking lot, but did little to stave off the chill air. Pulling my coat a little tighter around me, I went out and walked with Nathaniel toward the bus stop. Beyond the fence that surrounded the IAC campus, kids waited with autograph books, hoping for a glimpse of one of the astronauts. They spotted Nathaniel, and once again settled for the lead engineer of the space program.

I let go of his hand and stepped to the side as the kids swarmed around him. Thank heavens they had no interest in the engineer's wife. It was like watching a feeding frenzy, with autograph books in lieu of teeth. He ran the gauntlet nearly every day, and I suspected that it was one of the reasons he often worked so late.

Well . . . that and my husband's inherent nature. The kids weren't the only rocket enthusiasts.

After he worked his way clear of them, Nathaniel waited until we had walked down the block toward the bus stop to get back to his news.

"Well . . ." He glanced behind us. "This is not technically classified, since the final list of the astronauts will make it clear, but . . ."

"I won't mention anything until the final list is published." Not even the first cut. I hadn't expected to make the final team—not really—but with my logged flight time, I thought I'd at least get past the first cut.

"Director Clemons did not select any women. At all."

Stopping dead in my tracks, I stared at him. The head of the IAC, Director Norman Clemons—a man I had worked with for years, and someone I had respected—had not selected any women. Breath steamed in front of me as my mouth hung open. "How is that supposed to make me feel better?"

"Well . . . because you know it wasn't you. Right?"

"But there wasn't anything in the requirements about being male."

Nathaniel nodded. "Clemons said he thought it would have been self-evident. Because of the dangers."

"Oh my God. I accepted that piece of patriarchal stupidity for test flights. But now? We're trying to establish a *colony*. How exactly does he expect to do that without any women?"

"I think . . ." He hesitated and looked down the street, his eyes squinted against the breeze. There were times when Nathaniel really couldn't tell me things, because they were classified, and when he hit one of those walls, he always looked vaguely constipated. Right now, it looked as if he were holding something huge.

"What?"

He licked his lips and shifted his weight. "There was some . . . concern about the stresses of space."

"Stresses. Women handle G-forces better than men. The WASPs established that during the war and—" I broke off at the sudden compression of his lips, as if he were biting back words. "You are kidding me. They think we'll get hysterical in space?"

Nathaniel shook his head and gestured toward the bus stop. "I thought we might go dancing tonight."

Grinding my teeth, I jammed my hands into my coat pockets. "Why not a show, while we're at it." If I had to lay money on who had objected to the fitness of women for the space program, I'd pick one man: Stetson Parker.

*   *   *

I will grant that Nathaniel was right, in that I wasn't sad anymore, but anger was, perhaps, not what he had intended to inspire. By the time we reached the weekend, I was still angry. If I had tried my best and failed, it would have been different. I could have dusted myself off and tried harder next time.

This? This was maddening, because there was nothing I could do to change it. If you haven't gathered by now, I don't do well with "helpless." So I headed out to the private airfield where our local branch of the 99s Flight Club met. The first rule of flight club was—well, actually, the first rule was "safety," but after that it was, "Ground is for griping. Planes are for planning." In-air conversations did not return to the ground.

Which is why I started this particular conversation on the ground. I wanted at least some gossip to arise from it. I looked around at the circle of women. When the original 99s formed, they took their name because there were only ninety-nine women pilots in the United States. Now there were thousands of us in different clubs across the nation, and I was betting that all of us had the same ambitions. "Who else applied for the astronaut corps?"

Everyone's hands went up, except Pearl, who was still plump from having triplets, and Helen, who didn't have her license yet. (I'd gotten her hooked on flying at the Fourth of July party last year. Her father still hadn't forgiven me.)

It was Betty's turn for preflight refreshments and she had brought lemon-beet cookies. I'd been dubious when they first made an appearance, but these could be made despite the sugar shortages, and they were tart, sweet, and delicious. She set the plate down on the rough wooden picnic table set up in the corner of the hangar. Her movie-star red lips twisted into a pout. "I didn't make the cut."

I snatched a bright pink cookie from the plate. "None of us did."

The other women turned on me with expressions ranging from surprise to suspicion. Pearl wrinkled her pert little nose. "How do you know that?"

"Because." I broke the cookie in half. "They didn't take any women."

"Why? On what grounds?"

Betty snorted and grabbed her bosom, which was magnificent. "Obviously, these get in the way of the controls."

"Speak for yourself." Helen ran her hands down her flight suit, which accentuated her boyish figure.

"Seriously, though. I thought they were trying to establish colonies."

Nodding, I avoided any of the things Nathaniel had hinted at. "They'll be doing a formal announcement of the list at a press conference next week."

Betty perked up and grabbed for her bag. "You don't say." She pulled out her reporter's notepad.

I cleared my throat. "Obviously, *I* don't say, but someone with a tie to a major newspaper would probably be invited, and—"

"Nuts." She glared at the pad. "They'll probably give it to Hart. He's getting all the prime international stuff. I swear to God, if I have to cover one more garden club—"

"You'll do it, and be grateful for the paycheck." Pearl twisted her gloves in her hands.

Betty sighed. "You could have at least let me rant a little longer before bringing reality into this."

"The thing is—" I cut in, pointing my cookie at Betty. "Do you think he'll notice an all-male list?"

She narrowed her eyes, and I could see her formulating the pitch she'd use with her editor. "Can I cite you as a source at the IAC? Not by name."

"I . . . I don't want to get . . . um . . . *my* source in trouble."

Betty snatched the cookie out of my hand. "If you think that little of my—"

I snatched it back and crumbs went flying. Laughing, I popped the tart morsel into my mouth. "I just want to make sure the parameters are clear."

"Parameters confirmed." She grabbed her flight jacket and stood. "Shall we fly?"

"Absolutely." I tucked another cookie into the pocket of my flight jacket and glanced at Helen. "Going up with me, or one of the other girls?"

"Wouldn't miss it."

My little Cessna 170b could carry four people. Betty had a Texan, but it wasn't any good for conversation, so she decided that, given the topic, she'd start with us, so we didn't have to use the radio to talk. We piled into the cockpit, and put the conversation on hold while I went through the preflight checklist.

There is something magic about takeoffs. I know people who are afraid of flying who say that the takeoffs and landings are the only hard parts, perhaps because that's when the act of flying is most apparent. I love the way you get pushed back into your seat. The weight and the sense of momentum press against you and the vibrations from the tarmac hum through the yoke and into your palms and legs. Then, suddenly, everything stops and the ground drops away.

It never feels like I'm rising, but that the ground is falling away from me as if I were light as air. Maybe that's what frightens people? Or maybe I'm not frightened because my dad flew with the Air Force when it was still part of the Army, and had taken me on my first plane ride when I was two years old. I'm told that I laughed the entire flight. Clearly, I don't remember that. I do remember begging him to do barrel rolls when I got a little older.

Most kids? Their dad teaches them to drive. Mine taught me to fly.

Anyway. Once we were up in the air, I turned us in a lazy spiral away from the airfield, just to get a feel for the air today. Betty sat in the copilot seat, with Helen behind us.

Betty turned to address both of us, shouting a little over the engine. "All right. Flight Club rules are in effect. Am I right that they want to turn the moon into a military base?"

"From all the things Nathaniel isn't saying, I think it's actually that women are too emotional to go into space."

Betty shook her head, and I'm fairly certain she cursed under the sound of the airplane. "Right. This is hogswallow, and we need to change it."

"How?" Helen leaned forward in her seat.

"I can pitch this to my editor as discrimination, but that's not going to take if I can't also talk about some of the women who were passed over." She looked at me. "I can do it in ways that won't make my sources clear, and . . . and I can also prime Hart to ask the question and bring it front and center at the press conference."

I glanced sideways at her. "How? I mean . . . that feels very direct."

"Mr. President, with an all-male astronaut corps, is there a danger that the Communist bloc will perceive this as a military outpost rather than a colony?"

Helen raised her hand, as if to remind us that she was from Taiwan. "He'll counter with international cooperation."

I nodded. "We've got people at the IAC from Taiwan, Algeria, Spain, Brazil, France, Germany, Serbia, Haiti, the Congo . . ."

Helen chimed in, "Belgium, Canada, Denmark, France, Iceland, Italy, Luxembourg, the Netherlands, Norway, Portugal, the United Kingdom . . ."

"And the U.S."

Betty shook her head. "And none of those are Communist countries."

"Okay . . . but it still doesn't talk about the hysteria aspect."

"No, but it does highlight the all-male astronaut corps, and that gives us leverage for a follow-up about why there are no women." She snorted. "And it's an election year. Eisenhower is running against Brannan, so I'm going to bet money, right now, that a return to 'normalcy,' with women relegated back to being 'homemakers,' is going to be a key election issue."

Cold ran all the way to the center of my body. "But . . . but the director of the IAC doesn't answer to the president, he—" Even as the words left my mouth, I knew I was being stupid. The IAC might be an international effort, but because the launch center was on American soil, we had more influence on the program than other countries— even with a British director. And I'd seen the list of astronauts. Fully three-quarters of them were American or British. All of them were white. "Everyone buckled up?"

They both said yes, but didn't ask me why. They knew me well. I pulled the plane up, gaining altitude, and looped us over. Centrifugal force kept us pushed into our seats. The Earth lay spread out below in a quilt of green and brown. There was enough haze in the sky that the line between ground and air was indistinct and the edges blurred away into the silver-white of the sky. I'd seen pictures from orbit, the Earth turned into a blue-green globe. I wanted to float weightless in space and see the stars with all their startling clarity. If these men with their constant jockeying for dominance dragged us back into the dark ages, I would . . . what?

Bringing the plane out of the loop, I took us into a barrel roll. Silver and green spun about, with us as the center of the pinwheel. Behind me, Helen laughed and clapped her hands.

Coming out of the roll, I considered my next option. People were losing sight of the greenhouse timeline, since this was a slow disaster. We needed to establish colonies on the moon and the other planets while we had the resources to spare. If their excuse was that establishing a colony wasn't safe for women, then we'd need to prove that women were just as capable as men. "Do you think your newspaper would be interested in covering an all-women air show?"

"Hell yes." Betty jabbed her finger at me. "But only if I get to use your name."

"I'm not anyone."

"You're married to the lead engineer at the IAC. That story about you flying out after the Meteor? I can use that."

I swallowed. Being the center of attention was . . . necessary. And it would just be talking to Betty. "Sure. You can do that."

TWELVE

MEN OF THE SPACE AGE

National Times photographs by SAM FALK

March 26, 1956—The rocket specialists—those who think up, design, engineer, and fire the mighty engines to carry scientific instruments aloft—are the men to whom the country looks for achievement in the Space Age. They work in many fields, ranging from fuels to computer systems and from alloys to communication techniques. The best known of these is Dr. Nathaniel York, who is the lead engineer for the International Aerospace Coalition.

The press conference went exactly as Betty predicted. When questioned about the exclusively male list, Norman Clemons, the director of the IAC, said that it was "for safety considerations." And it was "much the same as when Columbus discovered the New World." Or Shackleton's trip to the North Pole. No one had been concerned that there were no women on those expeditions. He was sure that the "international effort" made it clear that this was entirely a peaceful, scientific expedition.

Some of the women's magazines, which had been founded to agitate for suffrage, picked up Betty's story and joined her in rallying for women to be included in founding the colony. No men paid any attention to the women's magazines. I know—shocking.

Basira sat down on the opposite side of our shared desk at the IAC. "He's back."

I glanced around to see if anyone had heard her. Not that it really mattered, but the other women in the computing department were all busy at their calculations. The scratching of pencils across paper and the shush of glass cursors brushing over Bakelite slide rules were punctuated by the rattle of our Friden mechanical calculator. And even if anyone *had* been paying attention, there was nothing wrong with Basira reporting that Director Clemons had returned from the testing range.

Besides, most of them knew what I was hoping to do. I nodded and closed my notebook. I set it to the side of my desk, pencil lined up neatly against it. Opening my desk drawer, I pulled out another notebook, labeled "WASPs," which had the figures I'd collated about the Women Airforce Service Pilots of the Second World War.

Standing, I hugged the notebook to my chest. Basira smiled at me. "Operation Ladies First is go."

I needed the laughter rather desperately. Helen glanced up from the desk she shared with Myrtle. She nudged Myrtle, who turned and gave me a thumbs up. Nodding to them, I headed out of the room and down the corridors to Director Clemons's office.

There was no reason to be afraid of him. We had enjoyed multiple conversations at holiday parties, or company picnics. He was always a calming presence in the "dark room" on launch days. But before, Nathaniel or my work had always been there as a shield.

My palms left damp imprints on the cover of my notebook. I stopped before I got to Clemons's office door, which was always open, to wipe my hands on my skirt. Today, I'd opted for a simple gray pencil skirt and a white blouse, which I hoped made me look more businesslike. Any type of armor would be welcomed.

Swallowing, I went to the door, and Mrs. Kare, his secretary, looked up with a smile. "Mrs. York. What can I do for you?"

"I was hoping I could make an appointment to speak with Director Clemons." This was me chickening out. I had the notebook, and he was *right there.*

He was reading with his feet up on the desk, one of his cigars clenched between his teeth. Smoke belched around him like a misfiring engine. The book he held had a rocket in front of a dusty red landscape on the cover, and looked more like a novel than a technical paper.

"Let me check his schedule."

He lowered the book. "Send her on in."

"Oh—" I swallowed. Something about his crisp British diction always made me feel as if I'd come in unwashed from a field. "Thank you, sir."

He held up the book as I approached his desk. "Have you had the opportunity to read this yet?"

"No, sir."

"It has a Captain York in it, who sounds remarkably like your husband." He gestured toward a chair. "Sit, sit. Have you ever met this Bradbury chap?"

"No, sir."

"Well, I think he must be a fan. The notion of an ancient civilization on Mars is rubbish, but I will happily accept any press that excites people about space." He set the book on his desk. "The American Congress is getting huffy about appropriations again. Is that what you're here for? Do you need another one of the IBMs for the computing department? They are offering."

I shook my head. "That's really Mrs. Rogers's decision, but for myself . . . well, they aren't very reliable."

"So the engineers keep telling me. Overheating." He grunted, nodding. "What brings you here?

"Oh—well. It's actually about keeping people excited about Mars, sir. You see . . . I wanted to talk to you about considering women for future missions."

"Women?" He sat forward and gave me his full focus. "No, no. If we want people to be excited, we need the most highly qualified pilots on these missions, or the public will have our heads."

"I understand, but if we want to establish viable colonies, they'll need families, and that means convincing women that it's safe." I opened my notebook to the chart of statistics I had drawn up. "Now, certainly, you don't want to send the average woman into space, any more than the average man would be a good candidate. But as an example, I thought that maybe you might consider some of the WASP pilots. There were 1,027 women who flew during the war for the United States alone, and they averaged seven hundred flight hours each, with 792 of them going well over a thousand flight hours. The average fighter pilot, on the other hand—"

"No."

"I . . . I beg your pardon?"

"I am not sending women into space. If a man dies—well, that's tragic, but people will accept that. A woman? No. The program would be shut down in its entirety."

I stood, putting the notebook on his table and spinning it so he could see. "I think we could shift public perception, though. With these numbers—"

"No. You are speaking of women who ferried planes around as if they fought in combat."

Pressing my hands against the comforting grid lines,

I took another breath. He had said "combat" as if that was a consideration for the space missions, but you wouldn't need that on a colony. I chickened out, the way I always do, and didn't call him on that slip. "We're doing an air show. Maybe you could come out and see it? As an example of how we could shift perception of women pilots. The amount of training the WASPs had to go through was more rigorous than the men, because of the variety of planes that we flew."

"I appreciate your efforts, but I have to keep this project running. I do not have time for charity work." He picked up the novel again and started to read. "Good afternoon, Mrs. York."

I closed the notebook and bit down hard on the inside of my lip. I couldn't tell you if I was trying to keep from yelling or crying. Probably both.

The weeks marched on and my attention was pulled away from the idea of an air show, partially from despair, but mostly because the IAC was working nonstop toward a lunar landing. While the American branch was doing that, our European counterparts were preparing to establish an orbiting space station. Teletypes flew back and forth across the Atlantic as the rocket scientists shared notes.

We were all pulling long hours. Still, Nathaniel and I tried to leave before sundown on Fridays so we could observe Sabbath. Not that either of us was especially observant, but it was good discipline.

I leaned on the doorframe to his office as the heavy gray shadows of evening dulled the parking lot outside. Nathaniel had his shirtsleeves rolled up and was glaring at something on his desk.

With one knuckle, I rapped on the inner office door. "Ready to go?"

"Hm?" He looked up and rubbed his eyes. "I've got a little more to do. Mind waiting?"

"You know . . . you'd think that we'd do a better job of leaving by sundown in the summer."

Nathaniel spun in his chair to face the parking lot. "What time is it?"

"Almost nine." I came into his office and set my purse and coat down on one of the chairs. "Did you take a break today?"

"Yeah . . . I had a lunch meeting with Clemons." He turned back to the desk and picked up the paper he'd been studying. "Elma, if you were in orbit, would an r-bar or a v-bar rendezvous make more sense to you?"

"Okay, first of all, a lunch meeting does not count as taking a break." I leaned over the back of his chair, so I could see the paper he was so fixed on. It was a report called *Line-of-sight guidance techniques for manned orbital rendezvous,* which seemed to consist of more questions than answers. "Second . . . what's the assumed orbit?"

He flipped through the pages. "Um . . . hang on. Let's say four thousand miles."

Putting my hands on the base of his neck, I dug my thumbs in while I considered the question. One of the challenges of orbital mechanics was that the faster you went, the higher you orbited, and thus the slower the orbit. It was completely counterintuitive without equations or a model. So my instinct as a pilot to do the v-bar rendezvous couldn't be trusted.

The v-bar rendezvous got its V from velocity, which you used to catch up to the target by flying in the same direction that it was speeding. I dug my finger into the muscles that ran up the back of Nathaniel's neck. His head dropped forward until his chin rested on his chest.

But an r-bar rendezvous might work . . . if we dropped

into a lower orbit than our target. That would make the ship move faster than the target, and we'd catch up with it. Once close enough, we could just fire thrusters to push back up toward the target, which should use less fuel.

I had a possible answer, but given the little grunts of pleasure that my husband was making, I wasn't entirely sure he would hear me. His trapezius was a solid mass of knots down to between his shoulder blades. "I'd lean toward an r-bar rendezvous. Less fuel, plus the orbital mechanics mean there would be natural braking action if the thrusters failed."

Lifting his head, he leaned forward to stare at the page. "See, that's what I thought, but Parker wants v-bar."

My hands paused and then smoothed out his dress shirt. "Well. He's been in space and I haven't. As a pilot, I'd probably give his opinion more weight than mine."

"That's part of my problem. Everyone gives his opinion more weight because he's one of the original Artemis Seven." He threw the paper back on the table. "Even on things that have nothing to do with piloting. I mean . . . he's still going on about the Soviet—excuse me. The 'Communist Threat.'"

"The long winter hit them harder than us. The Soviet Union dissolved, for crying out loud. What's he thinking?"

Nathaniel rubbed his forehead. "The Soviet Union is gone, but Russia is as big as ever."

"And starving." The long winter had affected the nations closer to the poles more than others. "China isn't in any better condition."

"I think he's trying to curry favor with Eisenhower by trying to . . . I don't know, and I'm totally talking out of school."

With the elections, people were starting to lose sight of

the reason for getting into space. At least they weren't dismissing the importance of a space program. Yet.

It's not always Nathaniel who keeps us late at the office. The next Monday I got caught up in a series of equations for translunar trajectories. It was fascinating, because I was trying to account for the shift in gravitational pull as the spacecraft transitioned from the Earth's sphere of influence to the moon's. It affected everything, including the amount of propellant required. By the time Nathaniel and I got back to our tiny apartment, I had a head full of porridge.

Throwing the day's mail on the table, I dropped into the closest chair. My fingers were smudged with ink but I still rested my head on my hands with a sigh. "Space sounded so romantic."

Nathaniel chuckled dryly behind me and bent down to kiss the back of my neck. "I thought I wasn't going to be able to pry you out of the office tonight."

"Well, Sanchez needs the propellant calculations by tomorrow so he can adjust the payload parameters." I massaged my temples, trying to ease some of the strain from staring at numbers all day. "Becky was working on it, but then *someone* told Director Clemons that she was pregnant and . . . She was just barely showing. It's not like we do anything but sit at a desk."

"And run back and forth to the labs. And sit in on tests when we're firing experimental engines. And propellant tests, and—"

"You are just as bad." I straightened and glared at him.

He was leaning against the kitchenette's counter with his coat off and his tie half-undone. "Oh no . . . no, I would have let her keep working, but maybe kept her out of the test sites. But I understand why the director made the call he did."

"Because, and I quote, 'Pregnancy has a direct effect on women's brains'?"

He snorted. "Politician. Not a scientist. If something happened to a pregnant woman working at the IAC, it would set back public relations."

I opened my mouth to retort and snapped it shut. He was right, darn it. People were already trying to shift funding from the space program because they couldn't grasp the scale of the disaster that was coming. Turning back to the table, I picked up an envelope. "I'm going to go through the mail."

"You can pay the bills tomorrow."

"I won't be any less tired." Part of our marriage agreement was that I handled the bills and balanced the checkbook. We were both good at math, conceptually, but I could do it in my head, and Nathaniel needed to write things down, which meant I was faster.

Behind me a cabinet opened, followed by the rattle of crockery. "Baked potatoes and . . . we have a little bit of ground beef. Chili sound good?"

Yes. Yes, I have a husband who cooks. He does not have a wide array of dishes, but the ones he does know how to prepare work well with our ration books. The chili would be mostly beans, but tasty. "That would be welcome."

There was a letter from Hershel, which I put aside to answer over the weekend. If I tried now, he'd get nothing but a string of numbers and symbols. Electric bill. Phone bill. Those went in another stack to pay tonight.

A heavy white envelope, which fairly screamed invitation, caught my eye. We got a lot of those from different people wanting to have The Doctor York at their soiree. He was front and center at every press conference explaining trajectories and mission parameters in ways that anyone could understand. Doing the same thing at a dinner party was just tiring.

But . . . but this invitation had Senator Wargin's return address. I knew his wife: Nicole Wargin had been a pilot with the WASPs during the war. And Senator Wargin was a vocal supporter of Dr. Martin Luther King, Jr. I was hoping that the combination of his progressive politics and his wife's interests would make him sympathetic to my own hobbyhorse.

I opened the envelope, sliding out the heavy white card.

SENATOR AND MRS. KENNETH T. WARGIN
REQUEST THE PLEASURE OF
DR. AND MRS. YORK'S COMPANY
AT A DINNER PARTY AT HALF PAST SIX O'CLOCK
ON THE SEVENTH OF AUGUST.

"Nathaniel?" I turned in my chair.

He had his shirtsleeves rolled up and was rubbing a potato with oil. "Hm?"

"Senator Wargin and his wife have invited us to a dinner on the seventh. Shall I say yes?"

He shook his head, setting the potato on the counter. "That's only a week before the next launch. I'll be exhausted."

I stood and leaned against the counter next to him. "That's your natural state."

"Yours too." He grabbed the other potato and rubbed oil over its surface. The muscles in his forearms rippled with the motion. Oil had splashed just above his left wrist and glistened with each movement.

"True . . ." I set my finger in the streak of oil and drew it farther up the inside of his arm. "This way, someone else will cook dinner for us."

"And I'll have to make witty conversation."

"Oh no. No one expects *witty* from you."

He laughed, and leaned down to kiss me. "Why this one?"

"I used to fly with Nicole Wargin." I slipped around to stand behind Nathaniel. Running my hands around his ribcage, I leaned into him. "And . . . and I'm hoping that the senator might have thoughts about the need for women in the colony."

"Ah-ha." He turned in my arms, still holding the potato. Keeping his oily hands away from my clothes, he kissed me on the cheek, then at the base of my jaw, then nibbled a trail down my neck.

Between gasps, I managed to squeak out, "And you could use the same time to argue for the need to get off planet."

"Well . . . I'm still going to be exhausted."

"I could make it worth your while?"

"These potatoes still need to go into the oven."

Laughing, I released my hold on his waist and stepped back. "Fine. Far be it from me to distract you."

He bent down to open the oven door, giving me a look at his well-tailored trousers. Have I mentioned recently how fortunate I am to be married to Nathaniel? The warm air from the oven stirred a strand of his hair, and the light caught on that glinting oil again as he set both potatoes directly on the wire rack. He stood and kicked the oven door closed with his heel.

The heat from the oven seemed to warm the entire apartment. Nathaniel lifted a hand still glossy with oil. "I figure . . ." He traced a line down my throat. "It'll take about an hour before those are ready."

"Is that so?" My breathing was fast and heated. "Do I have time to make my argument for going to the dinner party?"

His finger continued its path, gliding along the collar of my shirt until he reached the top button. "As long as I get to make an argument for staying in."

"Counterargument, confirmed."

THIRTEEN

SPACE RECORD SET BY LEBOURGEOIS

Colonies in Space Would Aid Humanity

By HENRY TANNER
Special to The National Times.

KANSAS CITY, KS, Saturday, April 13, 1956—Lieutenant Colonel Jean-Paul Lebourgeois has given the International Aerospace Coalition another space record by staying in orbit more than four days. With this advancement, the IAC has demonstrated that working and sleeping in space is possible, a necessary step for the space program.

Nicole Wargin perched on the arm of the sofa in her living room, her glass filled with pre-Meteor champagne. The diamonds around her throat glittered above a glorious peacock green dress. Around us, the living room was filled with the cream of society in tuxedos and rich jewel-toned evening gowns, enjoying the kind of food that a ration book wouldn't get you. If you couldn't hear what Nicole was saying, she might have been any society maven.

Thank God she was more interesting than that.

"So the mechanic had sworn that the Hellcat was flightworthy, but I was at six thousand feet and my fuel gauge suddenly bottomed out."

"Over the ocean?" Mrs. Hieber clasped a hand over her bosom in dismay. Earlier she had regaled us with stories of how she'd saved her prize roses from the Meteor winter through heroic use of glass and steam. Too bad she wasn't interested in growing vegetables. I'd saved us by prompting Nicole to tell war stories. That I had another agenda was beside the point. At the moment, we weren't hearing about aphid invasions.

I'd heard Nicole's story before, so I just sipped my cocktail and enjoyed the show as Nicole pointed a manicured nail at her. "Yes. Over the ocean. Well, I hadn't any other choice, had I, but to circle back to the aircraft carrier and tell them I was coming in."

"No! Without an engine?"

"It was that or land in the ocean. When I landed, it turned out that the mechanic had missed a damaged fuel line. You should have heard the chief tear him up and down." Unpowered landings were part of training, but landing on an aircraft carrier was a whole other ball of wax. She caught my eye and gave a wink. "Tell them about the Messerschmitts, Elma."

I had been perfectly content to sit among the other women and listen to Nicole tell stories, but when your hostess invites you to take the floor . . . "Oh. Well. We weren't supposed to be flying combat missions, because it was too 'dangerous' for women."

Nicole snorted and shook her head. "Not that the Germans could tell who was flying a plane."

"Exactly. So, I was delivering a Mustang to the Ambérieu-en-Bugey Air Base and a trio of Messerschmitts comes up out of nowhere." The crowd around us had gained a few men, which I'd been hoping the topic would draw, but still . . . there were suddenly a lot of people listening to me. I took a sip of my champagne. "Bear in mind that I was flying a fighter plane, but it didn't have any ammunition."

"Oh no." That came from Senator Wargin, who had joined his wife. He was a stout man who carried the weight well, beneath a full head of hair that was just beginning to gray.

"Oh yes. I had just enough time to radio for help, and then they started firing. All I could do was evade, and hope to outmaneuver them. And of course the day was utterly cloudless. But there's this river valley that runs toward the base, and I thought that maybe I could find some cover there."

Nicole leaned forward. "Which comes with its own set of problems, because you're flying low, and there's no room for mistakes."

"But it was better than being shot at. So I'm tearing down the valley, with this da—dratted—German on my tail, and another one flying cover for him." I tried to demonstrate where the other planes were in relation to me without spilling my drink. "I have no idea where the third is. All I'm trying to do is use the river bends to make sure they can never get a straight shot at me, and praying that our boys are going to find me in time."

"And clearly they did." Ah . . . the sound of smug masculinity.

I turned in my chair. "Actually, Colonel Parker, they didn't."

Of course he'd been invited to the dinner. Senator Wargin was excited about the space program, so naturally, he would want the first man in space there as another trophy guest, like Nathaniel.

Nicole laughed at the look of shock on Parker's face. "She got one of them to shoot the other, flew the second into a cliff, and . . . what happened to the third?"

"I never saw him again. I'm assuming that when our boys *did* arrive, they chased him off."

"Wait—" Parker held up his hand. "You're telling me you downed two Messerschmitts without ammunition?"

The nice thing about anger is that it overrides my anxiety about being the center of attention. "I had the advantage of knowing the terrain. I'd been ferrying planes in for months and knew where the river forked. They clearly didn't."

"I don't believe it."

"Are you calling my wife a liar?" Nathaniel does this thing with his voice when he's angry that always reminds me of my father. It gets very low, and very controlled. Right now it was so tense, you could have stabilized a rocket with it. He stood just behind me, only a few feet from Parker.

"No, no . . . Of course not, Dr. York. I just wondered if it was really a Messerschmitt." He smiled, charmingly, and winked at Senator Wargin. "You know how excited ladies can get—one plane becomes three. A biplane becomes a Messerschmitt. Maybe the sun was in her eyes on this 'utterly cloudless day'? I'm sure she's not lying, but maybe a little confused. That's all."

I set my glass down on the nearest table so I didn't crack the stem in my fist. "Oh, Colonel Parker, you're so clever! Why, that must be just what happened." Laying my hand on my bosom, I turned to Nicole. "Don't you think?"

She joined me, like the world's best wingman. "I'm sure you're right. And to think, all these years, we've been confused by the wreckage. Why, that prisoner must have lied about what kind of plane he was flying to make himself look good."

"I declare! I think you're right." Turning back to Colonel Parker, I beamed up at him. "Thank you *ever* so much for straightening that out for me. I feel like such a fool."

Perhaps that was a tactical error. His face had red blotches at the cheeks, and it wasn't from embarrassment. He inclined his head. "Still. The danger you were placed in demonstrates why letting women near a combat zone was a mistake."

"I'm curious, Colonel Parker. How would you have handled being unarmed? As a man?" Tactical mistake or no, this got right to the heart of the astronaut issue.

He held up his hands. "Look. You were clearly very fortunate. I'm just saying that you should never have been put in that position."

"I agree. My plane should have been armed. As a woman, I'm smaller and lighter. That means that my plane needs less fuel and I handle G-forces better than a man." That last was skirting the truth, because I was tall for a woman, and the ability to handle G-forces was more related to height and blood pressure. "In fact, I would argue that women should already be in the astronaut corps, for exactly those reasons. To say nothing of the fact that we're trying to establish a colony."

"And men are better suited to do that work." He glanced around the room and parroted what Clemons had said during the press conference. "Christopher Columbus didn't take any women on his voyage, did he?"

"That was about conquest." Sweat beaded under my brassiere. "The pilgrims, on the other hand, did bring women. If you want to establish a colony, we need women in space."

"I see no compelling reason for that."

"Here's a reason." Nicole laughed, lifting her glass over her head. "Babies!"

Laughter bubbled around us, breaking the tension. Senator Wargin stepped forward and guided Parker away, chatting amiably about golf. Small kindnesses, sometimes, are the best ones. Nicole left her perch and came to join Nathaniel and me.

Standing, I picked up my glass and saluted her with it. "Sorry about that."

"Please. I remember Grabby Parker from the war." She took a sip of her champagne. "Have you met his wife?"

I shook my head. "We don't socialize."

"You'll notice that she's not here tonight. Not that I'm saying anything by that . . . I'm just noting that Mrs. Parker was invited."

"Speaking of invitations . . ." I glanced at Nathaniel, who seemed content to stay with me rather than mingle. "I'm putting together an air show featuring women pilots. I don't suppose—"

"Yes. If you're about to ask me to fly, yes." She held up her hand, diamond bracelet glittering. "Wait. Darn it. I need to check with Kenneth to be certain it's okay. Politics and all. But I can usually talk him round. So, if there's no conflict, then yes. 'Might be confused,' my aunt Fanny."

"Swell!" That would delight Betty's journalistic soul. Having a senator's wife on our roster would make pitching an article about the air show to her editor at the *National Times* that much easier. And, as an added bonus, it meant I wouldn't have to be front and center.

I spent a surprising amount of time in concrete bunkers. The smell of kerosene filled the air of the testing range, even in the control bunker; having the test range three miles away from 203,400 gallons of kerosene still seemed uncomfortably close. I rolled a pencil between my fingers, waiting for the static firing test of the new Atlas rocket.

This one was an easy assignment. All I had to do was calculate the amount of thrust and see if it would be enough to get a rocket into orbit. Any of the computers could have done it, but I was here because it was Leroy Pluckett's project. Damn good engineer. Couldn't keep his hands off the computers, but as his boss's wife, I had very few problems with him.

Relatively few. He leaned over my chair, one hand sliding across my shoulders to rest on the chair back. "How's it going, Elma?"

I sat forward so he wasn't touching me. "Can't do much until it fires."

Across the room, one of the other engineers lifted his head. "Dr. Pluckett, we're adding the liquid oxygen now."

"Great." He smiled down at me, and by "me" I mean my bosom. "Just let me know if you need anything."

"Absolutely." I tapped my pencil on the table, trying to draw his eyes away. "I should probably finish getting ready."

"Can I help with—"

An explosion rocked the room.

Sound and heat roared through the bunker, carrying the stench of burning carbons. It wasn't the first time we'd lost a rocket, by any stretch, but that didn't make it any quieter.

Engineers flinched, throwing their hands up to plug their ears. I twitched away and nearly fell out of my chair as the thunder died, leaving just the distant crackle of a fire. Sirens joined the cacophony. Pluckett reached for me, as if he were trying to help, only his meaty hand "somehow" landed on my chest.

Standing, I straightened my skirt and stepped back from him. My pulse shook through my hands, as much from anger at Pluckett as from the explosion. "You'd best attend to your rocket. Or do you need me to calculate the size of the misfire?"

The weight of the bowling ball pressed against my palm as I stared down the lane. Letting out a breath, I advanced, swinging back, forward, and releasing the ball. It left my hand in a momentarily perfect line, then curved to the side to hit just off-center.

A split. Darn it. Again.

"You can do it, Elma!" Behind me, Myrtle clapped her hands. "You can do it."

I spun back, skirt flaring around me, while I waited for the pinboy to clear the ones I *had* knocked down. "You'd think that a physicist would be better at this."

With an arm around his wife, Eugene shook his head. "Theory and practice. Two different things. It's like saying being a physicist should allow you to fly."

"I *can* fly, thank you very much." My bowling ball thunked against the end of the return trough and I stooped to pick it up, waving a little thank you to the pinboy who'd rolled it back. We had to remember to tip them well.

"Speaking of flying . . ." Eugene said.

Myrtle nudged his foot. "Let her bowl. I want to see the fireworks."

"We'll get you out in time to enjoy the Fourth." Eugene shook his head and pointed his beer toward the lane. "And I'll wait till after Elma's turn for my question."

"I'll be fascinated to see where this segue takes us." The Fourth was what had made me suggest bowling. After the Meteor, I found fire raining from the sky considerably less appealing. I turned back to the lane, where the pinboy had cleared the last of the pins and was safely perched on his high stool. He had a comic out, and even from here I could recognize Superman's distinctive red-and-blue costume.

But, back to bowling . . . To knock down both pins, I'd have to strike one at just the right angle to cause it to fly across and hit the other. I could see the trajectory. Give me a piece of paper and I could describe it for you with mathematical precision. I swung the ball back, its weight tugging on my arm like additional G-force, then brought the pendulum forward, aiming at the pin on the right. The ball released, and, for a brief instant, arced weightless through the air, before thudding against the smooth poplar floor. It rumbled down the lane and I stood there, arm outstretched, as if I could will it to hit the pins correctly.

It brushed the pin on the right, which wobbled, and then tipped to land spinning on the floor. The other pin stayed perfectly upright.

A commiserating groan rose from our little group. Laughing, I turned back and curtsied.

"Next time!" Nathaniel patted me on the shoulder as he took his place on the lane.

Myrtle laughed. "Next time . . . I keep waiting for them to throw us out *this* time."

"My bowling isn't that bad."

Eugene and Myrtle exchanged a look like I had just said something adorable. And then, belatedly, my brain caught up with my mouth. The "us" Myrtle meant wasn't our bowling party, but Eugene and her.

Before the Meteor, they wouldn't have been allowed in at all. This place would have been filled with white people, and I wouldn't have noticed. Now, with Kansas City being the capital, Myrtle and Eugene weren't the only brown people in here. They were still outnumbered, but at least no one was glaring at us.

Embarrassed that I hadn't noticed the imbalance until she pointed it out, I marked my score down on the sheet and dropped onto the bench next to Eugene. He handed me my beer and raised an eyebrow. "So, what's this I hear about an air show?"

"I don't know if it's going to happen." The beer was cold and had a bright acidity. "The idea was to prove that women pilots have the ability to be astronauts."

"But . . . ?"

Nathaniel's bowling ball careened down the lane and slammed into the pins, throwing them clear in a beautiful strike.

"Yes!" I lifted my beer to my husband's success. "But we only have leisure craft. The more I think about it, the more I realize that no matter how good the show is, it won't look as flashy as a show with military planes."

"That's a pity. Pilots would know it was a feat, but the general public looks at the trappings." Eugene shook his head as he stood for his turn. He clapped Nathaniel on the back. "Good job, York."

Nathaniel picked up his beer and leaned against the back of the bench. "The air show?"

"Yeah."

Myrtle peered over her glasses at him. "You make your wife follow through on that. It's a fine idea."

Nathaniel held up his hands, and laughed. "You have a very different idea of our marriage than I do. I don't make Elma do anything."

The pins cracked and bounced, but Eugene had left one standing. "I don't know why she thinks any husband can make his wife do anything. Never worked with us."

"You hush." Myrtle threw a wadded-up napkin at his back.

Laughing, Eugene waited for the pinboy to clear the pins and roll his ball back to him. "So you need Mustangs."

"Wouldn't that be nice?" I sighed and took a deep sip of my beer. I hadn't flown a Mustang since the war, but they had been, by far, my favorite of the planes we had to ferry. Swift, agile, and a beautifully responsive machine. It might not be the highest tech these days, but it had been glorious back then.

Eugene's next bowl knocked that pesky pin down. He

let out a hoot and pumped his fist. "Now who's cooking with gas!"

Myrtle rolled her eyes and stood. "He loses his train of thought so easily."

Giving her a peck on the cheek as they traded places, Eugene grinned. "Do not." He leaned down to pick up his beer. "How does six Mustangs sound?"

I stopped with my beer in midair. "Six? Six Mustangs? Where—?"

Eugene grinned. "My airclub has six of them."

My jaw literally dropped. "Are you serious? I've called all the—no. Wait." I pinched my nose. "Someday, I swear to God, I will learn this. I called all the white airclubs."

"*Ha!* Take that!" Myrtle jumped in the air. All of her pins had scattered in a strike. She spun around. "And none of you saw that, did you?"

I shrugged. "Six Mustangs."

Myrtle exchanged a look with Nathaniel and shook her head slowly. "Pilots."

He sighed and raised his beer to her. "I don't know how you do it."

I let them have their laugh and just grinned at Eugene. Six Mustangs. We could do proper formations with that, and smoke tricks, and . . . "Are there any women pilots in your group?"

"Yeah. Come to the club and I'll introduce you." He gave me a wink. "We can go for a spin and leave these two on the ground."

FOURTEEN

IAC LAUNCHES MANNED SPACE PORT MADE OF AN INFLATABLE FABRIC

By BILL BECKER
Special to The National Times.

KANSAS CITY, KS, April 21, 1956—The world's first space station is a huge spinning wheel of four sausage-shaped links.

The Kansas City Negro Aeronautics Club had a nicer facility than our women's club did. There was a little house next to the hangar, both of which had been painted blinding white, with red shutters and lettering.

As soon as we walked into the social room of the house, I became self-conscious and grateful for Eugene's presence as a shield. I was the only white person in the room. The brown faces ranged from a magnolia tan to a deep blue-black, with no one who was even as light as Myrtle.

I stood out like a dirty handkerchief dropped on a clean table. Clutching my purse tighter, I planted myself in the door to keep from backing out. Everyone was staring at me. I tried to smile. And then I realized that the way I was hanging on to my purse, they probably thought I was worried someone was going to steal it. I let go, and that probably looked just as bad.

Eugene turned back, smiling, and beckoned at me to

follow him to a table with three black ladies sitting at it. Conversation started up again in the social room, but I kept hearing snatches of "what's she doing here" and "white" and "no business." Some of them, I think, weren't trying to keep their voices down.

Two of the women stood as we came up to the table. The third stayed seated and stared at me with a neutral expression, with only a pinching of the nose to indicate disdain.

"This is Miss Ida Peaks." Eugene gestured to the younger of the two standing women. She was short, with generous curves and ruddy brown cheeks. The other standing woman wore her hair in an elegant French twist, pinned with green Bakelite combs. ". . . Miss Imogene Braggs, and . . ." He gestured to the seated woman. Her orange dress with a narrow white collar gave her a warmth that her expression countered. ". . . Miss Sarah Coleman. Some of the finest pilots you'll ever meet."

"Thank you for meeting with me." I took off my gloves and, at Miss Braggs's gesture, sat down. "I believe Major Lindholm has explained our aims to you?"

Miss Coleman nodded. "You want to be an astronaut."

"I—well, yes. But my main goal is to get the IAC to consider women as pilots. The current group is entirely composed of men." I turned to smile at the two friendlier women. "I was hoping that you would consider flying with us."

Miss Peaks tilted her head to consider me. "So you can use our planes?"

Something about this conversation was off. I glanced at Eugene, but he had stepped back. "That . . . that is a separate discussion, I think."

"And if we turn you down—about using the Mustangs— would you still want black women to fly with you?" Miss Braggs's tone was gentle, with mild curiosity, but the words held a challenge.

"It depends upon the reasons for turning us down, I suppose." That answer caused Miss Coleman to sniff. "If it was because you doubted me as a pilot, then that doesn't seem like it would be a good collaboration. But, otherwise, yes, I should still like you to fly with us. Major Lindholm has spoken very highly of your performance in the shows your airclub has put on, and I need experienced pilots."

"Good! I'm game, then." Miss Peaks grinned at me. "Any chance to do some more formation flying is fine by me. You . . . you are okay with formation, right?"

"Absolutely. I was definitely planning that." It would take a liquid ton of rehearsal, but precision flying was mission critical if we were going to convince people that women pilots were as good as men.

Miss Coleman shook her head. "There's no point in it."

"Sarah—"

"No. Don't hush me. You know good and well that even though we're qualified—even if this air show scheme were to work—we wouldn't be allowed in the astronaut corps." She glared up at Eugene. "Would we, Major?"

He cleared his throat. "Well, now . . . they only took seven men, and had to take those from different countries, and—"

"And none of those countries selected anything but a white man."

"The makeup of the list bothers me as well. That's why we're trying to change things with the air show. Once they see how qualified you are—"

Miss Coleman leaned across the table, face intense. "I was accepted into the WASPs during the second war. Until they realized I was black, and then they asked me to withdraw my application. What makes you think that the IAC is going to be any different?"

"I—well . . . well, because we're talking about a colony,

and . . . and . . ." And I remembered what had happened in the days after the Meteor hit, when the people in the black neighborhoods were left for dead until Eugene and Myrtle had used their leaflets. "And we'll make them. But to do that, we have to show them we can fly first."

Miss Peaks shrugged. "I already said I'm in. Y'all can keep arguing, but nothing's going to change if we just sit here."

Slowly, Miss Braggs nodded. "If nothing else, it'll be fun."

Miss Coleman stood. "I've got better things to do with my time than help yet another white lady exploit us."

"Exploit?" I stood too. "Now, see here. I'm inviting you to fly, not to mop floors or serve dinner."

She smirked. "See? That's the only way she can picture us. I'm a mathematician and a chemist, working in pharmacy, but all you could think of were servant roles for me. So, no thank you, ma'am. You can just go on and convince yourself that you're trying to save us. It'll be without me."

She strode off, leaving me gaping and with my skin too hot. I'd probably gone bright red with anger and embarrassment. I should have known better. I'd made the same mistake with Myrtle when we first moved in and I assumed she was just a housewife. She'd been a computer for a black business that had manufactured hair-straightening chemicals. I hadn't even known such things existed.

"I'm a fool . . . Would you please convey my apologies? She's absolutely right." I gathered up my purse and started to pull my gloves back on. "Thank you for your time."

"Did you say there was formation flying?" Miss Peaks stared after Miss Coleman.

I stopped with one glove half-on. "Yes." I didn't say *If we can get the planes,* but I thought it.

"And when's the first practice?"

"I—does this mean you're still willing to fly with us?"

She turned her gaze back to me, and a corner of her mouth curved up. "I already said yes." Then she winked. "Besides . . . that went better than I thought it would."

I laughed, relief making it too loud. "I can't see how."

She cocked her head, and her smile didn't change, but the meaning of it did. "You apologized."

Have you ever gotten exactly what you wanted, and then realized that it had unintended consequences? That was me and the air show. In addition to Nicole Wargin, we also had commitments from Anne Spencer Lindbergh (yes, that Anne Lindbergh); Sabiha Gökçen, a Turkish fighter pilot in the Second World War; and Princess Shakhovaskaya, who had fought in the First World War before having to flee Russia.

I hoped the fact that she was an actual fighter pilot, and a princess, would draw some attention. Betty had been ecstatic, because the princess was a publicity gold mine.

And Nicole, bless her, had worked her political contacts and come up with a list of guests that staggered the mind. Or, at least, my mind: Vice President Eglin's wife. Charlie Chaplin. Eleanor Roosevelt.

Which is how I came to be sitting in a borrowed Mustang on an airfield surrounded by bleachers and camera crews. More than one crew. All I have to say is "Thank God for princesses"—even aging ones who no longer had a country. It turns out that given a choice between interviewing a physicist housewife and a princess who flies with a tiara, they opted for the tiara.

I was fine with that.

I was even happier when it was my turn to fly. Nicole, Betty, and I were set to do some formation flying with Miss Peaks and Miss Braggs of the Kansas City Negro Aeronautics Club. They'd supplied us with the Mustangs, and, as

Eugene had promised, they were damn good pilots. And . . . they'd convinced Dr. Martin Luther King, Jr. to attend.

Have I mentioned that the crowd was immense?

We queued for takeoff, following Miss Peaks with military discipline. The first part of the routine was simply a tight V formation, buzzing the airfield. I say "simple," but during our second pass over the field, we rolled into a vertical bank of 180 degrees while keeping the V tight and even. After years of puddling around in my Cessna, flying at speed in a Mustang with a group of amazing pilots . . . a part of me came back to life. A part that might have withered and died even before the Meteor struck.

The seat pressed against my spine with the G-force of our turns, and the little blips of turbulence from the planes around me gave a tangible sense of the other pilots. These women made me feel vibrantly alive.

The people in the stands below? They might as well have been asleep, for all they mattered in that moment. We roared past them, banked to climb into a steep arc, and then split apart.

This next bit was Senator Wargin's idea. It was cheesy as all hell, and I couldn't wait. Six planes, seemingly flying out of formation, and yet perfectly in sync. Over the radio, Miss Peaks said, "On my mark, ladies." It was a formality when she said, "Mark" a moment later, though, because we were all already where we should be. I hit the button to release a stream of colored smoke in time with the others. We each dipped in an individual arc, passing the other planes in an intricate choreography designed to avoid the wake of turbulence from each other's slipstreams.

Behind us, in red smoke against a silver sky, we wrote the word MARS.

I finished the final upstroke of the M and glanced over my shoulder. The ground lay at my back, past the red mist.

My angle was all wrong to read it, but from here, it was enough to see that our individual strokes all connected. Damn, we were good.

I turned forward again, and hit a bird.

Then three more smacked into me. Feathers and blood flashed past the plane with meaty thuds. I had to tilt my head to the side and scrunch down to see past the carnage on my windscreen, but, by God, I managed to stay in alignment with my teammates.

My position is probably why I didn't see my coolant levels drop. Or the engine temperature rise. Or the thick, dark smoke pouring out of the back of my plane to mix with the red.

I thought I had escaped the bird strike unharmed until my propellers sputtered and failed. A bird must have been sucked into the radiator and cut a coolant line. Not that it mattered in that moment what had caused it. I had no engine.

My plane was pointed straight up. No engine. No lift from the wings.

The ground rolled overhead as the first turn of the incipient spin. There was a moment of zero G as the plane stalled out, and everything seemed to float.

Then the spin started in earnest.

The urge to pull back on the stick was so strong, but that would have killed me. The plane flipped over again, showing sky, and then earth, and then nothing but the fairgrounds spinning like a toy below me. Red and black smoke whipped past my windshield, blending with the blood of birds.

G-forces pressed me against the right side of the plane and squeezed the breath out of my chest. Right-side spin. I kept my hands lightly on the stick and pushed the throttle all the way forward. My vision started to go dark from the outside from the G-forces as I fought to stop the roll. Stick, hard left, full opposite the spin.

The muscles in my arm burned, trying to fight the pull, and I just braced myself harder, pushing. Goddamn it. I knew how to get out of a spin—I just had to get control again. My altitude ticked away. The rudder fought me every inch, but I got it to the left.

With that, the spin slowed, but I was still aimed at the ground in a dive. My canopy was smeared with blood and feathers. All I had were instruments.

According to the instruments, I still had enough height to pull the canopy and bail out, but, by God, I wasn't going to crash a borrowed plane while I still had space to maneuver. Dragging in a breath against the G-forces, I yanked back on the stick to pull the plane out of her dive. The tunnel vision got worse as I pulled at least three Gs, but it was that or ditch the plane. I. Was. Not. Going. To. Do. That.

I tightened my legs and abdominal muscles, trying to force blood back to my brain as the G-force increased. Blacking out was not an option. I kept my eyes on the instrument panel, relying on it to tell me when I was finally, finally back to straight and level.

My vision started to clear and I took a full, deep breath before looking for the runway. I still had to land, but that was the easy part, even with obscured vision. The Mustang was a darn good glider, and I had enough height to bank and come around to the runway. I passed over it once to get a sense of range, then pulled a 360 to make another approach, so I could come in to land. And to try to kill some speed. My flaps were useless from the bird damage, so it was going to be a really fast approach. I peered right and left, using the spots of clear windshield to gauge my position relative to the ground.

It rose up to meet me and I slapped the wheels down,

bouncing harder than I liked from the speed. Braking the plane, I brought her to a rolling halt at the end of the runway. I'd need someone to tow her to the side until we could look at the engine.

Birds. God, I hated birds. Well. When flying, I hated them—although, to be fair, the bloody birds had come out of this a lot worse than I did.

A giggle came on me out of nowhere. Bloody birds.

I was a terrible person. But I was alive.

Sliding back the canopy, I hauled myself up as the remaining pilots flashed past overhead, back in formation. They'd given me clearance to get under control, but should be heading in to land now. I was clear of the runway, wasn't I?

I turned to look over my shoulder.

The runway was clogged with people. Cameramen and reporters and audience members and everyone was running toward my plane. *Everyone.* I waved from the cockpit so they'd see I was okay. I didn't need help.

They didn't need to come running out here. Not all of them.

The flight helmet was pinching around my throat. I could barely draw breath. Fumbling with the strap, I couldn't get my fingers to unbuckle the thing. My gloves— too bulky. I couldn't even get them off.

"Mrs. York! Mrs. York! Are you all right? What happened up there? Was that part of the show? Or did you lose control of the plane? Over here! Mrs. York! Over here!"

Who was talking? There were so many people. If I hadn't still been in the cockpit, they would have crushed me in their midst. All of them crowded around the plane, and I couldn't tell where the voices were coming from. Just a mass of people, shouting my name over and over again.

A man climbed up onto the wing, talking into a microphone. "I'm standing on the wing of a Mustang flown by Mrs. Nathaniel York, who just survived a near fatal mid-air accident. Mrs. York, can you tell us what happened?"

On the other side of the plane, a man with a camera had set it on a tripod on the ground. Another man stood in front of him, gesturing back at me.

They hadn't even let me get out of the cockpit. I ripped at my gloves, trying to yank them off my hands. "Let me down, please."

"Poor thing! She's shaking." Around us, more people called my name.

The man on the wing shoved the microphone at me. "Can you tell us how you feel?"

I turned and scrambled over the opposite side of the cockpit, hopped down, and slid off the wing. Like an idiot, I landed next to the television reporter.

"Oh! And here she is now. Mrs. York, it must be quite a fright to have something like that happen. You're lucky to be alive."

"Lucky?" He thought I was frightened because of the tailspin. They all thought I was shaking because of it. I pressed my hand against the wing and tried to steady myself. "I lived because of training that I received as one of the Women Airforce Service Pilots during the war."

"Of course, but it still must be frightening."

"Not really. The birds in the air startled me, of course, but surprises like that are why we were put through such rigorous training as WASPs." I gestured to the air, where the other women in our group were still circling. If I could only turn the attention away from me as easily as they circled. "Any of the other women in our group could have overcome that spin the same way I did. In fact, we have it easier than men in those circumstances, because our bodies are not subject to the same degree of strain from the G-forces in a spin."

"And how did it feel, to be in that spiral of death?"

"Well . . . the death spiral is a different type of spin." I tried to do the society smile that Nicole used to such good effect. "But when you're in the middle of a tailspin, if you've been trained, you only think about what to do next. I save the panicking for when I'm talking to reporters."

That got a chuckle from the crowd. I kept my hand pressed against the warm wing of my plane. It had kept me alive, even after those damn birds. "One good thing about the moon and Mars missions: those pilots won't have to worry about hitting birds."

Another laugh. "I do hope that people will enjoy the rest of the air show, and think about what our lady pilots can do for the space missions. If we want colonies . . . we'll need women in space."

"That's interesting that you say that. Can you tell me why?"

"Oh dear . . . I'm not sure if I should explain where babies come from on television." Through the crowd, I saw Nathaniel. Or, I didn't even really "see him," because he was still fighting his way through; I felt him, his terror and the way he drove through the crowd to try to reach me. "And now, if you'll excuse me, I need to go reassure my husband."

The crowd laughed even louder. I didn't intend that last bit of double-entendre when I said it, and I was fairly certain that no amount of "reassurance" would calm Nathaniel down anytime soon.

Wading into the crowd, I kept my head down, concentrating on the hard tarmac. Men's shoes, ladies in heels, gray cuffs, stockings with crooked back seams, and hands—hands touching my shoulder, or arm, or back as people said my name. "Mrs. York!"

And then, finally, "Elma!"

Nathaniel's arms went around me in a shield. I wanted to cower into them, but I used his strength to draw myself up. People were watching, and I could not disappear. People were watching. That thought did not help. I could barely breathe.

But my husband was here. I lifted my head to seek his eyes as a guide wire. Their crystal blue was covered by a sheen of tears, and their edges were rimmed with red. His hand shook where it pressed against my back.

I put a hand against his cheek. "I'm fine. Love, I'm fine. It was just a tailspin."

"Thirty percent of aviation fatalities are from tailspins." He clutched me close and pressed his cheek against mine. "Goddamn it. Don't 'just a tailspin' me."

I don't know where the laughter came from. Because I wasn't dead? Because panic and hysteria are two sides of the same coin? Because he loved me so much he'd just resorted to statistics to express it? "Well, now you'll have to revise the numbers, won't you? Because I didn't die."

He laughed at that, and picked me off the ground. The crowd stepped back as he swung me in his arms.

That's the image they showed in the *National Times*. First there's my plane, tumbling out of control. And beside it, a photo of me, laughing in the arms of my husband with a crowd of people standing around us.

Those are the only photos of me, because as soon as we got off the airfield, I locked myself in the bathroom. Every time I thought I was together enough to go back out, I could hear the voices of reporters in the hall and got queasy all over again. So I waited until the air show was over, and my stomach was empty, and Nathaniel's worry when he knocked on the door was too much to ignore.

It would make more sense to be afraid of the crash, but I was afraid of the reporters.

And I was ashamed to be so weak.

FIFTEEN

LADY PILOTS THRILL AIR SHOW THRONG

By ELIZABETH RALLS

Special to The National Times.

KANSAS CITY, KS, May 27, 1956—Hundreds of aviation enthusiasts turned out at the municipal airport here yesterday to watch the first international show of women pilots. Of particular interest to the throng was Princess Shakhovaskaya, formerly of Russia, who flew loops in her vintage biplane.

The smells of garlic and ginger wafting around Helen's kitchen had my mouth watering. I was on cocktail duty, and was mixing another batch of martinis for the lot of us. Women pilots perched on every available seat, leaned in doorways, or—in Betty's case—sat on the counter.

Betty held a newspaper clipping in one hand and the remnants of a martini in the other. "I quote: 'The lady pilots acquitted themselves with admirable skill and thrilled the attending crowd. The pilots performed many astonishing feats, not least of which was the military precision of their formation flying, led by Miss Ida Peaks of Kansas City.'"

Ida sat at the table in the corner, next to Imogene. Opposite them, Pearl, who had found a babysitter for her triplets, kept blinking around the group as if she were startled to be out of the house after dark. We'd even managed to get Sabiha Gökçen to join us before she headed back to Turkey, although the princess had "declined our kind invitation with regrets."

"The most breathtaking moment of the air show came as Mrs. Nathaniel York—"

"Why they not use your name?" Helen glared at the large pot of vegetables she was stirring as if it were the newspaper.

"It's standard convention." I poured a measure of vermouth into the pitcher of gin. "And I like being married to Nathaniel."

"Just wait until Dennis asks you to marry him." Betty waved the newspaper at her. "And you're Mrs. Dennis Chien."

"Wait—what?" I turned from the martinis. "You have a beau?"

Helen stared at me, holding the spoon in one hand and shaping the word with her mouth.

"B. E. A. U. It's French for boyfriend," supplied Pearl. "And why don't we know about him?"

Helen rolled her eyes and looked back to the pot of vegetables. "Just because he's Chinese doesn't mean we're dating."

I blinked. "Wait. Dennis Chien? From engineering? He's a lamb."

"We're. Not. Dating." She spun and pointed the dripping spoon at Betty. "You. Read article."

"Aye aye, ma'am." Betty took a healthy sip of her martini and lifted the paper again. "The most breathtaking moment of the air show came as Mrs. Nathaniel York hit a flock of wild geese and lost power to her engine."

I winced and glanced over to Imogene. "I'm still so sorry about that."

"Yes. I'm sure you control the flight pattern of geese." She shook her head. "And you paid for it, so . . . hush."

Helen snorted. "Good luck getting her to not feel guilty on something."

Raising my hand, I said, "Jewish." It was also why I'd insisted that Nathaniel and I cover the damages, even though it wiped out our savings, because I didn't want anyone to think we were being cheap. "And Southern. It's encoded in my DNA."

"Try being Catholic." Helen said from the stove.

"Agreed." Pearl nodded. "I'm feeling guilty just sitting here."

"The point—" Betty cut in and waved the newspaper clipping over her head. "Is that my article got picked up by the AP, which means it went out to all the major papers, and millions of people read it. So we need to start talking about our next move."

Sabiha Gökçen raised her hand. "Another air show? Is popular. Yes?"

"Maybe we could do one in another city." Ida said. "Like Chicago or Atlanta."

Nodding, I added ice to the martini pitcher. "Or Seattle. Nathaniel's been talking with Boeing about their KC-135 refueler. And, no, we can't fly her, but still . . ." Even getting Boeing to loan us one of the first production models to be a static display on the field would draw a lot of attention. "There are probably local pilots there that might be good to pull in."

Betty shook her head. "The decision makers are here in the capital. We need to do something here. Like getting an air show televised. Live."

I nearly dropped the ice tray. Facing all of those reporters had been bad enough when it wasn't live. But being broadcast to the nation? No thank you.

"Ooo!" Pearl clapped her hands together. "What about the Dinah Shore show? She has guests on sometimes."

"And she's Jewish." Betty leaned across the counter toward me. "What about it, Mrs. Nathaniel York? Want me to see if I can get you on there?"

"Pretty sure I'd have to sing to do that." I left alone the assumption that all Jews must know each other and stirred the martinis, focusing on the chilling pitcher as if my life depended on it. Condensation began to form on the outside as the gin cooled. "I think just flying in an air show will be enough for me. What about Ida?"

"This better not be an assumption that because I'm black, I can sing."

"That article lists you as the leader of the formation segment."

"Has Dinah Shore ever had a black guest?"

I pulled the spoon out of the pitcher. "A more immediate question is . . . who wants another martini?"

Everyone did. Me? I wanted a double.

Back at work, the goal of reaching the moon carried on. I had been working on a series of calculations for orbital rendezvous. In theory, the astronauts would be able to ask the computers on Earth to do their calculations, but there would be times when they would be out of radio range, so we needed a way for the astronauts to work it out on their own. If the IBM was smaller or more reliable, that might be an option, but even that would require them to do preliminary calculations.

A shadow fell across my desk. Mrs. Rogers, who ran the computing department, stood there with a frown. Her steel-gray hair was pulled back in a bun that made her look more severe than she really was. "Elma? You have a call in my office."

A call at work? I ran through the list of people who would call me at work and came up with exactly two. Nathaniel, who was just down the hall. And Hershel. My heart dropped into my stomach. Swallowing, I pushed back my chair. "Thank you, Mrs. Rogers."

Basira looked up at me from across our shared desk. "Everything okay?"

I shrugged to hide my concern. "Let you know in a minute."

Was hurricane season about to get really bad? Had one of the kids been injured? Was it his wife? Or, God—what if Doris was calling because something had happened to Hershel? Polio could reoccur. What if he'd fallen and hurt himself?

Wiping my mouth, I followed Mrs. Rogers to her office. She gestured me inside, where the phone lay off its hook on the desk. She stopped at the door. "I'll give you some privacy, but try not to take too long, hm?"

"Of course." I went in and only belatedly remembered to say, "Thank you."

Taking a breath, I wiped my palms on my skirt before I picked up the phone. "Elma York here."

A masculine voice—someone I didn't know—answered. "Sorry to bother you at work. This is Don Herbert."

Don Herbert? The name was vaguely familiar, but I couldn't place it. In the absence of any other clues, I fell back on my mother's training. "How do you do?"

He chuckled, which I prayed meant it wasn't something terrible. "Well, thank you. And yourself?"

"Fine, thank you." I fiddled with the phone cord and waited.

"I don't expect you to remember me, but we met during the war a couple of times. You ferried a couple of bomber planes to me when I was with the 767th Bomb Squadron in Italy."

"Oh! Captain Herbert. Yes. Yes, I do remember you." What he hadn't mentioned in the "we met" statement was that he'd called down some fighter pilots who were making catcalls at me and my copilot. Whatever this was, it wasn't about my brother, so I let myself sit down. "What can I do for you?"

"Well . . . funny thing. I had a bit of a career change after the war, and I saw the newspaper article about you and that spin you pulled out of and the whole thing about astronauts and . . . Have you heard of the show *Watch Mr. Wizard*?"

"I—" That was not at all where I thought this conversation was going. For a moment, I'd thought he was going to invite me to be an astronaut, even though I knew that invitation would have to come from Director Clemons. "Yes. Yes, I have. My niece is very fond of it, although I have to admit I've not seen it myself."

"That's all right."

"It's just that we don't have a television."

He laughed. "It's all right. Really. It's just me doing the kind of science that you're so far beyond it would bore you to tears."

"Wait. You're Mr. Wizard?"

"Told you I had a career change." His laugh hadn't changed, and I suddenly wished that I *had* watched the show so I knew what he looked like now. "The thing is, my producer's daughter saw the clip on television of you pulling out of that spin and declared that she wanted to be a pilot like you."

"That's . . . that's very flattering."

"So we got to talking, and I was wondering if you'd like to be on the show."

I hung up the phone and pushed back from the desk so fast I nearly knocked the chair over. Sweat coated my back and prickled under my arms. Was this a rational response? No. It wasn't. But, be on television? Be on *live national* television? No. No. That was impossible. All of those people staring at me? And what would happen if I made a mistake, which I would? What would people think?

The phone rang and I jumped like a test launch had misfired. I think I squeaked. My hand pressed against my chest, and beneath my palm the beat of my heart pounded in double-time. The phone rang again.

I could be rational. I wasn't, but I could act like it. Wetting my lips, I picked up the phone. "Mrs. Rogers' desk. Elma York speaking."

"Don Herbert here. Sorry about that. I think we got disconnected."

"Yes. I . . . I was wondering what happened." Liar. I covered my eyes and leaned forward to rest my elbows on the desk. "You were saying?"

"That we'd like to have you on the show. I thought we could talk about the physics of flight, maybe do a simple experiment about lift? The format is real simple."

"I wish I could, but we're so busy preparing for the next launch. I just don't know if I could get the time off."

"We can work around your schedule."

"That's very kind, but . . . maybe I could suggest another woman pilot?" Betty would be brilliant at this.

"Sure . . . it's just that, well, my producer's girl is kinda keen that it be you. I don't need an answer right away, but think about it, eh?"

"Sure. Sure. I'll think about it." I would think of a way to say "no," is what I would do.

⁎ ⁎ ⁎

The next couple of weeks were genuinely busy at work, which seemed to be a constant, so I hadn't needed to lie much when Don called back a week later, just to see if I had any questions. I'd pretended to be too busy to talk—the launch, the fate of humanity, and all that—but he gave me his number so I could call back. I hadn't. But life outside the IAC continued on.

After work, Myrtle and I hopped off the streetcar outside the Amish Market. It was midway between our apartments, and I liked the owners better than at the grocery closer to where Nathaniel and I lived.

"How long you think he'll stay at work?" Myrtle jumped over a puddle to reach the sidewalk.

"Long enough for me to bake cookies and then go back for him?"

On the sidewalk near the bus stop, a homeless man sat with his knees drawn up in front of him. A little girl leaned against him, clutching a scrap of blanket. I steered over to them and dropped a dollar in his cup. Some might see it as extravagant for tzedakah, but Nathaniel and I could have been them.

Myrtle trailed after me, and I heard the rattle of coins hitting the cup before she caught up. "So we have enough time for talking."

I pushed open the door to the market. "Not you, too."

"What?" Her eyes were wide and innocent. "Just thinking we could have a girls' night. Eugene's on rotation out at the Edwards Air Force Base, so I'm at loose ends."

"Mm-hm . . ." I picked up a shopping basket and nodded to Mr. Yoder, who ran the Amish Market. Even with his broad straw hat, his simple dark suit always put me in mind of the Hasidic Jews back home in D.C. Entire family lines of which had been wiped out by the Meteor. I dug in my purse to check my ration book. "Darn it, I'm out of stamps for meat."

"You should go on *Mr. Wizard*." She picked up a bunch of radishes and put them in her basket.

My heart started racing, just at the name of the show. It had been a mistake to tell the women in the computer department, but I thought they'd laugh. I hadn't expected them to encourage me to go. In hindsight, that was stupid.

"You're bringing it up just like that, no lead-in or sliding up to the subject?" The lettuce looked good, but we had some growing in the window box at the apartment. I hadn't considered the orientation of the fire escape to the sun when we rented the place, but we'd gotten lucky. So long as one of us remembered to water the boxes, that is.

"Tried that. Girls' night, remember? So . . ." She weighed a bunch of grapes in her hand but put it back, *tsk*ing at the price.

"I don't know . . ." How could I explain that I panicked? In a way that made sense to her—or to anyone, really? Even me. "Are those tomatoes?"

Nestled among the greens was a box of pale-greenish orbs with only the barest blush of pink. It hadn't been warm enough for tomatoes in ages. Sure, you could get greenhouse tomatoes from farther south, but they were almost always mealy and tasteless by the time they reached Kansas City.

Behind me, Mr. Yoder said, "We had some ripe ones earlier today, but they went fast."

"That's fine." I picked up three of them and grinned at Myrtle. "Come over. I'll treat you to fried green tomatoes, and you can make martinis and try to convince me to go on *Mr. Wizard*."

SIXTEEN

PUNJAB FACES FOOD SHORTAGES

Special to The National Times.

KARACHI, Pakistan, June 26, 1956—Mian Mumtaz Daultana, chief minister of Punjab, Pakistan's granary, has told the Legislative Assembly that Punjab will face an acute food shortage next year if the Meteor winter continues.

I hate vomiting, and this was the second time today. The taste of the morning's coffee still clung to the back of my throat.

Goddamn it. I was going to have to fix my makeup again, after those nice women had taken such pains to make me presentable for the television cameras. What really angers me when my body betrays me like this—and I try to focus on the anger—is that I haven't *always* been terrified of crowds.

But I can't shake the memory of being in college and all those young men staring at me. And the mockery. The teasing. The . . . the hate. I could solve problems in my head that they couldn't even do on paper, and the teachers, damn them, kept shoving that in their faces until I just wanted to quit and hide . . . but I was also my father's daughter. He believed in me so thoroughly that I couldn't shame him by not trying. And I still want my father to be proud of me, even though he and Mama have been gone for four years.

Let's just say that I've learned how to vomit discreetly. And I still hate it.

Someone knocked on my dressing room door. "Mrs. York?"

I gripped the edge of the toilet as my stomach cramped again. Swallowing, I snatched a piece of toilet paper. "Just a minute."

It took only a minute to blot my face and reapply a thick red layer of lipstick. As I walked to the door, I pinched my cheeks back into brightness. My hands were still shaking, but if I kept them by my side, it shouldn't be too obvious. I had tried smoking in college so they'd have something to do, but it just made the shaking worse, and it tasted like a rocket fueled by a pigsty.

"Sorry to keep you waiting." My voice might have even sounded normal—if you didn't know me. As it was, all breathy and low, I sounded more like Marilyn Monroe than myself.

The waiting assistant smiled over his clipboard. "Not a problem, Mrs. York."

But he led me down the hall at a brisk clip toward the studio. My stomach cramped again.

3.1415926535897932384 . . .

At least *Watch Mr. Wizard* was a children's show, so there wouldn't be that many people watching. Only ninety-one stations. That was just two million viewers. Or more?

How could new studios have such poor air circulation? *2, 3, 5, 7, 11, 13, 17, 19, 23, 29, 31, 37, 41 . . .*

The soundstage was brilliantly lit. They'd given me a quick tour earlier, and the assistant now led me onto the fake back porch of Mr. Wizard's house. *43, 47, 53, 59, 61, 67, 71 . . .* This would just be a conversation with a man I knew from the war. If I didn't think of him as Mr. Wizard—if I could remember him as Captain Don Herbert—I'd be okay. I just had to talk to him. Only him.

Beyond the door, someone said, "We're live in five, four, three . . ."

Live broadcast is go.

Confirmed live broadcast.

I pressed my hand against my stomach and breathed through my mouth. Don was a good man, and there wasn't a live audience. It would just be him and the child actor. Goddamn it. Why had I said yes?

The assistant—he'd had a name, I should know his name—held his clipboard and nodded to the stage. That was my cue.

Beyond the wall, Don was talking, waiting for me to walk through the door. I just had to open the door. The knob was right there. *Get it together, Elma. If your father could see you, standing here trembling in the dark . . .*

The assistant solved my problem by knocking on the door.

On the other side of the fake wall, Don said, "Come in."

And then my mother's voice sounded in my head. *Shoulders back. Head up. You're a young lady, not a camel.*

Shoulders back, head up, I opened the door and walked onto the stage. Don was standing by a kitchen counter with his shirtsleeves rolled up. A young girl, no more than ten, stood at the counter with him, in a cherry red skirt and snug pink cardigan. Her glossy brown hair had been smoothed back from her face in ways that wouldn't have lasted five minutes when I was a child.

Don had a model airplane in his hands as I entered. "Well, look who's here!" He set the plane down on the counter and turned to the little girl. "Rita, this is my friend Elma York."

"How do you do, Mrs. York?"

He held up a finger. "Actually, you should call her Dr. York—she's a doctor, but not a medical one."

"Gee, really?"

My eyes stung a little. He hadn't told me he was going to do that. "I suppose that's right. I have doctorates in physics and mathematics from Stanford. But most people just call me Mrs. York."

"Well, you're Dr. York today, because I need your help with some physics." He picked up the plane again. "I was just trying to explain aerodynamics to Rita, here."

"I'd be happy to help with that."

As I walked to the mark they had chalked on the floor for me, Mr. Wizard leaned down to Rita again. "You see, Dr. York is also a pilot."

Rita smiled like a consummate child actress. "Keen! She's the perfect person to help me understand how airplanes fly."

"And rockets, too." Mr. Wizard grinned. "But more on that later. For now . . . let's look at the wing of an airplane."

Nathaniel had my overnight bag in one hand as we walked up the stairs to our apartment. He swung it to the side when we passed the bottle blonde from 3B. She was tottering down the stairs in heels and bright red lipstick, which suggested a night out. She smiled at me. "Saw you on television last night."

"Oh. Um." I gripped the banister and smiled vaguely at her. Did you say thank you for that?

"I didn't know you were so smart!" Her front teeth were stained with smoke, though God knew how she could afford both tobacco and rent.

"Thank you?"

Nathaniel took a step back down toward me. "I'd better get her home. She just got back from Chicago."

"Chicago! That must have been something."

I edged past her. "I hardly saw it at all. I went to the television studio and then straight home."

Turning on the stairs to watch me, she clasped her hands together and just beamed. "To think, I know someone who's been on television."

Know me? We lived on the same hallway, but I had no idea what her name was. We just saw each other on the stairs sometimes. "I can hardly believe it myself."

"What was it like?" She took a step up to follow me.

Nathaniel put a hand on my arm and sort of drew me to him. "Now, I'm sure you ladies could talk all night, but I haven't seen my wife in two days. We'll talk to you later?"

"Oh, sure!" She giggled. "That would be swell. Good night!"

With a "Good night" of our own, we escaped onto our floor. Nathaniel glanced over his shoulder and rolled his eyes at our neighbor. "Was I right that you needed an escape?"

"God, yes." I kept my voice low, because sound could echo down the stairwell. "Do you know her name?"

He shook his head. "I was hoping you did. We'll check her mailbox tomorrow. Tonight, though . . . I've missed you very much."

"Likewise." I leaned over to peck his cheek as he fumbled with the keys. "How shall I make up for being gone?"

"Hm . . ." He turned the key in the lock, and pushed the door open. "I was thinking more of ways to convince you to stay home."

"It was just two nights. Can't you—" The phone rang. "Bother."

Nathaniel flicked the wall switch. It clicked. The room stayed dark. "Sorry—must have burned out."

The phone jangled on the other side of the room. "Don't worry about it."

I made my way across our apartment, which really wasn't that dark with the light from the hall and the city outside. A beam of orange sodium-vapor light fell across the phone as it rang again. "York residence. Elma York speaking."

"Is this the famous Dr. Elma York?" My brother's laugh conjured his face in the dark. The corners of his eyes always crinkled when he smiled.

"Oh, stop. No one calls me that."

"Except for Mr. Wizard. Elma, you were great."

Beaming, I wrapped the phone cord around my hand and sat on the sofa. "A compliment? You must be getting soft in your old age."

"Well, I'd better get with the program. Look at you. I thought the newspaper clippings you sent were keen, but television? And Doris tells me you were in—what was that?" His wife said something in the background. "*Women's Day.* Mama and Pops would have been so proud of you."

I wiped my eyes with the back of one hand. "Well, I almost threw up all over the set."

"Couldn't tell." There was a little hesitation there, as if he wanted to ask something, but he just said, "You were great, really great. And your fan club starts here. Speaking of . . . there's a fan who wants to talk to you."

The phone rustled as he passed it to someone. Nathaniel was fumbling in the junk drawer, still in the dark. I stretched over to reach for the table lamp on the other side of the couch.

"Hello, Aunt Elma." The sweet breathy sound of my niece's voice filled the receiver.

"Rachel! How's my favorite niece?" I pulled on the lamp's chain, but it stayed dark. Like an idiot, I tried again. "Hang on, darling. Nathaniel? I think it's the fuse."

"Yeah. I'm trying to find the flashlight."

"Oh—sorry. It's at the airfield. The Shabbat candles are

in the bottom drawer." I returned to the phone. "Sorry, Rachel. I had to help Uncle Nathaniel find something."

"Was Mr. Wizard nice?"

"He was very nice, sweetie. Did you watch the show?"

"I always watch *Mr. Wizard,* even before you were on, but I like you better than him."

I laughed, tucking my feet up under me on the couch. In the front of the apartment, Nathaniel lit a candle and brought light to our tiny studio. I gave him a thumbs up and he grinned. "Well, you *know* me."

"That's not it. I thought I wanted to be a scientist like him, but I want to be an astronaut like you."

"I'm not . . . I'm not an astronaut." I racked my brain, trying to remember what I'd said on the show. "I'm just a pilot."

"But you *want* to be an astronaut. And you're a doctor. And Daddy says that you're really smart and you can be anything you want to be and you'll be an astronaut someday, so I want to be one too."

Pressing my hand over my mouth did nothing to stop me from crying. "Your daddy says a lot of things. Wanting something isn't enough by itself."

"I know that." Ah . . . the scorn of a nine-year-old. "You have to work hard, too. What do I need to do to be an astronaut?"

"Things you won't necessarily like. Like . . . eating your vegetables, so you can be nice and strong. And doing all your math homework."

"Now you sound like Daddy."

I laughed. "You were the one who said you wanted to be an astronaut."

"Well, I do."

"And I do too." The little girl on the show had also said she wanted to be an astronaut, which I thought was part of the script, but she'd said it again when we went off the air. I was too limp with relief to really reply, but I wished I had now. "So, you need to make a list of all the things you need to learn, and then start working, all right? Someday, you and I are going to be on Mars together."

"Really?" Her voice grew muffled, and fabric rubbed against the phone. "Aunt Elma says we're going to Mars together."

I could hear Hershel laughing in the background, and then his voice was in my ear again. "Now I'm going to have to buy her model airplane parts."

"I'll mail her a kit for her birthday."

"That'd be swell. Oh—say. Have you gotten the invitation for Tommy's bar mitzvah?"

I stood, grabbing the phone by its base. "Hang on. Let me check." This was one of the benefits of our tiny apartment. Not only did I have less to clean, but I could drag the phone across the room to the kitchen table and the cord would reach. "I was out of town the past two days."

That was a good excuse, but the truth of the matter was that once we started working on the air show, I'd been ignoring the mail. And since then . . . well, I hadn't anticipated any of this attention. Nathaniel was unscrewing a fuse from the box, but when he saw me, he lit another candle. I took it from him, cradling the phone between my head and shoulder.

There was a stack of mail in the table and I flipped through, looking for the envelope. By candlelight, it was almost romantic. Maybe when I got off the phone with Hershel, I'd suggest to Nathaniel that fixing the fuse could wait. "When is the bar mitzvah?"

"December 15th. Doris says to tell you that we've got the guest room all set for you."

"That's wonderful—" One of the envelopes was yellow.

On the outside, in bright red ink, a stamp read OVER-DUE. "Um . . . Hershel. May I call you back? Tell Tommy that we'll be there. I wouldn't miss it."

As we said our goodbyes and hung up, I wasn't really listening. I'd torn open the envelope and had slid out the overdue bill inside. My stomach twisted as if I were about to address a crowd of thousands, but this time it was only an audience of one. I'd been so busy with the air show and interviews and television that I'd gotten behind on the bills.

"I . . . I forgot to pay the electric bill."

The silence remained after my words vanished. Candle-light flickered on the table and I finally saw the rose stand-ing in a vase on the table. At current prices, it was as if he'd bought me a dozen.

"Nathaniel . . . I'm so, so sorry."

He left the fuse box hanging open. "Hey, you've had a lot on your mind. It's all right."

The stack of mail on the table all but glared at me. I had barely been cleaning the apartment, and now this. "I'll go through the accounts tomorrow. Make sure I didn't miss any others."

"It's all right." He blew out his candle and walked around the table to me. "I'm just happy to have you home."

Then he blew out my candle. I think he meant it to be romantic, but it left us standing in a darkness of my making.

SEVENTEEN

**INSULATING CONCERN HEATS HOUSE
FOR $12 A MONTH IN A 2-YEAR TEST**

KANSAS CITY, KS, July 14, 1956—In cooperation with the UN's Climate Committee, the Owens-
Corning Fiberglass Corporation undertook a two-year
test program involving 150 new houses in all climatic
regions of the United States, Europe, and parts of Af-
rica. The test homes were "comfort-engineered" and
required trees and trellises for shade, a wide roof overhang or heat-repellent screening, and attic ventilation.

Before we got home from the synagogue, I needed to take
my coat off. It felt like it must be in the mid-seventies. On
the one hand, thank God it was finally warming up. On
the other . . . I knew what the warming meant. We were
hitting the beginning of the greenhouse effect.

I stood, my coat over my arm, as Nathaniel crouched to
open our mailbox. He tipped his hat back on his head.
"Huh. I wonder what this is . . ."

Inside the box, a large padded envelope nearly filled the
entire space. He wrestled it free, and the thing seemed to
expand as it came out of the box. The last edge came loose
suddenly, and Nathaniel lost his balance and fell back on his
rump.

"You okay?" I bent to retrieve a couple of other envelopes that had dropped on the floor.

"Fine, fine . . ." He reseated his hat and clambered to his feet, staring at the envelope. "It's for you."

I stopped in the process of slipping the other envelopes into my purse. "Me?"

"From NBC." He tucked it under one arm and bent down to shut our mailbox. "Betcha someone got fan mail."

"Don't be silly. It's probably just a thank-you gift or some such thing." We started up the stairs, but my heart was pounding before we even reached the first landing. I wanted to believe that no one had watched the show.

And yet, when we got to the apartment and settled in, the giant envelope taking up most of the kitchen table, I circled around it as if it were a cobra or something equally deadly. Nathaniel sat down at the table and pulled out the rocket booster design he'd been working on when I'd talked him into leaving the office yesterday.

"That looks suspiciously like work . . ." I opened the refrigerator and rummaged through it, trying to figure out what we'd have for lunch.

"And you look like you're about to start cooking." He looked up at me and winked. "You knew I was a terrible Jew when you married me."

"I just made a comment."

"Mm-hm . . . and you don't get to use Shabbat as a weapon if you're going to ignore it too."

"Fine." I shut the refrigerator door. For me, the observation was as much about discipline and reminding myself of who I was as anything else. It had seemed important after the Holocaust, and then again after the Meteor, because Grandma would have . . .

Grief pops up at the strangest times. "I'll cook after

sundown, which isn't until nine tonight, if you'll take an actual day off."

"Wait . . . let me see if I understand this. You're trying to convince me to not work by offering to not feed me?" Nathaniel tapped his pencil against his chin. "Hm . . . there's something not quite right here."

"Oh, I'll feed you. Cold cuts and guilt." I laughed and pulled the envelope toward me. Best to get it over with. Sitting down opposite him, I patted the giant envelope proprietarily. "Besides, I have to see what's in this."

He laughed and stood, giving me a kiss on the back of my neck. "I'll make sandwiches, and if I'm right and it's fan mail, then . . ."

"Then what?"

"You'll have to think of some way to reward me for being right."

"Righteousness should be a reward in itself." I pulled the envelope open and more envelopes fell out. "Damn."

"Ha!" Nathaniel opened the refrigerator and said again, "Ha!"

"Sandwiches, husband." Some of the envelopes had beautiful penmanship, others had been addressed in actual crayon. Bemused, I picked up one of the crayon-addressed envelopes and laughed aloud. "This is addressed to The Lady Astronaut—well . . . more accurately, it's the Laddy Astronot."

"That will be my new pet name for you." Nathaniel set a cup of iced tea on the table next to me. "Chicken on rye okay?"

"Mm-hm . . . a little onion, too, please?" I opened the Laddy Astronot letter and pulled out a sheet of grubby primer paper. "Oh . . . My heart is going to break. Listen to this: 'Dere Laddy Astronot I want to go into space to. Do you have a roket ship? I want a rokket ship for Christmas. Your fred, Sally Hardesty.' And there's a picture of a rocket."

"Just wait until you actually get into space." Dishes rattled behind me as he worked on the sandwiches. "We'll have to get a bigger mailbox."

"If. And that's a big if, with a lot of other ifs before it." I put Sally's letter back in the envelope and set it aside. I wouldn't be able to answer her until Shabbat was over, but I could triage the letters. I didn't know if I was going to be able to answer all of them, but at least Sally Hardesty and the other crayon writers.

"I have faith—"

"I thought you were a bad Jew."

"I have faith in you. Speaking of which, I could use your help on an orbital parameter question." He pulled a loaf out of the breadbox and set it on the counter.

"Use a cutting board."

"I was going to." Releasing the knife he'd grabbed, Nathaniel bent to retrieve the cutting board from under the sink. "I think we can skip the translunar orbit and go straight to a lunar orbit, which would save a lot of time and materials."

"And risk the astronauts' lives through inadequate testing?" I pulled another letter toward me and ran my finger under the flap to open it.

Dear Dr. York, I didn't know that girls were allowed to be doctors . . .

"I'm not saying we'd skip the Earth orbit, just the translunar one. We're sending an unmanned mission around the moon to get pictures in September, so we'll know that orbit can be done. Having someone orbit the moon, though . . ."

. . . I would like to be a doctor . . . "A lunar orbit involves transferring in and out of orbit, which is a whole different

set of orbital mechanics. You have to change from the sphere of Earth's influence to the moon's and—"

"I know. I'm not asking about the mechanics of it. You already worked out fuel consumption and a flight plan . . . What I'm asking is if there's any compelling reason to do the translunar orbit as a manned mission."

"Seems like something you should be asking Parker." I slapped the letter down on the table, not even sure why I was irritated with Nathaniel.

"Well, he's not a physicist, is he?"

Ah . . . that was it. We'd been here before, where he asked me for advice because he wanted to prove Parker wrong about something. It reminded me too much of my college days, and being used as a tool to keep young men in line in math class. Nathaniel only knew about that in the most general sense, mostly as stories that I managed to make sound funny.

I took a slow breath and folded the letter carefully. Pressing down on the fold with my thumbnail, I creased the paper with a fair bit of vigor. "Sorry. I just . . . Okay. The primary reason to do the translunar orbit first is so that if we're wrong about fuel consumption for the transit, it gives the crew a larger margin of error for getting home. And they only get one shot."

"But the math—"

"Sweetie . . . I'm a physicist, but I'm also a pilot. If you're asking me to tell you that skipping steps is okay, I'm not going to do it. They get one shot at getting home. If the math is off, even a little, and they don't have the fuel to correct, then they go shooting past the Earth, or burn up on reentry." I shoved the letter into the envelope. "And I also don't want to work on Shabbat."

"You're answering fan mail. Doesn't that involve writing?" His voice was consciously lighthearted, and I loved him for making the effort.

"I'm reading, not writing."

He set a sandwich next to me, the bread sliced in a diagonal. Leaning down, he kissed the top of my head. "You're right. And I'm sorry."

"I shouldn't have gotten cranky."

"Well, let's eat lunch, and then . . ." He walked to the shelf and pulled down a book. "And then, I'll read."

Narrowing my eyes, I stacked the letters on the side of the table until after lunch. "I see the word *Mars* on that."

He laughed and showed me the cover. "It's a novel. Clemmons lent it to me. Says it's a comedy, at least in terms of spaceflight. Does that count as taking the day off?"

"Yes." I beamed up at him. "Yes. And thank you."

We had been sitting in the "dark room" with nothing to do for the last two hours and twenty-three minutes—and yes, we were all counting—as we waited for them to resolve an "issue" so the countdown clock could continue. It wasn't even anything wrong with the rocket itself, just an automatic cutoff that tripped when it shouldn't have at T-minus thirty seconds and holding. It had to be worse for the three men strapped into the giant *Jupiter V* rocket outside.

At the Capsule Communicator station, Stetson Parker tossed a tennis ball into the air, his headset pushed back behind one ear. Every couple of minutes he grinned and said something into his comm. As CAPCOM, he was in charge of filtering all the information from the scores of engineers and computers down to the stream that the astronauts needed in their capsule.

Was he talking to Jean-Paul Lebourgeois, Randy B. Cleary, or Halim "Hotdog" Malouf? For the first time, none of the astronauts going up were Americans, and to my eternal surprise, Parker had turned out to be a polyglot. French, Italian, and, of all things, Gaelic.

Helen leaned across our shared table. "Hey. You going to the 99s this weekend?"

I shook my head and straightened the pencils on my side of the table. "I'll be wiped out after this."

She *tsk*ed and turned back to the chess game that she was playing with Reynard Carmouche.

That *tsk* had been a masterful use of a single noise to convey disappointment and resignation. I lifted my head and stared at her dimly lit profile. "What?"

"Last week you said you were trying to stay rested for the launch." She moved a pawn a space forward and Carmouche cursed in French.

"I was." The graph paper stuck to my fingers as I picked it up to tap it straight on the edge of the table. "And you've got your solo license, so it's not like you need me in order to fly anymore."

At this Carmouche looked up. "You can fly?"

"Yes." Helen pointed at the board. "Are you going to play or just stare?"

"I am thinking!" he protested, crouching closer to the board as if putting his nose between the pieces would solve the puzzle for him.

Helen turned back to me and leaned across the table. The desk light focused down on our papers, leaving an unearthly uplit glow on her face. "Why don't you come to the 99s anymore?"

"I—I just . . . there are a lot of new members." Our core group still came, and Ida and Imogene had joined us, but after *Mr. Wizard* and the articles about me, we'd gotten a sudden influx of members. There were only so many times I could handle being asked for an autograph or to pose with someone. I shrugged and straightened my pencils again. "I just . . . I miss the small group."

Helen nodded, tapping her fingers on the desk. "Give it time. They lose interest if you aren't there. The ones that are just tourists, I mean."

The tension sighed out of me. Thank God for friends who understood my fears without me having to spell them out. Especially not here, in the dark room, where I wanted to be as professional as possible.

Carmouche finally moved a knight. Helen turned back to the game and immediately moved a bishop. "Check."

Stetson Parker's voice cut through the room from the CAPCOM desk. "What's the word on the delay? Prayer time is coming up for Malouf."

"He cannot get out of his chair to pray." Clemons jabbed a cigar toward Parker.

"He's not asking to. He just wants to avoid being mid-prayer if the countdown starts again."

"When the countdown starts, we shall let him know." Clemons turned away from Parker and barked, "York! Status!"

Nathaniel looked up from the console he was leaning over. He had a telephone pressed to one ear and was jotting down something, his nose wrinkled in concentration. He held up one hand to silence Clemons. God, I loved my husband.

Parker snorted. "I'll tell him to go ahead and pray. Might speed things up." He pulled the mic back into place and murmured to the astronauts.

I glanced at the big clock on the wall. If this went another hour, we'd lose our launch window and have to wait until tomorrow. It wouldn't be the first time we'd scrubbed a flight, but it was never pleasant.

"Checkmate." Helen leaned back in her chair and crossed her arms. "Checkmate is go."

The Frenchman's jaw hung open, and he stared at the board as if he were tracing all of the steps that had led to his doom. I stood and cracked my back. "I don't know why you keep trying, Dr. Carmouche."

"Someday . . . someday, I must beat her. It is simply the law of averages, no?" He rubbed his forehead, still staring at the board. "Confirmed checkmate."

"York—Elma York." Parker gripped the ball he'd been tossing in one hand and beckoned me with the other. The harsh light of the comm desk threw heavy shadows under his brows.

Helen and I exchanged glances before I crossed the room to Parker. Nathaniel, still on his call, watched me with enough intensity that the room started to heat up. I put on my most careful neutral face and stopped in front of Parker. "Yes?"

"Hang on." Having called me over, he now made me wait as he listened, nodding at something one of the other astronauts said.

I stood, resisting the urge to brush my skirt smooth, fidget with my hands, or do anything, really, but wait. Nathaniel's gaze still burned the right side of my body, but I didn't turn to look at him.

"Got it. *Elle se tient ici . . . Ouais, ouais. Vous et moi à la fois.*" He released the talk button on the mic and sat back in the chair. The ball flew up from his grasp and smacked back down into his palm. "Lebourgeois's wife is doing all the American things. So their daughter is in a Girl Scout troupe, and they want you to come talk to them."

I blinked a couple of times before I found my voice. "Me?"

"Yeah, they formed a 'Lady Astronaut' club. I figured they would want an actual astronaut, but . . . girls, huh?

Kinda adorable that they want to talk to you." He grinned, showing his dimples, as if that helped. "You'll do it, right?"

There is no possible way to say "no" to an astronaut who is sitting atop what is, essentially, a giant bomb. Even if I spoke French and could rip the microphone off of Parker, I couldn't decline. I smiled. "Sure. I'd be happy to do that. Just tell me when."

Parker turned back to the mic and rattled off more French, "*Elle va le faire, mais Dieu sait ce qu'elle va parler. Les bébés dans l'espace, probablement. Les femmes, eh?*" Then he listened for a moment before he turned back to me. "His wife is watching from the roof. If you could go chat with her after the launch, he'd appreciate it. It'll distract his daughter while he's in space."

"Sure. Gladly." The thing was that I didn't resent Lebourgeois's wife or his daughter, or even him for that matter. If it were me, I would be thinking of everything I could possibly do to distract Nathaniel and make him more comfortable. It was just Parker and his shit-eating smugness. Yes. Yes. He was the first man into space. Yes. He was a damn good pilot and, in fact, very brave. But he was also a self-serving schmuck. "Soon as I'm finished, I'll head up to the family area."

"Great." He grinned again, all dazzling white teeth. "See if that husband of yours will tell you what's holding us up."

"I'm sure he'll tell us as soon as we're clear." I glanced at Nathaniel, who had begun massaging his right temple. That was not a good sign. "And how's your wife?"

Parker looked down and rolled the ball along the table. "Better. Thank you."

That was not . . . that was not the response that I had expected. "I was sorry that she couldn't make the Wargin dinner."

"Well. Maybe next time, hm?" He cleared his throat. "You were going to check with your husband? About the launch?"

"Of course." That was not my job. Of course, my actual job required a rocket to be launched, so I had something to track and compute. I brushed off my skirt and swung away, heading toward Nathaniel. If nothing else, it gave me an excuse to talk to him.

My husband had stopped writing anything but still gripped the pencil in one hand hard enough that his knuckles had turned white. His jaw was set. He stared at the desk while Clemons paced behind him.

Clemons saw me approach and snatched the cigar from his mouth. "What?"

"Colonel Parker had some questions for you, Director Clemons." It was at best tangential to the truth, but he'd be better able to answer Parker's questions about the launch than Nathaniel would. Clemons stalked off in response without actually acknowledging me.

My poor husband seemed in danger of stabbing himself with his pencil. And I couldn't touch him. Not at work, without making everything more complicated for both of us. I stood for a moment, wishing I could rub the tension out of his neck as he nodded and grunted in response to whoever was on the other end of the line.

Taking a breath, I turned and walked back to my station. There was nothing I could do for Nathaniel, and under the circumstances, I was a distraction.

Carmouche was putting his chess pieces back into their case. He looked up as I rejoined the table and leaned in close. In a hushed voice, he said, "That Colonel Parker . . . he does not like you very much."

"I know." I tucked my skirts under me as I sat. "Helen? I'll come to the 99s this weekend if—if you'll promise to

fly with me so I don't have to share the Cessna with someone I don't know."

"*Āiyō, Āiyō!*" Her grin of triumph did the translation,
and I couldn't help smiling back.

"Ha!" Nathaniel straightened. "We've worked around
the automatic cutoff. Start the clock again and tell Malouf
his prayers worked. Let's light this candle."

EIGHTEEN

ALGERIAN FRENCH KILL THREE IN RIOT

By MICHAEL CLARK

Special to The National Times.

ALGIERS, Algeria, Aug. 22, 1956—Riots flared in Algiers today as thousands of Frenchmen demonstrated during the funeral of Amédée Froger, chairman of the Algerian Mayors Federation. He was assassinated by an anti-space terrorist yesterday.

Betty volunteered to come with me to meet the Girl Scout troop that Lebourgeois's daughter belonged to, which was great, because I was scared senseless. Betty was thrilled about the "Great Publicity," and had been gushing since we'd met at my place, imagining headlines with her hands spread wide like she was cupping the words.

"Lady Astronaut Meets Astronaut's Daughter!" She laughed and swung on the streetcar's pole. "I wish you'd let me bring a photographer."

I reached for the pull cord on the streetcar. "This is our stop." The doors opened and I trotted down the steps to the street. "First, please stop calling me that; I'm not an astronaut."

"That's what the public calls you." She hopped down next to me, coat pulled tight against the wind.

"Yes, but I haven't been into space, and it's disrespectful of the men who have." I pulled the address out of my purse and steered us down the street.

"Whoa. Elma." Betty put up her hands in mock surrender. "I thought you were the one who was all keen to get women into space."

"I am, but that doesn't mean I want a title I haven't earned." We were meeting the Girl Scouts in the common room at a Catholic church in a newer part of Kansas City I didn't usually visit.

The broad streets had modern buildings with narrow windows and low, thick walls. Half of them probably had several stories below ground, in the fashion that had become popular right after the Meteor hit. Idiots. They were building for an impact that would never come. At least the floors below ground would be fairly easy to cool.

The church itself was easy to spot from several blocks away from its redbrick facade and the thrust of its bell tower. Given the number of cars parked outside, it clearly had some sort of event going on. Likely a wedding, which was nice.

Right after the Meteor, there'd been a trend toward free love as a sort of reaction to Doomsday. It was good that people were still getting married, since it meant that they weren't as scared about the future.

On the other hand, if people were becoming complacent about the planet's future, that was a different sort of problem.

"Don't be mad." Betty grabbed my arm. "Just smile. You've got a great smile."

"What are you—?"

The sidewalk next to the church was filled with reporters. Sweat drenched my back and ran down my inner arms.

If Betty hadn't had a hold of my arm, I would have probably made a run for it. My stomach heaved and I had to swallow hard to keep from hurling on the spot.

"Smile, Elma." She kept her grip on my arm and spoke through a fixed smile of her own. "We need this."

"I didn't even want a photographer, and you arranged *this*?" I wrenched my arm free, heart hitting my ribs like a punching bag. Any moment now I was going to cry, and that was monumentally unfair. I was angry, damn it. I turned my back on the reporters.

"You can't walk away. Elma. Elma . . . the little girls are coming out. Elma, you can't leave them. There's an astronaut's daughter here, and her daddy is in—"

"Damn it." Mr. Lebourgeois's daughter had asked me to come because her father was in space and she was scared. "Goddamn it."

So I turned to face the cameras, and all the expectations, and—and eight little girls, all wearing cardboard-and-tinfoil space helmets.

"Elma . . . please don't be mad." Betty stayed by my side, talking through a smile. "Please. I knew you'd say no, and you're so good on camera. Please don't be mad."

I gave her my brightest, most Stetson-Parker smile. "Well, bless your heart. Why would I be mad?" One little girl. I was here for one little girl. I tried my damnedest to block out the cameras and the men shouting for us to look at them and smile. One little girl. Her name was Claire Lebourgeois and her daddy was in space.

I could keep from throwing up for long enough to reassure her that he was coming home.

Fourteen days after they went into space, Lebourgeois, Cleary, and Malouf safely returned to the ground. They hadn't accomplished all of their objectives, but they'd proven the main point that the lunar module would sustain life long enough for an exploratory moon mission. That just left it up to us to get them there.

Sitting at my shared desk with Basira, I tried to ignore the constant bouncing that the engineer next to us was doing. I'd offered him a chair when he came in, but he was too eager. Resting my head on my left hand, I tried to surreptitiously rub my temple while studying the figures that Clarence "Bubbles" Bobienski had brought from the latest engine test. I'd been on the radio this morning before work, and getting up two hours earlier had left me with a headache that ran from my left eye, over my scalp, and down to the base of my neck.

I was fairly certain it wasn't fatigue that was the problem, though. "Bubbles, this doesn't make sense."

"I know!" He jabbed a finger, raw with chewed cuticles, at the paper. "That's why I want you to go over the calculations."

I shook my head, running the tip of my pencil over the machine-generated numbers. "It's not an error in calculation."

"Please. That machine adds wrong if the temperature is over sixty-five." The cuffs of his shirt were smudged gray with pencil lead. "I need a computress."

As a group, we hated that nickname. Lifting my gaze, I fixed him with a dead stare that I'd learned from Mrs. Rogers. Out of the corner of my eye, I could see that Helen had done the same. "You need a *computer*."

He waved my correction away. "Can you help me?"

"I *am*. I'm telling you that there are no errors in the calculations, so it's either an error in the initial data set, or you've found a spectacularly effective engine arrangement." It *was* possible that going to a star pattern in the middle of the solid propellant could lead to a more efficient burn ratio. In fact . . . "This structure reminds me of a theory that Harold James Pool had."

"Yes!" He bounced on his toes, and behind him, Myrtle covered her mouth to stifle a laugh. There was a reason he had the nickname Bubbles among the computers. "See! That's why I need you doing this, because you understand. That contraption doesn't. I mean, great Scott!— you've got a PhD."

That was the first time my degree had come up at work since I was hired. Mrs. Rogers knew my credentials, of course, but after our interview, I'm not sure I ever mentioned it, even when trying to make a point. I guess he watched *Mr. Wizard* or listened to *ABC Headline Edition*.

It wasn't as if it made me a better computer, and trotting it out always sounded like posturing. I mean, anyone with a background in physics would have been just as capable of the type of work we did. And several of the women in the computer department didn't have college degrees at all.

"My degree is irrelevant here." I flipped back through the pages that Bubbles had brought me. "Do you have the raw data?"

"Of course!" He shrugged as if I'd asked a stupid question. I waited, smiling at him, until he snapped and pointed both fingers at me. "Oh! You need it. Right. Got it. It's over in the lab. I should go get that. I'll go get that."

"Thank you." I stacked the pages on my desk as he bounded out of the room, tie flapping with each step.

The moment he was out of the room, giggles escaped from almost every desk. We loved Bubbles, but oh, he could be *such* an engineer sometimes. We had a saying: *Engineers caused problems. Computers solved them.* Bubbles? Perfect example of the type.

Basira pushed back her chair and jumped up, bouncing from one foot to the other. With an exaggerated American accent, she kept bouncing like Bubbles. "Ah need a computress! Lord help me, ah need a computress!"

"Bless his heart." I laughed and rested against the back of my chair. "He means well."

"Oof. Harsh words." Myrtle left her desk and came over to join us. "But, seriously, what do the numbers look like?"

I slid the paper over to her so she could flip through it. Helen appeared at her elbow, head tilted to the side as she studied the printed output. "Something must have been mistranscribed on the punch cards."

"That's why I wanted the raw data, which really . . . how hard is it to figure out that you need to bring that with you?"

Nathaniel came into the computer room. The giggles stopped and everyone returned to work mode. He was my husband, but he was also the lead engineer. I winked at Helen as she returned to her seat, then turned to give him my full attention.

His mouth was compressed in a narrow line, and a muscle bunched at the corner of his jaw. Between his brows, concentration furrows had appeared. He had a magazine rolled up in one hand and was slapping it against his thigh as he walked. "Elma. May I speak with you? In my office."

"Of course." Exchanging a look with Basira, I slid my chair back from my desk. "If Bubbles returns before I'm back, will you just tell him to leave the raw data on my desk?"

As I followed Nathaniel out of the computer room, the other women did a pretty poor job of pretending not to stare at us. Nathaniel's back was rigid, and his strides ate up the length of the corridor that led to his office. My heels clattered against the linoleum as I hurried after him.

Nathaniel held the door to the office for me, staring at the floor. That muscle in his jaw kept clenching and unclenching, and my heart seemed to be joining it in a race. The last time I'd seen Nathaniel this furious was when he had fired Leroy Pluckett for grabbing one of the computers.

The usual organized chaos dominated his office. The blackboard on one wall had been filled with what looked like equations for a lunar orbit, which made sense, given the next phase of the space project. Nathaniel shut the door carefully, so it barely made any sound.

He strode across the room and tossed the magazine on his desk. It unrolled as it hit—the issue of *Life* I had been in. I wasn't on the cover, thank God, but there was a one-page write-up about my Girl Scout appearance. At some point, I was going to forgive Betty for ambushing me. Maybe. She didn't understand how much being the center of attention terrified me—but that didn't stop me from feeling panicked that she would pull a stunt like that again. Especially with how thrilled she'd been because her story had made it to a national market.

Nathaniel loosened his tie, still staring at the floor. "Elma. I'm furious. It's not at you. But it's going to sound like it is."

"That . . . that sounds ominous." I sank into the chair near his desk, hoping it would inspire him to do the same.

He grunted, sweeping his hand over his hair, and then just . . . stood there, with one hand on his hip and the other gripping the back of his neck. "It's fucking stupid."

"Nathaniel!" I think that reaction is a permanent imprint from my mother.

"Fucking. Stupid." He turned and glared at me. "I have just spent the last fucking hour in the office of Director Norman Fucking Clemons who fucking said, and I quote, 'Control your wife.' I don't think he appreciates the fact that I did not fucking slug him."

My mouth hung open. Brilliantly, I said, "What?"

"Control. Your. Wife." He brought his fists together and pressed them against his forehead. "Control your—fuck him."

"Wait—because of the magazine?" If Clemons had said that to me, I might have been furious. As it was, I was just horrified that I'd gotten Nathaniel in trouble. "Or the Girl Scout appearance? I didn't . . . what did I say?"

He snatched the magazine from the desk. "This? This isn't the problem, except that he's an asshole and a coward."

"You didn't say that to him, did you?" The headache I'd been fighting all day spiked and ran a line of current through my right eye.

"No." Nathaniel scowled. "No. I told him I would talk to you. And I am. We're talking."

"I'll stop doing interviews. I'll call and cancel things as soon as I get home tonight."

"Stop? I don't want you to stop."

"But if it's affecting your job . . ."

His anger transformed to horror. "No—no. It's not you. I'm not angry at you. Clemons is the one who's out of line. And it's because what you're doing is working. He spent the majority of the time ranting about how he's getting criticism for not including women in his plans, and pressure from some pretty influential people to add them. All of them talked about having seen you or listened to you or read an interview with you."

My stomach churned. "I'm so sorry."

"You haven't done anything wrong."

"But if it's getting you in trouble . . . I don't want to cause any problems." I held up my hands, but they were shaking, so I folded them in my lap. This was just like being in college again. Every time I stood out, it made someone angry, and now it was causing Nathaniel problems too. "I'll stop. It's fine. I'll stop."

"I'm not asking you to stop!"

"I know, and I love you for that, but still—" I swallowed, tasting bile at the back of my throat. The room was too warm, and my headache sent lines of green and white across my right eye. "I mean. I don't need to prove anything. If I keep going, it'll be bad for morale. Distracting. The astronauts don't like having me out there."

"Parker asked you to talk to the Girl Scouts! Aside from expressing some jealousy that you'd been on *Watch Mr. Wizard*, even he admitted that you'd done a good job. In his usual way, I mean."

"*He* watched the show?" I was standing. I didn't remember standing. Had *everyone* seen me on television? My stomach was a fireball of tension, and seemed set to launch itself up my esophagus. I tried to catch my breath, but all systems were critical. "Tell him I'll stop. Tell Parker that I'll ask Don to invite him next time. I'm so sorry. Tell him I'm sorry."

Nathaniel was staring at me like I was some sort of freak. I was messing everything up. His mouth hung open, and his brows were drawn together like he'd never seen me before. "Elma . . ."

I vomited. Noisily, and without discretion. What little I'd managed to eat at lunch spattered in messy chunks on the linoleum floor of his office. Nathaniel flinched back, and my stomach heaved again. I managed to make it to the trash can, but the damn thing was wire frame.

"Oh God." He had me by the shoulders and braced me as I threw up again, sobbing.

"I'm sorry. I'm so sorry. I'm sorry. I'm sorry."

"Hey . . . hey, sweetie. No. Shush. No. You have nothing to apologize for." He smoothed the hair back from my face and kept murmuring at me. I have no idea what else he said.

But he eventually got me calmed down and sitting in his office chair. He knelt in front of me, holding both of my hands. I don't know what his face looked like because I was too ashamed to lift my eyes.

Somewhere in the back of my brain, a rational part remained, screaming at me to pull it together. Or maybe it wasn't rational, because it was my mother's voice, sounding mortified. *Elma! What will people think?*

I wiped my eyes with the handkerchief—when had I acquired a handkerchief? Oh, it was Nathaniel's. In one of my few early domestic fits, I had embroidered NDY in the corner with dark blue floss. "I'm sorry."

"No, no. It's my fault. I should have waited until I wasn't so angry." Nathaniel squeezed my hands. "Elma, I'm not angry at you. At all. You've done nothing wrong."

"I got you in trouble at work. I didn't pay the electric bill, and we were behind on the gas, too. My housecleaning isn't much more than doing the dishes and making the bed. I'm having trouble concentrating at work. If I weren't trying to make trouble—"

"Okay. Stop. Shh . . ." He squeezed my hands and rose up on his knees. "Elma. Elma? What's 441 multiplied by 48?"

"21,168."

"Divided by twelve?"

"1,764." My breathing eased a little.

"Square root of 1,764?"

"Forty-two."

"Okay. Good." He wiped the tears from my cheeks. "Can you look at me?"

I nodded, but gravity seemed to keep my gaze chained to the floor. I used my next breath as a propellant to look up.

Nathaniel's sky-blue eyes were pinched and worried. "I love you. I'm proud of you. I'm sorry for whatever I've done to make you doubt that."

"Nothing. I mean . . ." I wiped my eyes with the back of my hand. "This is just . . . I'm sorry."

"If I accept your apology, will you stop apologizing?" He tried for a smile, but his voice still cracked with worry. "Tell you what. Let's take the rest of the day off and go home."

"No—I don't want to pull you away from work. And Bubbles still needs my help with calculations, and if I'm not there, Mrs. Rogers will have to reschedule people, and I don't want to be trouble."

He put a finger over my lips. "We'll stay here, then. Okay? But I want you to stay in here with me. I need your help on some calculations. Okay? Can you help me with those?"

I nodded. I could be helpful. That I could do. I could do all the math he wanted.

"Good. Now, Elma, here's . . ." He stood and rooted around on his desk until he found a piece of paper and drew it toward me. "Here's the equipment list for the moon landing. What I want to know is how many launches we'll need to do to get everything there."

I pulled the chair closer to the desk. "What type of rocket am I assuming?"

"The Jupiter class, unless it's more efficient to do something else." He rested a hand on my back. "Just sit here and work. I'll be right back."

NINETEEN

BIRTHS IN SPACE HELD POSSIBILITY

Psychologist Believes Man Could Produce
Children Fit for New Environment

By GLADWIN HILL
Special to The National Times.

LOS ANGELES, CA, Sept. 19, 1956—The possibility of husband-and-wife scientist teams voyaging through space and begetting children on the way was seriously cited today at a gathering of leading space scientists.

By the time I'd figured out that the lunar mission could be done with five launches using the Jupiter class rockets, or two using the Sirius class that was still in development, Nathaniel had cleaned up my mess, brought me a lemonade, and . . .

And I'd realized that he had given me equations to do so I would calm down.

It had been a good choice. The line of equations was clearly either wrong, or right. Having that certainty gave me a lifeline back to . . . sanity, I guess. It had been a really long time since I had broken like that. It hadn't happened since before I met him. Not to that degree, at any rate. Now

I just had small panics. The desire to flee. Sweats. The occasional vomit session before a television appearance.

That train of thought was not going to lead me anywhere useful. I checked the numbers again, and they were beautifully correct. Taking a slow, deep breath, I set down my pencil and looked up.

Nathaniel was sitting in a chair he'd drawn up to the other side of the desk. It wasn't designed to be a two-person desk, so he was hunched over its edge like a worried gargoyle. He had a report in front of him and was tapping his pencil against it as he read.

"I think I'm okay now."

He put his pencil down and regarded me. "Do you want to talk about it?"

"There's not much to say."

He grunted, nodding, and tapped his pencil against the desk. "May I ask a question?"

"Of course."

"If it distresses you, then we'll change the subject."

"I said I was okay now."

Nathaniel held up both hands in surrender. "Okay. Good." He set them back down on the desk and cleared his throat. "I understand why you haven't mentioned it, so I'm not upset, just worried. So . . . can you tell me the due date?"

"The what?" I looked back at the papers. Due date for the launch? That hadn't been in the paramet— . . . And then my brain caught up. I laughed outright. "I'm not pregnant."

"I don't know if that reassures me or makes me more worried. Are you sure?"

"I had my . . . my period last week. You remember that."

"Oh. Right." He rubbed his forehead. "Maybe you are now? I mean . . . we've been intimate since then."

And more than once, at that. "That's not how it works."

"But you've been vomiting more."

So much for thinking I was being discreet about it. "Ah. I didn't know you knew. It's not . . . I'm not pregnant. That's not . . . that's not what this was."

He watched me, and I could feel the question taking shape. It took up space and left little room for air. "Can you tell me what 'this' was?"

I dragged in a breath. As much as I wanted to, I could not pretend that he was being vague. Dodging the question would only worry him more. "You know . . . you know how I tell stories about being the youngest in my class? Okay. Well. I try to make them funny stories, because that helps. But the truth is that I was . . . Mama called this 'having a spell.' It didn't happen that often, and hasn't happened in years. I was just . . . I'm sorry. I wish you hadn't seen it."

"You understand that I'm just worried about you, right?" He reached out for my hand.

"I do." Mostly. The science part of my brain could describe what was happening. "The anxiety that I get sometimes—I mean . . . It hasn't been this bad since I was eighteen."

I'd been tutoring one of the boys—by request of my professor—and was subjected to six months of "My grades would be better if you knew anything about teaching." Being eighteen, I believed the boy. Being eighteen, I'd thought that I couldn't quit. I'd told Nathaniel stories about the student, but only as jokes. I never told him about going to the bathroom to sob, and then wiping my face and continuing the session.

Until one night when I couldn't.

All I will say about that is, thank God Hershel was at Stanford too, or I probably would have—he's a good brother. Never told our parents. Although, in hindsight, he probably should have. It had been exactly the thing that Mama had been afraid of, that I would be too fragile to handle the stresses of going to college when I was fourteen. I got so good at hiding my distress that I don't think my parents ever knew.

"I am . . . terrified, every time I have to address an audience. You remember Mama and her 'What will people think?'"

He nodded, but was otherwise very still and focused on me.

"I think . . . Mama was concerned about appearances because she had married up. I didn't know that. I just knew that I had to be perfect. Always. And, and . . . I think what just happened is that—well . . ."

"Clemons represents what people will think."

Pressing my hands over my mouth, I nodded and tried desperately not to cry again. Crying was weak. It was for children. Or grief. I was my father's daughter, goddamn it. Nathaniel was already worried enough. He didn't need me dissolving again.

Nathaniel stood and came around the desk. He knelt next to my chair and wrapped his arms around me. "He doesn't. Okay? He called me in today because what people think is that you are smart, and brave, and funny, and kind, and they want to be like you. Do you know what President Brannan said?"

I shook my head, my hands still pressed over my mouth.

"According to Clemons, President Brannan said that his daughter asked him why she couldn't be an astronaut."

I laughed a little. "Oh, that must have been a fun conversation."

"And he asked her why she wanted to do that, and she said, 'I want to go into space with Dr. York and be a lady astronaut like her.'"

And that was when my attempts to not cry failed. Completely. But these tears were of an entirely different sort, and welcome. Nathaniel was crying with me, because that's the sort of wonderful man I married.

Anyone looking at us would have thought that we were grieving, but it was the happiest I'd been in months.

You know you've worried your husband when he makes a doctor's appointment for you. I couldn't blame him. I was angry about it, but I couldn't blame him. He drove me to the doctor's office and sat in the waiting room. He probably would have come in, if I'd let him.

Instead, I was sitting in a gown on a cold table with my feet up in stirrups while a man I didn't know did unmentionable things to my nether regions. Really, though. Would it be too much to ask that they warm these things?

The doctor pushed back his rolling stool. "You can sit up now, Mrs. York."

He had a beautiful Scottish accent, which made his appearance a little less forbidding. Lean and intense, he studied me with pale blue eyes under heavy eyebrows. One focuses on such things, rather than the indignities of being a woman.

Clearing his throat, he turned away to a pad of paper. "Well, you're definitely not pregnant."

"I know. Thank you, though."

"Can you tell me a little more about the vomiting?" His nose bent down like a hawk.

"Vomiting?"

"Your husband mentioned it when he made the appointment."

I was going to kill Nathaniel. Pressing my lips together, I ground my teeth, before forcing a smile. "Oh, it's nothing, really. You know how husbands get."

He wheeled around to face me. "You have every right to be angry at his interference, but I'll ask that you not use social niceties when I'm inquiring about symptoms. I need to know the frequency and nature of the vomiting to make certain that it isn't related to another matter."

"Oh." I rubbed my forehead. The doctor just wanted to know how things were without Nathaniel's misdiagnosis, the same way I wanted to see the raw numbers before they ran through a machine. Not that my husband was a machine, though I was aggravated with him as if he were. "It's not . . . it's not an illness. I just get nervous when I have to speak in front of a large group. That's all. It's been happening since I was a teenager."

"Just before speaking?"

"Sometimes . . . sometimes after." I twisted the hem of my gown, my head bent.

"What other times?"

"If I . . . it really doesn't happen very often." I hadn't been preparing to speak this last time. My cheeks burned with shame, remembering. "But there have been times . . . when I feel . . . overwhelmed? If I've made a number of mistakes or feel like I'm . . . shirking?"

He grunted, but provided no other commentary. "And did anyone ever treat you for it?"

I shook my head. Hershel had wanted me to go to a doctor, but I was afraid that he would say I wasn't fit for university. Or tell my parents, which would have amounted to the same thing.

"Do you have shortness of breath at these times? Sweating? Racing heart? Before vomiting, I mean."

My head came up of its own accord. "Yes. Yes, I do."

He nodded and pulled a prescription pad toward him. "You have anxiety, which is unsurprising, given the age we live in. The papers are calling it the Meteor Age, but I think the Age of Anxiety is more apt. I'm going to prescribe Mil-town and refer you to—"

"I don't want to take any drugs."

He lifted his pen from his pad and turned to glare at me. "I beg your pardon."

"I'm not sick. I just get upset sometimes." This was exactly why I hadn't wanted Hershel to take me to a doctor. Next thing you knew, I'd be in a sanatorium filled with women getting shock treatment and hydrotherapy for "nerves."

"It's perfectly safe. This is, in fact, the most common prescription I write."

"But I'm fine." I did not want to join the brigades of women taking "mother's little helpers."

The doctor pointed his pen at me. "If I had told you that your vomiting was caused by influenza, would you also refuse to take any medicine?"

"But that's different."

"It most certainly is not." Rolling his stool closer, he held out the prescription. "My dear lady, your body is not supposed to react to stress in this way. You are, in literal fact, being made ill by forces outside yourself. Now, I want you to take this, and I'll give you a referral to my colleague, who can discuss some other therapies as well."

It was easier to take the piece of paper than to argue. So I did, and I thanked him, but I would be damned before I was going to drug myself into oblivion.

In the waiting room, Nathaniel was sitting in a chair by the window where I'd left him. His right knee bounced up and down, which it only did when he was really nervous. He had a magazine open, but I'm certain that he wasn't reading it, because his gaze was just staring at the same spot on the page—until I walked over.

He closed the magazine and rose to meet me. "Are you—?"

I glanced around the waiting room, which had people in half the chairs. Mothers with infants, women great with child, and men as nervous as Nathaniel. Clearing my throat, I took his arm. "Not. As I told you."

He rested one hand on top of mine and his brows were drawn together, as if he were trying to solve an engineering problem. "I'm not sure if I should be reassured or disappointed."

I tilted my head. "I'm sorry."

Kissing my forehead, he released my hand to pull the clinic room door open for me. Cool air rushed in from outside and carried with it the hubbub of downtown Kansas City. "I want you to be happy."

"I am." I didn't tell him about the doctor's actual diagnosis, because that was just going to lead to arguments, and this was close enough to the truth. I leaned against him, feeling the wool of his coat beneath my cheek. "I'm sorry I worried you."

"I've been thinking about taking a vacation."

I laughed. "You? The man who dreams in rocket engines? Please."

"Not long, but you know—careful." Nathaniel steered me clear of a woman running down the sidewalk, clutching a shopping bag. He scowled after her before continuing. "We're going out to California for your nephew's bar mitzvah, so why not make it into a proper vacation? We could stop by JPL while we're out there."

As if stopping at the Jet Propulsion Laboratory was a vacation. "I see how you are . . ." Another woman ran past, carrying a bag of flour. "Your idea of vacation involves looking at rockets."

"Just trying to be efficient."

"Mm-hm . . . 'Efficiency' is not usually a word I link to

vacation." The street got emptier as we walked, and yet the noise of Kansas City seemed to become louder and angrier.

"Ha! You're the one who calculates our fuel consumption even when we're driv—what in the . . ."

I'd already tightened my grip on Nathaniel's arm before we rounded the corner for our streetcar stop. A gang of reporters filled the street. A runaway rocket ignited in my chest and I twitched back. Cameras, microphones, and . . . none of them were pointing toward us.

A police line stretched across the sidewalk, and on the other side of it, a crowd surged. The gang of reporters stood just this side of the line, holding their cameras over their heads. Occasionally, the police line would part and let a civilian through.

Every time, the reporters mobbed around them.

I tugged on Nathaniel's arm. "Let's go back."

"Hang on. I want to see—" He glanced down at me and stopped with his mouth open. I don't know what he saw, but he nodded. "Yeah. Sorry. Right."

Goddamn it. I wasn't that fragile. I relaxed my grip on his arm and nodded toward the police line. "Do you want to find out what's going on?"

He shook his head. "Nah. Let them do their job. We can read about it in the paper tomorrow."

TWENTY

U.S. CAPITAL ROCKED BY FOOD RIOTS

By GLADWIN HILL

Special to The National Times.

KANSAS CITY, KS, Sept. 22, 1956—The area around the capitol was cordoned off after rioters, headed by housewives, attacked butcher shops and grocery stores today protesting high prices. They broke into stores and tossed goods onto the streets. At least fifty persons were injured and twenty-five arrested as the result.

One of the luxuries of our apartment building was that it had laundry facilities in the basement. That was fortunate, as I'm not entirely certain that Nathaniel would have let me go out to a laundromat alone after the food riots we'd seen the day before. Not that there would be laundry riots anytime soon, but still. My husband was a worrier sometimes.

Even so, schlepping the laundry bag up four flights of stairs left me huffing by the time I got back to our floor. It was tempting to drop the bag and just drag it down the hall, but I kept it hugged against my body, then propped it on my knee between myself and the wall as I unlocked our door.

Pushing it open with my shoulder, I grabbed the bag and carried it into our studio. Nathaniel was sitting on the couch with his feet up on the coffee table, talking on the phone.

"Uh-huh. Oh, hang on. She just came in." He set the phone down on the table and jumped up. "Let me get that for you."

I relinquished the bag with a sigh. "Who's that?"

"Hershel." He carried the bag over to the dresser and set it down.

"Anything wrong?" It wasn't our usual day for a phone call.

He shook his head, busy with the knot on the laundry bag. "Just wanted to talk to you, I guess."

I sat down on the sofa and picked up the phone. "Well, hello. To what do I owe the pleasure?"

My brother laughed in my ear. "I need a favor."

"I'm not doing your math homework."

"It's more dire than that." His voice took on the overly serious tones of a radio star. "It's the most dire thing a man could face and hope to survive."

"Dancing?"

He laughed out loud at that, and I could picture his eyes crinkling until they almost closed. "Worse. Doris's entire family is coming for Tommy's bar mitzvah."

I whistled, which isn't ladylike, but he'd taught me to do it when we were kids, so I figured he wouldn't mind. "That is rough. And what's the favor?"

"Will you come early? To the bar mitzvah. I need . . ." His voice faltered a little, which made me sit up on the couch. "Ah, hell, Elma. I was planning on joking about it, but I realized that I was going to be . . . There aren't any other Wexlers. It's just you and me and the kids."

You'd think that at some point the grief would stop. I put my hand over my mouth and leaned forward, as if I could somehow fold over the pain and keep it from escaping into the world again. There might be cousins out there somewhere, but between the Holocaust and the Meteor . . . it was just the two of us.

I had to swallow hard before I could speak. "Yeah—I mean, I have to check the launch schedule, but yeah. I can come out early."

"Thanks." His voice was a little ragged. "Plus, California has actual food. Nathaniel said you got caught in those riots yesterday?"

I let Hershel change the subject, and shot my husband a look. He was engaged in trying to figure out how to fold my panties, and it seemed to be taking more effort than a differential equation. "That's a wild exaggeration. We had to go to a different streetcar stop, that's all."

"He made it sound like you were right in the middle of it."

"The police were doing a fine job containing it." I sighed, remembering the gossip I'd heard in the laundry room. "Although . . . it sounds like our favorite market got hit. Poor Mr. Yoder is Amish, and I think he had to just stand there and let them take stuff."

"Oof. Well, come out here and we'll pamper you. You need it, eh?"

There was a consciousness in the way he said it that made me purse my lips and stare at my husband. What, exactly, had he said to Hershel before I came into the apartment? To ask Hershel would be to invite him to discuss my well-being, and that was not something I wanted to do. Not now, at any rate. Maybe when I was out there, if there was time around the festivities. Maybe. "Listen, I should probably go. Nathaniel is about to wrinkle all the laundry."

"Give him my best, huh?"

"Likewise. Same to Doris and the kids." When I hung up the phone, I stayed on the sofa for another moment, with my hand still on the receiver. "Did you call Hershel?"

Nathaniel straightened, lowering my underwear. It might have been funny, if his face hadn't been so serious. "Yes."

"Did you tell him?"

"No." He set the underwear down on the dresser and faced me. "I didn't. I did say that you'd been working too hard."

"Don't." I got to my feet and crossed to the laundry bag. The clothes inside were still warm from the dryer as I pulled them out. "I know you mean well, but don't."

I didn't work all the launches. I was on the Maroon Team, which rotated in every third launch. Even there, we were further divided into shifts, which rotated to try to minimize exhaustion, because all stations had to be staffed the entire time astronauts were up.

Sometimes, though, even when you weren't scheduled, you wanted to be there. We'd sent an unmanned launch up three days ago that Basira and the Green Team had control of, so Helen and I should have had the night off. We did, in fact. But this was the flight that was going to circle the moon.

At five o'clock, Helen came over to my desk and put her purse down on Basira's empty half. It clunked as she set it down, seeming abnormally heavy for a cloth purse.

Putting a finger by the last row of numbers I'd been double-checking, I stared at the bag. The cloth seemed to contain a faint outline of a bottle. "Nice bag."

"Refreshments." Helen grinned and patted it. "You're staying, right?"

I nodded and wrote a dash in the margin so I'd know where to start up again tomorrow. "Yes. If for no other reason than that it's the only way I'll get to see Nathaniel."

"He could take a night off."

"Ha. You've met my husband, right?"

"Not good if he burn out." She drummed her fingers on the desk. "What do you think it will look like?"

I shrugged and stacked my papers. Around us, the other women were wrapping up their work for the day, pages rustling as they slid reports into their drawers. "Gray? I mean . . . there's never been a hint of color in the telescope images. And we won't have really clear images until the rocket gets back."

"They are still pictures from the moon."

Grinning, I pushed back from my desk and stood. "I admit that I'd probably stay, even without Nathaniel." It was an amazing thing we were doing. We'd managed to program a rocket so that it could do a giant orbit around the moon without a pilot. We hoped.

It was different from what we'd be doing later when we sent men to orbit the moon. This didn't involve needing to transfer in and out of orbit, though, because we'd just set up a highly elliptic orbit with the apogee on the far side of the moon. That math was fairly straightforward.

I followed Helen out of the room and joined the tide of IAC employees headed for Mission Control. We wouldn't all fit in, of course, but there was a viewing room, and then, for those of us with the keys, a second control room.

Someday we'd have two missions in space at the same time, so they'd built two duplicates of Mission Control. One of them was in use training the next flight crew, but one was, in theory, empty. Or, at least, not in official use.

Helen and I peeled off from the main throng and headed to the stairs that led up to the other control center.

"Hey! Wait up." Behind us, Eugene and Myrtle Lindholm slipped through the door and into the echoing cement block stairwell.

"Eugene!" I grinned down at them. "I didn't know you were coming."

"The way Myrtle has been going on about this? If I missed the first fly-by, we'd have nothing to talk about."

"I must learn her bargaining techniques."

Eugene overtook Helen and me on the stairs with no problem. "She doesn't so much bargain as deliver ultimatums."

"Don't listen to him."

"See!" With a laugh, Eugene turned to look at me as we proceeded up the stairs. "What do you think we'll see? Myrtle thinks it will only be gray."

"She's probably right. The pictures are only getting scanned at a resolution of one thousand horizontal lines, and because we're so far, the transmission is at a slow-scan television rate . . ." I trailed off. "I just started talking jargon, didn't I?"

"Mm-hm. But it's close enough to what we've been doing over in comm, so I've got a decent idea. It'll be fuzzy?"

"Yep. But we should get better images as the probe swings back toward Earth."

We reached the top of the stairs and Eugene opened the door. "Speaking of . . . how's Nathaniel?"

Raising an eyebrow, I nodded at Eugene to thank him as I walked through the door. "He's going to love being called a probe."

Eugene laughed. "You know what I mean. Is he still as cranky about the IBMs?"

"According to him, they are an abomination, and he won't consider any manned lunar mission that doesn't include human computers." Which was fine by me, as it increased my chances that they'd have to include a woman. Not that men couldn't do math; it's just that most of them went into engineering instead of computing. The world of numbers on paper didn't seem to have the same appeal as the hardware and explosives of rocketry. Their loss.

There were people in this hall, too, but not as many. Most of them were from the Green Team. There were a few astronauts, though. Derek Benkoski and Halim "Hotdog" Malouf were leaning over a console, chatting with Parker. Mrs. Rogers was with another knot of people standing near the large display that would show the images from the probe as they came in.

"Where do you think we should watch?" Helen stood on her toes, trying to see over the crowd.

I scanned the room and spotted some empty chairs near what would normally have been the flight surgeon's desk. Steering our group over there, it was hard to keep my eyes off the big dark screen. This would get us one step closer to the moon. After this, they'd pick a landing site, and then . . . then someone would go to the moon. "Helen, I'm suddenly delighted that you brought 'refreshments.' "

"That sounds promising." Eugene grinned down at her. "Running into you all was definitely the right choice."

Helen patted her bag. "Better than watching baseball."

At the surgeon's station, she pulled out some paper cups and a mason jar filled with her homemade blackberry wine. It was an unctuous beverage, but there were days when sweet and strong were exactly what you needed. Then Helen pulled out some soda water. "Found cocktail recipe."

"Good lord." Eugene leaned forward to peer into her bag. "Do you have an entire bar in there?"

"No ice." She frowned at the two liquids. "Not cold, though."

"Don't need it cold." Myrtle picked up two cups and held them so Helen could pour. "Just need it strong."

I laughed and took the cup. The bubbles lifted a scent

that held the memory of summer warmth. When Helen had hers filled, I lifted mine. "To the moon."

"To the moon—and beyond." Eugene tapped his cup with ours.

The sparkling water cut back some of the cloying sweetness and brightened the dark fruit. "Say. This isn't bad."

"Bad before?" Helen narrowed her eyes and gave me one of her patented *tsk*s.

Drawn by the promise of alcohol, a couple of engineers drifted over, including Reynard Carmouche. I was a little afraid that he was going to bring Parker with him, but fortunately he was more interested in staying with the other astronauts.

Someone had brought gin, and of course that meant we had to experiment with other cocktail variations. For science. Chemistry is a very important part of rocketry.

Holding a gin and blackberry "bramble," Helen leaned in to bump me with her shoulder. "Betty asked about you."

"That's nice." Which is Southern for "fuck that." "Did I tell you we're going to California for my nephew's bar mitzvah?"

"She meant well. And she's sorry."

All of the "she meant well" in the world would not make up for that betrayal. "I think I've even talked Nathaniel into taking a vacation. Can you imagine? He'll probably sit on the beach with a report on orbital insertion."

"Maybe you could at least come back to the 99s?"

"Hey!" A voice from the front of the crowd cut through the murmur of conversation. "It's starting."

I rose onto my toes to see over the heads of the other folks, using the motion as an excuse to step away from Helen, who really did mean well. Betty had just been interested in breaking into *Life* magazine, which that visit had done for her. Bless her heart.

But none of that mattered today. Today was all about the moon. I took another sip of the sparkling blackberry concoction and let the excitement of the group pervade me. This kind of group I didn't mind. It was just being the center of attention that distressed me.

The room quieted, and we began to hear the voices of the people in the main control room. It was like being at a launch run by ghosts. It was weird being on the outside of the main Mission Control. I was so used to being in that room and doing the math. I closed my eyes for a moment and listened for Nathaniel's voice among the others.

Beside me, Myrtle inhaled sharply. "What is that?"

I opened my eyes. There, on screen, the first grainy images had appeared. It took me a moment to make sense of the grays and blacks flickering on the screen.

Over the loudspeaker, Nathaniel's voice resonated through the room. "What you're seeing, ladies and gentlemen, has been rendered in ones and zeroes, transmitted through the depths of space, then translated back into an image. This is the surface of the moon."

And, like a magic trick, I could see the curve of the horizon.

Joy erupted out of me in a cheer. Around me, people jumped into the air like we'd won a race. I guess we had, or at least the first heat of it. I raised my glass to the success of the *Friendship* probe and the team who had planned the mission.

Malouf raised his hands in triumph. Mrs. Rogers danced like a girl. Parker punched the air with a hoot. Eugene lifted Myrtle off the ground, spinning her around in a hug. And I laughed and laughed.

"Me next!" Helen punched Eugene's arm and he chuckled.

Eugene picked Helen up and spun her around and around. I stared at the screen, grinning so hard my cheeks hurt. The moon. Someday. Someday, I would go there. Someday, I would walk on the moon.

Funny how seeing your goal made manifest can change things. When we started to get the higher-resolution images in, the stark beauty of the moon became even more real. Yes, it was forbidding, but there was also a majesty to the austere landscape.

I think everyone at the IAC felt a renewed energy for the project. I put my head down and buried it in calculations. But there was another thought that kept running through my mind.

It turned out that Bubbles's figures were correct. The change in interior structure of the fuel core made it significantly more stable, which in turn allowed it to generate more thrust. With that, we'd be able to increase our payloads by a good 23.5 percent, which would drastically reduce the number of launches needed for the moon base.

Nathaniel was working on a new scenario with those numbers. It was complex enough that he was running our calculations through the IBM, no matter how much he hated it. The program would take hours to run and he liked to babysit the machine, even when Basira, its actual programmer, was there. It's not like he could fix anything if a punch card failed to feed or something, but . . . men.

"So . . . I got another invitation to go on *Mr. Wizard.*" I fiddled with the edge of a discarded punch card I'd pulled out of the trash. When you stacked a couple of them together, the holes from the punch cards let specks of light through and almost sparkled.

"Is that so?" Nathaniel looked up from the abstract he was reading. "Have you responded?"

I shook my head.

"I haven't been to Chicago in a while." He shifted in his chair. "Maybe we could take a vacation?"

"You keep using that word. It wouldn't be a vacation if I were working."

"Well, a vacation for me, then."

Smiling, I tore the edges of the card into little strips. With the notched corner of the card, the strips almost looked like feathers on a wing. "I haven't said yes."

"Whatever you decide, I'll support you. No matter what."

"I know."

He meant it to be supportive, I know he did. But it put the decision squarely on me. Either I would cause strife at work if I continued fighting for women's inclusion in the space program, or I would disappoint Nathaniel. Oh, he would never *say* that, but if he was proud of my success, then it followed that he would be disappointed if I quit.

I know. I know that's not a logical progression. I do. I just . . .

Basira sat on the other side of the room, oblivious to our conversation, as the compiler rattled. The cards ran through the feeder with a *thwick, thwick, thwick* as each hit the metal guard. I pulled out another card from the trash and flipped it so the notch mirrored the first one. Wings. That was the crux of the matter, wasn't it? Wings and flight and space, and I wanted to go into space in ways that did not make sense, even to me.

I had a life I should be content with. And I was. I liked being Mrs. Nathaniel York. If I turned down *Mr. Wizard* and the interviews and the invitations to dinner parties, then I could go back to concentrating on my husband and my job. I loved both, and . . . and I could do more.

Was I really going to be content running calculations for someone else's ideas? It would remove the immediate stress, true, and leave . . . what?

I curled the leading edge of the "wings" and held them together so they cupped the air in tandem. Paper planes might be a good project for *Mr. Wizard*. I could show Rita how to make a wind tunnel. Oh.

I lowered the wings, light peeking through the hole punches in little sparkles.

Oh. I had been thinking about who I would disappoint— *What would people think?*—but I knew the answer to that. The little girl on the show. The Girl Scouts in their tinfoil helmets. The crayon letter writers. My niece.

What would people think?

Those little girls thought I could do anything. They thought that women could go to the moon. And because of that, they thought that *they* could go to the moon, too. They were why I needed to continue, because when I was their age, I needed someone like me. A *woman* like me.

"I'm going to say yes."

Nathaniel nodded, watching me. "I'll come with you."

"There's a launch that week."

"It's a supply launch with construction material for the orbiting platform, and unmanned. The team is solid, and I won't be needed for any press conferences." He stood up, and even though Basira was right there, he came over and kissed me.

"Nathaniel! What will Basira think?"

"She'll think that I love you, and she'd be right."

TWENTY-ONE

ROCKET GROUP TOLD OF RUSSIAN RESPECT

***

Special to The National Times.

PRINCETON, N.J., Dec. 3, 1956—The International Aerospace Coalition was told today that the "tremendous admiration the people of Russia hold for IAC scientific and technical advances" was a key to future understanding and cooperation between Russia and the IAC.

I flew us into Chicago a day early, and Nathaniel did his level best to keep me well and thoroughly occupied until I went to the studio. As much as I'd been wanting him to delegate some of his work, it was odd knowing that there was a launch happening without him. I never thought we would hit a point where rocket launches were routine, but when you have one or two a month, your views change.

"How about a boat tour?" I stopped by a sign for the Mercury SceniCruiser as we crossed over the Michigan Avenue Bridge.

"That sounds . . . chilly." Nathaniel had given up fighting the wind blowing off the lake and carried his hat in one hand. His ears had turned pink with the chill.

He was probably right. The wind had been brutal, but

in the rare moments when it wasn't blowing, the sun was actually fairly warm, and this was December.

The winter might finally be breaking. Of course, then summer would come and never leave. I peered down the stairs toward a boat docked on a walkway right next to the river. "Looks like they have an interior cabin. Come on. It'll be fun."

"And the fact that it won't have a pay phone has nothing to do with your interest."

I tucked my arm into his. "The fact that its lack of a phone is the first thing you thought of is rather telling, don't you think?"

He laughed and turned us to the stairs. "Busted. Sorry. Really. I am *trying* not to think about work."

"I know . . ." I patted his arm as we started down to the river. I'd already caught him on two different pay phones today. "We can go back to the hotel, if you'd rather."

Shaking his head, he sighed. "They're fine. I'm disrupting things every time I call."

"It's so touching when they grow up."

The wind wasn't so bad when we got below street level. There were some tourists, mostly folks with kids, but not too many given that it was a Tuesday. We only had to wait behind one couple for tickets. As the gentleman talked to the young man in the ticket booth, his wife turned to smile at us, in that way you sometimes do with strangers in a line.

Then she did a double take.

I braced myself. No. That's not true. I suddenly developed a fascination with the river, as if watching the water and the scum at its edges would keep me from having to acknowledge someone who had clearly recognized me. Yes, I wanted to change the public perception about women and our ability to be astronauts, but I had not wanted to be a pinup girl for spaceflight.

In my peripheral vision, I saw that the woman was still staring at me. There was the intake of breath as she prepared to speak. A hand reached toward me, just a little, to try to catch my attention. "Excuse me."

"Hm?" I glanced at her, but tried to look like the boat was now the most interesting thing I had ever seen.

"I hate to bother you . . . only you look familiar."

I shrugged, and reached for Nathaniel . . . except, goddamn it, the woman's husband had finished his business at the window and Nathaniel was stepping forward. I put on a neutral smile, just so I wouldn't look angry. "I must have one of those faces."

"Are you Elma Wexler, by any chance?"

Wexler. At the sound of my maiden name, my head snapped around of its own accord. "Yes. Yes, I am." I didn't recognize her. Plump and blond going to gray, she looked like someone's mother. Probably one of the kids staring at the boat was hers. "I'm sorry, but . . ."

"Oh, it's been years. I'm Lynn Weyer. I lived next door? In Wilmington?"

My jaw dropped. "Oh my goodness. Lynn Weyer?"

"Well, Lynn Bromenshenkel, now." She turned, reaching for the man she'd been standing with. "Luther? This is Elma Wexler—"

"York, now. We lived next door to each other for two years."

She jumped right in, the way she had when we were kids. "It was the longest I'd lived in one place, on account of Daddy moving around." When she smiled, I could see her ten-year-old self buried under the intervening years. Her nose always wrinkled when she smiled. "Do you remember the 'Mud Pie Incident'?"

"I got in *so* much trouble for that. And then the Glass House Affair, when Hershel tripped and split his knee open?"

Lynn's laugh hadn't changed at all. It burst out of her like the sonic vibrations of a rocket. "Oh, the blood." She put her hand on her husband's arm. "Honest, it's not as bad as it sounds. It's just—honestly, I don't know why I'm laughing. I'm just so happy to see you."

Neither of us asked about the other's parents. It had stopped being a thing one did at some point.

Nathaniel turned from the ticket booth, then, our tickets in hand, and we had to do introductions all over again. One of the boys was hers, but he had his nose in a book the entire time, and even if he had seen me on *Mr. Wizard,* he didn't see me on the boat.

As we pulled away from the dock, Nathaniel and I found a space in the inside cabin with Lynn and her husband. I settled into the crook of Nathaniel's arm and watched Chicago roll past outside.

The captain's voice crackled over loudspeakers set into the ceiling of the boat. "Afternoon, folks. Take a look on your right and you'll see the Hotel Murano, designed by Jette Briney. All those round balconies are supposed to remind you of the petals on a tree. And, like a tree, it goes underground, with a whole network of bunkers that are designed to be warm and inviting. Mind you, I've never been in there, 'cause you have to have a whole lot more ready cash than a boat captain makes." He laughed at his own joke.

I leaned my head back to look up at Nathaniel, who was shaking his head slightly. Probably at the same thought I had, which was that underground bunkers were all well and good if you were worried about another impact, but right on the river? When the temperatures went up again and the water table rose, that was going to be a disaster.

"Now, we have a real treat for you today: we'll get to go out and cruise around the lake." The boat slowed as we reached the locks out to Lake Michigan.

Nathaniel shifted in his seat to peer out the window to watch the locks in action. He was never going to stop being an engineer. "Huh . . . I wonder if—" His jaw snapped shut.

"You wonder if . . . ?"

He cleared his throat. "Ah. I wonder . . . if we should have Myrtle and Eugene over for dinner when we get back."

"That is not what you were going to say."

The corners of his mouth twisted into a wry smile. "No. But allow me this course correction."

Which meant it had been something about rocketry. I patted his thigh in appreciation. "That would be nice. Maybe we could have—"

The captain's voice cut in with just enough volume to make conversation difficult. "Last year we weren't able to go out at all because the lake was frozen solid, but this winter is mild enough that we'll be able to give you a good view of Chicago and cruise around Navy Pier and Adler Planetarium. Interesting trivia: Did you know that the astronauts are using our planetarium to practice navigation?"

Nathaniel and I met each other's gazes and I started to giggle. "There's no escape, is there?"

In mock tones of horror, he said, "The space program is *everywhere*."

Across the cabin, Lynn's husband grunted. "And a damn foolish thing it is, too."

"Luther." Lynn smacked her husband's arm. "Language."

Nathaniel stilled beside me. "What do you mean?"

"A couple of years of bad weather, and they're telling us we have to go into space?" He shrugged, the flesh of his neck bunching over his collar with the movement. "Even if I believed this nonsense, why not spend the money making things better here on Earth?"

"They are." I rested my hand on Nathaniel's knee to let him know that I would take this one. "That's why we have rationing—they're trying to eliminate anything that will add to the greenhouse effect. The space program is just one aspect of it."

"Eternal winter. Please." Luther waved his hand toward the front window, where we were starting to draw level with the top of the lock. "You heard the captain."

"I think you've misunderstood. The winter was temporary. The problem is that the temperature is going to start rising soon. 'Eternal summer' is what we're actually concerned about." Being in Kansas City, at the IAC, we were surrounded by people who understood that, and were all striving for the same goal. "Besides, it's not a good idea to keep all your eggs in one basket, right? All the space program is doing is making another basket for eggs."

"Ma'am. I appreciate your thoughts, but there are economic forces at work here that I don't expect you to understand. This is all about big business seeing an opportunity to make a buck off the government. It's conspiracies and shadows all the way down."

Nathaniel drew a breath. "I'm the le—"

I dropped my purse on the floor to stop him. "Oh! I'm such a klutz." Having him say that he was the lead engineer for the space program? While we were trapped on a ship with these folks? I was already too angry to continue the conversation, and it wasn't going to go anywhere better from there. "Lynn, do you remember how I was always dropping things?"

She joined me in changing the subject, bless her, and from there on the conversation was perfectly ordinary.

What did we talk about? I don't even know. Everything? Nothing? It was just . . . normal. Until I ran into Lynn, I hadn't realized how far outside of normal our life had become. They had a son. They were hoping for another. They had a mortgage, for God's sake.

A mortgage. Nathaniel and I were too afraid of the future to even move out of our studio apartment, and the Bromenshenkels were planning twenty years into the future with a mortgage.

The next day, Nathaniel came with me to the studio. It was a relief to have him there. At a show about science, Dr. Nathaniel York of the IAC was quite the celebrity, so I was able to fade back and just be Mrs. York for a while.

Mind you, I think Nathaniel was turning up the charm in order to draw attention from me. It meant that I didn't have to carry on small talk with anyone. More than once, I thought about the doctor he'd taken me to, and had some regret for not having that prescription filled. But I only threw up once, and I don't think that anyone except Nathaniel knew.

And then it was time to go to places.

The assistant, whose name I still couldn't remember, appeared at the makeup table. "Dr. York? We're ready for you now."

Nathaniel turned toward him and opened his mouth, then shut it again with a laugh. "You're not talking to me." He bent down to kiss my cheek and whispered, "Prime numbers are your friend."

He knew me so well. I whispered back, "Later I'll have to see if you're divisible."

A coughing laugh was my reward, and he blushed a little, which was always a bonus. "Only divisible by one."

Straightening, he gave me a wink and stepped back.

It was marginally less terrifying to go with the assistant this time, though whether that's because I knew what to expect or because I hadn't had as much time to get worked up, I couldn't tell you. I was mostly fine, just mild butter-flies. I didn't need to be drugged, thank you very much—

Until the assistant turned to Nathaniel and said, "I'll be back to show you where you can watch, Dr. York."

"No." The word was out of my mouth before I knew why I didn't want Nathaniel watching. It was why he'd come, after all. And he'd seen the other broadcast. It wasn't as if I was about to do something shocking, or even diffi-cult. "I—never mind. It's fine."

Nathaniel watched me for a moment. "You know . . . I think I'd rather watch from the control booth. See how they do this stuff."

What will people think . . . He knew me so well, and it made no sense that I was afraid to make a mistake in front of him. Goodness knows he'd seen me be foolish plenty of times, like the "dandelion greens salad" disaster. And yet, I was nodding at him now. "That sounds like a fine idea."

Then it was off through the hallways of the studio, onto the soundstage, and then on my mark at the fake door. Be-yond the door, the assistant director said, "We're live in five, four, three . . ."

Three was a prime number. So was five. I breathed through my mouth. Seven. Eleven. Thirteen.

The assistant held his clipboard and nodded to the stage. That was my cue. I put my hand on the knob and walked through, smiling.

Don looked up with a grin. "Dr. York! Boy, am I glad you're here. Rita and I were just trying to figure out what fuel to use for our bottle rocket."

Beside him, Rita had a bottle with fins on the side like a toy rocket. This time she wore a blue dress, spangled with stars.

"As it happens, I can help with that." I walked to the mark like an old hand, and found myself smiling at Rita. She smiled back. It might have been acting, but still . . . this was why I was here.

And now I wished Nathaniel were there to see me.

The miniature rocket we'd made from a bottle filled with baking soda and vinegar lifted off the makeshift launch-pad in a spray of foaming gas. It arced above the height of the set. Off camera, a pair of stagehands with a blanket caught the rocket as it dropped back down.

Rita clapped her hands with delight. "Golly, that's keen, Dr. York!" She turned to Don. "Say, Mr. Wizard, what would happen if we used a bigger rocket?"

He laughed and put a hand on his hip. "You remember those calculations that Dr. York showed you?"

"Oh, sure." She beamed at me. "So all I'd have to do is figure out how much the new rocket weighed . . . I could do that!"

Mr. Wizard handed her the sheet of paper we'd been using earlier. "All right, then. I'll see you next week."

From behind the cameras, the director said, "And we're out. Good work, people."

I sagged against the counter and sighed as a sort of brightness drained out of me. TV was nothing like doing calculations—not really—since these problems were all things that we'd discussed beforehand. But the precision with which the entire studio worked to pull off this live broadcast . . . it did remind me a little of the dark room on launch day, as dozens of competent people focused on one goal.

Don joined me in leaning on the counter. "You're a natural at this."

I barked a laugh. "There is nothing natural about television."

"Heh. No, I suppose not." He loosened his tie and beckoned me to walk off the set with him. "Still. You make math seem interesting."

"Well, it is." I shrugged. "Oh, I know it isn't for most folks, but I think they've just been put off by people who taught them to be afraid of numbers."

"That's a nice perspective." He held the door to the soundstage for me so we could head into the labyrinth of hallways back to the dressing rooms. "Did Nathaniel stick around?"

"He was watching from the control room." He might still be there, in fact, watching them wind up the loose ends.

"If you ask me, the IAC could do worse than create a show with the two of you—like *The Johns Hopkins Science Review,* but for space." Don paused at the door to his dressing room. "Say, how long are you two in town?"

"We're flying home tomorrow." I was not going to even remotely address his idea of me hosting a show. About the only comfort I could derive from the suggestion was that I was doing an adequate job masking my terror.

"Well, if you don't have dinner plans, why don't you join me and Maraleita?"

"That would be lovely, but we've got a date with Adler Planetarium." I shrugged ruefully. When Nathaniel had manfully *not* suggested heading over to check in on the astronaut training program, I made the offer. "It's supposed to be a mini-vacation, but we're both working."

"Next time, then."

I kept the smile on my face as I said goodbye, and managed to make it down to my own dressing room before I started shaking. *Next time.* This was never going to stop. I shut the door and sat down on the little couch. Nothing bad had happened to me. I was fine. *3.14159 . . .* Leaning forward, I rested my head on my knees and let the wool of my skirt cocoon my face.

My dear lady, your body is not supposed to react to stress in this way.

I needed to pull myself together before Nathaniel got back from the control room, or he would worry. I was not sick. I was fine. Deep breaths. Slow, deep breaths, pushing past the knot of tension in my abdomen. *2, 3, 5, 7, 11 . . .* The show had gone well. Don was pleased. I hadn't been eaten by bears.

Someone knocked on the door. I sat up fast enough that the room grayed a little at the edges of my sight. Wiping my eyes, I pasted on a smile. "Come in!"

Don opened the door. His face was tight, and worry pinched his brows together. "Elma . . . you'd better come with me. It looks like Nathaniel has gotten some bad news."

The room went cold. I moved from sitting to standing at Don's side without a transition. "What sort of bad news?"

"I don't know for sure." He led me down the hall. My hands were numb and I couldn't feel the floor. I think I knew, even before he said it. "But on the radio, they're saying that a rocket exploded."

TWENTY-TWO

PROPANE IS URGED TO END BUS FUMES

————

*Air Control Head to Ask City
to Use "Bottled Gas"*

————

CHICAGO, IL, Dec. 4, 1956—Dr. Leonard
Greenburg, City Commissioner of Air Pollution Control, asserted yesterday that the use of propane gas,
familiarly known as "bottled gas," could eliminate
noxious fumes from buses. These fumes are said to
contribute to the alleged "greenhouse" effect caused
by the Meteor. However, the mayor of Chicago questioned whether such an overhaul of the bus system was
really necessary.

In the writer's room, there was a long table with chairs for
ten people. Nathaniel sat alone on one side of the table,
hunched over the telephone. He had a hand pressed over
his eyes as he listened to whoever was on the other end of
the line. A broken pencil lay on the table in front of him.

When I came in, he didn't look around. Don pulled the
door shut behind me. My heels were unnaturally loud as I
crossed the room, and still, Nathaniel kept his head down.

"Yeah . . . if you have the altitude, the computers should
be able to tell you how much propellant was left."

Pulling out a chair, I tried not to let it scrape against the linoleum. I sank into it with a rustle of crinoline. I lay a hand on Nathaniel's back, to let him know that I was there, I guess. As if he hadn't heard me. His back was rigid and soaked with a cold sweat.

"No, no—I understand. But—right. It will at least tell the firefighters how bad the burn is going to be."

I could just barely hear the person on the other end of the line. Someone from the IAC, I presumed, and probably Director Clemons.

"Oh. Oh, I see." He sighed and bent his head even farther down. "No. We can't account for fuel on the farm itself."

My heart stuttered. Farm? The flight path of the rockets was carefully calculated to not pass over any towns or farms. From what Don had said, I thought the rocket had exploded on the launchpad. That happened in tests, but not with proven rockets like the Jupiter class.

"Right. Yeah . . . Elma's done, so we'll head straight back." He nodded, pulling the base of the phone closer. "Mm-hm. I understand."

Then he hung up. He sat there staring at the table, or maybe with his eyes closed. I couldn't tell which with his hand still shielding his eyes.

"What happened?"

He sat back, finally dropping his hand. His eyes were bloodshot, and tear tracks stained his cheeks. "They're still sorting that out. But it looks like the booster separated too soon, knocked it off course."

"Oh God."

"Rocket fell on a farm." He pressed his hands against his face again. "Goddamn it."

What do you say to that? "Was anyone . . . there?"

"Whole place is in flames. Gah." He wiped his eyes with his sleeve and pushed away from the table to stand. "I need to get back."

"Of course." Though what either of us could do, I didn't know. "It's not your fault."

"I'm the lead engineer." Nathaniel turned away from me and stood with his hands on his hips, head bent. The seconds passed between us in ragged breaths.

I shouldn't have asked him to come. "I'm sorry."

All the tension drained out of his shoulders and he slumped. "No. Elma, no." When he turned his face was drawn and haunted. "Don't take this on yourself. You're right. It was a routine launch, and my being there wouldn't have changed anything."

I wish he believed that.

Flying back from Chicago, four hours after the rocket went down, we could still see the column of smoke rising from the farm. Flames licked the bottom of the column with hungry orange tongues. It had been a rocket, not a meteorite. That gave no real comfort, not when death had still dropped from the sky.

In the seat beside me, Nathaniel moaned. His fists were clenched into tight balls on each knee, and his shoulders hunched inward. "Can you fly over it?"

"I don't think that's a good idea." My husband had been near silent since the phone call. Packing our bags had fallen mostly to me, because when we got back to the hotel, he had been distracted by the radio, which had live coverage from the disaster. There had been children on the farm.

"Near it, then?"

"Nathaniel—"

"Yes or no?"

"Yes." We were flying with visual flight rules, so I didn't have to check with a tower to alter our flight plan. I steered us toward the farm. Most of the fire had been concentrated on the fields, but it had spread to the house and barn. And the outbuildings. The drone of our engine and the hiss of the wind over the wings matched the lapping of flames.

I kept looking at the sky, my hands tense on the yoke. There was a part of me that saw that fire and thought that a meteorite had just hit. Even after I realized that I was looking for ejecta that wasn't going to be there, I still kept scanning the sky. It was better than watching the ground.

"It shouldn't have gone south." Nathaniel had leaned forward to press his face against the window, trying to look down. "Something must have been wrong with the gyroscopes."

"They'll have telemetry back at Mission Control."

"I know that," he snapped.

"Okay. Okay . . ."

He stared out the window, fists still knotted. Smoke roiled in front of us, and I banked the plane away from the farm.

"What are you doing?"

"Avoiding updrafts." I leveled out and pointed our course toward the IAC, which was alarmingly close. It had a runway for the astronauts to use with their T-33s. "Call the tower for me? Get permission to land at the IAC instead of out at New Century AirCenter."

The window held his attention for another few seconds, and then he nodded and reached for the mic.

When we landed, Nathaniel went straight to Mission Control. I had to taxi the plane to the hangar and tuck it in next to the T-33s. Sleek and gorgeous, they were designated for the astronauts to use so they could go to different training locations.

My little Cessna looked like a child's toy next to them. I could have pushed it into the hangar by myself. I'm ashamed that even amid this tragedy, I had a moment of coveting those planes. When I climbed out of the Cessna, the stench of burning kerosene and wood and flesh filled the air. I swallowed a gag.

Before I could cross the tarmac, another T-33 taxied up to the hangar. I stopped where I was to give the pilot clearance. They were great in the air, but their visibility on the ground was pretty limited.

The engine shut down and the cockpit popped open. Stetson Parker climbed out from the front, with Derek Benkoski in the trainer seat. That had to have irked Benkoski. Parker hopped down so fast that I wondered if he'd had time to run through the complete shutdown checklist. More likely he made Benkoski do it.

Parker saw me and changed course. "How bad is it?"

I shook my head. Behind him, Benkoski was climbing out of the cockpit, focused on us like a long-range scanner, seeking any glimmer of information. I had none. "We just got here. You fly over?"

He nodded, face grim, and turned back to the building. "I wonder how long they'll ground us."

"That's what you're thinking about? People are probably dead, and you're worried about the next flight?"

Stopping, he drew himself up straight and cracked his neck. Then he turned. "Yes. That is what I'm worried about. I ride these things and I ask the men on my team to ride them, so yes. I'm wondering how long it will take them to figure it out, because this was an unmanned flight. But that rocket could have been carrying me, or Benkoski, or Lebourgeois, whose daughter you so charmed, Lady Astronaut."

As much as I wanted to make a withering comeback, he was right. "I'm—I'm sorry. I didn't think."

"No. You didn't. You never do. You just go after what you want, and to hell with anyone who stands in your way." He turned and stalked off toward Mission Control.

Benkoski gave a long, low whistle. "What was that?"

"He hates me."

"I know. I meant, why?" The astronaut was lanky and stood with his head half-cocked to the side, like he was trying to get a sighting on my brain. "There aren't that many people he hates."

"I—we knew each other during the war." I shook my head. It wouldn't do any good to go into it. I walked back to my Cessna to push it into the hangar. "Doesn't matter. And he's a damn good pilot, which is all that counts now, huh?"

Benkoski shrugged and followed me to the plane. He took up a spot on the other side. "I've seen better."

"Like you?" I leaned my full body weight against the strut of the plane.

He grinned, even with the scent of smoke filling the air, and helped me push. "You know it."

After we got the plane situated, Benkoski fell into step beside me as we walked to Mission Control. Fishing in his pocket, he brought out one of the little black notebooks that most of the astronauts carried. "Say . . . my niece saw you on *Mr. Wizard*. Any chance I could get an autograph for her?"

"Sure." My stomach churned as I took his pen and signed my name on a blank page. On the horizon, the world burned.

Nathaniel stayed the night at Mission Control. There were crew quarters, and he decided to bunk down there. He sent me home. I expect he slept about as much as I did, which was not at all.

When I got into work, I walked down the hall to his office, carrying a change of clothes for him. Everyone I passed had the look of soldiers fresh out of the trenches in the war. Their faces were tight and somehow more gaunt than they'd been three days before.

I knocked on Nathaniel's door, even though it was open, so that I wouldn't startle him as I went in. His blond hair stuck up like a haystack, and dark circles ringed his eyes as he looked up. "Thanks."

"Have you eaten?" I laid his clean shirt across the back of a chair.

On his desk were stacks of telemetry readings. He had a pencil in one hand, going down the list of numbers. "Not hungry."

"The cafeteria will be open."

"I'm not." The muscle at the corner of his jaw ticked as he worked. "Hungry."

"All right. I'm sorry." I backed toward the door. I had just wanted to help. But I was in the way.

Nathaniel sighed and dropped his head so his chin nearly rested on his chest. "Wait." Wiping a hand across his eyes, he stood with part of his face shielded. "Elma, I'm not mad at you. I'm sorry. I'm being curt and rude and I'm . . . Will you shut the door?"

I nodded, pushing the door closed. When it latched, Nathaniel let out an enormous sigh and sank into his chair. "I'm a mess."

"Why don't you take a break?"

"Because . . . everyone wants to know what happened. And I don't know." He tossed his pencil on the desk. "I don't know. The range safety officer should have ordered the self-destruct when it went off course, and he didn't. But I don't know why it blew up in the first place, and I should."

I came around his desk and stood behind him. Putting my hands on his shoulders, I leaned down to kiss the top of his head. He smelled of sweat and cigarettes. "You will."

No. No, that wasn't cigarette smoke. It was the stink of

the burning farm. Nathaniel shook his head, and the muscles under my hands jerked with the movement. "There's probably going to be a government inquiry."

I dug my thumbs into his tight muscles and he grunted. Working in little circles, I leaned all my weight on him. "Parker was wondering how long they'd be grounded."

"It'll take months to go through everything." He rubbed his forehead. "We'll have to push the moon launch back too."

The moon launch wasn't scheduled to use the same type of rocket, so it shouldn't be affected by the flaw in this one. On the other hand, this one wasn't supposed to have a flaw. Plus, the orbital platform would be set back with the loss of the payload.

Nathaniel cleared his throat, and the muscles in the back of his neck tightened again. "Say . . . Elma?"

"Right here."

He swallowed. "I don't think I can . . . I think I'll need to stay here for the next couple of months."

"I figured." Any chance I had of getting him to take a vacation was pretty much out the window now. I grimaced. I'd chastised Parker for wondering about being grounded, and here I was worrying about vacations. I was a jerk.

"That means I won't be able to go to your nephew's bar mitzvah."

My hands stopped moving of their own accord. "Oh." I bent my head and resumed the massage as I tried to sort out my thoughts. I didn't want to leave Nathaniel alone, not with the amount of pressure he was under. But Hershel needed me there, and it was Tommy's bar mitzvah, for crying out loud. "Do you . . . do you mind if I go by myself?"

"Thank God." He spun in his chair to face me. "I was all prepared to convince you that you needed to go."

I brushed the hair back from his face. "See, you needn't have worried. I'll abandon you at a moment's notice."

He grinned, but the movement was pained. "Falser words were never spoken." He slid his arms around me and pulled me close. "Thank you."

"For?"

"I can't yell when I go out on the floor. I want to. I want to scream and gnash my teeth. So thank you for giving me a place where I can be awful, and find my way back again."

TWENTY-THREE

JUPITER ROCKET EXPLOSION
IS LINKED TO HUMAN ERROR

KANSAS CITY, KS, Dec. 12, 1956—(United Press International)—Failure to transcribe a program correctly—apparently a human error—was blamed for Tuesday's explosion of a second stage for the Jupiter moon rocket in a preliminary report. The rocket flew off course and crashed onto a farm, killing eleven. Government inquiries are scheduled to determine if the disaster was preventable.

I was not happy about leaving Nathaniel behind, but, as he predicted, the government scheduled inquiries about the crash. Besides the IAC's own work looking into the explosion, they also needed to prepare documents that laymen could understand.

The smart thing to do would have been to take a commercial plane to California, but I wanted to clear my head, and flying seemed an excellent way to do that. However, Nathaniel insisted and maybe, occasionally, I can be not an idiot. Whatever. The end result was that I wound up on my first commercial flight.

I was not impressed. The only good thing about it was that they served cocktails, which I couldn't have enjoyed if I were the pilot. The view was terrible. The pilot bounced twice when landing, and he didn't even have any cross-winds as an excuse.

But just being able to stand up and leave the plane with-out running through a checklist? That was nice. Walking off the plane and seeing my brother waiting? Glorious.

My brother stood with Doris, Tommy, and Rachel at his side. It looked as if California continued to treat him well. He had a tan and wore a light Hawaiian shirt printed with arcing hibiscus. The kids had sprouted like weeds, and Tommy was nearly as tall as his father. It had been three years since I'd seen them. Rachel hung back a little, but she was grinning, with dimples in her round cheeks.

"Aunt Elma!" Tommy wasn't shy, though—never had been. He was the first to fling himself across the space be-tween us, rocking me back with the force of his hug. "You came! There's a great place to throw gliders from our new house. And I made a really cool one, and it's not from a kit, either."

Hershel rocked forward on his crutches. "Easy, tiger. Let's get Aunt Elma home before you plan her whole itin-erary."

Releasing my nephew, I beckoned to Rachel. "Do I get a hug?"

She nodded and submitted to an embrace. I had to crouch, but not nearly as much as I had last time I saw her. Doris rested a hand on her daughter's shoulder. "Tell her about your club, Rachel."

Her face turned up toward me, with wide eyes. "We started a Lady Astronaut club. It's really neat."

"That's great, sweetie." My stomach twisted as the rea-son that she was suddenly shy became clear. I wasn't just her aunt anymore. I was Someone. The Lady Astronaut had come to call. "Maybe I can visit it, huh?"

Rachel nodded, and her eyes got bigger and brighter,

then she turned back to her mother, her hands pressed together like she'd won a prize. What did I expect? I hadn't seen her in three years and now I was . . .

If I were an actual astronaut, I wouldn't mind it so much. I think. It's just that people called me "Lady Astronaut" *because* I wasn't allowed to be one. That was the thing that rubbed. The reason I was known at all was because I was agitating for a role I couldn't have. Having folks call me that? Having my niece do it? It was like being jealous of a character on TV, except that character was me. Can you be jealous of yourself?

I straightened, and finally the path to hug my brother was clear. He'd shaken off the cuff of one of his crutches and transferred it to his other hand so he could hug me without the metal pole knocking into my back. I wrapped my arms around him. Despite the hibiscus printed all over it, his Hawaiian shirt smelled like lavender. "Oh . . . I've missed you."

"You've lost weight." He pulled back, eyes pinched behind his glasses. "We'll talk."

It was a damn good thing that Nathaniel *wasn't* with me, or I'd have given him such a look right then. "Well, that won't last long with Doris's cooking." I let go of my brother to greet my sister-in-law.

"I don't know." She gave one of her trilling laughs, which ran up and down a scale. "I'm planning on putting you to work. Hershel didn't tell you that?"

"That's why I'm here. I wouldn't know how to take a vacation if one fell on me." Although that *is* what our vacations had a disturbing tendency to do.

I remember when Hershel had his bar mitzvah. He's seven years older than I am, but it's one of those early memories that stuck. Or parts of it did. I remember that I had to stretch up to see him over the top of the pew, and that he stumbled over the words when he was reading the maftir portions. Afterward, being six and full of belief in my own infallibility, I announced that I wouldn't make that sort of mistake when it was time for my bar mitzvah.

He didn't laugh at me like a lot of boys would. I remember him, balanced on his crutches, looking with pain at our father. That distress, on what was a happy day, is the part of my memory that is still so strong and so much my brother. He sat down and patted the sofa beside him, then explained that girls don't get to have a bar mitzvah. It's different now, but that's the way the world worked in 1934.

I cried. And he held me. That's my big brother for you. In a nutshell.

It was also the first time that I understood what being a girl meant.

As we sat in the pews for Tommy's bar mitzvah, I wanted to pull Rachel onto my lap and tell her that she could do anything she wanted, but it would be a lie.

That sorrow for Rachel didn't stop me from being proud of my nephew as I watched him. My nephew had spent the week practicing his Hebrew over and over. Apparently, he'd heard the story from Hershel about how he hadn't practiced his maftir enough. Tommy wouldn't make that mistake. He said it while he was running up the stairs. He said it carrying out the trash. He said it while he was throwing gliders on a hill overlooking the ocean with me.

When they called him up to the bimah, he looked like such a dapper young man, in a suit, with his bow tie snugged up against his collar and a neatly pressed prayer shawl draped over his shoulders. Hershel slid out of the aisle and followed Tommy to the front with the rattle and click of crutches and dress shoes.

Beside me, Doris gave a little sobbing breath and pressed

her handkerchief to her eyes. I was glad mine was already in my hand.

Hershel's voice cracked as he said, "Blessed is He who has now freed me from the responsibility of this one."

Thank God for handkerchiefs. Mine was going to be soaked by the end of the service.

Then Tommy pulled back his shoulders and recited, "Lo marbechem mikol ha'amim chashak Hashem ba'chem, va'yichbar ba'chem ki atem hahm'at mikol ha'amim . . ." No wobble. No fear. Just a clear, youthful voice, reaching toward Heaven and God's ears.

. . . It is not because you are the most numerous of peoples that the LORD set His heart on you and chose you—indeed, you are the smallest of peoples . . .

I was going to need another handkerchief.

Hershel and I sat at a table off to the side of the banquet room they'd rented. Doris was across the room, talking to one of her many cousins. In the middle of the dance floor, Tommy gyrated with a gaggle of his friends, resplendent in a white evening jacket.

They looked so young. What sort of world would they inherit?

Hershel nudged me with his shoulder. "What was that sigh?"

"Doomsday stuff." I waved it away and picked up my champagne glass. This party must have cost them a fortune. France hadn't been able to get a vintage ripe since before the Meteor.

"Ah . . . you're also looking at those kids and doing weather projections forty years out, huh?" He nodded and picked up his own glass, lifting it in a toast. "To the long summer."

"To space." I clinked my glass against his and sipped it,

bubbles rising up to bring flavors of apricot and flint along the top of my palate. "Do you think they'll remember what the stars looked like?"

He shook his head. "Rachel doesn't."

My breath caught in my throat. Of course. She'd only been five when the Meteor hit. By the time the dust settled, there was enough steam in the air to give us near constant cloud cover. "That's appallingly tragic."

"Not for her." He pointed with his champagne flute toward where she spun with some of her friends. Her little taffeta party dress twirled out around her. "She thinks all of this is normal and just the way the world works."

"Even with a father who is a meteorologist."

"Oh . . . she has an intellectual understanding of it, but, it's like . . . I don't remember what it was like to walk. The polio hit when I was so young, you know?" He rested a hand on his crutches where they sat propped against the table. "This is my normal. Intellectually, I know that it's not. That a disease paralyzed my legs. But I have no memory of being able to move them."

I hadn't known that, oddly. But I suppose my own memory was just as skewed. My brother had used crutches since before I was born. That was just normal. So, I guess I had firsthand experience that proved his point. These kids wouldn't realize how much things had changed. "How . . . how bad *does* the global climate look? I'm so focused on the IAC that I haven't been tracking it."

"Well . . . the cold went a little longer than we projected, but I think that's because our models were based on volcanic eruptions, and ash is nonreflective. Plus, we didn't take into account how long things burned. I mean, we did, but the data from the early days was pretty scarce, so . . ." He shrugged, light glinting off his glasses as he looked toward the ceiling. "The greenhouse effect is still going to hit, but it's looking like the ozone wasn't damaged as badly as we thought it would be. Again, modeling based on A-bomb testing."

"So . . . it's not an extinction event?"

"This is why I'm not allowed to talk to the press." He wiped the back of his hand across the back of his mouth. "The Earth is going to heat up. That's going to be permanent. But if we can limit the amount of greenhouse gases we generate, then we might—and I stress the word *might*—be able to keep the Earth habitable. Or at least habitable longer."

"Well . . . that's something." After that, what do you say? We sat and watched people dancing. Doris's brother had pulled her out on the dance floor. I was a little jealous of her for getting to dance with her brother. Or anyone, really. I cleared my throat. "Nathaniel is sorry he couldn't be here."

Hershel waved that away. "The crash. I understand."

"Still." All of these people, and we were the only Wexlers. I wasn't even properly a Wexler anymore, and Rachel wouldn't be when she got married.

"How's he doing?"

"Fairly well, all things considered." The actual answer was "poorly," but if I was going to complain about him discussing me with my brother, I couldn't very well go disclosing Nathaniel's troubles. Across the room, the jazz band struck up another tune. I don't remember what, because I could feel Hershel's next question gathering.

"And you?" His tone was too quiet. He rolled the stem of his glass between his fingers, but he was staring at me.

I could blow off his question. Answer it socially. Lie. But on the day of my nephew's bar mitzvah, when I was sitting next to one of three blood relatives I had left in the world . . . I kept my gaze on the dancers, maintaining the placid smile Mama had taught me how to use. "Remember *that* semester at Stanford."

"Yeah." Not needing me to specify which semester, he reached over and put a hand on my arm. "God. Elma. I'm so sorry. I'd wondered . . . when you talked about *Mr. Wizard*. I was hoping you were joking."

"Twice. Before the show." In this beautiful ballroom, with all of these smiling people, I couldn't bring myself to say the word "vomit." My muscles were so tight they started to tremble. I took a breath and tried letting it out again, trying to let the tension go with it. "And before every interview."

"And . . . has it—" He wet his lips. Looking around us, in case anyone was going to approach, he leaned toward me. "Have you tried—tried it again?"

I was already shaking my head to stop him. "No. I broke down, and that's the worst Nathaniel has seen. He knows that I had a breakdown in college and why, but not the details. Please don't tell him. Please, please don't tell him."

"I won't." He squeezed my arm. "I won't. I promised I never would, and that's going to my grave—even if that's the worst possible metaphor I could have used."

My own laugh surprised me. It cut through the ballroom in a space between notes and bounced off the far wall. Heads turned our way, but I think that all they saw was a brother and sister, sitting together while nervous giggles rocked them.

They certainly didn't see the memory of the year that I tried to hang myself.

TWENTY-FOUR

SPEED IS KEY TO SUCCESS
OF SPACE PROGRAM

By DR. NATHANIEL YORK
Lead Engineer, International Aerospace
Coalition, Feb. 4, 1957

TIME is the scarcest resource, and the most essential to humanity's space efforts. Since there is no way to increase the supply of this resource, the only sane choice is to make the best use of the small and rapidly dwindling quantity available.

The contrast between the ballroom for Tommy's bar mitzvah, which had been all baby blue plaster and gilding, and the congressional hearing rooms of the New Capitol could not have been stronger. The New Capitol stood as a testament to the austere and modern aesthetic of post-Meteor fashion, stainless steel framing squares of granite. I was there to support Nathaniel during the inquiry into the *Orion 27* crash. When I got back from California, he'd requisitioned me from the computer department to help him prepare the data for the hearing. Other computers could have done the work, but I knew his shorthand.

In the two months since the crash, we had prepared exhaustive reports with a host of charts and indices, but if the congressmen asked for a number Nathaniel didn't have, then I could supply it. At least, that was the plan.

On the second day of the hearings, Senator Mason from North Carolina scowled down from his bench. I almost expected him to have one of those ridiculous wigs judges wore in England. "Now, wait a minute, sir. Wait a minute. Am I to understand that the entire rocket program is so fragile—so fragile, sir, that a single symbol can undermine it?"

Director Clemons shuffled his papers. "No, sir. Although in this instance, it is true that we are looking at a transcription error."

"I find that . . . yes, sir, I find that hard to believe, sir. I find that hard to believe." If Mark Twain had been an idiot, this man might have been his embodiment. "I find that very hard to believe."

One might think he found it hard to believe.

Senator Wargin, who was one of the few bright spots on the committee, cleared his throat. "Perhaps if we let them explain the equation in question."

My heart seized in my chest as if someone had hooked a live wire to my spine, sending current through my body. That was my cue. This was why I was here. I tried to draw a breath, but it was too shallow. I tried for another. God. Panting wasn't going to help.

As I wiped my hands on my skirt, Nathaniel stood. "Let me try to walk you through it."

My gaze had been fixed on the polished wood of our table. I dragged it up to follow Nathaniel. He walked away from the table, drawing the eyes of everyone in the room off of me. He didn't—he didn't have to do that. I could have explained it. That's why I was there. I wiped the sweat off my forehead and watched him inch through the explanation.

Explaining that a single superscript had been dropped by the man responsible for transcribing our handwritten formulas onto punch cards was simple. Explaining what that superscript did? You had to understand the entire formula.

I should be the one explaining it. Nathaniel was doing it because he'd taken one look at my sweaty, shaky self and seen me as a liability. Pressing my hands against my skirt, I bowed my head and waited.

When he sat down, I leaned over. "You should bring Helen tomorrow. She wrote most of the program."

"Helen is Chinese." He sorted his papers as Director Clemons answered a question about the range safety officer's duties.

"Taiwanese."

"The point is, Mason wouldn't get past her accent." He rested his hand on my knee. "I need to—" But then he turned away in answer to something Mason asked from the stand. "Yes, sir. All of the rockets are equipped with a self-destruct device in case of malfunction."

"So! This is something, sir, that happens often enough that you plan for it."

"We would be irresponsible if we did not have contingency plans, even for theoretical occurrences." Clemons's voice sounded like he'd been sucking on lemons and still trying to smile. "Sir."

For the rest of the session, my role stayed that of a spectator.

The only silver lining to the whole ordeal was that, since Senator Wargin was on the committee, Nicole came in to watch at some point. As we stood to recess for lunch, her lemon yellow dress was a welcome spot of color amid the stainless steel and granite of the hearing room.

"You look peaked." She swirled over to Nathaniel, skirt billowing out. "Both of you. No offense, but you need to get out of this tomb. Join me for lunch?"

Nathaniel stood, stretching. "Thanks, Mrs. Wargin, but I have some things to go over with Director Clemons before the next session."

"Sandwiches for us." Clemons rose from his chair. "Thank you for the offer, though."

"Well, may I at least steal Elma?"

I shook my head. "I should stay."

Nathaniel took me by the shoulders and turned me away from him. "Go on. You can bring me back a piece of pie."

Nicole linked her arm through mine. "Pie? Perfect. I know just where we're going." She half-dragged me out of the hearing room and into the bustling, hushed halls of the New Capitol. Congressional aides hurried down the thick blue carpet that lined the halls. It was the only spot of softness amid the crisp right angles and stone.

"We can't go too far, though." I kept having to blink to get my eyes to focus. "I need to be back when the session starts."

"Well, I happen to know that one of the senators—who shall remain nameless—always takes a two-hour lunch. We've got plenty of time. Besides, you and I? We need to talk."

The restaurant that Nicole took me to was pre-Meteor splendor, with tall ceilings, crystal chandeliers, and mirrors everywhere. It had gilding like something out of a Regency romance novel, and I felt hopelessly out of place. For the hearings, I had confined my wardrobe to dark pencil skirts. Today's was navy, with a plain white blouse, to blend as much as possible with the sea of men and their suits.

The floral scarf Nicole had tied about her neck framed her face with a softness more appropriate to our luncheon setting. She broke that illusion when the waiter came to take our order. "Two martinis. Doubles. Deviled eggs to start us, and then filet mignon for both. Rare and bloody."

"Oh, I shouldn't—"

"Two-hour lunch. Plenty of time to absorb and recover." She folded her menu. "Besides, you look brittle enough to crack. And I want to soften you up before I make my suggestion."

"You mean, ordering for me doesn't count as 'suggestion'?"

She waved her hand, diamond bracelet sparkling. "Please. You would have ordered a salad and eaten a third of it. At least when you just pick at the steak, you'll get a little nutrition."

"That bad?"

"You and Nathaniel both." She shook her head and placed a hand on mine. "Elma. Dear. I've seen more than my fair share of inquiries, and you are both textbook cases. Your clothes are loose, so . . . Not eating. Foundation is heavier under your eyes, so . . . Not sleeping. Probably barely talking outside the chamber."

She wasn't wrong. I was saved by the arrival of the martinis. "What's your suggestion?"

Nicole pushed mine firmly toward me. "Drink."

"Oh? That bad?"

"Drink." She lifted her own glass in a salute and waited until I touched mine to hers, and then to my lips. She took a healthy swallow, closing her eyes with relish, then set the glass down. "Why isn't Nathaniel using you?"

My mouth tasted of brine and juniper as I swallowed. "Well, we did all of our preparations before arriving, and there hasn't been a call for new calculations yet."

"I'm talking about having you testify."

I nearly dropped my martini. "Testify? Me? Why in the world would they want to hear from me?"

She tilted her head, and I wasn't sure how I thought that the scarf made her soft. "Elma. Senator Mason is going to try to use the accident to stop the program."

"Yes, well, he's always hated it." He kept trying to funnel the money to his own state for disaster recovery. To be fair, North Carolina needed it. They got hit with a lot of the fires, and then the acid rain afterward killed most of the farming land. "What does that have to do with me?"

"Because you're the Lady Astronaut."

"I am *not* an astronaut!" My voice cut through the low hum of conversation around us. Wealthy and powerful people turned to stare. What must they think? Bending my head, I applied myself to the martini and let the cold burn of the gin distract me.

"And the Lady Astronaut clubs?"

The deviled eggs arrived. There was not a chance that I could eat even one of the glistening ovoids. *Your body is not supposed to react this way . . .* Swallowing, I pushed the martini away from me. "That was NBC's idea. I had nothing to do with it."

"Bullshit."

"It's true. And Don—Mr. Wizard—objected to the name, because boys *and* girls should be able to be astronauts, or in his Mr. Wizard Science clubs."

She shook her head and leaned across the table. "That's not what I mean. You may not have organized the clubs, but the fact that they exist is *directly* because of you. And Nathaniel isn't taking advantage of your popularity?"

"I'm not—"

"You're photogenic. You make rocketry sound exciting and easy. You're funny and—"

"I throw up." Clapping my hands over my mouth, I closed my eyes and concentrated on breathing. Nicole was trying to help. If I were someone else, her suggestion might work, but not with me. "I can't."

"When?" Her voice was softer.

Lowering my hands, I opened my eyes. "Before every filming. Sometimes after, too."

"But not during?"

"I can't."

Nicole bit her lower lip, then sighed and slid her chair a little closer. "I . . . you have to promise me you won't say anything. Lord help me, if the paper gets wind of this—promise me, Elma."

I shook my head, trying to figure out where this was going, and then realized it looked like I was saying no. "Sorry. Yes. Of course I promise. Though you're alarming me a little."

Lowering her voice until it was barely audible over the clink of cutlery, she leaned closer still. "After the Meteor . . . I had some trouble. Similar trouble. And then when Kenneth was running for office it became . . . it became a problem. *I* became a problem." She looked around as if we were in a spy novel. "I can introduce you to my doctor."

"I don't want to take drugs."

She pulled back, her face frozen in a social smile. "I didn't say anything about medication, of course. The wife of a senator? What would people think?"

That fear, I understood all too well. I held up my hands to try to soothe her. "It's not—I wouldn't. It's just . . . I talked to a doctor and he recommended *them*, but . . ."

"I know." She picked up her martini and stared into it, mouth twisted in an odd smirk. "Believe me, I understand all about the 'but.' And I was wrong."

✳   ✳   ✳

It took another week of hearings before I realized that Nicole was right on two fronts. First, that although Nathaniel resolutely was not asking me to testify, he needed me to. Or, rather, he needed a computer to testify, and of the ones who worked for IAC, I made the most sense, because I'd been helping him prepare; and . . . and because of my existing visibility.

And, second, that testifying would make me ill. No, wait . . . that's not the part she was right about. I already knew that about myself. What Nicole was right about was that I shouldn't *have* to get sick every time I addressed a group of people.

It's funny how, once something comes into your consciousness, you begin seeing it everywhere, like seeing your birthdate in random places. After talking with Nicole, I began seeing ads for Miltown constantly. At the pharmacy there was a sign that read "Ice Cream!" and then under it, just as large, "Yes! We Have Miltown!" Or, at the grocery store, leafing through a magazine, there were ads for the "happy pill." Heck, Milton Berle was even joking about renaming himself "Miltown Berle." I know that we're pattern-seeking creatures, but at a certain point the prevalence of anxiety began to seem like a Fibonacci sequence of emotion.

So, I called Nicole's doctor. Who also specialized in psychotherapy. This new doctor turned out to be a woman, which was a surprise and a relief. I didn't tell Nathaniel where I was going. He would have understood, and gone with me. I just . . . I just didn't want to admit that I was this weak. I was so ashamed of needing a drug to do something as innocuous as talk. I was smart. Heck. When I wasn't being modest, I was brilliant. I knew that. But the doctor and Nicole were both right, and if this had been any other condition, I would not have balked at medication.

So I bundled up and pretended to be stepping out to run some errands. It is the closest I have ever come to outright lying to him, and my skin felt as if it were coated with a layer of slime. I nearly turned back to tell him, but if I had done that, I don't think I would have made it out the door. I would have stayed home instead, just so that I didn't have to lie to him.

Dr. Haddad's office was on the ground floor of a brownstone. It felt more like someone's parlor than a medical office. Lamps stood in the corners and created a dim, intimate space. The doctor herself was slender, with sleek dark hair that she wore straight and cropped at her shoulders. Her black trousers were so alarmingly fashionable that covetousness suddenly overran me.

She guided me to an armchair. "Tea?"

"No, thank you."

Pouring a cup for herself, she smiled. "I find it always soothes me, especially in this weather."

"It's starting to get warm again."

"Mm-hm . . . but it isn't there yet." She held up the cup and smiled over the edge at me. "So . . . what brings you in this evening?"

I swallowed, and immediately regretted declining the tea, which would have given me something to do with my hands. "I seem to be suffering from anxiety and . . . and I don't know what to do about it."

She set her cup down and leaned forward. "My dear. That's what I'm here for."

And I wept.

TWENTY-FIVE

PEIPING MAY ORBIT SATELLITE BY 1958

U.S. Intelligence Data Note Increasing
Indications of Active Space Program

By JOHN W. FINNEY
Special to The National Times.

KANSAS CITY, KS, Jan. 9, 1957—A Government intelligence report predicts that Communist China will be able to launch an Earth satellite in two years.

The small white pill sat in the center of my palm. The palm itself was coated in a thin sheen of sweat. Overhead, the bathroom fan rattled like an unbalanced airplane engine and masked most of the sounds from the apartment.

Nathaniel had been sitting in a chair with Ray Bradbury's new novel. I kept hoping he'd go out, but he hadn't yet, which was probably for the best. If anything went wrong, I should have someone with me.

Telling him that I was about to take a tranquilizer would be sensible—but I didn't.

Don't ask me why. It wasn't that I didn't trust him, it's just . . . I don't know. I didn't trust myself? Does that make any sense?

Taking the pill was a sign that I had failed. No matter

what the doctors said about anxiety being a genuine illness, I couldn't shake my mother's voice: *What will people think?* What would my husband think?

Wetting my lips, I placed the pill in my mouth. The bitter coating curled my tongue and I swallowed a mouthful of water to wash it down. I set down the glass. Done. In the mirror, my face stared back at me unchanged. Brown eyes. Nose slightly askew. Chin a little too rounded. No horns . . . yet. I know it sounds melodramatic, but that two-hundred-milligram pill carried a potent possibility. *Please work.*

Twenty minutes. It would be twenty minutes before I could possibly feel the effects. I opened the vanity drawer and hid the bottle among my sanitary napkins. There were few places in our tiny apartment that I could be certain Nathaniel wouldn't go. This was one.

Wiping my hands on my skirt, I opened the door and left the bathroom. Nathaniel barely glanced up from the book he was reading. Given the congressional hearings, it was a wonder that he was willing to take the day off. On the other hand, since we couldn't resume our launch schedule until the hearings concluded, there wasn't that much he could do at work.

Right. I pulled out one of the chairs at our table and sat down. There were bills to be paid. I pulled the stack toward me and got to work.

An hour later, the bills were paid. I'd balanced the checkbook. And . . . I felt fine.

I drew a blank sheet toward me and began plotting a trajectory for a moon landing. Possibly, if I thought about it, I was a little slower. Maybe. But no more so than toward the end of a long day. Not that I felt tired, just . . . muted? That's not even the right word. I just felt . . . normal. Whatever that means.

The next morning, I checked the bankbook, looking for errors. There were none.

One of the curtains let in a thin stream of amber light from the streetlights outside our apartment. I curled against Nathaniel and nestled my head on his shoulder.

He ran a hand down my arm, leaving a contrail of goosebumps in his wake. His touch explored the contours of my hand and circled my wedding band.

"I've been lying to you." Sometimes, the things I blurt out surprise me. This one didn't.

His breath stilled, but under my cheek, the beat of his heart sped. "About?"

"The class I'm taking . . ." Errands hadn't cut it as an excuse, after the first session. "I'm . . . I'm seeing a therapist."

All the tension drained out of his body. "Oh, thank God."

"That . . . was not the response I expected."

He pulled me closer and kissed my forehead. "I'm glad you're taking care of yourself."

"You're not upset that I lied?"

"Well, yes, but the relief outweighs that." His hand found my hair and he stroked it back from my face. "And . . . I'll admit to being a little hurt that you didn't feel safe telling me. But not angry. Okay? I'm not angry."

My eyes stung and I blinked them clear. "You are amazing."

"I am in love. That's an important distinction." Nathaniel turned to kiss my forehead. "Without you, I'm just an average guy."

I laughed and poked him in the ribs. "You. Are not an average anything."

"Eh. I'm a pretty good administrator. Not bad with numbers."

My hand drifted lower. "Good with rockets."

He grunted and stretched under my touch. When he relaxed, he pulled me on top of him so that our bodies were pressed full length against each other. "I . . . I would say that you're better at handling rockets than I am."

"Is that so?" I pinned his arms to the bed and lifted myself up to kneel, straddling him. "Well, Dr. York . . ."

"Yes, Dr. York?"

"In that case, I have a very . . ." I kissed his neck. "Serious . . ." My tongue licked the sweat from his jawline. "Question."

"Yes. Whatever it is. God, yes."

"Would it help . . ." There was a rough spot under his chin that he'd missed while shaving. My heart sped up and I raced ahead to get my words in front of my fear. "If I explained the equations to the committee?"

Nathaniel twisted to look at me, though I couldn't have been more than the same sort of shadowed blur that he was. "Elma . . ."

In my name was a wealth of unsaid thought. Yes, it would help. No, he didn't want to ask me to do it. Yes, he was terrified I would break. No, he didn't want to see me hurt. Yes, he loved me for offering. No, he couldn't accept.

I slid off of him to sit on the bed at his side. "Remember how when I was in university, I was the only girl in class, so instructors would ask me to explain a math problem in order to show the boys up?"

"I know. That's why I can't ask you—"

"Hush. I'm not done."

"Okay . . ." He sat up next to me, shoulders hunched forward. "Sorry."

"The thing is . . . it worked. They were always shamed into doing better because they couldn't stand to have a little girl understand something that they couldn't."

"And it was hellishly cruel of the professors."

"Yes. Yes, absolutely. But . . . but if I'm *choosing* to do it, it's different." True, but I was still sweating, and it was no longer from sex. "And . . . I'm taking Miltown now."

"Oh."

"It helps."

"Good." He kissed my forehead. "Thank you for telling me."

"So . . . With this new dataset, let's return to my point." The faster we could stop talking about my anxiety, the better. "Senator Mason keeps making you go over the equation that caused the rocket to go off course in the first place."

"Yes . . ." I couldn't see his face, but I could imagine his brows knit together in concentration.

"He will keep making you explain over and over again that the problem was a transcription error when the program was transferred to punch cards. Let me explain exactly how leaving out a single superscript bar caused the program to break. If a woman tells him, he'll have to either pretend he understands it, or admit that he's not smart enough to be making a decision on this."

"Huh." He rubbed his head. "Okay. So that might hopefully, finally, make Mason stop harassing us about the error, but . . . the real problem wasn't the transcription failure, and they'll still hound us on that. God—"

I reached for his hand and pulled it away from his head. "Are you still having nightmares?" The nights that he'd woken in a sweat or cried out in his sleep didn't leave this much of a question. It was more an opportunity for him to come clean with me. And yes, I'm aware of what it means that we had both been lying to each other, and ourselves, about how we were feeling.

His shoulders slumped farther. "Yeah."

"I told you mine . . ."

"Heh." His thumb found my ring finger and rolled the wedding band left and right. "The latest was that I was the idiot range safety officer and knew the rocket was going to crash, but couldn't order the destruct sequence. I was glued—literally glued—in my chair. Only, of course, it wasn't my chair, it was a seat on an airplane, and I had to watch the whole thing."

When the rocket veered off course, the range safety officer, who was responsible for making the call about the self-destruct sequence, didn't. He waited to see if the course would correct. It didn't. As a result, eleven people had died on the Williams farm where it crashed. Two of them were kids.

He sighed and bent forward at the waist, pulling his hand free of my grip to wrap his arms around his head. "Senator Mason is going to use this to tank the space program. People are already agitating about the resources that are going into it instead of relief here on Earth. It's dead simple for him to use the deaths to sway public opinion."

"So let me explain about the new safety procedures. Let me recommend moving the launch site to the equator." We'd wanted to do that years ago, but couldn't get budget approval, since the Sunflower facility had already existed. "Let me explain what's going to happen to our planet, and why space is so important."

"This is going to be offensive, and yet . . ." He sat up. There was enough light from the street that I could just see his eyes, pinched with concern. "Why would he listen to you?"

"Because I'm the Lady Astronaut."

The morning I was to address the congressional hearing, I wasn't afraid of speaking. I was afraid that the medication wouldn't work. I sat there next to Nathaniel as I always did, a litany of "Am I calm?" running through my head.

I wasn't. I was terrified, but the reaction wasn't as . . . bright? Does that make sense? I was still afraid, but it was like a cloud had come between the fear and me. Yes, it made the whole room a little dimmer, but it also meant that the fear itself didn't cast such dark shadows. The actual test would come when—

Nathaniel rested a hand on my knee. "Ready?"

I managed a nod. I think I smiled. Swallowing was not possible, as my throat had gone completely dry. Nathaniel kept his hand on my knee, out of sight of the committee, as Clemons stood.

1, 1, 2, 3, 5, 8, 13, 21, 34 . . .

"Gentlemen . . ." Clemons paced around to the front of the table so all I could see was his back and his hands clasped behind him. "During our deliberations, it has occurred to me that we have neglected to give you an adequate foundation in understanding the root of the accident."

. . . 55, 89, 144, 233, 377 . . .

"The 'transcription' error." Senator Mason drawled as he leaned back in his chair.

"Correct. I would like to return to that error, and have one of our computers explain, in detail, the effects of that error and the steps that will be taken to ensure that such an error never occurs again." He turned to the side and gestured at me. "May I present Dr. Elma York. She's the physicist responsible for recognizing the effects of the Meteor on our climate, and is the pride of our computer department, although you may know her better as 'the Lady Astronaut' from *Mr. Wizard.*"

The Fibonacci sequence dropped out of my mind. This? From Director "Control Your Wife" Clemons? Whatever his intention, the shock was enough to jar me out of my pattern of fear. Was I calm? No. But I didn't think I was going to throw up, either.

Taking a deep breath, and amazed that I could, I pushed my chair back and stood. "Thank you, Director Clemons. Distinguished gentlemen of the committee." I focused on Senator Wargin, who did not smile, exactly, but his eyes were kind. "If you will turn your attention to the blackboard, I'll walk you through the equation that governed the rocket . . ."

Senator Mason jabbed his finger at me. "We've been over that, ma'am. Yes, we have."

"Oh." I paused to smile. This man, for all his power, was a child in mathematics. "I'm so sorry. I thought you were still asking questions because we hadn't explained adequately. I must've misunderstood, of course, so to help me . . . would you explain the part of the equation that you had questions about?"

His mouth worked, pursing and grimacing, before he nodded. "Maybe you had best proceed. To make certain my colleagues are on level ground."

At his side, Senator Wargin had covered his mouth. His eyes were decidedly crinkled with smile lines. He cleared his throat. "Yes, Dr. York. Please start from the beginning."

"Very well. To calculate an ascent track, we have the following equation for the acceleration in the direction of the flight path: $V = \Delta V/dt = [(F_1 + A_{e,1} * (P_{e,1} - P_a) \ldots$ Now, the F_1 is, of course, referring to the thrust of the first booster. That was calculated at, as you can see farther down in the equation, 12.8 times ten to the ninth G's of thrust . . ." I glanced at the bench. Senator Mason's eyes had begun to cross. "Am I going too fast?"

"No . . . no, not at all. Carry on."

And I did. By the time I finished, they either understood or pretended they did, which was actually more useful for Nathaniel's purposes. I didn't throw up. Not even once.

And the cherry on the cake? Senator Mason asked for my autograph for his granddaughter.

It would have been nice if that had ended the inquiries, but my testimony at least allowed them to move from "who to blame" to "budget."

Three weeks later, I stood outside Director Clemons's door. Even from the hall, the stink of his cigars announced that he was in. Taking a deep breath, I stared at the ceiling. The Miltown was not a miracle pill, or my heart wouldn't be racing, but it helped. I could do this. I had an appointment. This was only one man, and not a congressional committee.

Letting out my breath, I rounded the corner and smiled at Mrs. Kare. His secretary looked up from her typewriter. "Oh! You can go right on in, Dr. York."

"Thank you." When had she started using my title, and why?

In his office, Director Clemons bent over a stapled report, one of his cigars clamped between his teeth. Behind him, Parker scowled. "Oh, please . . . like that'll work."

I stopped in the door. "I'm sorry. Am I early?"

"No, no . . . come on in." Clemons waved me into the room and I realized that there was another man here. Tall, and blond, he looked somewhat familiar, but in my shock, I couldn't place him. "You know Lieutenant Parker. Have you met Wernher von Braun?"

Oh God—that was Wernher von Braun, rocket genius and Nazi scientist, sitting in a chair by the window. Nathaniel had worked with him years ago, but I knew him only by reputation.

They'd brought me into a room with a literal Nazi. Had that been Parker's idea? Probably.

"How do you do?" Saved or damned by social niceties,

I was able to make it through his response, which I barely heard, and even shake his hand. Yes, I'd heard the stories about how he wasn't "really" a Nazi—about how he had been "forced" to use Jewish prisoners or risk losing his own life. But he'd made that choice. *1, 3, 6, 10, 15, 21, 28 . . .*

"Colonel Parker suggested that we might need some assistance in understanding your report." Clemons waved at the chair in front of him. "Have a seat."

Did Clemons even know I was Jewish? I sat and smoothed my skirt as if I could rub the taint of von Braun's touch off my hands. If I walked out of the room, my chances of convincing Clemons were over. "I take it that you were concerned about Nathaniel's impartiality?"

"Exactly so." He leaned back in his chair. "Now, explain it to me very slowly, like I'm a congressman."

Wetting my lips, I nodded. "I hope you'll bear with me if I start with a history lesson, which is not in the report. It will give some context."

Clemons waved his cigar, smoke trailing it like a plane going down. "Go ahead."

"When sewing machines were first introduced, people were frightened because they were new and moved with an unprecedented speed. There was concern that you could go blind from watching the machine. So the manufacturers made them beautiful: they added gilding and floral motifs."

Parker snorted. "So you want to send some Lady Astronauts up as decoration?"

"As we explained to the congressional hearing, our goal is to expand humanity to other worlds. You will need women on those worlds or they will never be self-sustaining colonies." I glared at Parker. "I trust you don't need me to explain the biology of babies?"

"Babies or no, it's not safe." Parker shook his head and smiled. "I appreciate your ambition, I really do, but surely the *Orion 27* accident demonstrates that we can't put women in the line of fire."

"No. That is the wrong tactic to take. If you point to the explosion as a sign that rocketry is not safe, the space program will fail." I looked back at Director Clemons, but with the cigar in his mouth, it was hard to read his expression. "You know it will. If you want to demonstrate that the program is safe, then you need to demonstrate that these rockets are safe enough even for ladies."

Parker shrugged, as if none of that mattered. "And we will . . . after the moon base has been established."

I pressed my hands flat against my skirt to keep me from balling them into fists. "If you refer to page six of my report . . . After World War II, there is no shortage of women who flew as WASPs and have the right skills. But if you wait too long, those women will be too old, which will raise the barrier of creating the colonies."

"She has a point." Wernher von Braun, of all people, stepped into Clemons's smoke cloud to support me. "The Russians used their Night Witches in the war to devastating effect."

Parker tilted his head at the mention of the Russian women's air squadron. "I always thought they were propaganda."

"Propaganda, perhaps to begin with. But real and effective." Von Braun shrugged. "And even propaganda has its uses. We want the space program to continue, yes?"

Propaganda. Yes. I was well aware of what propaganda could do.

Clemons grunted and tapped his cigar in the brass ashtray on his desk. "All right . . . so let's go through this point by point."

I took a breath and stood to join Parker behind Clemons. I kept both of them between me and von Braun. Not because I thought he was going to pick me up and haul me off, but because it sickened me that people forgave him for what he'd done simply because he was a brilliant rocket scientist. A "nice" man. A "gentleman."

Yet here I was, giving tacit approval to his presence by saying nothing. Because if I did? Then Parker would use that to talk about how hysterical women were.

And worse . . . if the space program failed, then humanity was going to be trapped on Earth as it got hotter and hotter. So I leaned over Clemons's shoulder and turned to the first page of my report. "Right . . . We begin by looking at the budgetary benefits of using women as astronauts, due to our lower mass and oxygen consumption."

And from there, it was all about numbers, and I was home.

TWENTY-SIX

ROBOT DESIGNED TO EXPLORE MOON

6-Legged Crawling Device
Would Report Over TV

March 22, 1957—What has six legs, one claw, television, and sleeps sixteen hours a day? It could be a robot exploration vehicle small enough to be landed on the moon in a Project Reconnoiter package, according to a report to the International Aerospace Coalition yesterday. A working model of the proposed moon crawler has been built. The full-sized object would stand about five feet tall on its walking shoes, weigh 110 pounds, and be powered by little more than a square yard of solar cells.

The first launch after the hearings was unmanned.

It was a requirement that came out of the hearings and a smart thing to do when you're still trying to make sure that your system is robust. In our department, we computers had always employed a safeguard procedure, in that any calculations intended for a rocket were looked over by two other women. In the past, we had sent it to the Air Force, and they had used one of their men to transfer it to program cards. And that was that.

Now, two computers would look at the output of the

IBM machine's run to make sure no errors had been introduced. It was fairly straightforward. The first launch went smoothly.

The second launch was manned. No one was treating it as though it were straightforward.

Oh, we were all pretending like it was business as usual, but you could have ignited the atmosphere in the glassed-in viewing area above Mission Control. I wasn't on duty this shift, but there was no way I was going to miss the launch.

If this launch went smoothly, the astronauts would demonstrate that the lunar module could dock and rendezvous with the command module. We could go back on schedule, and we'd be another step closer to the moon.

If it didn't, then we'd have killed Derek Benkoski, Halim Malouf, and Estevan Terrazas.

There was a whole range of possibilities in-between, including a launch abort, or just scrubbing for weather. Those lesser evils were not the things filling anyone's minds as we milled around the viewing area. At T-minus four, the wives and children of the astronauts would be escorted to the roof to watch the liftoff from there. It would also sequester them from the press if things went badly. We all laughed and chattered, pretending that nothing could go wrong.

All of the astronauts and their wives—except Parker's—had turned out for this one to support the men in the capsule. Mrs. Lebourgeois separated from her husband and floated across the room to me. She was a diaphanous blonde with a long neck like a swan's and a tendency to purse her lips into a kittenish pout.

But she smiled when she saw me, and came up to give me a kiss on each cheek. "Ah, my dear! Our daughter is still talking of you. Not even her father is so impressive."

"She should be impressed with him! He's been in space. I just dream about it."

"It will not be so long for you, I think." Her swan's neck bent down in a curve as she winked. "My husband, he is making me take flying lessons so I can be ready."

That was optimistic, and more than a little charming. "Has he . . . heard anything?"

"No." She pouted. "But he has told Director Clemons that he believes women should be included. I think he just wants to . . . you know . . . have his wife in space?"

Her hand covered her mouth as she giggled at what must have been a stunned expression on my face. My mouth hung open a little and then I laughed with her. It had not occurred to me that one tactic would be to appeal to the male astronauts about the benefits of . . . marital duties in space. "Oh my heavens. Maybe I should try to talk to all the wives."

"Oh, we talk amongst ourselves."

"I'll bet. Have you . . . have you met Mrs. Parker?"

"No. She is always 'ill' with something or another, or busy. I think she just does not want to spend time with foreigners, but who am I to guess, hm?" She gave a little shrug and dismissed the absent woman. "Did you know . . . the weightlessness, it does, how shall we say, 'interesting' things to our husband's anatomy. The blood flow is quite . . . unrestricted by gravity."

"Well, now I want to get my husband into space." I glanced through the glass window to where Nathaniel stood hunched over his desk. They should really just make his station a standing desk, since he had trouble sitting when he was tense. Which was always.

Wait. I couldn't hear them. They'd turned the speakers off.

When had they . . . ? Something was wrong. Nathaniel

had the phone pressed to his ear and a broken pencil in one hand. Clemons stood at a different phone and was clearly shouting. Randy Cleary, the astronaut manning the CAP-COM desk, was talking into his headset and making sooth-ing gestures with his hands as if the astronauts in the capsule could see him.

The countdown clock had stopped at T-minus twenty-eight.

Other people had noticed and were moving toward the window. Mrs. Lebourgeois caught her husband's sleeve as he walked past. "*Que se passe-t-il?*"

"*Je ne sais pas. Ce ne fut pas une explosion ou nous auri-ons senti.*" He winced and looked at me. "Dr. York can tell you. An explosion we would have felt, is that not so?"

"Yes. It's probably just a glitch that they'll get sorted out soon." I smiled at his wife. "Honest, we have to stop launches all the time. It might just be the weather."

Except I'd been on the floor when there was a weather scrub, or a cutoff switch failed, or a system didn't come online as expected. We had procedures and manuals that were inches thick on what to do in every possible contin-gency. Everyone stayed aggravated but calm. Whatever was happening down there was not routine.

I leaned closer to the glass, looking for Basira, who was on duty for this launch. She was leaning together with Myrtle. Both women had dropped their pencils and looked shocked.

Behind me, Parker spoke. "All right, everyone. There's no need to be concerned. Nothing is wrong with the rocket."

I turned, along with most of the rest of the room. He stood next to one of the couches, holding the viewing room's phone receiver in one hand. I wouldn't have called down to bother them, but I guess the first man in space had more privileges than I did.

He hung up the phone as we all leaned forward in anticipation. "It's just a weather delay. Things are in a holding pattern."

That was a lie. I knew what a weather hold looked like. If it was weather, you'd see a lot of bored engineers spinning in their chairs. I opened my mouth to challenge him, then shut it again. This wasn't the time.

Parker caught my eye and gave this weird little nod. Almost like he was thanking me for not interfering. Something was very, very wrong, but I trusted him—which surprised me—to have a compelling reason for wanting the lie to stick.

I turned back to Mrs. Lebourgeois and laughed, shaking my head. "Oh, weather delays are the worst. There's nothing you can do but wait it out."

"I am glad that it did not happen when Jean-Paul went up. I should have died from the waiting."

"Well, the astronauts will probably just take a nap." I kept having to pull my gaze away from the window. "When Cristiano Zambrano went up, we had a two-hour delay, and I actually heard him snoring."

Someone approached and I stepped back a little to let them enter our circle of conversation. Stetson Parker stood next to me. He smiled, showing his outrageous dimples. "You wouldn't expect a person to sleep under these circumstances, but the couches are custom made to fit our bodies. Surprisingly comfortable. Say . . . Mrs. York, may I borrow you for a moment? Got a question about your Lady Astronaut speaking engagements."

I met his gaze and smiled as brightly as he was. "Of course, Colonel Parker."

My first thought was that something had happened to Nathaniel. We stepped a little away, facing the window so that our backs were to the viewing room. My husband was still talking on the phone. Every moment I looked down there, I became more convinced that something terrible had happened. Myrtle had tissues out.

Parker leaned in, voice low. "I'm trusting that you're not going to scream."

"Gee. Thanks."

"There's a bomb." He glanced from me to where Benkoski was standing by the switch for the speaker. "There's a man with a sign and explosives, and he's strapped himself to the gantry. That's all we know."

A thousand questions ran through my head. How did he get out there? What kind of bomb? What would happen if it went off? "Copy. What do you need me to do?"

"I want you to get all the wives and children to the cafeteria without scaring them. Keep them away from the press." He glanced over his shoulder. "Especially Malouf's and Benkoski's kids—keep them from hearing anything until the situation is handled."

Of course. Their fathers were on the rocket, waiting for launch. "Have they told the astronauts?"

"I don't know." He grimaced and looked down at Mission Control's floor. "It looks like that's what Cleary is doing, though."

"I'll tell the wives, discreetly."

"I wouldn't." He shrugged. "Astronauts' wives already have to live through enough stress and worry for a lifetime. Save them this."

It was tempting to make a comment about his own absent wife. Later. I could score points later. I spun away from him, clapping my hands. "Ladies? I'm going to suggest that we adjourn to the cafeteria where, I'm told, there is cake. It will be a much more agreeable wait than in here."

I do not do well when there is a problem that I can't do anything to solve. The two hours we waited in the cafeteria were awful. I spent the entire time listening for an explosion.

Listening for an explosion, while trying to amuse small children who had been promised a rocket launch and were long past their naptime. Mrs. Lebourgeois's daughter was an unexpected help, even without knowing what was happening upstairs. She borrowed tinfoil from the chef, and I sat next to one of Mrs. Benkoski's little boys and helped him smoosh tinfoil into a pointed column. "Good! That can be the body of your rocket."

While I was chattering with children, I was trying to mask all the questions stampeding through my brain. What was happening upstairs? What could I do? My tactical training consisted of listening to my father and his friends tell war stories.

What would my father have done? Stormed the gantry? No. Sat next to a five-year-old who was making a mess of his fuselage? Maybe. "Oh—Max, that's very good."

The cafeteria door opened. All of our heads turned toward it as if we were in a formation drill. Parker entered, followed by Benkoski, Malouf, and Terrazas. Still in their flight suits.

"Daddy!" The little boy next to me abandoned the table and ran across the cafeteria, holding his tinfoil rocket up in the air. "Look what I made!"

His mother was slumped against the table, eyes closed and crossing herself repeatedly. I stood more slowly, letting families reunite. I somehow managed not to scream "What happened?!"

Instead, I tidied tinfoil. That's right. There had been a bomber threatening the space program, and I spent that time making rockets and cleaning up tinfoil. I turned my back on everyone and began gathering up the supplies we'd been using. Little scraps of foil littered the table where Mrs. Lebourgeois had shredded them while chattering idly about a film she'd seen recently.

Parker swept some of the scraps into a neat pile. "Thank you."

Stopping, I stared at him. "What happened?"

"The astronauts used the emergency slide. When they were clear, the Air Force moved in." He glanced over my shoulder to the happy noises of children being adorable.

"That's it? The Air Force moved in?"

"They shot the bomber." Parker's gaze hardened on mine. "He was opposed to 'abandoning God's creation on Earth.' The rocket was 'a sin and a violation of God's plan.'"

I bent my head and shredded a piece of tinfoil, finding satisfaction in tearing the metal. "Well. I'm glad that's over."

"Good work, by the way."

Lifting my head, I stared at Parker. He stood at ease in a well-tailored suit that hinted at the blue of flight suits, though not quite as vivid. His hair was a little mussed, which was unusual for him. "That is, I think, the first compliment you have ever given me."

"It's the first one you've earned."

The muscles in my right arm burned with the desire to punch him. The urge pulled the breath out of me. If I moved at all, I would lose the battle, and I'd never punched anyone before, so I had no idea if I would be any good at it. "Do you practice being offensive? Or do you come by it natural?"

He winked. "For you? I practice." Parker looked past me to smile and wave at someone. "I'll be honest. I needed someone who knew how to talk to women and children.

And while I may not like your whole Lady Astronaut routine, you do it well."

"Two compliments in one day? You're slipping."

"Then let me leave you with this. You're never going into space if I have anything to say about it."

That was so much blunter than anything I had expected from him. Sniping at each other, sure. But actually coming out and saying he'd keep me grounded? I couldn't even fire back. "Why?"

"Really?" He shook his head, brows drawn together. "You tried to have me court-martialed, and you think that's not going to have consequences?"

"What—I didn't. I never tried . . . What are you talking about?"

He spread his hands on the cafeteria table and leaned toward me. "What, exactly, did you think was going to happen when you reported me for 'conduct unbecoming an officer'? Did you think I wasn't going to go on trial? Please. You're a general's daughter. You know exactly what happens with that kind of charge."

"Yes." I kept my voice clipped and low, conscious of all the kids behind us. "Yes. It gets ignored. I wasn't the first person to report you for harassing women."

"You're the only one I know about." Parker pushed back from the table, spreading his hands as if he could brush it all away. "And when they looked into it, you know what? None of the girls had a problem with me. None of them."

A laugh came out of nowhere. "They were *afraid* of you. They were afraid they'd be grounded."

"And you weren't? Please."

"I wasn't. Because, as you say, I was a general's daughter." I shook my head and backed away from him. "How did you ever get anyone to marry you? Or—maybe that explains why no one ever sees your wife?"

His face hardened and closed. "My wife is off limits."

"I'll bet she is." I turned my back on Parker and walked over to rejoin the other wives. Anger was shaking my veins with the force of my pulse. Bastard. Self-centered, self-righteous bastard. He thought he could keep me from joining the astronaut corps? I'd like to see him try.

And then the anger bled into cold resignation. He already had. And it was working well.

The IAC sent Nathaniel to a hotel that night, with a military guard, just in case someone decided to take a shot at the program's lead engineer. That was a depressing thought. I went with him, and the agency sent someone to our apartment to get clean clothes for us.

He sat on the edge of the hotel bed in his stocking feet, staring at the carpet. I sat next to him, leaning into his warmth. "Can we pretend this is a vacation?"

Nathaniel laughed, sliding an arm around my back to pull me closer. "The agency is doing something wrong. We have to change the way we're selling the space program to the public."

"There's always going to be someone who disagrees."

"Someone with a bomb?" He flopped back onto the bed, pulling me with him. "I think we're going to relocate the center."

I was willing to follow Nathaniel to whatever random place his thoughts took him. Turning so that I was on my side, I nestled against him and rested my hand on his chest. "That seems a little extreme."

"Clemons was already talking about it before this. He was going to use the *Orion* disaster to try to get us away from population centers."

"May I put in a request for somewhere equatorial?"

"Still trying to get a vacation, huh?"

"Trying to get better orbital trajectories." The button on his shirt shifted under my hand, and I rolled my fingers around it. "Where were you thinking?"

"It's all Clemons. I just build the rockets. While we were waiting for the situation to resolve"—which was such an engineer way to describe a bomber—"Clemons was going on about how many jobs we create . . . I don't know. It might actually turn into a bidding war."

"So, equatorial location and a pony?"

"Heh." His hand came up behind my back and pulled me closer. "You know . . . I kept having flashes of what it would have been like if you were on that rocket."

"Well, that's a worry you can put out of your head." I rolled away from him to stare at the pebbled plaster ceiling. It might be the surface of some unfamiliar planet. "Parker declared today that he was going to do everything in his power to keep me from being an astronaut."

"What?" Nathaniel sat up, staring down at me. "He said what?"

What, exactly, did you think was going to happen when you reported me . . . I cleared my throat. "He said something about how I was never going into space if he could help it. But, sweetie, don't say anything about it."

"Don't—why the hell wouldn't I?"

I sat up to face him. "Because it was just him and me. No one else heard, and you know how he can play things off." As the first man in space, the agency had good reason to want to keep his image spotless. If they had to sacrifice a computer for him? I knew what would happen, and Daddy wasn't here to make sure it didn't. "Besides, at the moment, they aren't even accepting women as astronauts. When they do? Then we'll talk about it."

*　*　*

Two months passed. The U.S. committee that had looked into the crash finally voted to continue the United States involvement with the IAC, in part, I think, because they were afraid the other nations would colonize the moon without us. There were changes, of course, which we implemented over the winter.

Higher security at the IAC required a fancy new electric fence and armed guards roaming the edges. Clemons used the bomb and the Williams farm tragedy like budgetary weapons to get upgrades and add staff.

As Nathaniel predicted, the IAC pushed to relocate the launch facilities to Brazil to limit vulnerabilities. Mind you, we'd asked for this at the beginning, but hadn't been able to get building a new launch site through the budget because the U.S. was afraid that other countries would use rocket technology for weaponry.

The rockets would be assembled and tested at the Sunflower facility in Kansas, then shipped to the new center near the coast in Brazil for launch. It finally got us near the equator, which was going to help with the moon and Mars programs.

And it meant that the computer department was busy redoing all of our trajectories to account for the new launch site, although it would likely be another two years until it was fully operational. I was hunched over a page doublechecking my differential equations when a shadow fell across my desk.

Blinking, I looked up. Nathaniel stood by my desk. He had that serious, constipated expression, as if there were a secret he couldn't share.

"Sorry to bother you, Elma, but I thought you'd like to see this." He laid a single sheet on the desk in front of me. "It's a carbon, so you can keep it."

Across the table, Basira lifted her head and gasped. She was staring at the same line I was.

PRESS RELEASE: IAC DIRECTOR ANNOUNCES NEW CALL FOR ASTRONAUTS: WOMEN ENCOURAGED TO APPLY.

Someone shrieked. That was me. I had jumped up and thrown my hands into the air like I was some sort of gymnast. Around the room, the other computers had stopped, pencils frozen mid-equation. They were staring at me, and I didn't care.

"They're taking women astronauts!"

Pencils, laughter, papers, and hurrahs filled the air. My fellow computers jumped up and hugged each other. We were all laughing and crying and it was like the war had just ended again. I grabbed Nathaniel in a hug that left him gasping. He kissed me, bending me over in a dip that defied gravity.

At the door, engineers poked their heads through the door to see what all the hoopla was about. Bubbles bounced into the room. "What in the—?"

"Lady astronauts!" I shouted from my husband's arms. "The lady astronauts are headed for orbit!"

TWENTY-SEVEN

"SUPER-FUEL" TO DRIVE ROCKET
INDEFINITELY IN SPACE

April 18, 1957—A "breakthrough" on the path to
a super-fuel for rockets that will drive themselves in-
definitely with an atomic oxygen captured in the upper
atmosphere was reported last week by Peter H.
Wyckoff, rocket specialist at the Air Force's Sunflower
Research Center. Oxygen in the upper atmosphere
consists of molecular oxygen, each molecule composed
of two atoms of the element. However, in the region
sixty to seventy miles above the Earth, ultraviolet rays
split the molecular oxygen into single atoms. Dr. Wyckoff reported a catalytic agent has been found that would
cause the recombination of the atomic oxygen in the
upper atmosphere into molecular oxygen, such combination resulting in the release of great amounts of
energy.

I had not been to the 99s in months, but the Sunday after
Nathaniel put the draft of the press release on my desk, I
went. And I took applications with me.

Walking across the tarmac to our hangar, the scent of
petrol and black tar whipped around me on the breeze. Such
a strange combination of scents to be nostalgic for.

No one was sitting on the picnic bench outside the hangar, which wasn't surprising, with October's first chill in the air. Nicole's Cadillac was parked near the door, so I knew at least one person was there.

Outside the small door set in the bay doors, I stopped, almost tempted to knock. Then I shook my head and pushed the door open. They were using my plane, and I still contributed to the rent, so it wasn't as if I were a stranger.

I stepped through into laughter that dissipated as I took off my hat.

Pearl looked up from a slice of cake and her gaze widened. "Well, hello, stranger."

Or maybe I *was* a stranger. When Pearl stood, she had an obvious bump which said that her triplets would soon have a new sibling. Or two. I waved, a little sheepish that I hadn't known. "Hi."

Ida Peaks and Imogene Braggs were at the table, along with some women I didn't know. There were more planes in the hangar, too. One of the Mustangs seemed to have made its way over. And a P-38 Lightning—whose was that, and how could I become their best friend?

Nicole had been perched on the end of the table with a cigarette held lazily in one hand. She stood when she saw me, smiling. "It's about damn time."

And Betty . . . she kept her gaze fixed on the table.

But Helen bounced up from the table, grinning like I'd given her the best present. "I was just telling them!"

Of course. Helen had been in the computing department when we got the news. "Well, just remember, it's not public yet. The press release won't go out until Tuesday."

"I won't tell anyone." Betty spoke to the table. "If that's what you're implying."

To respond or not to respond, that is the question.

Whether 'tis nobler to suffer the bait of defensive posturing or to . . . "Hell, I wasn't worried about that. You're good at keeping secrets when you need to."

Nicole stepped between us. "Now, girls . . ." She hurried over and gave me a kiss on the cheek. "I'm so glad you're back. You get me hooked on flying again, then up and vanish. It's too much, really, darling."

"Anyway." I fished in my bag. "I have the applications for the astronaut progr—"

Women surrounded me like a bank of clouds. One minute, clear skies; next, zero visibility except for a flurry of white as the pages were whipped away. The laughter that had been present before I came in resurfaced, bouncing off the walls.

Though not all of the cries were of delight. "Advanced degree?" One woman's shoulders drooped. "I didn't even go to college."

As quickly as they had surrounded me, the women dispersed to fill out their applications. I had already filled mine out. It was sitting in a box on the secretary's desk outside Clemons's office.

Helen had snatched one from my hands, too. She'd seen the announcement, but not the application form. The grin sagged off her face. "A thousand hours in high-performance aircraft with four hundred of that as pilot-in-command? And fifty hours of jet time? How—that not fair. What woman has that?"

I winced. "I do. A lot of the WASPs do."

"Chemistry counts? Oh my God. Oh my God." Ida Peaks bounced on her toes. "I have a master's in chemistry—and I meet all the qualifications. . . . goddamn it. Except for the high-performance aircraft."

Imogene stared at her application as if she were trying to decide whether to kiss it or flush it. "Same . . . I keep thinking about Sarah Coleman and how she was asked to withdraw her application during the war."

"They can't ask us to withdraw if we don't even qualify."

Imogene nodded, still staring at the document. "And the reason that only white women qualify is because of that policy decision about the WASPs. This is an extremely neat way to keep the astronaut corps all-white while pretending that it's open to everyone."

That hadn't even occurred to me. I blinked, trying to decide what to do or say, but before I could get my thoughts in order, Ida snorted.

"Well, that's bullshit. And I bet Dr. King will have things to say about it. Very loud and pointed things." Ida turned back to the table. "I need a pen."

With a flourish, Imogene raised her pen. "Got one right here, and you can have it when I'm finished filling this damn thing out. Fifty hours pilot-in-command of a jet aircraft my aunt Fanny's ass. The spaceships aren't even jet powered, are they, Elma?"

"They're not." I hesitated, not wanting to promise something I couldn't deliver. It had taken this long just to get women even considered. "I'll mention it to Nathaniel and see if he can convince the director to change the requirements. The forms haven't gone out to anyone except you all yet. I think."

From the table, Betty said, "They'll send it out with the press release. Once that happens, it'll be set in stone."

I nodded, lips pressed together. Swallowing my pride, I walked over to the table where she sat and put one of the applications down in front of her. "You have enough flight experience."

"And a master's in journalism. Pretty sure that's not the sort of advanced degree they're looking for."

"It's still worth trying." I slid it toward her. "Right?"

She nodded, but didn't reach for the application. Instead, she shook herself like a dog just out of a pond and reached for her purse. "I've been carrying this around for months, hoping you'd come back. I should have just forwarded it, but . . . I don't know. I think I was afraid you'd throw it out."

Cocking my head, I stared at her as she fumbled around inside her purse. "Why would I throw it out?"

"Because it was from me." She pulled a battered envelope from her bag and put it on the table. "Or, at least, it would have been if I'd forwarded it."

Curious, I picked it up. The return address was from *Life* magazine. Just the name sent a flash of red across my vision with the memory of that anger. She was probably right—I probably would have tossed it if it had come right after the Girl Scout incident.

Betty kept talking, fingers twisting the strap of her bag. "They sent it to me because I was the writer on record. It was addressed to you, but they didn't know where to send it, and . . . I could have just sent it with Helen, I guess."

Inside the *Life* envelope was another one, in better shape, with an unfamiliar looping signature and *Red Gables Home, Red Bank, South Carolina*, as the return address. I sat down.

Betty had opened the interior envelope, but I couldn't find it in myself to care. The curiosity would have been too much for her journalistic heart. I suppose I should be grateful that she didn't try to hide that she'd read it.

The writing was the same looping, unfamiliar hand from the envelope.

Dear. Dr. York,

I am writing on behalf of one of our patients, who saw you on Watch Mr. Wizard. *At the time, she said that you were her great-niece, but called you Anselma Wexler. We assumed that she was confused, as she is quite elderly and not always lucid.*

But when Life *magazine came out, she saw you there, and again referred to you as her niece. In this article, I noticed that Wexler was your maiden name, so I thought it best to reach out on the off chance that you are indeed related to our Miss Wexler—Esther Wexler.*

She had been living with a sister who has since passed away, but to the best of our knowledge has no other living family.

Sincerely yours,
Lorraine Purvis, RN

The page shook in my hand and became impossible to read. I read it again. Aunt Esther was alive?

I pressed my hand to my mouth to try to stop the noise I was making. It was high and thin and rose and fell and I don't even know what to call it but that my aunt was alive and Hershel and I weren't alone and I had to call him and then we could go to Red Bank, South Carolina, and get Aunt Esther and—

"Elma?" Nicole had a hand on my shoulder, then pulled me into an embrace. "Elma, sweetie—there, there . . . shush, now . . . There, there . . ."

"I call Nathaniel." Helen's words helped me catch my breath a little.

"No—no. I'm fine." Or at least that's what I tried to say. Whatever sound I made was enough to stop her, though, and it cut off my keening. I wiped my eyes with both hands, the paper of the letter scraping against my cheeks. "Sorry. That was . . . that was embarrassing."

Nicole kept me in an embrace. "Nonsense. Embarrassing

is spilling wine on His Excellency, the Prince of Monaco, at a state dinner. This was just a moment of being human, and being human isn't embarrassing. Well. Except maybe farting."

I laughed. God. Oh, thank God for Nicole. And then Helen put her lips together and blew out a raspberry. Perhaps my laughter was a little desperate, but at least that breathlessness made sense. Straightening, I wiped my eyes again, leaving streaks of mascara along the sides of my thumb. I must have looked a mess.

"Sorry. It was actually good news. My aunt . . ." I had to take an unsteady breath to be able to continue. "My aunt is alive."

When I pushed the door to our apartment open, Nathaniel was lying on the sofa reading a report. He lowered it, smiling. "You're home ear—" He sat up, pages dropping all over the floor. "What's wrong?"

Five different sentences competed for priority. What won was perhaps the least helpful. "I need to make a phone call."

Fortunately, Nicole had followed me upstairs after driving me home. She rested a hand on my shoulder. "Everything's okay, but Elma had a bit of a shock."

Right. I needed to give Nathaniel context, or he would only worry more. "Betty got a letter from the *Life* magazine article, only it was for me, and—" I shook my head. None of that mattered. "Aunt Esther is alive."

"Oh my God." Nathaniel crossed the room and pulled me into his arms. "That is wonderful."

I sagged into his chest, and the weight of Nicole's hand left my shoulder. Behind me, the door closed with a quiet click. Nathaniel rocked me in his arms and let me cry out the past five years of grief.

I'd thought Hershel and I were alone. And yes, there was some small part of my brain that wondered: if Aunt Esther had survived, then who else might have? Maybe my parents were alive? But some of the tears came from knowing that they weren't. That no one who lived within fifty miles of Washington had survived. But, oh—we had an aunt again.

Sniffling, I pulled back, wiping my eyes for the umpteenth time that day. I fished in my bag to pull out the letter. "I'm going to call the nursing home."

I had made so many compromises with myself to find happiness. I had sat shiva and gone through the entire mourning process for my family. I had put them in a box and buried them in my memories, in lieu of the earth. This exhumed them, and left a raw scar in the ground of my mind.

But it was a time of great joy, too.

Nathaniel's eyes were red. He gave a lopsided half-smile. "Well . . . if there's ever been a time to say l'chaim . . ."

L'chaim. To life.

Stepping back, he cleared the path from me to the phone. "Do you want me to go out, or . . . ?"

"Don't you dare." Walking to the phone took an unreasonable amount of energy, like escaping the gravity well of grief. "I'll need someone to hand me tissues."

"Tissues, check. Confirmed tissues are Go."

Snorting, I sat down on the sofa and reached for the phone. The number of the Red Gables nursing home was on the letterhead. Two letters and five numbers later, the phone was ringing.

"Good afternoon, Red Gables Home." The voice on the other end of the line was the soft mellifluous stream of a native Southerner.

I felt the shape of my words shift to match hers. "Yes. Could you please connect me with one of your residents? Esther Wexler?"

"I'm sorry, Miss Wexler is at dinner now."

I'd half expected her to say "dead." Clearing my throat, I picked up one of the papers that Nathaniel had dropped. "May I leave a message, then?" The page had a preliminary trajectory for a launch from Brazil. "This is her niece. I—"

"Dr. York?"

"Um. Yes."

"This is Lorraine Purvis. I wrote to you." She gave a little laugh. "Lord. I can't believe you're really her niece. We just . . . Well. She just gets so confused sometimes. Sweet as anything, but . . . Listen, why don't you hold on for just a minute and I'll go get her."

"Oh, I don't want to be any trouble."

"It's fine. I won't pull her out of the dining room if she's still eating. Be right back." The phone clunked against a desk or counter and I could hear her footsteps tapping away in the distance.

Nathaniel had moved across our studio to the kitchen and was taking the dishes out of the drying rack. The plates clattered against each other as he put them away in the cupboard. Cleaning was probably a good way to distract myself. I reached down to pick up the rest of the papers Nathaniel had dropped.

The report had pages covered with equations in Helen's handwriting. Stacking them, it was hard not to look over the calculations. As a sign of how disordered my mind was, it took me a moment to recognize them as orbital trajectories for Brazil, Kenya, and Indonesia.

All three spots were equatorial and had lower fuel consumption than anywhere in the United States or Europe. And all three had eastern coasts, which would be nice, since it meant that a failed rocket would drop into water instead of—

The phone rustled and clattered as someone picked it up. "Dr. York?"

"Yes."

"One moment, I have your aunt here."

"Thank you." I set the pages down on the coffee table and closed my eyes, waiting.

The phone rustled, then a voice like an aged and beloved canary flitted through the line. "Anselma?"

"Aunt Esther." My voice cracked and the room blurred behind yet another veil of maddening tears. It was like hearing a ghost. What do you say to someone you thought was dead? For that matter, she must have thought the same of me until she saw me on *Mr. Wizard*. What came out of my mouth was a banal and safe social noise. "How are you?"

"Well . . . well, well, well. As I live and breathe. Isn't it wonderful to hear your voice."

"I'm sorry. I only just got the letter. I didn't know."

"Lands, child, I didn't know you were alive, either. After Rose and I got out of Charleston, well—I thought it was just the two of us."

It was good that there was a phone line between us. At the sound of my grandmother's name, I had to move the phone away from my mouth and cover it for a moment. She had lived. When I read the letter—*She had been living with a sister, who has since passed away*—I hadn't known which sister.

Goddamn it. My grandmother had survived the tidal waves that swamped Charleston, and I had done nothing to find her.

TWENTY-EIGHT

ASTRONAUTS SUFFER BONE LOSS

Special to The National Times.

KANSAS CITY, KS, April 18, 1957—The medical report on the astronauts who recently spent 43 days aboard the *Lunetta* orbiting space platform illustrated how their organisms responded to the unprecedented conditions of prolonged life in space. The astronauts were found, for example, to have about 14 percent fewer red cells in their blood when they returned. Projecting the impact of such changes on future astronauts coming back after a long stay in space suggests that these returnees could become instant invalids on Earth. One goal of *Lunetta* will be to see whether increased exercise in space slows down these adjustments so that future spacemen can become earthmen again with minimal trouble.

When I put the phone down, Nathaniel looked up from the newspaper he had been reading. He'd long since finished putting the dishes away.

"That sounded like a good phone call."

"She's doing well." Standing, I rubbed my forehead, still a little shocked. "But I don't think she's happy there. I was thinking . . ."

"You want her to move in with us?" He lowered the

paper and leaned back in his chair. "What about going to live with Hershel?"

I shrugged, crossing to join him at the table. "Sure. She could. But he already has two kids, and I don't know that they need another mouth to feed."

He grunted and drummed his fingers on the table. "We'd need a bigger place . . . and I'm willing to do that . . ."

"But?" The studio was fine for the two of us, but adding a third really would be too much.

"We can't afford a house yet, and paying more in rent for a larger place . . ." He spread his hands, trying not to call attention to the fact that we'd spent our savings to cover the damage to the plane in the air show. "It's something to think about."

"Housing prices have come down. We haven't really looked for a place in a while, and there are those new subdivisions out by the Sunflower facility."

"It's not just . . . My hesitation isn't just about the space. If the IAC is moving the launch facilities to Brazil, then that might not be a good choice for Aunt Esther." Nathaniel shrugged. "I mean, I could continue to work at Sunflower doing designs. For a while anyway."

"Oh." I gnawed the inside of my lip, thinking. "Well, we aren't likely to make that move for at least a year while they do construction. Right?"

"More likely two, since we still have to pick the site." Nathaniel sat forward in his chair and took my hand. "But if you're accepted as an astronaut, then . . . I know what their training schedule is like. Is that going to be fair to her?"

"You think I should leave her in a nursing home?" I'd just found my aunt again, and now he expected me to leave her with strangers?

"God, no." He ran his free hand over his hair. "But if Hershel is willing to take her in, that might be a better choice in the long run. We don't have to make any decisions now, but it's worth thinking about."

Two weeks after I spoke with my aunt. Two weeks after I called Hershel to let him know that she was alive. Two weeks later, I was on the phone with my brother again, holding another letter in my shaking hand.

I had taken a Miltown, but that only slowed my heart from a gallop to a trot.

"National Weather Center, Hershel Wexler speaking."

"Hey, it's Elma . . . Have you got a minute?" The black plastic of the phone trapped sweat in my palm.

"What's wrong?" Through the receiver, I could hear the sound of his office door shutting.

"I was just invited to move into the first round of testing for the astronaut program." The letter still shook in my hand. I'd somehow thought that they would tell me at work, but I'd gotten a form letter along with . . . I didn't know how many other women.

"Mazel tov! Wait until I tell Rachel. She's going to be . . . over the *moon*."

I groaned at the joke. "You are the worst."

"Seriously, though, I'm so proud of you. When do you go in?"

"Well, that's the problem." I finally sat down on the sofa and put the letter on the coffee table in front of me. "It's the week we're scheduled to go visit Aunt Esther. And it's five full days of testing."

"Oh." Hershel shuffled some papers on his desk. He sighed. "Well, let me see if I can change my vacation request."

"I'm sorry." I twisted the cord in my hand.

"Or . . . there's really no reason for us both to go. You could do the testing and then come out to visit once we've got her settled."

The room seemed to get colder. "I thought—I thought we were going to decide that once we saw her in person. You know. And talked to the nursing staff about what she needed?"

Hershel laughed in my ear. "Yeah. Well . . . at that point the concern had been your schedule, not whether you were on the planet."

"We don't know that I'm going to get in."

"Please. Elma. They'd be idiots not to hire you, for publicity reasons, if nothing else."

"That's not how the space agency works." Everything about the space program was complex and dangerous. There's no way they would fly someone unqualified just for publicity reasons—at least not until things were established. "Everyone who goes up now has to be able to work. Who knows what testing will show?"

"Right. Uh-huh. You'll owe me the newest *Blackhawk* comic if I'm right. Which I am." My big brother could sound so cocksure sometimes. "And you also needed time to find a new place, right? That's why we were waiting until next month."

"Yes . . ." The newspaper lay across the room on the kitchen table, still folded in a tidy bundle. Nathaniel and I would have to go through the classified ads tonight.

"Do you really want to be house-shopping and moving while preparing for these tests?"

Why did he have to be right? I leaned forward to rest my elbow on my knee and rubbed my forehead. Parker, after all, had said he'd make sure I never saw space, so maybe I should focus on what I could do for my family. "Maybe that's not where my priority should be. I mean . . . shouldn't I be planning for what I can control, instead of some random thing that might happen?"

"Elma." I could imagine Hershel glaring over the rim of

his glasses at me. He'd confessed once that he actually couldn't see that way, but it looked fairly intimidating. "You are not going to be happy unless you try for this."

"But what if I don't get in?"

He laughed at me. "If you don't get in, I'll buy you a subscription to *Mystery in Space*."

"Good. I'll need it to drown my sorrows."

"Look . . . The flight will have to do a layover somewhere. Why don't I see if I can find a route through Kansas City? Aunt Esther will probably need to rest anyway, so we can spend the night, and you can see her. Hm?"

"Gee. You mean it?" His ability to reduce me to a kid again is remarkable. And my hands had stopped shaking, to boot. "Maybe you'll even be here for a rocket launch."

A living aunt and making the first cut in the astronaut application process . . . When I went to work the next day, I was still vibrating with joy. Even the linoleum of the IAC seemed brighter.

Before we went down our separate hallways, Nathaniel leaned in to kiss my cheek. "Careful. You're going to blind someone with that smile."

"Don't worry. It'll go away as soon as I see what your engineers have mucked up this time."

He laughed and gave my hand a squeeze before sauntering down to his office.

Even from down the hall, the computer department had the hum of morning arrival, the air chirping with bright conversation full of recipe exchanges and compliments on dresses. Once we started working, it became all math and slide rules and the rattle of the Friden calculator. Lately there was the occasional curse as the IBM overheated. Again.

When I rounded the corner into the room, Basira was sitting on our shared desk waving her hands in the air as if she were conducting a symphony. ". . . chandeliers everywhere. I had no idea. And the singing! Oh, they were wonderful."

Myrtle shook her head. "Gee. All we did was go bowling. It was our league night."

"What's going on?" I set my bag on the desk and began working at the buttons on my coat. As much as I wanted to blurt out that I'd been selected for the first round of testing, Basira had the floor.

"Hank took me over to the Missouri side to see a show last night." She clapped her hands. "It was to die for. The Midland Theater—it was as if someone said, 'Could we put more decoration here?' and then answered 'yes' every time. Even the toilets were ornamented."

I shrugged out of my coat, resolutely not saying that I'd made the first cut. "I can't think of the last time we went to a show."

"Well, if you get a chance—" She broke off, looking past me. "Geez, Helen. Are you okay?"

"Just allergies." Helen waved her hand with a smile, but her eyes were red and swollen. Her shoulders drooped. Her voice had a rough burr.

Oh hell. She hadn't made the cut.

I did not announce at work that I'd made the first cut, but at the 99s? Well . . . I wouldn't be able to avoid the topic there. When Sunday rolled around, I went out to the airfield with the letter in my bag. I still wasn't comfortable around Betty. True, she had reunited me with my aunt, but she'd carried the letter around for months. She could have given it to Helen or Nicole to deliver, so once again, I felt like she was manipulating and using me.

Pearl had brought a pound cake, which was sitting in the middle of the table inside the hangar. Ida and Imogene huddled inside their coats. Nicole had taken off one glove to eat cake. Even with the doors closed, my breath frosted white until I got right next to the table and the tiny space heater under it. My ankles scorched while my fingers froze.

"Ooo! Cake." Brilliant conversationalist, I know. It was that or talk about how big Pearl was getting. If she wasn't carrying twins, I'd be stunned.

"I was just in a baking mood, I guess." She rubbed her stomach with one hand.

Nicole looked at the clock. "Just missing Helen . . ."

As if that had summoned her, the door to the hangar opened with a bang. Helen stood in the door with a bag over her shoulder. She came in, slamming it behind her. At least she wasn't sad anymore?

She looked at me, then the rest of the group. "My application was rejected."

"Mine too." Ida raised her hand. "Not that it surprises anyone."

I cleared my throat. "I'm in."

"Me too." Nicole set her cake down, brushing the crumbs off her skirt.

Imogene shook her head. "Rejected due to insufficient experience with jet engines."

"They took me." Betty shifted to look at Pearl. "What about you?"

"I didn't apply." She ran her hand over the arc of her stomach. "We'll wait until the colony is established and then see."

The silence in the hangar grew palpable. Outside, the buzz of airplanes said that the world continued on, but in here, something had broken. Even though we were all bunched together around the table, a jagged line ran through our group. Having some in and some not was bad enough, but the racial lines were so clear.

Helen broke the silence and upended her bag on the table. Manuals and textbooks flopped open. I caught one as it slid toward the edge of the table. It was a manual for a T-33. From the pile, Helen pulled out a steno pad. "These are the airfields with jet planes."

"But the deadline has passed . . ." Nicole shook her head. "I mean, it's terrible, but what can you do?"

"I can be ready next time." Helen glared at her, then turned her attention to Ida and Imogene. The ferocity in her stance reminded me that she was a champion chess player. "You too."

Leaning forward, Ida picked up a manual and flipped through it. "Sounds like we've got some flying to do."

"And some letters to write." Imogene turned to Betty. "You gonna publicize this as well?"

"I don't know . . ."

Imogene had perfected the art of the raised eyebrow. She added in a pursed lip, and the disappointment cracked off of her like a whip.

Betty raised her hands, palms out in a conciliatory motion. "I just have to figure out the angle."

"How about 'Racists Running Astronaut Selection'?" Imogene grabbed the knife from the table and nearly stabbed the cake. "Dr. King is going to have a field day with this. Bet all the candidates are white."

"I can . . ." I stopped and cleared my throat. Was I really about to offer this? "Would it help if you had a list of who got in?"

Ida nodded and broke off a piece of her cake. "It would. And don't worry, Betty, we've got black papers that are going to be more than happy to run this story. They won't have any trouble understanding the 'angle.'"

TWENTY-NINE

**LUNETTA ORBITING PLATFORM
POISED TO SET NEW RECORD**

KANSAS CITY, KS, April 26, 1957—Tomorrow morning, if all goes as scheduled, the three astronauts of the *Lunetta* 2 crew will blast off for a record 59-day mission in the orbiting international station in space. Successful completion of the astronauts' assignment will represent another milestone passed toward attaining the capability for long-term manned spaceflight, whether in orbit, as with *Lunetta,* or on some future crew's flight toward Mars, Venus, or Jupiter.

On Monday, most of my morning went to helping Bubbles with data from his latest engine tests. He bounced on his toes as he leaned over the desk. Across from me, Basira had her lower lip firmly clamped between her teeth and a smile tugging at the corners of her mouth. His enthusiasm was just so . . . enthused.

"All right, Bubbles . . . The amount of thrust is consistent." I slid the sheet of calculations over to him. "Even with a payload, you would only need two stages instead of three to get to orbit."

"I knew it!" He punched the air, tie flapping. "Launch-pad, here we come!"

I cleared my throat. "On *paper* the Sirius is ready. But that's Dr. York's call."

He grinned. "You're Dr. York too."

Rolling my eyes, I shook my head. "You know which one I mean . . . I'm just a computer, he's the lead engineer." That said, the engine tests had been very consistent, and it was the most stable fuel structure I'd seen come through our department. This had the potential to be a game changer for the moon missions because it would consume fewer resources. More importantly, a two-stage launch process meant less opportunity for failure. "Go on. Show him."

He picked up the pages, shrugging. "Ah. He and the director are off-site right now. But when he comes back, for certain! Thanks!"

Of all the engineers, Bubbles was probably my favorite. He bounced out of the room, paper and tie fluttering with each step.

Basira gave up her battle with laughter and bent forward to bury her face in her arms. "Does he end every sentence with an exclamation point?"

"I heard one question mark in there." There were at least three other computation requests on my desk that I needed to work through. Ah . . . the glamorous life of a computer. "It's a really lovely engine, though. At least on paper."

Helen pushed back from her desk and came over to ours. "He said the director is off-site?"

My skin prickled with unease. Crap. We'd talked about this at the 99s. "Right . . . I think it's a visit to Lockheed-Martin to look at the command capsule for the moon landing."

"I guess that'll take the rest of the day, huh?"

"Probably." I stood up and stretched as casually as I

could. It's a good thing that the fate of our nation didn't depend on Helen's or my espionage skills. We were about as subtle as a cat in heat. "Be back in a bit. I'm going to visit the powder room."

Nodding, Helen went back to her desk and picked up a pencil, as if she'd never stopped working on equations. Myrtle looked between us with some confusion, but thankfully didn't ask what we were up to.

I headed out, skipping the ladies' room in favor of Clemons's office. Though Helen and I both had access to the same areas of the IAC base, I had less risk than she did. With Nathaniel working here, I could always claim to be on an errand from him. She would probably be fired, which would mean getting sent back to Taiwan.

The door to Clemons's outer office stood open, as usual, and the sound of typing popped out of the room in staccato bursts. Mrs. Kare sat behind her desk, copying over a report. At least three layers of carbons filled out the pages.

She smiled, fingers still moving. "Well, hello, Dr. York. What can I help you with?"

"I need a copy of the astronaut candidates list." Bluffing, as if this were totally something I should have, seemed safer than trying to dig through her filing cabinets.

"Oh . . . I wish I could help you, but I just sent all of that over to Stetson Parker's office." She brightened. "You might check over there."

"Thanks. I'll do that." Of course the head astronaut would have some involvement over was chosen. He must have been livid when Clemons made the decision to add women to the roster. And why had he let me on the list, after he'd sworn to keep me grounded? Waving, I backed out of Clemons's office and headed down the hall. Now I steered into the bathroom. Stepping into one of the stalls,

I locked the door and leaned against the cool metal partition until my heart slowed down.

I wanted to help Ida, and Imogene, and Helen, and whoever else had been knocked out of the running, but Parker hated me. I had to be on the list against his wishes, and going to his office would be the least inconspicuous thing I could do.

That left the tests . . . I'd be able to find out who was there at the tests.

On Monday, May 13, 1957, at 9 a.m., I showed up at the testing facility, which was not on the IAC campus but at a military testing facility at Fort Leavenworth. It was a pre-Meteor building with huge windows set in redbrick walls. At the front desk, they checked me in and then gave me a medical bracelet with the number 378 written on it.

"That's a lot of women," I joked, trying to get an opening to look at the list. "Anyone I know?"

The receptionist shook her head. "There's only thirty-four of you. That was your number in the application stage."

Even with a mission, my jaw fell open a little as the scope of the operation became clear. They'd already discarded . . . who knew how many applications . . . and I'd made that cut. Only thirty-four in, though . . . At least that would make collecting the names easier. "I'll get out of your way, then."

"Down the hall and to the left." She had already returned to her ledger, leaving me to my own devices.

Down the hall and to the left led me past a line of women. All of them white. Would I have noticed, if not for Ida and Imogene joining the 99s? Probably not. As I walked down the line, Nicole leaned out to wave at me.

I paused next to her. "Fancy meeting you here. Anyone else we know?"

"I've seen Betty, Jerrie Coleman, and Jackie Cochran, but I haven't been keeping a list. It's not all white people, though." She shrugged, and the fabric of her dress rippled with the movement. It was a navy blue dress that had a white collar to seem serious and a tightly girdled waist to seem . . . we'll say "approachable." She pointed farther down the line. "See? Maggie is here."

"Oh, yeah." Six or seven places back stood a lone Chinese woman. Maggie Gee had been a WASP during the war. She and I didn't really know each other, but she had been one of two Chinese women there, so hard to miss. I waved as I headed to the rear of the line, but I don't think she recognized me.

Around us, women circulated in a susurration of crinoline and starched cotton. Not a single one was black. And the longer I stood there, the clearer it became that Maggie was the only person who wasn't white.

Pulling a notepad out of my purse, I jotted down the names of everyone I recognized. Fifteen or so had been WASPs, even if I didn't remember all of their names.

I stood there, heels aching, as we all waited. I attempted small talk with the woman behind me—Francesca Gurrieri, from Italy—but our silences were filled with wondering what would happen. The line ended at a pair of double doors. Periodically, a woman would emerge and we would shuffle forward.

I tried to make guesses about what was happening inside based on the way they came out, but all I could really tell was that some people had done well—they walked with shoulders back and chins held up. If anyone ever forgot that these women were all pilots, all you had to do was look at the cocky edge in their stride.

Sabiha Gökçen sauntered out of the doors. I jotted her name down on my list and then did a double take.

She was wearing a pantsuit and tennis shoes. Darn it. That was brilliant. I'd fallen into the trap of trying to present myself well, but they were looking for pilots, not ladies.

It would be all right. I smoothed the wool of my skirt and took a breath. Most of the other women were also in skirts, and it didn't seem to make a difference to the way they came out of the double doors.

Nicole vanished inside along with four other women. I shuffled forward.

I was beginning to regret not taking a Miltown that morning, but the drug slowed my thoughts just enough that I hadn't wanted to chance it. I didn't think they would ask us to do any flying, but there might be a simulator. All this waiting, though . . . it did make a girl's stomach flip over.

Nicole came out smiling and strode straight down the hall to me. She leaned in. "This part's a cake walk. It's just blood tests and blowing in tubes—like the screening they did when we applied to be WASPs."

I let out a breath. "It would have been nice if they'd told us."

"I suspect they're trying to see how people do under pressure." She winked. "Got an ace up my sleeve there."

My eyes widened, then I managed a laugh. She'd taken a Miltown? "I guess being a senator's wife makes you a little immune."

"That's exactly what I meant. And now . . . I'm off to take a written test on the second floor." She rested a hand on my arm. "You'll do great."

After she left, I went back to shuffling forward until it was my turn through the double doors and into a stark white-and-chrome ward filled with nurses in equally stark white uniforms.

The nurse assigned to me got me settled on a chair next

to a low enameled cart. She was a brisk white woman in her mid-fifties with steel gray hair tucked up under her nurse's cap. Her name tag said "Mrs. Rhode." "Now, Mrs. York, we're just going to draw a little blood."

"Of course." It made me glad I'd opted for a sweater set, since that made my arms easy to access. I pulled off the cardigan. "The veins on my left arm are easier."

Mrs. Rhode raised an eyebrow. "Medical background?"

"My mother was a doctor in the first war." I held out my arm so she could wrap a rubber cord around it.

"That explains—oh!" She sprang up, moving past me to the woman on my other side.

The nurse attending the woman was trying to keep her from slumping to the ground. Mrs. Rhode grabbed her other arm. It was the woman who'd been standing behind me in the line. Her face was pale as a cloud bank, and almost that damp. They got her propped back up in the chair.

"I hadn't even stuck her yet." The other nurse shook her head, feeling for the woman's pulse.

Mrs. Rhode shrugged. "Saves us time." She turned and waved for an orderly to come over. "When she can stand, escort her to the waiting room and make sure she's okay before discharging her."

I shivered. Just like that. It wasn't as if the astronauts needed to do blood draws in space, but that little bit of a weakness and she was out.

Maybe I should have taken a Miltown that morning. Or maybe it was best that I didn't. I could second guess for days. All I knew was that I was not going to faint over a needle. At least I had that.

My nurse came back to me, brushing her hands off. "Sorry about that."

"It's quite all right." I turned my chair so the woman who had fainted was outside my line of sight. She must be mortified. The least I could do was try to minimize her embarrassment by pretending not to have noticed.

Mrs. Rhode had good technique with the needle, and I barely felt it go in, past the initial sting. The glistening steel tube stuck out of my arm like someone had welded a fuselage to me.

Was it completely necessary for me to watch her? No. But I wanted to be sure she knew I wasn't afraid. "You must be fatigued, with all of us to go through."

She shrugged. "It's better than the men. Ever tried taking a medical history from a pilot? They've apparently never been ill and were born through immaculate conception."

I laughed. It was shockingly loud. "You know we're all pilots, right?"

"Yeah." She pulled the tube of blood off the needle and capped it. "But they were all indoctrinated with the fact that an illness would get them grounded."

"Ah . . . the brass didn't pay as much attention to the WASPs." I took the gauze she handed me and pressed it against the crook of my elbow when she withdrew the needle. "So . . . what's next?"

"Just a few questions." She jotted my name on the vial of blood and stuck it in a tray. Picking up a clipboard from the low cart, she pulled a pen from her uniform pocket.

The questions were all standard and dull. My last period. History of illness. Pregnancies. Allergies.

"What medications are you currently taking?"

That one stopped me. I hadn't taken a Miltown this morning, and even when I did, it wasn't really for an illness. That's what she was trying to find out about, right?

"Mrs. York?"

"Does aspirin count? Or vitamin C?" I chewed my lower lip, trying to make it look like I wasn't being a Pilot with a capital P. But goddamn it, I wasn't going to let my anxiety ground me. "And there's Dristan when I can't shake a cough."

She shook her head. "I just need to know about things you take on a regular basis."

"Oh. Well, there's nothing, then." And that was true. Right?

The second day, I wore a pants suit and tennis shoes. Entering the hospital lobby, it became clear that I was not the only one to change their wardrobe strategy. Once I checked in, the receptionist directed me to a lobby on the second floor.

This room had wooden chairs lining the walls and another row, back to back, down the center. A single ivy plant struggled in the corner near the window, as if it could escape the bland white walls. The chairs were occupied by more women in trousers than I'd previously seen in my life.

Nicole spotted me and waved me over. She sat with Betty and two other women I hadn't met yet: Irene Leverton, a rancher's daughter, and Sarah Gorelick, a mother of eight.

Sarah laughed at what must have been a priceless look on my face. "I get that all the time. The way I figure it, if I can survive eight children, space is nothing."

Nicole leaned forward to put a hand on my arm. "Did you hear? They've eliminated three of us already."

"I know one woman fainted."

"Plus another for anemia, and . . . they say that Maggie had a heart murmur." She arched an eyebrow suggestively.

Maggie, the only Chinese candidate, just "happened" to have a previously undiagnosed heart murmur. Ida would be livid when I told her tonight.

An orderly with a clipboard appeared at the entrance to the lobby. "York, Coleman, Hurrle, and Steadman."

"See you later." I waved the little group a cheery farewell and joined the other three women. The orderly led us down a hall and dropped us each off at a different room. Mine was a small room, with an examination chair, as if for an eye doctor.

It smelled of sweat, and a tinge of vomit. I suddenly became very glad that I'd spent the last month exercising to get ready for this. Which led me to wonder where Hershel was right now. He should be arriving in South Carolina to meet Aunt Esther soon.

Mrs. Rhode, the nurse from the day before, gestured me over to the chair.

Did Aunt Esther look the same? She had sounded the same, certainly, but how had the five years since the Meteor treated her? Wait—Mrs. Rhode had just said something. "Sorry?"

"I need you to take your shirt off so we can monitor your heart."

"Oh—" The orderly had left the room so we were, in fact, the only people here. I fumbled with the top button of my blouse. "Of course."

As she pasted discs to my chest, her hands were cold. Goosebumps rose on my arms, and I had to fight not to cross them over my chest. With wires trailing over to one of the machines, I settled into the chair. The cold metal stung my back, which really wasn't used to being exposed like this.

"All right, Mrs. York. I want you to keep your eyes open for this procedure. Tell me about how you met your husband, and be sure to keep talking for the next five minutes." Behind me, metal clanked against metal. "No matter what, keep talking and keep your eyes open."

"All right . . . I met Nathaniel three times before we started seeing each other—" Something cold brushed my

ear. "The first time was at Stanford. I was assigned to tutor his roommate in—ohmygod what—"

Freezing liquid filled my right ear, and my equilibrium
was suddenly gone. The room spun around me in frantic
circles. I clenched the seat of the chair with both hands.
Eyes open. Keep talking.

"Tutor . . . I was assigned to tutor his roommate in math.
Differential equations. But the fellow wasn't always there
when I came and . . . and . . ."

This was worse than being in a tailspin. There, at least,
you could do something to pull out of the spin.

". . . and so Nathaniel and I would talk. A little. About
rockets, mostly. The next semester, his roommate had a different roommate." God, I was barely making any sense. "I
didn't see him—Nathaniel. I didn't see Nathaniel again
until the war. I was a WASP. I ferried some planes and did
some training in New Mexico. He was there. He remembered me. I was less shy. We talked about rockets again."

I couldn't get my eyes to focus. Even keeping them open
took effort as the room whipped around me.

"The third time was Langley, at NACA. I was visiting
with my father—I mean, my father took me with him
to visit NACA. Nathaniel was there. We talked about
rockets. And he asked me a question about trajectories. I
answered . . ."

The edges of the chair dug into my fingers as I fought
to stay in my seat. Had other women fallen out? Had the
men?

"I answered and he offered me a job. He shouldn't
have—I mean. Computers weren't his department. Engineer. He was the lead engineer."

They'd done this to Stetson Parker. Whatever she'd
stuck in my ear was something that had happened to Stetson Parker. The one thing I knew for certain about the test-

ing was that we were being subjected to the exact same tests as the men. If he could survive this, so could I.

"He later said that he had wanted me for the engineering department, but then he couldn't have asked me out."

The doorknob had a beam of light shining on it. I fixed my gaze on that and tried to let the room swing around that point. It helped. A little.

"It never occurred to me that a woman could be an engineer, and the computer department was all women, so that seemed like a natural fit. I was there for two months when he asked me to go to the Christmas party with him. I told him I was Jewish. It turned out that he was too, but it was the company party, so—"

Mrs. Rhode stepped in front of me and clicked a stopwatch. "Very good, Mrs. York. Four minutes, thirty-eight seconds. That's quite good. You may close your eyes now."

The darkness was a welcome relief. The room still spun, but not as badly.

"What was that?"

"Super-chilled water to freeze your inner ear. It's an equilibrium test to see how well you can function when unbalanced. We look to see when your eyes stop rolling as a sign that you've gained a measure of control."

"And I could only focus after four minutes and thirty-eight seconds?" In a plane, it would have killed me if it had taken me that long to pull it together.

"Yes, but you were able to function the entire time. You may put your shirt on, but we'll leave the heart monitors in place for the next test." Something cloth, presumably my shirt, landed in my lap. "And thank you for not vomiting."

The rest of the day followed similar baffling and unpleasant lines.

There was a table that they strapped you to, turned you upside down for five minutes, and then jerked it upright to see if you'd faint from the sudden change in orientation. A treadmill that rose at a steady rate as you ran to simulate a run up a mountain.

There were other examinations, some of them less dignified than a trip to the gynecologist, which is saying something.

When I was sweaty, tired, and annoyed, they gave me written tests about orbital mechanics. With each round, there were fewer and fewer of us. Some hadn't been able to get through a crucial part of the testing—I nearly didn't make it through the run "uphill"—and other women changed their minds. Those of us who stayed, though, had an odd mix of camaraderie and fierce competitiveness. We were, after all, pilots.

THIRTY

34 WOMEN TOOK ASTRONAUT TESTS

KANSAS CITY, KS, May 16, 1957—(AP)—
Thirty-four women were chosen to undergo a preliminary testing program to be Lunar Astronauts. All 34
are airplane pilots and their ages range from 23 to 38.
These beauties range from blond to brunette and are
among the best feminine specimens on the planet.

By day four, there were just twenty-one of us left. Betty
and Nicole were still in the running, as was Sabiha. Sometimes we were in the same testing room, other times it was
a solo ordeal like the inner ear test.

After I endured the joys of having a metal cup pressed
against my eyeball to test for glaucoma, I walked into an
interview room. Stetson Parker sat at a table, flanked on
one side by Benkoski and the other by Director Clemons.

"Bloody hell." Clemons threw his pen down on the table.
"We don't really need to interview her, do we?"

Thank God I was already sweaty from the treadmill earlier, because it masked the cold sweat that broke out of
every pore. "I know that I've tried your patience, but—"

Clemons waved his hand and I stopped talking out of
habit. He picked up his pen again and aimed it at me. "You
misunderstand. We are supposed to see if the candidates

have the drive an astronaut needs. That is hardly a question with you."

"Oh." I looked back at the door. "Should I . . . should I send in the next person?"

"No . . ." Parker leaned back in his chair. "I think we should do this right, so no one can accuse us of favoritism later. Why don't you sit down, Mrs. York, and tell us why you want to be an astronaut."

Favoritism. Ha. But I sat down in the chair facing the men and rested my hands on my knees with my ankles crossed, the way Mama had taught me. Don't ask me why I wanted to sit like a lady when I was wearing rumpled pants and a sweat-dampened shirt. It might just have been the only armor I owned.

For once, I was glad for all the interviews that I had done, because this was a question that I had answered over and again. "Why do I want to be an astronaut? Because I believe that women have a necessary role in establishing colonies on other planets. If we have—"

"I'm not interested in your speeches." Parker sat upright with a thump. "If I wanted those, I could read a magazine."

"Colonel Parker!" Clemons glared at him. "This is not how we treat candidates."

"We all know why she thinks *women* should go into space." He turned to face me again. "I want to know why you, specifically you, want to be an astronaut. And why you want to do that *now,* at this stage of the program."

I stared at him. I didn't have an answer. Or at least not one that I could articulate. I just wanted to, in the same way I wanted to fly. I discarded the truth—which was that I didn't really know—and instead reached for answers like the ones that I'd seen the astronauts give in interviews. "I feel that it's my duty to—"

"To serve your country . . . That's the answer someone

gives to the press corps." Parker shook his head. Neither of the other two men stepped in this time.

All three men stared at me, waiting.

I closed my eyes and took a deep breath. If I could talk to Congress or appear on national television, I could answer these men. "I don't remember a time when flying wasn't a part of my life. My father was a pilot. I used to beg him to do barrel rolls when I was little because I loved the way the earth spread out below us and gravity didn't seem to matter . . ."

I opened my eyes, but still stared at the polished linoleum floors as I felt my way through my answer. "Space seems . . . I'm a pilot, you know? Space seems . . . necessary. Or inevitable. Or . . ." I spread my hands, struggling to find words I was willing to say to them about how I *yearned* to go there. "Maybe it was all the science-fiction novels and comic books my dad gave me, but the idea of not going into space seems more impossible than anything else. Even if the Earth weren't damaged, I'd still want to go."

Benkoski gave a little grunt, his pencil scratching on a form. Clemons had his arms crossed over his chest and his lips pursed as if he were holding a cigar.

And Parker was nodding.

God help me, the man who had said he would keep me grounded was nodding as if he understood. Then he shrugged and picked a notebook off the table. "What's the reliability data on the Atlas booster?"

"Um . . ." The sudden shift in topic left me a little startled. "Fewer than nine out of ten Atlas launches were successful. That's why we moved to the Jupiter design."

Clemons kept his arms crossed over his chest while Benkoski jotted down my response.

"What are the advantages of pressure carburetors over float carburetors?"

"Pressure carburetors are less likely to exhibit carb icing, which can initially lead to the engine running more rich, but will eventually restrict the airflow and cause a complete blockage. And they provide a stable fuel-air ratio under negative-G conditions, such as a rapid dive or inverted flight." It is astonishing how much more comfortable I am with technical questions than personal ones.

From then on, the interview was almost simple.

When Hershel asked for a hotel recommendation, I sent him to the Aladdin, which is where Nathaniel and I had stayed after the bomb threat. Its lobby had a second-floor balcony with a martini bar. The balcony was supported by black marble pillars, and the gilding on the railings and at the top of the columns gave a pre-Meteor golden-age elegance to the place.

As appealing as the martini bar was, after surviving five days of testing, it was probably not a good plan to drink before meeting Aunt Esther. Maybe after that I would have all the martinis they could make.

We made our way through the lobby and back to the restaurant attached to the rear of the hotel. It was intimate, with pretensions of elegance. When we'd been here before, the food had been solid, if uninspired.

The maître d' glided forward to meet us, menus in hand. "Two this evening?"

Across the room, Hershel leaned out from a booth and waved.

Nathaniel shook his head. "No, thank you. We're meeting someone."

He may have said other things, but I was already past him and hurrying between the rows of tables. Hershel had grabbed his crutches and was pushing up to his feet as I got close. He'd brought Tommy with him, and he looked every inch the young man. He wore his dinner jacket from the bar mitzvah and had his hair slicked down with Brylcreem.

Hershel braced himself on one crutch and held out an arm for an embrace. I hugged him, suddenly shy about greeting the poof of white hair I'd passed. He gave me a good solid squeeze and murmured. "You look beat."

"Good to see you too." I thumped his back before releasing him and facing my aunt.

She beamed up at me with the strong Wexler stamp from my father's side of the family. I don't know why Aunt Esther never married, but she had a sort of kittenish charm, even over ninety. Her white curls had been pinned into place in a style held over from the 1880s. There was powder caught in the wrinkles on her cheeks, but her eyes were as bright as ever.

She held out both hands to me. "Anselma! Let me look at you."

"Only if I get to look back." I sank onto the seat beside her, hoping that Tommy would forgive me for not hugging him yet. "You haven't changed a bit."

"Once you hit a certain age, it's hard to look older." She reached up to pinch my cheek. "They aren't feeding you enough at that school of yours."

"School?" I shot a glance over to Hershel, who was just shaking hands with Nathaniel.

"The tests you were doing." Hershel put a hand on the back of the booth and lowered himself to sit next to Tommy.

"Oh. That's not school, really. I'm applying to be an astronaut."

Tommy perked up at that. "That is just the keenest thing. What was it like? Did you meet Stetson Parker? How do you get tested? And Dad said we're going to see a rocket launch while we're here."

"I'm not sure which question to answer first."

Aunt Esther had a hand cupped around her ear. "What did he say?"

"He asked how the astronaut testing went."

She frowned, cocking her head to the side like a bird. "Well, now, that's what I thought he said. But I have to confess I'm not real clear on what an astronaut is. I keep hearing it on the news, but it just sounds like some sort of story."

"Um . . . an astronaut is someone who goes into outer space."

"Well, that's the silliest thing I ever heard of. Why would anyone want to do that?"

I'd spent the day trying to explain that to a series of shrinks who seemed determined to ask many of the same questions that Clemons and the gang had. Defending the desire to an aunt I'd just rediscovered lay beyond my abilities. "Let's just say that I'm sort of applying for a new job."

She shook her head and said something in Yiddish, but too quickly for me to catch. I'd never really spoken Yiddish, since my parents hadn't. I used to love listening to Aunt Esther and Grandma and the other aunts kvetch, though. I put my hand on her papery thin one. "Sorry? Can you repeat that in English?"

"Why are you working?" She gave Nathaniel a meaningful look. "Why is your wife working?"

"She likes it, and I try to make sure she has what she likes." Nathaniel winked at Aunt Esther as he settled on the bench next to Hershel. "You want me to make sure your niece is happy, right?"

"She's just like her father. And her grandmother." She pinched my cheek again and I began to see why Tommy was sitting next to his father. I'd forgotten this aspect of Aunt Esther. She was the baby of the aunts, which is a funny term to apply to someone who was over ninety. "I would be dead, were it not for Rose."

I cleared the tears from my throat. "How did y'all get out?"

She laughed a little and clapped her hands. "We went to church."

Glancing at Hershel, I raised my eyebrows questioningly, but he shrugged. "Aunt Esther, I thought you said that you drove out of Charleston."

"Oh . . . oh. Yes. Later, that's what we did, but first Rose took us to the church in town—you remember the one with the big steeple? It's the first time I set foot in a Christian church, but, Rose, she said we had to, and so we climbed all the way up to the top of the bell tower. I've never seen so many steps in my life."

The church with the big steeple . . . I had no idea which one she was talking about. We'd moved around so much when I was a kid that my knowledge of Charleston was limited to how to get from Grandma's house to my cousins', and the synagogue, cemetery, and grocery store. The priorities were clear, at least.

"That's amazing. And how—"

"Good evening, everyone. Have you had an opportunity to look over the menu?"

That poor waiter—I don't think I've ever hated anyone quite as much as I hated him in that moment. It wasn't his fault. He had a job to do—and, truly, I should eat something—but I wanted to hear more about the church. "I'll need a minute."

"I can order for you, if everyone else is ready." Nathaniel looked up from his menu. "The menu hasn't changed from when we were here before."

"Take your time." The young man flashed his teeth in a way that said that he was really an actor. He was handsome, if you go for the Clark Gable type, but he was never going to land any roles if his next line was any indication of his acting ability. "Say, aren't you the Lady Astronaut?"

"Only on TV. Not when I'm having dinner with my family." Which was maybe a little too sharp, so I gave a sugar-laden smile to counterbalance it. "You understand, right, honey?"

Poor kid. He'd thought he could suck up by "recognizing" me. His face fell and you could see him thinking that he'd kissed his tip goodbye. Hershel had covered his mouth and was studying the menu with the intensity of a man trying not to laugh.

"Sorry, ma'am." The waiter made a vague gesture to another part of the restaurant. "There were just . . . there's a family with some little girls, and they recognized you. I said . . . They were shy, and I said I could help them out."

Oh. Well, that changed things. And I had to give him credit for not backing down from a promise to kids, even if all I really wanted to do was spend time with my aunt.

Aunt Esther watched the whole conversation with quiet interest. Her head tilted to the side as each of us spoke, which just made her look more like a little bird. When I had visited as a child, she and Grandma had always made time for me and my endless questions. Did I repay that by giving her my attention now, or by following her example and visiting the little girls?

Sighing, I turned to Nathaniel. "Would you order for me? I'll be right back."

It says something that I wasn't nervous walking over there. Maybe I was just worn out from the testing, or maybe I was finally getting used to the spotlight. I could hope for the latter.

The family was sitting at a table close to the entrance. The wife wore a small Star of David on a chain. My heart lifted a little at that. Funny how, even though I was there with my family, just seeing someone else who was visibly Jewish made me feel less alone in the room.

The younger of the little girls spotted me first, and her brown eyes went wide. Her rosebud of a mouth dropped open. She poked her sister in the side.

"Ow! Mama! Shoshana is poking m—oh my gosh." The older girl was perhaps ten, and had the same dark brown curls as her little sister. "Oh my gosh."

The father looked around in the direction of his daughters' stares. Seeing me, he pushed his chair back and stood. "Thank you for coming over, Dr. York. I hope we didn't interrupt your dinner."

"Not at all. It's just a family gathering." Telling him that it included an aunt who I'd thought was dead would only make him feel guilty.

"Robert Horn. My wife, Julia."

"A pleasure." I shook her hand. The skin was rough and chapped, as if she spent a lot of time washing dishes.

"And these are our daughters, Chanie and Shoshana." The obvious parental pride shone through his smile. "They are big fans of yours."

"I'm going to be an astronaut!" Shoshana announced.

"I bet you will." I turned my attention to Chanie. "And how about you?"

"A writer." And then, as if seeking my approval, she added, "But I'll write about space."

"Well, then. It sounds like the future will be a wonderful place."

We chatted about nothing, which I had become very practiced at over the past several months. What I'd come to realize is that, with kids like these, it was less about *me* and more about elevating them—not because it was *me*, but because I was something out of the ordinary.

It was easy to confuse that with extraordinary. I wasn't.

I could have been anybody so long as I was Somebody, if that makes any sense. They would have been just as excited to meet Hedy Lamarr.

Though, to be fair, I would also be excited to meet Hedy Lamarr.

For me, the out-of-the-ordinary person that I met that night was Aunt Esther. When I got back to the table, she had Nathaniel, Tommy, and Hershel crying with laughter. Literally crying. Nathaniel had gone red in the face and was blotting his eyes with his napkin.

I slid onto the bench, jealous at missing whatever the story had been. Aunt Esther's cheeks had a flush of red to them, and her wrinkles were twisted up in a bow. Fortunately, Nathaniel had ordered a martini for me, so I had that for consolation.

Tommy grinned at me. "The damn thing's hot!"

"Look what you've done." Hershel shook a finger at our aunt, who did not look even a little abashed. "He's going to teach that to his sister, and my wife will have my head."

"Eileen won't mind."

"Doris." Hershel wiped his eyes and sobered a little. Our cousin Kenny and his wife Eileen had died in the Meteor. Presumably—like most, they'd just vanished. "My wife's name is Doris."

"I know." She picked up a low tumbler, which smelled like a rum and Coke, and gave him a wink. "How is she doing?"

"*Doris* is doing pretty well. She's looking forward to seeing you. So is my daughter, *Rachel*." Hershel also had a martini. He lifted it. "Now that we're all here . . . l'chaim!"

To life, indeed.

I lay sprawled across the bed while Nathaniel rubbed my feet. His thumbs dug into the ball of my right foot in a searching circular pattern, like a tension-finding radar.

"So . . . I take it dancing is out?" He ran one thumb down the arch of my foot.

I groaned and pulled a pillow over my face. "I'll need a compelling reason to leave this bed. Ever."

"I might be able to provide that." The motion of his hand changed to a softer pressure that sent shivers up my spine.

"That feels more like a reason to stay *in* bed." I pressed the pillow more firmly over my face.

My husband has a wonderful laugh. "Fine. Stay in bed."

"What was the story Aunt Esther told tonight? While I was with the little girls."

"Oh God. I nearly died." His fingers worked around the back of my heel to my Achilles tendon, and then up my calf. "I don't think I can tell it the way she does, though. Apparently, when your father was little, they're having a party, and your dad sees his first electric light. He touches it and says, 'The damn thing's hot.' Now—you have to picture your aunt Esther saying that."

I could just see her, with her delicate features and bright eyes, chirping, "The damn thing's hot."

Things you don't expect small children or little old ladies to say. "I'm sorry I missed that."

"How about you? I didn't get to hear anything about the testing today."

"Mm . . ." Under the pillow, the world was warm and had the suffused light of dense cloud cover. Low visibility was fine by me. I'd spent the past five days being tested along every axis they could think of, and some I hadn't known existed. "The centrifuge was fun."

"Ha! You are the only person I know who would say that unironically."

I pushed the pillow up so I could stick my tongue out at him. "Any idea how long before we hear back?"

He shook his head and lifted my foot a little higher.

"Not my area. I'm more concerned with the health and morale . . ." Nathaniel bent down so his hair fell across his forehead, and took my big toe into his mouth. His teeth nibbled the tip, and my back arched as he withdrew his mouth. ". . . of specific candidates."

"I see." Pulling my foot back, I slid it down his chest to nestle into the place where his thighs met. "And what is your candidate criteria? Besides an ability to handle being placed in a centrifuge chair, of course."

Nathaniel's hips flexed to match my pressure, and, for a moment, his eyes flickered closed. A lazy smile ghosted across his face as he leaned forward. "Well . . . Clearly the centrifuge indicates an ability to work with compromised blood flow, which is . . . ah . . . necessary for a pilot."

"Is *that* why women are able to handle higher G-forces than men?" I traced a line up the inside of his thigh. "What other qualifications does your candidate possess?"

The bed creaked beneath me as Nathaniel shifted to his knees. "It's critical that suitable candidates have experience with rocketry."

"What type of experience? Should I demonstrate my experience ensuring that the rocket is topped up and ready for launch?" Beneath my hands, his body seemed supercharged with heat. His shirt bunched under my touch as I found my way to his belt.

Nathaniel leaned down, his breath hot against my cheek. "That would be acceptable."

"Acceptable!" I wrapped my legs around his waist and pulled him down against me. "I plan on being excellent."

THIRTY-ONE

DR. KING TO LEAD ANTI-BIAS TREK

15,000 Southern Negroes Going to Capital
to Observe 4th Year of School Decree

MONTGOMERY, AL, May 18, 1957—Next week, a young Negro minister will lead a pilgrimage to the Meteor Memorial in Kansas City to mark the fourth anniversary of the Supreme Court's school desegregation order.

Saturday morning we all went to synagogue together. Several times during the service, I had to press my handkerchief to my eyes because I would look at Aunt Esther beside me and half-expect to see Grandma on her other side, or Mama and Daddy behind me. I was so very glad to have her back, but she brought ghosts with her.

Nathaniel hadn't been able to join us because it was a launch day. Ever since the *Orion 27* disaster, he wouldn't miss a launch. Rockets still blew up occasionally when they were being tested, but those were just data points.

That evening, we all went over to Mission Control to watch the launch. It was a manned craft, heading for the orbital platform. I say "platform," but it was more donut-shaped than flat, rotating to create a limp artificial gravity.

The night was warm and banks of clouds bounced the

lights of the launch tower back down to the Earth in a sodium-orange haze. Baffles gave some shelter to the roof-top, but wind snuck past it and cooled the sweat from the back of my neck. I still hadn't gotten used to being warm outside again.

The loudspeakers punctuated our conversation with the countdown.

The public affairs officer on duty kept up a running commentary for the spectators both at the IAC and listen-ing via the radio. "Four minutes, fifteen seconds. The Test Supervisor now has informed the Launch Vehicle Test Conductor that they are Go for launch."

Perhaps with the weather warming, folks would start coming to the roof earlier for launches. We tended to wait until T-minus four minutes because it was too cold, even in the summer.

"Three minutes, forty-five seconds and counting. In the final abort checks between several key members of the crew here in the control center and the astronauts. Launch Operations Manager wished the crew, 'Good luck and Godspeed.'"

Aunt Esther had produced a painted fan from some-where and created a miniature breeze of her own.

I smiled at her. "What a lovely fan."

Aunt Esther preened, waving it in a lopsided circle. "Rose gave it to me. I hadn't thought to grab my own when we left home, but she always had one in her bag."

"Three minutes, twenty-five seconds and counting; we're still Go at this time. We'll be coming up on the auto-matic sequence about ten or fifteen seconds from now. All still Go at this time."

"Really?" Memories of sitting on the front porch with lemonade, and Grandma stirring the air with her fan, tick-led the back of my mind. "It's beautiful."

"She got it in Spain!"

"T-minus two minutes, forty-five seconds and counting. The members of the launch team here in the control center are monitoring a number of what we call red-line values."

Hershel had gone ahead with Tommy and leaned against the railing at the far side of the roof. Downstairs, my nephew had met Benkoski's son, Max, with whom I'd made tinfoil rockets. They were becoming fast friends.

I smiled at my aunt, unsure if this was a true story or her spotty memory. "Grandma . . . Grandma went to Spain?"

"She and your grandfather went for their honeymoon."

It had never occurred to me that they must have had a honeymoon. Granddaddy died before I was born, and Grandma had seemed eternal. "I had no idea. Did you ever—"

"T-minus one minute twenty-five seconds and counting. Our status board indicates the third stage is completely pressurized."

Things would start moving quickly now, and I didn't want her to miss a thing. Night launches were spectacular.

"There are some seats over here." I beckoned Aunt Esther to the folding chairs set up on the roof.

"T-minus sixty seconds and counting. Randy Cleary just reported back: 'It's been a very smooth countdown.' We've passed the fifty-second mark. Power transfer is complete—we're on internal power with the launch vehicle at this time. Forty seconds away from liftoff. All the second-stage tanks are now pressurized. Thirty-five seconds and counting. We are still Go with thirty seconds and counting. Astronauts report, 'It feels good.' T-minus twenty-five seconds."

Aunt Esther's cheeks blossomed with roses, and she

settled into her chair like an eager child. Truly, she wasn't much bigger than one. She had been a small women my entire life, but I swear she was a good four inches shorter than before the Meteor.

"Twenty seconds and counting. T-minus fifteen seconds, guidance is internal. Twelve, eleven, ten, nine, ignition sequence starts . . ."

". . . eight, seven, six . . ." We joined in the countdown with everyone else on the roof and my stomach knit itself into a tight ball.

". . . five, four, three . . ."

Every time we launched, I worried that this one would fail. That we would watch three astronauts lost in a massive explosion.

". . . two, one, zero, all engines running."

In the distance, the base of the rocket sprouted the vivid yellow-white fire of a successful ignition. In silence, it rose on this cushion of flame. The night around us lit up like day.

"Liftoff. We have liftoff."

Beside me, Aunt Esther rose to her feet, hands clasped in front of her chest. The light of the rocket reflected off her bright eyes as if the fire of her soul were coming out to push the rocket into the sky.

Then the sound hit us, a heavy rumble that you felt more than heard. The force of the waves beat against my chest. What must it be like to ride that sound and fury? I held my breath, praying for the rocket to keep going. The blaze of fire pushed it faster and higher into the air until it disappeared into the cloud cover and left us with just a traveling glow that faded back into the night.

Aunt Esther turned to me and grasped both of my hands. "Thank you."

"For?"

"I never thought I would see such a thing. I didn't know why you'd want to be an astronaut, or even really what one was, but now . . ." She looked up to the clouds, where all trace of the rocket had vanished. "You must."

After my family left, it was back to the grind of computing. That makes it sound like I didn't enjoy it, when I did. It's just that, having spent a month preparing for those tests and then five days immersed in the potentiality of becoming an astronaut, it was hard to go back to something mundane.

It's true that I was still helping the program, but I wanted to go into space. The fact that Helen hadn't gotten in also rankled. She had bounced back to her usual cheer on the surface, but she, Ida, and Imogene had stopped coming to the 99s. They were using their free time to rack up jet engine hours.

The really absurd thing about that requirement was that astronauts barely *flew* anything. Sure, they had to go into outer space, but there was a reason that Chuck Yeager called it being "spam in a can." Most of the systems were automated.

It would be different on the way to the moon, but even that would be nothing like flying a jet.

Meanwhile, the Sirius rocket that Bubbles had designed was ready for a launch test. All the static firings in the world wouldn't count until we actually sent it into the air.

I tapped the trajectory pages together into a stack and tucked them into a folder. "Be right back. I'm going to run this down to Bubbles."

Basira looked up from her desk with a pout. "Oh . . . let him come for them. He's so adorable."

"You should ask him out on a date." I slid my chair back and stood.

She barked a laugh. "I'm pretty sure he's supposed to ask me."

"That would involve him realizing that the computers are women."

"A man who asks for a 'computress' doesn't know that?" She snorted and turned back to her pages. "Please. I just think he doesn't know what to do with us."

"Which is why you should ask him out . . ." I winked and headed for the door. "Should I tell him you asked about him?"

"Don't you dare!" She flung a wadded-up piece of paper after me, and hit Myrtle by mistake. Which set the whole room to giggling.

Still laughing, I headed down the hall to the engineering wing. The practical labs, which is where Bubbles usually worked, were in a different building from us, because they tended to blow things up. Thank heavens for the "gerbil tubes" that connected our buildings. Otherwise, I would have to step into the heat to run the report over.

I opened the door to the stairwell up to the sky bridge.

Down a floor, a conversation cut off. ". . . . told you, I'm fine—Sh."

That hush echoed up the stairwell. It took a second to identify the voice, only because I'd never heard Stetson Parker sound stressed. Not even when there was a bomber on the IAC campus.

I leaned over the railing and looked down. He sat on the bottom step with one leg stretched out in front of him. Halim Malouf stood over him, hands on his hips.

"Y'all need any help?"

At the sound of my voice, Parker's head jerked up and around. "Everything is fine."

"Are you sure?" It was tempting to leave him, but the lines of his face were drawn tight. "I can get a medic."

"No!" His voice echoed up to the top of the stairwell and back down again. Parker closed his eyes and let out a slow breath. "No. Thank you. That won't be necessary."

"I think maybe it is." Malouf rubbed the back of his neck. "Stetson . . . it's been getting worse."

"Don't you say another word." Parker jabbed a finger up at him, then glared at me. "And you. I don't want to hear a peep about this from you."

Pulled down the stairs by their gravity, my heels clicked against the concrete steps. "If there's nothing wrong, then there's nothing for me to tell."

"You really like pushing things, don't you, York?" Parker grabbed the railing and hauled himself upright. His left leg hung loose under him.

"What happened?" I stopped on the stairs, clutching the trajectory folder as a shield between us.

"Nothing happened. I just slipped on the stairs, that's all." He took a limping step away from the stairs and his left leg buckled under him.

"Oh, hell!" Malouf caught him, easing Parker to the ground.

I ran down the stairs to try to help. "Are you okay?"

"Yes. I'm fine."

"You can't stand!"

"I fucking know that!" Parker pressed his fingers to the bridge of his nose and squeezed his eyes shut. He held his breath for a moment. Then he blew it out and lowered his hand. "York. I'm going to ask you as a favor. One pilot to another. Please don't say anything. You have the power, right now, to have me grounded. Please, please don't."

"Well . . . I'm sympathetic to fears of being grounded."

"Please."

I took another step closer. As much as I might have dreamed about Parker begging me for something, this wasn't what I wanted. I wanted to be better than him. Winning because he was sick? No thank you. "What's wrong?"

"I don't know. If I go to the flight surgeon, he'll ground me."

As well he should. A leg like that could jeopardize a mission. And for that matter, why hadn't Malouf told anyone already? Maybe it was recent. My thoughts went to stories my parents told about when Hershel got sick. It had started with a weakness in his leg. "Have you had a fever?"

"It's not polio."

I pulled back, a little startled that his thoughts went there too. "How do you—"

"I know what polio looks like. All right?" He scowled at me. "Why are you still here, anyway? Shouldn't you be scampering off to report this to the newspaper?"

Behind his back, Malouf made a subtle shooing motion, but not unkindly. "I think everything is under control, Dr. York."

"Of course." I started up the stairs and stopped at the next landing. Even if Parker were grounded, that wouldn't keep him from having a say in who got selected. "I won't tell anyone, but you should see a doctor. Just, maybe, not the flight surgeon."

I almost offered to take him, but I wasn't that big of a person.

On launch days, there's usually nothing for a computer to do until after liftoff. We've already done the calculations about alternate launch windows or adjusted trajectories for rendezvous so that Clemons and the launch director can make decisions based on known information if there's a delay.

But we still have to come in to Mission Control with the rest of our team. Helen was playing chess with Reynard

Carmouche, while I was looking at the places where it was possible to abort the moon mission if something went wrong.

That thing we say about how engineers create problems and computers solve them? Yeah . . . Nathaniel had given the computer department a list of possible failure points, and then asked how we could get the astronauts home under these varying conditions.

To put this into perspective . . . The Sirius has 5,600,000 parts and close to a million systems, subsystems, and assemblies. Even if everything was 99.9 percent reliable, that would still be 5,600 defects. It wasn't a question of *if* something would go wrong on the way to the moon, it was a question of when and what.

And when that failure occurred, it would occur in a spacecraft that was traveling at twenty-five thousand miles per hour. We weren't going to have time to run calculations then, so the idea was to create a library of possible answers so we could access a month's worth of work in a few minutes.

Tonight, with three hours of waiting time before ignition, the failure state calculations were a pleasant way to pass the time. And yes, I'm aware that I'm odd. I wasn't alone, however.

At his station, Nathaniel had a pile of reports and was gnawing his way through a pencil. Bubbles had a similar binder in front of him—though, given that it was his baby we were about to launch, that wasn't surprising.

Not everyone was working, of course. Parker was up in the skybox with Clemons, hobnobbing with the journalists. Today, he didn't have a trace of a limp.

What the hell had it been? Not polio, for certain. Mama would have known what it was, but I didn't have anyone I could ask without it getting back to him. Maybe I could inquire with the doctor when I went in to see him for my Miltown refill.

"Again?!" Carmouche leaned back in his chair with a groan. "Someday . . . I swear that someday I will win."

Helen crossed her arms and smirked at him. "It is only check. You still have a chance."

He harrumphed and leaned forward to stare at the board.

I lowered my pencil. "If you just want to win, you could play against me."

Shaking his head, Carmouche continued to glare at the board. He reached forward for a pawn, glanced at Helen, and pulled his hand back. Under his breath, he muttered in French about either Helen's parentage or the options for play. Either way, it sounded irritable.

"*Est-ce qu'elle vous bat de nouveau?*" Parker walked up behind me and I flinched in my seat. I swear he did that on purpose.

"*Oui. Il est l'ordre naturel, je pense.*" Carmouche sighed and tapped his fingers on the edge of the board.

"*Il n'y a rien de naturel.*" Parker looked down at me. "York. Clemons wants you."

"And he sent you down all those stairs for little ol' me?" I am, at times, a complete idiot. Antagonizing him was the last thing I needed to do. I pushed back my chair, aware that Helen and Carmouche were staring at us. "Thank you."

I followed him across the floor of Mission Control. Across the room, Nathaniel had his head buried in reports, and didn't look up. "Any idea why?"

Parker pulled the door open, but did not hold it for me. I caught it, following him into the stairwell. He bounded up the stairs two at a time, as if he had something to prove.

"Feeling better, I see." I chased him up the stairs, grateful for the time I'd spent preparing for the astronaut tests. Even in a skirt and heels, I could run up a flight of stairs without getting winded.

At the top of the stairs, Parker waited beside the door with a face of stone. He was a handsome man, I'd grant him that. He and Nathaniel were both blondes with bright blue eyes, but where my husband was lean and angular, Parker had the "ideal" physique of a movie star, with a square jaw and cleft chin.

When I came up alongside him, he put a hand on the doorknob and suddenly smiled as if we were the best of friends. The speed with which he turned on the charm left me chilled.

Parker threw the door open, holding it for me to walk through. Of course he would hold the door and smile, now that there were witnesses. The room was full of astronauts, their wives, and reporters here to cover the launch of a new class of spacecraft.

Clemons turned, one of his cigars smoldering in his hand. "There she is. Gentlemen, meet Elma York. One of our computers, and responsible for the calculations that identified the potential of the Sirius engine. Dr. York is also our newest astronaut."

The room went hot. Cold. Hot. I must have misheard. Surely they would tell me that in private first.

Flashbulbs went off. Blinding me. I couldn't breathe.

Astronaut.

The room spun around me like I was strapped in a centrifuge chair. Breath pressed out. My vision darkened at the edges.

Astronaut.

3.14159265359 . . . Someone said my name. If I fainted, what would people think? Parker would like that.

Astronaut.

Why the hell wouldn't they tell me that in private first? You didn't blindside someone with a thing like that, unless you wanted to watch them flounder . . .

Parker. Parker must have suggested this.

Someone said my name again, and I turned to the voice. The room was a blur of sound and light. There wasn't enough air. *Keep your eyes open. Keep talking.* This was just another test.

"Gentlemen . . ." I fought gravity to raise my hands. "Gentlemen, if you all talk at once, I can't hear you."

They ignored me and kept shouting over each other. "When will you go into space?" "What does your husband think about this?" "How does it feel to be an Astronette?"

That voice belonged to a round, balding man with his tie pulled loose.

"An astronette? That sounds as if I should be doing kicks in a chorus line." The laughter gave me a boost to find a smile somewhere. "So, please, I'm just an astronaut."

Just an astronaut. Ha. I was a goddamned astronaut. Not that they would print that.

"Now, now . . . you're the *Lady* Astronaut, from *Mr. Wizard.*" Parker smiled genially beside me. "We wouldn't want anyone to forget that."

"Is she the only lady astronaut?" Another reporter fired at Clemons.

Damn Parker. That moniker was going to stick, and it would make sure we were always second class to the men.

Clemons waved his cigar, leaving contrails of smoke. "No, she is not. But you'll meet the rest of them next week at our press conference. I just wanted to give you a preview of the talent and beauty of our lady astronauts."

Goddamn it. I smiled until my teeth hurt. "Well . . . this astronaut has some calculations to do."

"Of course." Clemons waved me back to the door. "Sirius is waiting."

The reporters hollered for some more photos, so I had to stand there, smiling, between Parker and Clemons. Both men beamed at the camera, and in the pictures, we all looked like the best of friends.

Then Parker held the door for me, as if he were a gentleman. I stepped into the stairwell and the door shut behind us.

His smile dropped.

"This must really rankle you." I started down the stairs ahead of him. "After saying you'd keep me grounded."

His laughter bounced down the stairs after me. "Please. If Clemons hadn't hired you, it would have been a public relations nightmare. The other women? They've earned it. You're just a publicity stunt."

Bastard. My heart galloped as if I'd run up five flights of stairs instead of down one. I slammed the door open and stalked onto the floor of Mission Control. A few heads lifted as my heels clicked across the floor.

The reporters were probably still watching. Thank God my back was to them. Whatever Parker said in the stairwell, I was still an astronaut. I'd been selected, and, by God, I was going to go into space. Publicity stunt? Ha. I was going to be the best damn student they had.

Back at my table, the tableau was much as it had been before. Carmouche had evidently made a move, because he was slumped in his chair, shaking his head.

"Did you lose again?"

"No. But she has me in check again. A different one, at least."

Helen studied the board. "I will try to put you out of your misery quickly."

"The offer to play against me still stands." I settled into my chair, smoothing my skirt to wipe the sweat off my palms.

Helen nodded to the skybox, from which all the reporters were staring at us. "What was that all about?"

This was good news, despite Parker, so I smiled, and in smiling found the joy that should have been there already. "I—I made the cut. I'm an astronaut." Laughter bubbled out of me. "I'm an astronaut."

For a moment, Helen's mouth dropped open and then she jumped up. Grinning, she ran around the table and swept me into a hug. "I knew it!" She straightened. "Nathaniel! Your wife astronaut!"

Across the room, Nathaniel's head jerked up. "What?"

Carmouche had also stood up at some point. "Clemons just told her she made the cut. Dr. York is one of the new astronauts."

"Yes!" Laughing, Nathaniel jumped up and punched the air. "Yes!"

All around us, engineers and medics and everyone started to cheer.

Bubbles and Carmouche and someone else grabbed my chair and lifted me into the air like I was a bride. I laughed and wept and laughed again, clutching the chair as they paraded me around the room.

Above us, the skybox flashed with cameras going off. When my chair was back on the ground again, I got swept into a long series of hugs and congratulations.

And then Nathaniel had me in his arms. He spun me around, giving me a moment of weightlessness. Kissing him, in front of everyone, sent me into orbit.

When he pulled back, tears brightened his eyes and a smile threatened to split his face. "I am so, so proud of you."

This was the way I wanted to learn about becoming an astronaut. Not in a room of random reporters, but here. With my peers. With my husband.

"All right, everyone!" Clemons bellowed from the doorway. "We've got a rocket to launch. Back to stations."

I could not stop smiling. Neither Clemons, nor Parker,

nor a gaggle of reporters could take this away from me. I was an astronaut. I pulled the numbers for the calculations I'd been doing in front of me, and kept losing my place on the page. I was an astronaut.

Across the table, Carmouche suddenly threw his hands into the air and shouted. *"La victoire est la mienne!"*

Helen folded her hands in her lap. "Congratulations, Reynard."

"You won?"

"Finally!" He got up and did the most ridiculous victory dance I have ever seen, involving elbows and hips moving in unlikely ways. "Finally, I have won!"

"Good game." Helen pushed her chair back and stood. She bowed to him. "Please excuse me."

My friend, the champion chess player, walked to the ladies' room, with her head high and her shoulders back. Do I sound self-important to think that there was a correlation between my news and Helen losing a game?

I was an astronaut. Helen wasn't.

And that needed to change.

THIRTY-TWO

**TEMPERATURE ON UPGRADE
BUT FALLS SHORT OF '51 HIGH**

CHICAGO, IL, June 25, 1957—At 12:55 p.m.
yesterday, the temperature reached 87.7 degrees and
the Weather Man, sweltering among his gadgets at
Navy Pier, announced that it was heading toward the
highest level since the Meteor.

I suppose I should report that the Sirius flight went flaw-
lessly. Bubbles was thrilled. Nathaniel was as well, since
this would reduce costs for moon runs significantly. Not
that we'd landed an astronaut on the moon yet, but it was
just a matter of time.

And by God, I was going to be one of them.

When we left the IAC campus, close to dawn, the excitement still had me floating. I looped my arm through
Nathaniel's and anticipated another successful "rocket
launch" when we got home. We walked out with the other
folks, heading across the parking lot for the gates of the
IAC.

"There she is!" Flashbulb. "Dr. York!" Flash. "Elma!"
Past the gates, a horde of reporters lay in wait. "Over here,
ma'am!"

My stomach clenched. Nathaniel turned us around,
which is a good thing, because I was moving toward them

like a moth to the flame. Or a lemming to the cliff, more like.

He rested his hand on mine and pulled me closer. "We'll have the company send us home in a car."

"I didn't think."

"Parker should have. Hell. If I'd thought about what happened with him and the rest, I should have."

I don't think that Parker knew about my anxiety. In fact, I'm sure he didn't, or he would have used it to keep me out of the astronauts. But he couldn't have ambushed me better if he'd planned it.

One of the UN drivers assigned to the IAC took us home, but when we got to our block, he didn't turn.

Nathaniel leaned forward and looked out the window. "Damn it."

Huddled inside my coat, I shivered in the dark of the back seat. He sat back and put his arm around me. "Let's stay at the Aladdin tonight, to celebrate."

"They have our apartment staked out?"

"Yeah . . ." He squeezed me tighter, but my trembling didn't stop. Nathaniel rubbed up and down my arm as if he could chafe the blood back into my veins. "We'll send someone round to get our clothes."

"My prescription is in the apartment." It wouldn't make the reporters go away, but it would put a haze between us.

"Got it. What do you want to wear tomorrow?"

Clothes? I was supposed to think about clothes, instead of the wall of reporters waiting to talk to me? On some level, I knew this was coming. I'd seen what had happened when the Artemis Seven were announced. But after months of being "the Lady Astronaut," I thought the level of attention would remain the same.

Of course there would be a difference. I'd just gone from being a wannabe astronaut to the real thing. As the first

woman that they announced, it made sense that the reporters would all want a piece of me.

I tucked my head into Nathaniel's shoulder and let the
wool of his coat block out the streetlights.

"Sir?" Our driver turned the car down another street. "Is
there a different hotel you could choose?"

Against my cheek, Nathaniel's chest moved in a sigh.
"Let's head to the suburbs. Just pick the first hotel you spot
that doesn't have reporters."

After Nathaniel and I spent the night at a Holiday Inn off
the interstate, he called Clemons and explained the situation. I was told to avoid the IAC while the reporters were
still there, and that Mrs. Rogers had accepted my resignation with many congratulations.

They hadn't even let me say goodbye to the other computers.

I wept. Took a Miltown. Burrowed under the covers.
And when the first Miltown wore off, I took another.

Nathaniel stayed in the hotel with me while a UN guard
sat outside the door. That was probably a good choice.

In the afternoon, our phone started to ring. I don't know
how they'd tracked us down, but they had.

I was not an astronaut. That was made very, very clear on
Day One.

There were seven women selected, and our first meeting
was not at the IAC. It was not even in Kansas City. They
flew us out to the bunker where Nathaniel and I had met
the president right after the Meteor struck.

I guess after the circus I'd been through, they wanted
to keep the rest of us under wraps. When I walked into the
conference room, I recognized some of the faces. Betty and

Nicole had made the cut and were sitting together at the conference table.

Nicole squealed and waved me over. "I wanted to tell you, but they told me I couldn't say anything because of the reporters hanging all over you."

I rolled my eyes. "That was a nuisance." Nightmare. Much the same thing. "Betty. Congratulations."

She nodded and bit her lower lip. Swallowing, she looked up. "You too."

That bit of careful social nicety out of the way, I sat down next to Betty and gave the other women my attention. Naturally Sabiha Gökçen had made it in. I was glad she'd come back from Turkey for this, because flying with her had been a pleasure.

Mrs. Lebourgeois, on the other hand . . . Last we'd spoken at the launch, Violette had only just begun taking flying lessons. I smiled at her and leaned across the table. "Two astronauts in the family? Your husband must be very proud."

She blushed and waved. "It is an honor, and so unexpected."

"I can imagine." I hadn't even seen her at the testing.

Pausing, I looked around the room at the waiting women. No men. Interesting. I knew that they'd added more men to the corps as well, but they must be training them in a different location.

We weren't chattering or doing any of the clucking that you'd expect from the movies. All of us were turned out, though—in pants suits, yes, but with makeup and our hair done just so.

Four of us were American. One French woman. A Brazilian woman—Jacira Paz-Viveiros—and Sabiha Gökçen. Seven, all told, to match the original seven men.

If Ida hadn't primed me for it, I don't know if I would have noticed that there wasn't a black candidate in the group.

Clemons, Parker, and two other gentlemen that I didn't know walked in together. Clemons clapped his hands together. "There are my beauties. First of all, ladies, congratulations on being chosen as astronauts in training."

One of the men I didn't know, a slender fellow with a shiny white forehead and ears that stuck out past his regulation crew cut, started passing out binders.

"Now. Our first task is to get you ready for the press conference. This is Mr. Pommier." He beckoned toward the other fellow, who was in his mid-fifties and had that steel-gray hair that some men acquire as they age. "He's your stylist, and will help you select your wardrobe and hair for the event."

I exchanged glances with Nicole, but neither of us raised our hands to ask why we needed a stylist. They had probably gotten one for the men and kept him on for us. If I were going to rock the boat, which seemed inevitable, then it would be over a bigger question.

"Mr. Smith is handing out press kits for each of you. We're going to go through sample interview questions to prepare you for the conference." Clemons turned to Parker. "Colonel Parker here is in charge of all the astronauts, as well as you lady astronauts-in-training. He'll be able to help you understand what's expected of you in your new role."

Parker gave one of his trademark earnest smiles. "Good morning. I wish all conference rooms looked this lovely when I walked in." He caught my eye. "Now, I know some of you are used to being able to say anything you want, but we've got to be careful with the information that goes out of the IAC. Besides our security interests, we also have an exclusive contract with *Life*. Isn't that right, Miss Ralls?"

Betty nodded, her eyes on the table and her cheeks red. "Yes, sir."

Well, bless her journalistic heart. Betty hadn't made the cut. She'd cut a deal.

"To control the image of the space program, all communication with the press must go through the front office." Parker held up a finger. "And just to be clear, 'the press' includes entertainment broadcasts."

This was not the hardship for me that he seemed to think it was.

"Wait a minute—" Sabiha's voice cut through the room. She had her binder open and was frowning at one of the pages. "This question. What is this answer? 'No. I am not an astronaut.'"

I grabbed my binder and flipped it open, amid the sound of pages shuffling and covers slapping against the hard wood of the conference table. Sure enough, under the heading "Approved answers to common questions" were a variety of questions about what it was like to be an astronaut.

"Thank you, Colonel Parker. I'll take it from here." Mr. Smith, the fellow with the jug-handled ears, had a voice like a revival preacher. The deep resonance rolled out at complete odds with his slight build. "You've already opened your binders, ladies, so let me explain. We've realized that it would be confusing for the public if we start calling trainees astronauts. It would be like calling someone a pilot when they'd just signed up for flight school."

"When, exactly, are we considered astronauts?" My voice left frost on the table.

"Fifty miles." Parker shrugged. "When you've been fifty miles above the Earth's surface, you're an astronaut. That's in conjunction with the IAC and the Fédération Aéronautique Internationale in Paris. Until then, you're astronaut candidates. Abbreviated as AsCans."

Of course. All nice and proper and completely legitimate. I couldn't even complain that it was unreasonable—except, of course, that the rule hadn't applied until they'd added women to the corps.

At the press conference, I stood in the shadows backstage with Nathaniel holding both of my hands. A film of sweat separated us. The murmur of the crowd rumbled through the curtains at a constant low-frequency hum. You could feel it through the floorboards, like the buzz of an engine. Around me, the new astronauts—excuse me, the new AsCans—milled about in uncertain patterns. The seven women nearly vanished among the thirty-five men they'd chosen. Why had I signed up for this?

Nathaniel stood directly in front of me. "197 times 4753?"

"936,341."

"Divided by 243?"

"3853.255144032922 . . . How many decimal places do you want?" The dress that the stylist had asked me to wear had a tight-fitted bodice. It had seemed to fit well enough when I'd tried it on, but now I could hardly draw a breath.

"That's fine. Square root? To five decimals . . . if applicable."

At least I wasn't the only one who was nervous. "62.07459."

Sabiha Gökçen paced back and forth, shaking her wrists out. She kept touching her hair as if she'd be happier to have it back in a ponytail instead of the bouffant it had been teased into.

"What is the optimal pitchover angle for the gravity turn when entering low Earth orbit?"

"Gravity turn . . . With what rocket engine and configuration? And what should the final altitude be?" Bless him for trying to keep me distracted.

"Jupiter class, with a dual-Sirius engine. Final altitude would be—"

He probably said more than that, but Clemons walked onto the stage and through the curtains. The uproar from the audience rose to critical. I closed my eyes and swallowed and swallowed and breathed through my nose and swallowed down the bitter acid that coated the back of my tongue. Not now. Not now not now not now . . .

Nathaniel breathed into my ear. "1, 1, 2, 3, 5, 8, 9—"

"That's wrong." I clung to him. "The Fibonacci sequence adds the prior number to the current one, so it should be 3, 5, 8, 13 . . . Oh. Clever man."

"I can do more bad math, if that will help." He gave me a squeeze and stepped back to look at me. "Just remember that the astronauts get to fly T-33s."

I snorted. "Here I thought you were going to tell me to remember that you loved me."

"Eh. You know that. But a T-33? A jet? I know where I stand in relation to—"

"Elma! We're up." Nicole grabbed my hand and pulled me with her to the stage.

T-33s. Even as an astronaut candidate, I would get to fly a T-33 jet aircraft. As we walked onto the stage, I tried to hold the image of the cockpit in my head. The flashes going off were just lightning. I could keep this steady, and hold the course.

That image lasted long enough for me to make it to the table with the other women. They had us seated in front, with the men standing in two rows behind us like a frame. This was just another interview. It was just like the ones I'd given before. I'd even been trained this time.

3.14159265359 . . .

T-33. Teeeeeeeeeee-thirty-three. Astronaut. Astronaut. Astronaut. T-33.

"Dr. York? What does your husband think about your new occupation?" came a voice from the front row.

The speaker was a man with a rumpled gray suit surrounded by nearly identical men with rumpled gray suits. I had no idea that reporters had uniforms. Nicole kicked me under the table.

I was taking too long to respond. "He's been very supportive. In fact, he was backstage waiting with us before we came out."

Clemons pointed to another reporter in the ubiquitous gray suit. "Why do you all want to beat a man to the moon?"

Nicole leaned into the microphone. "I don't want to *beat* a man to the moon. I want to go to the moon for the same reason men want to go. Women can do a useful job in space. We aren't in a contest to beat men in anything."

Thank God for her. That was a great answer. Granted, there was one man I would happily beat to the moon, but mostly, I just wanted us to get there.

"What are you going to cook in space?"

"Science." The word popped out of my mouth before I thought about it, and the room rewarded me with a laugh. "Followed by a nice healthy dinner of kerosene and liquid oxygen."

Betty leaned into the microphone. "And without gravity, I'm looking forward to soufflés that won't fall."

That line got a bigger laugh than mine, and pencils scribbled across notepads. Clemons pointed to another reporter. I stopped trying to identify them in the crowd, because their questions were all just the same inanity, and none of them had questions for the men.

"What about your beauty regimen in space? Will you be able to use hairspray?"

Sabiha shook her head. "We will be in a pure oxygen environment. Hairspray would be foolish."

That list of questions that they had prepared for us? We got none of them. They'd have been better off giving us a coach for beauty contestants. The only thing they were missing was asking us how we would bring about world peace.

Behind me, the men shifted weight and I heard one of them mutter, "What about bra size?"

"Does the IAC have any plans to include men or women of color in the space program?" The man who asked the question looked white, with close-cropped dark curls. His suit was not rumpled, and he held himself with exquisite posture.

I swiveled in my seat to watch Clemons. He kept his smile fixed in place and raised a hand, as if he had a cigar in it. Changing the gesture into a wave of dismissal, he said, "The astronaut program is open to anyone who qualifies, but due to the nature of the mission, our standards are very high. These ladies are the best pilots on the planet. Best lady pilots. Naturally, our new male candidates are also outstanding, and our focus today should be on these fine men and women. I don't want to hog their spotlight."

"Then I'll ask the ladies a question." The man turned to stare at the stage, finding each of us with his clear hazel gaze. "Would any of you object to serving with a black woman in space?"

Everyone froze a little. It felt like a trick question. I leaned toward the mic. "I would be delighted, and know several black women who are brilliant pilots."

Betty recovered next. "I wouldn't object, of course, so long as the standards aren't lowered."

Being angry always helps control my anxiety. Ida could outfly Betty. Imogene was a better pilot than me. And goodness knows Violette shouldn't even be on the stage. "We wouldn't have to lower the standards."

"Now, ladies . . ." Clemons stepped toward us, dragging his microphone with him. "Let's move on to the question that people keep writing in to ask. Which of you will be the first one in space?"

As we'd been coached, all of us raised our hands. Nicole raised both, just like Parker had. Me? I didn't really care who was first, so long as I got to go.

THIRTY-THREE

**TWO WHO MAY LAND ON
THE MOON SELECTED**

*IAC Names Men Who May
Land on the Moon*

KANSAS CITY, KS, July 2, 1957—Today the International Aerospace Coalition named the two astronauts who may become the first humans to set foot on the moon. They are Col. Stetson Parker of the United States, and Capt. Jean-Paul Lebourgeois of France, both veterans of the space program. Today, they and Lt. Estevan Terrazas of Spain were named as the crew of *Artemis 9,* which may go to the moon and back in April of next year.

They separated the astronaut candidates into two classes. The men were together for one, and the women for the other. I will admit that the first class they put us into made me a little complacent. Orbital mechanics. That was most of what I had done in the computer department.

The other women responded with varying degrees of success. Violette picked it up faster than I had expected. Nicole struggled with basic math and kept forgetting to take the square root or where the decimal place was supposed to be on the slide rule. I helped her where I could, but since I've never struggled with math, it was hard to figure out what to tell her. I just . . . I just did it.

Betty went through the motions, but I think she knew she wasn't going to actually get into space. Maybe she didn't even want to.

Sabiha worked her way through the orbital mechanics lessons with uneven progress, but iron determination. Jacira got it, but also hated it. She frequently muttered under her breath in Portuguese. I didn't speak the language, but I can recognize cursing.

When we turned in our first homework assignment, it was like flashing back to being in fourth grade again. The instructor looked mine over and shook his head. "Elma . . . did Dr. York help you with this?"

The room went red and then seemed to cool to freezing. I half-expected my breath to steam white. "No. He didn't."

"It's just . . . you only have the answers listed here." He smiled, and his spectacles flashed white in a beam of sunlight. "It's okay to get help, but I still need you to do all the work."

It really was just like fourth grade. Only this time, I wasn't going to have to wait, sobbing in the office, for my father to come and rescue me. I'd been too young then to know that there was a simple way to prove that I hadn't cheated on a test.

"I understand your concern, so please, ask me any question that you'd like, and I'll answer it. Right now."

He tapped the papers together on the desk with a sharp rap. "We don't have time for you to work through an equation. Next time, just do the work."

I ground my teeth together. He wanted me to write out all the in-between steps instead of just solving the equation? Fine. I could take the time to do that, and he could take the time to grade it. I knew how this conversation went. It had happened too many times for me not to know, and I had been an idiot to think that my time at the IAC would count for anything. "Yes, sir."

At that, Nicole stared at me, then raised her hand, smiling. "Excuse me, sir?"

"Yes, Nicole?"

"Elma wrote most of those equations."

He sighed. "Thank you, Nicole. I know she wrote the answers. But I needed her to do the work to find them."

She put her hand on her chest and widened her eyes. "Oh, goodness me. I'm so silly. I just—"

I cleared my throat before Nicole could go full debutante on him. "What she means, sir, is that in my work at the computer department at the IAC, I originated a good portion of the equations in last night's homework, and the ones that I didn't write, I've used on a daily basis for the past four years."

He blinked. "Oh." He set the pages down and smoothed them. "I see. That would have been useful information to know earlier."

Between dozing through the orbital mechanics classes, we also had advanced pilot training. We were often broken into groups of three and sent to different facilities to use simulators or specialized equipment. Some of it was old hat, like the "Dilbert Dunker," which I'd done for flight school as part of the WASPs.

But there were some unexpected twists. When I showed up for the Dilbert Dunker with Jacira and Betty, they gave us swimsuits.

Specifically, they gave us little blue bikinis.

In the dressing room, I held up the skimpy material and frowned. "Last time I took this test, we had to do it in a flight suit."

Jacira shrugged and unbuttoned her blouse. "I have learned not to be surprised at what Americans do."

"Don't look at me." Betty pulled her blouse off over her head. "I didn't do any advanced training when I was in the WASPs."

Jacira and I exchanged a glance. The application had required four hundred hours in high-performance aircraft. I didn't know how they did things in Brazil, but skipping that as a WASP would have been a surprising lack.

Regardless of my training, I had a choice of wearing the bikini or doing the test in my clothes, so I pulled the scraps of fabric up and did my best to make sure that they covered everything they were supposed to cover. Maybe they were going to give us the flight suit when we got out of the locker room.

Betty finished changing first, and headed out of the dressing room. She stopped right outside the bathroom door, then turned around and came back in. "Elma?"

"Yes?" I grabbed a towel and wrapped it around my midriff in a vague attempt at modesty.

"There are reporters here." Strain tightened her face. "I didn't call them."

Nodding, I continued to secure the towel, as if it took all my attention. "Thank you for the warning."

The Miltown in my purse whispered promises of calm, but I was about to go through underwater training. I couldn't afford to have my reflexes slowed even a little.

Scowling, Betty strode to her bag and pulled out a tube of lipstick. "Goddamn it. What part of 'exclusive' don't they understand?"

Rolling her eyes, Jacira pulled her long, dark hair back into a ponytail. "They are about to dunk us underwater. Many times. And you are put on lipstick?"

Betty shrugged. "With the bikinis, it's pretty clear what

kind of a test this is going to be. I aim to pass, 'cause I sure as hell ain't going to pass orbital mechanics."

I almost went out the door as I was. I was a physicist and a computer and a pilot, not a pinup girl. And yet . . . and yet, I could hear Mama saying, *What will people think?* She had always been on me to "gussy up" a little. I knew what the rules were for women. "Goddamn it."

Turning back to my bag, I slammed it open and dug through it to find my own tube of lipstick. The pill case rattled in the bottom of the bag, and I hesitated over it. No. I needed my reflexes fast for this test. I'd survived the press conference, and for most of the trial, there would be thousands of gallons of water between me and the reporters.

The silver lipstick tube gleamed in a corner of my bag. It was slick beneath my fingers. I pulled the lid off, twisted it, and applied a thick red coat to my lips. The makeup ladies at *Mr. Wizard* would be so proud.

Jacira watched and shook her head. "No. This is not why my country sent me."

"It's not why I'm here either." I capped the tube and straightened. "But lipstick won't keep me from doing my job."

Betty snorted. "Wearing lipstick practically *is* my job."

"You don't really . . ."

"Yep." She surveyed herself in the mirror and dropped her lipstick back in the bag. "I didn't have the flight hours to make the first cut, but *Life* was able to pull some strings to get me into the testing. After that? That's been all me, but I still owe the devil their due."

Given a choice, would I have made the same bargain? Oh yes. Yes, I would have. "Well. Shall we face the devil?"

"Heh. Most of these are just minor demons." She strutted toward the door. "Wait until *Life* hears about this. *Then* you'll see the devil incarnate."

I followed her to the door and thanked God for the towel. Cameras snapped and flashes went off as the three of us made our way to the Dilbert Dunker. And I had my first heart-sinking moment of realizing that Betty was right.

Let Betty pose for the camera. I focused on the actual test. The Dilbert Dunker sat at the deep end of the pool, up on a stand. The bright red metal cage had a pilot seat inside and sat poised above a set of rails that led into the pool. Ah . . . I'd spent so many hours learning to escape a water landing that it seemed almost nostalgic.

The problem was that training for an underwater escape began in the pool, outside the Dunker, with an obstacle course. They hadn't set one up. They were going to start us with the Dunker. We were being set up to fail.

The Navy test admins turned around to watch us. Or, more accurately, to watch Betty.

I could hardly blame them. How did she manage to sway like that without coming out of the bikini? The fabric was blue, but you could see it turning red just from the heat of her walk.

She stopped in front of the Navy officers with Jacira and me at her back, making an impromptu triangle. "So . . . who wants to dunk me?"

They had to pull Betty out of the cage. Mind you, this wasn't unusual for a first attempt, even with proper training. The thing dropped down a rail at a fifty-degree angle, hit freezing water, and then flipped you upside down. You had to unstrap yourself and escape the cage and they had blinders over your eyes, so you were doing it all by feel.

This is why Navy divers were in the pool as a matter of course. Still, I will admit to a certain amount of petty satisfaction at seeing Betty pulled out of the pool like a drowned cat. They wrapped her in a blanket and set her down on a bench while they reset the machine. My satisfaction turned to shame as I watched her shiver. I remembered my first attempt at the Dunker.

I turned to the Navy officer in charge. "Shall I go next?"

He did not quite roll his eyes, but it was close. "Sure. Why not. Let's send all of you in."

And this was what they called training . . . Trying not to growl, I clambered up the ladder to the Dunker's cage. Here, I had to let go of my towel, and the last scrap of modesty my mother had instilled.

As it dropped, flashes went off from the bevy of reporters stationed around the pool. I lowered myself into the cage and nearly shrieked.

The cage was metal. Including the seat. It had been in a pool of frigid water. I was wearing a bikini.

I definitely squeaked, but managed to keep it from being more than that. Still, it was one more reason to wish I were wearing a flight suit.

The officer lowered the harness over my shoulders. The cold, damp canvas pressed against my bare flesh as he helped me get buckled in. "All right, sweetheart. This is going to drop into the water and turn upside down. Your job is to not panic until the divers pull you out."

"I thought my job was to release myself and swim clear." I ran my hands over the buckle, trying to memorize its position.

"Right. That's what I meant." He slapped the top of the cage and stood up.

I leaned out. "Blinders?"

He hesitated and knelt back down. "You done this before?"

"I was a WASP." Of course, Betty had been too, but I'd flown high-performance aircraft. "Ferried Mustangs and most of the fighter planes, so they sent me to Ellington to train."

"Huh." He drummed his fingers on the edge of the cage, then leaned in close. "Okay. Listen. They aren't giving you dames the blinders. We were told to just go through the motions. You want to do this for real?"

I stared at him for a moment. *Just go through the motions?* They weren't going to put any of us into space.

Somehow, I managed to unlock my jaw. "They have me wearing a bikini, but I'm a goddamned pilot. Yes, I want to do this for real."

"Hot damn." He slapped the metal and stood again, leaning over into the control chamber. In a moment, he was back with the black goggles. "Don't drown, hear?"

"It wouldn't fit on my agenda." I took the goggles and pulled them on over my hair. The visible world went away.

With my hands, I verified the location of the shoulder harness, the cold metal frame of the cage, the buckle of my waist belt. And then I put my hands on the "stick" and nodded. "Ready."

Part of the test is that you don't quite know when they are going to release the cage. I filled my lungs, listening to the hush of fabric as the officer stood. The water lapped below me. A click.

And then the seat dropped.

Water slapped against me, wrapping me in winter. It pushed at my mouth and clawed the inside of my nose as everything spun. Immediately, my lungs started clamoring for air.

Panic did no good. I ground my teeth together and put my hands on my shoulders. There. The rough canvas of the shoulder harness was dead easy to find against my skin. In a flight suit, I used to have to fumble a bit.

I followed the line down to the buckle and popped it.

The waist belt rubbed against my stomach above the line of the bikini, its buckle a point of ice. I unsnapped it, pushing the two sides apart.

Wriggling free of the shoulder harness had been the trickiest part the last time I'd done this, but with the bikini, nothing caught or snagged. I slipped free almost before I was ready. I reached out and caught the edge of the cage with both hands to orient myself. I kicked free of the cage, swimming down and then back away from the "wreckage."

We were supposed to swim at a forty-five degree angle in order to get clear of presumed flames and oil slicks. That was harder to judge when swimming blind, and I suspect I broke the surface too close to the cage.

Sound rushed back in as the weight of water fell away. "—fast was that?" "Was that a record?" "Elma! Elma! Over here!"

Inhaling had never felt so good. I pulled the goggles off, smiling . . . at the wall. So I was turned around. That was okay. I needed to do a 360-degree spin with my arms over the water to clear any "oil" from around me.

After spinning in the pool, I turned to face the photographers and waved at them. A record? No. Even if I'd been fast, it was because the variables weren't the same as under normal test conditions.

But that was science, and science wasn't what they wanted from me.

THIRTY-FOUR

TWO-HOUR "WALK" IN SPACE PLANNED

Artemis 4 *Astronaut to Float*
75 Feet From Capsule

KANSAS CITY, KS, November 3, 1957—
(United Press International)—Capt. Cristiano Zambrano of Mexico will try to set a world "space walk"
record of perhaps two hours during the forthcoming
orbital flight of *Artemis 4,* the International Aerospace
Coalition said today.

Sitting in the simulator after hours, my thick binder of
checklists rested heavy on my lap. I massaged the bridge
of my nose and squeezed my eyes shut trying to press the
correct sequence into my brain by sheer force. The interior
of the simulator was a replica of the actual *Artemis* capsule
and as snug as the cockpit of a fighter, but where there
should be a canopy, I instead had a wall and ceiling of
switches with arcane acronyms. I'd been hoping that if I
studied in the simulator, I might have better recall during
an actual sim. No such luck, thus far.

"You ever coming out of there?" Nathaniel's voice came
from below the capsule.

I let my head thunk back against the padded seat.
"B-Mag."

With a laugh, Nathaniel climbed the ladder to stand on the small platform outside the capsule. "Pardon?"

"The Flight Director Attitude Indicator is called 'the F, D, A, I.' But the Body Mounted Attitude Gyro is abbreviated B, M, A, G, which is pronounced 'B-Mag.' I mean . . . really?" The orbital mechanics and the flight training weren't giving me any trouble. The acronyms, on the other hand, were killing me. "And why is that pronounced like a word when the commander is C, D, R? It takes longer to say."

" 'B-mag' is faster than 'B, M, A, G.' "

"You know what I mean." I glared down at the manuals in my lap as if they were Parker. "We have whole conversations without any actual nouns. 'We were doing an LOI burn, and Sim Sup dropped the FDAI along with the MTVC. Then the LMP saw BMAG fail, and we had an O2 off scale low . . . Ugh."

"No one's ever done a manual Lunar Orbit Insertion burn."

"You. Are not helping." I shifted my glare to where Nathaniel stood framed by the open hatch of the capsule. I was staring straight up at him. He'd nicked a spot under his chin when shaving. "And then there's the POGO. The Partial Gravity Simulator, which isn't even an acronym. If any of the women named something that, we'd be laughed out of the astronaut corps, which we are already. Oh. My. God. Did I tell you about the photo shoot last week in the T-33?"

"Yes. But feel free to tell me again if it will help." Nathaniel leaned an elbow on the edge of the narrow hatch.

"No. Thanks." It still burned, though. I thought they were finally going to let us go up in the T-33s, but all we did was sit in the cockpit and powder our noses. Literally powder our noses. At least when I sat in the capsule, we were doing simulations and learning something. I reached up and took Nathaniel's hand, turning it so I could kiss his palm. "Sorry I'm being such a grump."

"Tell you what . . . if you come out of there and help me go over some numbers in a report, I'll drill you on acronyms."

I shut my manual so fast the slap of its pages echoed off the tiny capsule interior. "Yes. Please. Please, let me do math."

He leaned down and kissed me on the cheek. "Great." Reaching down, he beckoned for me to give him the manual. "I've been missing you."

"Aw . . . you say the sweetest things." Standing, I wriggled out of the capsule. How some of the men could fit in there with a spacesuit stretched my understanding of physics.

Nathaniel leaned against the rail of the tiny platform. Past him, lines of cables and support struts wrapped the capsule in a network of chaotic artistry, designed to simulate missions as closely as possible for the people inside. I stretched until my back popped. The clock on the wall said that it was past eight o'clock. Apparently we were having dinner in the cafeteria again. "What are you working on?"

"Nothing complicated. Helen has already done the calculations, but I need to make sure the data reduction is okay before I send it up to the House Appropriations Committee." He clambered down the ladder with the manual tucked under one arm. "We're looking at what a proposed move to Brazil would do for the engineering department."

"I thought that was already approved." I slid down the ladder and hopped the last bit to the floor.

Nathaniel sighed. "It was. And then Senator Mason raised questions of national security over whether the United States should cede its power to another country."

I stopped at the foot of the ladder. "Is he unclear on what's happening? This is a global effort. There's not going to *be* a United States of anything if we don't get off this planet."

"He doesn't believe it." Nathaniel walked across the simulator room, shoes clicking on the concrete floor.

I followed, more quietly. Since joining the astronaut corps, I tended to wear sneakers and trousers to work. "The weather has been warming up. Has he not noticed that?"

He stopped by the bank of light switches. "Yeah, but right now we're in the sweet spot where temperatures feel normal, if a little out of season."

We'd be there for another five or more years before things started really running away. That was long enough for people to forget about the Meteor. "Well . . . as long as he keeps the funding going to support the space program at home, I suppose that's something."

"Right. Better if we're in Brazil, though." Nathaniel snapped the lights off and held the door to the sim lab for me. "Oh—how's the Brazilian astronaut holding up?"

"Jacira? She's amazing. The other day, the Sim Sup gave us a GPC that was at odds with the MIS—"

Nathaniel started laughing as the door shut behind him. "Do you hear yourself?"

"Fair." I glanced down the hall to be sure we were alone, then kissed him. "I'm still holding you to drilling me on these, though."

I settled into my chair at the Monday-morning meeting with a cup of coffee and a donut. There weren't really assigned seats, but habit and routine led us to sit in the same places every time. Malouf's and Benkoski's seats were empty because they were up on a mission, but none of the new astronauts would dare sit there.

Jacira, Sabiha, Nicole, and I sat together at the right-hand table, farthest from the door. For the most part, women tended to clump together in the crowd of men, although Lebourgeois and Violette naturally sat together near the back of the room. Betty sat near Parker, up at the front of the room next to Clemons, surrounded by his usual cloud of cigar smoke.

An all-important table at the back of the room held the donuts and coffee. I had not realized how much of the man's world was fueled by donuts and coffee.

Clemons flipped open the duty roster, which I had come to dread. "All right . . . Cleary and Lebourgeois, you're going to head over to ILC to do trials on the newest generation of space suit. They think they've solved the binding in the shoulder area, but don't trust them until you've spent the day in it."

Unpleasant, but a fair point. According to all the astronauts, the amount of effort it took to move in a space suit became incredibly fatiguing by the end of an EVA, so something that was mildly annoying when you first put it on could become intolerable by the end.

"Zambrano and Terrazas, you're still doing simulations with Wells, Tayler, and Sanderson, as per the original schedule. See if you can avoid breaking the IBM this time?"

Even I laughed at that. The mechanical computer that was supposed to manage the simulations had an abort rate that would have wiped out most of the astronaut corps if the simulations were real.

"Violette, Betty, Grenades, and Gladstone, you're in the barrel this week." He slid a couple of stapled pages across the table. I passed them back, glad I'd dodged that bullet. Being "in the barrel" meant being on the publicity tour. "Highlights include doing a public school appearance tomorrow and then cutting the ribbon on the reopening of I-70 on Wednesday."

"Gökçen, Wargin, Paz-Viveiros, Collins, Aldrin, and Armstrong, you're heading over to Chicago for a date with Adler Planetarium. Time to learn to use the sextant." Then he turned to me and smiled. That never ended well for me. "York. You and Parker are testing the new T-38 trainer."

I nearly dropped my coffee. The T-38? They hadn't even let me fly the T-33 yet, and I had somehow landed a test flight in the brand new and incredibly sexy T-38. I managed to exchange my urge to say "Really?" for a more measured "Yes, sir."

Nicole gave me a shove. "Aw, man. You get to have all the fun."

"Hey . . . boss's orders." But it didn't seem possible that keeping my head down and just doing the work had actually changed either man's mind. This was not a gift horse that bore examining, though. I'd been longing to fly the T-38 for—well, basically since it was invented.

"Trust me. She won't enjoy this." Parker pushed back from the table. "Let's get to work, people. We've got a moon to catch."

When I finished changing into my flight suit and parachute, I grabbed my helmet out of its wooden cubby and headed out to the tarmac. My mother would have perished if she could have seen me. Not only was I wearing trousers, but the chute straps ran so tightly through my legs that in some cultures I would be considered married to them.

Parker was already at the plane, his helmet propped on the edge of the cockpit. He was chatting with the crew chief, but nodded when he saw me, and swung right into pedantic mode. "The preflight check begins as you approach the aircraft."

Which was true of every plane ever flown. I nodded, hoping we could skip that part. "Right. Check for oil spills, obstructions, and anything out of the ordinary with the plane."

The beautiful, beautiful plane. The jet. From its needle nose back to the exhaust for the jet engine, the T-38 was a thing of streamlined beauty. The IAC planes were made of polished chrome with the blue-and-white logo of the IAC emblazoned across the tail.

He crossed his arms. Even with his aviator sunglasses in place, I could feel the glare. "I know you think you're a pilot, but a jet is different from a prop plane."

"Yes, sir." *Smile and nod, Elma, just smiiiiiile and nod.* I mean, he wasn't wrong. They *were* different. "I'm just eager to put that desk training and simulator time into practice."

"All right, then." He jerked his thumb to the plane. "What's the first thing you do after checking the area?"

"Check the logs. Then the canopy and seat safety pins."

"Do it." He leaned against the wing of the aircraft and made a shooing motion.

I checked the tie-down straps for the oxygen hose and the bolts, then hesitated, because I really didn't know this plane. "What am I missing?"

"Make sure you check for obstructions." He headed for the nearest intake with a slight limp.

"You okay?"

"You usually have to crouch to get a good line of sight through it, like this. Wait—" He lifted his head and beckoned me down. "While you're down here, check this out. Look along the wing—see how you can see through the body of the plane?"

"Um . . ." Brilliant. I did as he told me, peering along the wing at the plane, which was a solid mass in front of me.

"Your angle has to be just right. The wings are actually a single piece that goes all the way through the plane."

"Seriously? That is—oh!" I saw the glint of light and then a narrow view of the hangar on the far side of the plane. "Oh, wow."

"All right. This intake's clear, so take a look, then check the other side to see if it matches." He stepped back, favoring his left leg. "Copy?"

"Roger." I wanted to push it, because a pilot who was injured could directly affect me, but right now Parker was being nice. Or, at least, Parker levels of nice. Actually—wait. I have to be fair: when Parker was in pedantic mode, he was a patient and often generous teacher. It was just all the in-between stuff where we clashed.

Both sides were clear, and he walked me through checking the intakes for the engines with patience. But when I climbed into the rear cockpit, I had to resist dancing in my seat. It was such a pretty plane.

The act of going through every step of the preflight checklist helped focus me. Especially knowing that Parker was looking for any mistake at all.

That's right. I was less worried about a mistake killing me than I was about looking bad in front of Parker. My priorities were, perhaps, not what they should be.

I snugged down my shoulder straps and pulled the helmet into place. The helmet hugged my head and muffled most of the outside world. I connected the oxygen hose, twisting it until it clicked into place, and clipped it to my flight harness. I let the face mask hang open until we were airborne and the oxygen started to flow. For the moment, the canopy stood open, letting in the breeze from the high silver overcast sky. Petrol and tar and the resinous funk of rubber.

"All right." Parker's voice crackled in my ear. "Ready to start the number two engine?"

"I'm ready."

"All danger areas clear?"

I leaned to my left to look toward the back of the aircraft. Only the hanger stood behind us, and it was far enough back to be clear. Then I strained against the shoulder harness and checked behind us on the right. "All clear."

In front of me, Parker went through the same motions. All I could really see was the dome of his helmet as he settled back in his seat and nodded. "Let's signal for air. Hands clear?" In demonstration, he lifted his hands over his head, one fist pressed against the middle of his other palm. It wouldn't do to accidentally hurt our crew chief by bumping something.

"My hands are clear." They were clear, but my pulse was steadily speeding up. I took a slow breath to calm down. If I got this excited about a jet, a rocket would do me in.

Outside the jet, our ground crew ran back to feed air in to assist the engine ignition. From inside the craft, the whoosh of air rose to a steady whine.

"Thirty number two. There's 14% rpm. Ready tach. Throttle to idle."

The throttle matched the movement he was doing in the front and moved up. I wouldn't do anything until he switched control over to me, but I could pretend that my actions were powering the jet. At least for a little while.

Parker kept up a steady monologue, letting me know what he was doing. "Fuel flow is two hundred. Oil pressure is indicating. EGT rising."

So was my blood pressure. He was actually going to take me up in the jet.

"Seven seventy peak. Engine instruments look good. Hydraulics look good. Caution lights are out. Crossover is good." He paused, his helmet turned a little as if waiting for a response.

There's this weird thing in flying that makes it almost like a religion. Pilots do call-and-response as a liturgy of our own. "My engine instruments are good. Hydraulics check good. Caution lights are out."

"Clear left?"

I checked again. "Clear."

"Okay. Let's divert air to number one. Hands clear?" Parker lifted his hands over his head.

"My hands are clear."

Outside, the ground crew ran to switch the hose to the number two engine. Again, I had to marvel at the difference between Parker the teacher and Parker the asshole. His voice through all of this was calm and patient.

"Ready to start number one?"

"Ready." My voice, on the other hand, might have cracked a little. It was all I could do not to cackle with glee as the aircraft came alive beneath us. We went through the same checks for the number one engine, and by the end of it, I had almost matched the calmness of Parker's voice.

"Throttle gate is engaged. Okay . . . let's disconnect air." He lifted his hands over his head. "Hands clear?"

"My hands are clear."

They were clear of all instruments and, somewhat remarkably, not shaking. All of my nerves seemed to be vibrating, but it didn't show in my hands. Jets are infinitely easier than crowds, and much, much more alluring.

When the ground crew pulled the hose away from the engine, Parker resumed his litany. "Battery switch checks out. Good start."

We went through the pre-taxi checks and nav checks with the same call-and-response. Then we got to "Time to pull the canopy and seat pins."

"Canopy and seat pins pulled." The bright orange plastic came out easily. I lifted them both over my head to demonstrate that I'd done it before stowing them in the pocket by my left knee.

"Chocks clear." Outside, the crew followed his hand signals.

We began to taxi.

A plane on the ground is an ungainly thing. It jostled me against my shoulder straps, but I followed along with Parker as we went through the rest of the nav and comm checklists during taxi.

"Arms clear." He lowered the canopies and cut off the breeze from the outside.

My God. Even in the rear seat, the plane had such a wide field of vision. What must it have been like in front?

The tower came across our radio. "Talon One One, Tower. You are cleared for takeoff."

Parker's helmet turned a little, as if he could look over his shoulder to see me. "You ready?"

"Confirmed, ready."

He nodded and replied to the tower. "Talon One One. Cleared for takeoff."

Parker brought the jet up to full military power and lit the afterburner. The jet jolted like someone had kicked me in the pants. He released the brakes and popped the burners.

The engine whine rose in pitch as the jet rolled forward, forcing me back into my seat. It wasn't like a prop plane, where the force is almost gentle. This thundered through me, dragging my back into the seat.

She lifted off the runway so smoothly, I almost clapped as the ground fell away. But this was a training flight, not a tourist ride, so my delight stayed inside.

I watched the gauges and the world outside. It was like

the air had become liquid and flowed around us. How can you feel heavy and light at the same time? The G-force of takeoff pressed me into my seat, but the air held me up.

God. This was a beautiful plane. My love for it probably broke all the rules about worshipping graven images.

"York." Parker banked to the south and pressed me farther into my seat.

"Sir?" He wasn't going to offer to let me take the stick, was he? Not yet.

"I . . . have a problem and I need a favor."

"Come again?"

"You heard me." The asshole Parker returned for a moment and then he sighed. There's an intimacy to the sound of another pilot in your ear. "Look . . . Look. You and Malouf are the only two who know about the thing with my leg."

"I . . ." Where was this going? "I haven't told anyone."

"I know." He sighed again. "Thank you."

"What . . ." Everything about this conversation confused me. He couldn't have said this on the ground? For that matter, why hadn't Malouf reported him? "May I ask what's going on?"

Above the canopy, the clouds sank toward us, changing from a featureless expanse of silver gray to crenellations of cotton. Parker took us up into them and the wisps brushed past, feathering away as we ripped through.

The jet punched out of the upper level of clouds into blue sky.

"God."

It was not profanity. It had been so long since I had seen clear blue . . . It ached, that blue. The unobscured sun flared across the clouds and brought tears to my eyes, even with my visor.

"Yeah . . ." Parker sighed again. "This? This is amazing,

but space . . . I need to see a doctor. My leg goes pins and needles and then randomly, just stops working. They'll ground me if they even suspect something is wrong."

"So go to a doctor who's not a flight surgeon."

Parker gave the bitterest laugh I'd heard from him. "You think I haven't tried. I'm the first man into space. I can't go anywhere without reporters following me. I can't sneeze, I can't play ball with my sons, I can't even visit my—"

He stopped talking, leaving only the hiss of oxygen, the sound of my own breathing, and the rush of air around us.

"Can't visit your . . . ?"

"Can't visit my doctor." Pretty sure that hadn't been what he was going to say. "If I certify you on the T-38, will you let me use the flights to mask my visits to a doctor?"

I asked questions to buy time. "How will that work, exactly? I mean . . . you're not going to let me go up on my own."

"No. But there's a clinic. We land near it. I go in. I come back out. We keep flying."

"Just the T-38? You're not offering me a seat on a rocket?"

"Can't." His helmet turned as if he wanted to look back at me. "I get some say in that, but not the final word. If I did, gotta be honest, there wouldn't be any women in the program at all. Not yet."

"You know I've logged more flight hours than you, right?"

"Yes. And I know about the Messerschmitts and the target practice and all the other things you WASPs did. None of that matches what a test pilot does, and it sure as hell doesn't match what we do up there."

"Well, we can't know that, can we? Besides, how hard can it be if you can do it with a bum leg?"

He put the plane into a roll, as if that proved some sort of point.

I laughed—giggled, really. "Sorry—wait. I wasn't laughing at you. It's just—the plane is beautiful."

"She really is." He leveled the T-38 out and left us nearly floating in our seats. "So will you do it?"

"You still hate me?"

"Yep." He sighed again, which was such an odd sound coming from him. It was as if he had to let his ego leak out before he could keep talking. "But I acknowledge that you will keep your word and are principled."

"And you aren't worried that those principles will lead me to report you?"

"I am."

"The problem is that you're asking me to risk lives and jeopardize the program."

"I've kept myself off crew lists. But there's a difference between deferring missions and being grounded."

"And now they want you to go to the moon." The thing that was tempting about his proposition wasn't the T-38. It was the chance to finally be in his good graces, even if he resented me for it. I don't know. Maybe before I'd been in the program, I would have been able to take him up on the deal . . . but now? Now I knew exactly how fit you had to be as an astronaut. To say nothing of what would happen if I got caught colluding. "I won't tell anyone, but . . . I'm sorry. I can't help you hide it."

The air hissed past in our silence.

"Well . . . you're honest, I'll give you that. Okay." Parker's head dipped forward and then lifted. "I know about the Miltown."

THIRTY-FIVE

HURRICANE DATA SOUGHT

---

3 UN Planes Detailed for Research Work

PARIS, Nov. 3, 1957—Three United Nations planes
will be detailed for special hurricane research work
next summer and fall, officials said today. The United
States Air Force will supply the United Nations with
two B-50 Superforts and a B-47 Stratojet for the project. They will fly the Atlantic, Caribbean, and the Gulf
of Mexico as part of an ongoing effort to understand
how weather patterns have shifted since the Meteor
strike in 1952.

How do you tell your husband that you're being black-
mailed? Over dinner? "Say, sweetie, a funny thing happened to me today. Pass the salad?"

Maybe in bed, while distracting him with sex?

Or you could just blurt it out while brushing your teeth.

"Parker's trying to blackmail me."

Nathaniel pulled the floss out of his mouth and turned.
"What?"

"He knows about the Miltown and wants my help with
something."

"What." Same word. Totally different meaning. His

hands were clenched so tightly around the floss that it cut into the sides of his fingers, turning them dead white.

I swallowed, and the minty freshness made my stomach turn over in sour knots. I drew a full breath that burned cold. The knot of anxiety in my chest would have sent me reaching for a Miltown, but not now. Damn Parker.

"You can't tell anyone." This is why I hadn't told him at work. If I had, he would have stormed into Clemons's office and made demands about Parker's attempts at blackmail.

"Clemons has to know." The tips of his fingers, past the floss, had begun to go purple.

Setting my toothbrush in the holder, I sighed. "Let's sit down."

Nathaniel looked down and blinked at the floss. He uncurled it, flexing his fingers, and dropped it into the waste bin. "Okay."

By the time we got to the sofa, trembles shook my arms and sweat coated my back. I swallowed and stared at my hands, which I held in a relaxed and ladylike posture on my lap. Mama would be so proud. "If you tell anyone, then Clemons will know about the Miltown and my anxiety and the vomiting, and then what will he think? That I'm fit to go into space? That I'm even fit for the program? He already thinks I'm a publicity stunt."

"Who told you that?" The sofa creaked as he leaned forward. "Parker."

I nodded.

Nathaniel pushed himself off the sofa and paced to the Murphy bed and back. He stopped in front of the coffee table, legs spread and hands on his hips. "Tell me what happened."

"Promise me that you won't tell anyone." Tendons

jumped under the skin on the backs of my hands, but I didn't clench them into fists. "Or do anything."

His body stayed rigidly still, but he turned to stare out the window at the lights of Kansas City. "I can promise you that I will talk with you before doing anything. I can't promise to do nothing, because that is a promise I won't keep."

I rubbed my thumb on one of the muscles that kept twitching. Why I bothered, I don't know, since my entire body was trembling with stress. "He's been having trouble with his left leg. Pins and needles, he says. A couple of months ago, I caught him in the stairwell and he couldn't stand. Asked me not to tell. Later, it looked like it had gone away, so I thought it was temporary."

And it had felt safer to keep waiting for someone else to see his symptoms. I could chalk my silence up to prudence or compassion, but it had been largely fear.

Drawing another breath, I told Nathaniel about the flight, and the request, and then the demand. "He took me with him to the clinic. I think he didn't want me out of his sight."

"Into the examining room?" Nathaniel's voice cracked.

"No—no. Just the lobby." There had been a phone at the nurse's station, and I'd nearly called Nathaniel from there. Thank God I hadn't. "When Parker came out, he was green. And he stopped in the bathroom to throw up."

The problem with small clinics is that the walls are thin. I am all too familiar with the sound of retching.

"After another five minutes, he came out. He was pale, but not green, and he'd put his aviators on."

I had some guesses about why he was wearing sunglasses inside. My eyes always got red after a bout of vomiting.

Nathaniel grunted. "So the news is bad. Did he tell you what?"

I shook my head. "I didn't ask. I let him pretend that everything was fine."

"That was kinder than he deserved."

I shook my head. "I just didn't want to feel sorry for him."

"Anything else?"

"He let me have the controls of the T-38 on the way back. I guess it was a reward or something." My fingers had gone to ice. How could I be sweating and cold at the same time? "So . . . that's it. Back at the IAC, it was like nothing had happened."

Nathaniel grunted again and turned back to pacing. He's tall, my husband, and our apartment doesn't give him a lot of ground to cover. With the Murphy bed down, he had even less. He finally stopped in front of the window, staring out. "I could . . . I could force the issue. With the Sirius coming online, the G-forces of takeoff are going to be harsher than with the Jupiter. I could insist on physicals for all the astronauts."

"He would see through that."

"I'm not going to have him jeopardize the program, or the people in it, for the sake of his ego."

Or for mine, for that matter. Nathaniel didn't say it, but here we came to the problem. I didn't want anyone to know that I had anxiety. While some of that was fear that they wouldn't let me go into space, the rest of it was the same old concern. *What would people think?* And then, beneath that, the fear that they were right. "He's been deferring missions while he tried to figure out what was going on."

"But now there's the moon." The streetlights lit his hair into a corona. "You really think he's going to defer that?"

I shook my head. "I've been thinking about it all day. I'll have to get rid of the pills, that's for certain. And stop seeing the doctor. The more time between my last refill and when Parker outs me, the better. He will, though . . . Not immediately, because if he did, I would have no reason to keep silent."

Nathaniel's head snapped back to me. "That seems like a very bad idea."

"What else am I supposed to do?" I spread my hands, but my fingers were shaking, so I rested them in my lap again. "He knows. I don't know how, but he does."

With a grunt, Nathaniel turned to pace again. "The driver—that night we stayed in a hotel because of the reporters, I sent a driver to pick up our clothes and your prescription."

So it wasn't just Parker who knew. How long—how long before everyone knew and I got booted from the program and it went into the papers and—

My stomach lurched and twisted in time with my thoughts. I staggered to my feet and barely made it to the bathroom before losing it. Huddled on the bathroom tiles, I clutched the toilet and retched. Nathaniel came in behind me and held my shoulders as all of the accumulated anxiety of the day heaved out of me.

And I hated myself. Daddy would have been so disappointed in me, unable to handle a little pressure. If I couldn't handle this, maybe I shouldn't be in the space program. I was stupid and weak, and it didn't matter how hard I worked: this sickness would always be a part of me.

Nathaniel filled the tumbler from the bathroom sink with water and held it out to me. "I won't let anyone hurt you."

"How will you stop him?" My throat hurt as I spoke, but I took the water and swallowed.

"I don't know." He ran a hand over my hair and down my back. "Not all of it, at any rate."

"I don't even know part of it." I rocked back to sit on the floor, leaning against the side of the tub.

Nathaniel stood and opened the medicine cabinet.

"No." My fingers tightened around the tumbler.

Ignoring me, Nathaniel pulled out the bottle of Miltown and crouched in front of me. "Elma . . . is this better? Throwing up and being miserable? Is that better than whatever it is Parker could do to you?"

"I don't—" My voice fractured on the pain in my throat. "I don't know."

"Then let me tell you what I see." Nathaniel shifted to squeeze in next to me against the tub. He put an arm around my shoulders and pulled me against him, the pill bottle in one hand.

"Okay."

"You're better. With this. I was so—so worried about you before . . ." He shook the bottle so the pills rattled inside it. "Before this. I could hear when you threw up. You'd stopped eating. We went to bed together, but you didn't sleep. And you weren't talking to me about any of it. I thought you might be pregnant, until . . . that day. In my office. I was really frightened for you. And right now? The idea that Parker might put you through that, deliberately, because he's made you afraid to use a tool that helps—I would like to punch him."

That last sentence was so matter-of-fact that a laugh surprised its way out of me. Wiping my eyes with the back of my hand, I looked up at Nathaniel, but his eyes were squeezed shut, a crease carved between his brows. "You . . . you aren't kidding."

He let his breath out in a controlled stream. "No." Rolling the bottle in his fingers, he shook his head. "I have never had such a strong urge for violence. If I had been there, I probably would have punched him. And then he would have beaten the tar out of me."

With each revolution of the bottle, the little white pills inside rattled and shifted. Their tiny clatter promised a blanket of soothing calm. "I don't know what to do."

"Do you think the pressure is going to get any lighter?"

Sighing, I folded in on myself, and sagged against Nathaniel. He pulled me tight, pressing his lips against the top of my head. "Here's what I think. You keep yourself healthy, and then we can deal with Parker. Together. I don't know how, but I know we can."

"How can you be so sure?"

"Because we survived the end of the world." He kissed me again. "And you are my lady astronaut."

I followed Nicole's maid back to her sunken living room, where most of the 99s were munching on hors d'oeuvres and sipping cocktails. Jacira and Sabiha had joined the mix, but I didn't see Betty or Violette.

"Sorry I'm late. Aunt Esther called, and it took a while to get off the phone."

"How is the dear?" Nicole rose from the arm of the sofa she was perched on, leaving Imogene with her head bowed over a flight manual. "Martini?"

"Please." The glory of knowing a senator's wife was that liquor was never lacking at the Wargin house. I'd taken the Miltown out of my purse, but hadn't gotten rid of it, and having something to take the edge off seemed very appealing.

Helen bounded across the room to hug me, still holding the manual she'd been studying. "Missed you."

"Me too. Maybe we can grab dinner sometime?" I'd gone past the computer department a couple of times after my "promotion," as they called it, but it had been awkward. I kept wanting to check numbers, but that would just annoy everyone. "What are you reading?"

She shrugged. "It's just orbital trajectory calculations. Pretty basic."

"Basic for you!" Nicole handed me a martini with a laugh. "Some of us struggle with that stuff."

"That's why we trade. You teach me about simulator. I teach you about orbital calculations."

I raised my glass. "And if someone can get the acronyms through my head, I would be greatly appreciative."

The clear, cold gin lit up my mouth with all its juniper glory. I closed my eyes and sighed with appreciation as my shoulders relaxed, just a smidge. I'd missed these women. Thank God Nicole had thought about setting up a study group. Opening my eyes, I carried my cocktail and my books over to join Helen on the sofa.

Kicking off my shoes, I settled down and tucked my feet up under me. "No Pearl?"

Helen shook her head and scowled. "She doesn't think there's any point in prepping for the astronaut tests."

"They have to open it up more widely at some point, if it's really going to be a colonization effort."

From her spot on the sofa, Nicole nodded. "And that's something my husband strongly supports."

"Wait—" I blinked, feeling like I'd missed something. "Are they still talking about keeping it a military venture?"

With a sigh, Nicole scooted forward to face me. "I know you hate the idea, but—"

"But nothing. We have to get off the planet. I mean, sure, they might—and I stress the word *might*—be able to keep the greenhouse effect from running away, but by the time we know if that's going to work, it'll be too late to try to establish colonies elsewhere. We have to do it *now*, while we have the resources and the time."

"Preaching to the choir." Nicole smoothed the pages of her book, then reached for her martini. She took a sip of it before she continued. All of us—it wasn't just me—were staring at her, waiting to see what she was going to say. "But. There are members of Congress—and, in fact, of the UN—who only respond to questions of military threat. So if having a military component to the missions is useful in getting funding and keeping the program going, then that's what my husband will do."

"That's . . . Why are people so stupid?"

Nicole shrugged and unbuttoned her blouse by one. "Hormones. And if men are going to be led by them, then I'm happy to play my part."

Ida raised her glass. "Hear, hear!"

"How are you ladies doing this evening?" Poor Senator Wargin chose that moment to wander into the living room. I'm pretty sure he wasn't used to a roomful of women laughing at him, but he didn't seem to mind.

"Does anyone know what a MITTS is?" Jacira looked up from the binder she had been studying. She'd stretched out on the floor with her legs kicked up behind her.

"Um . . ." That was all I could offer.

"Mobile IGOR Tracking Telescope System," Ida said, without even looking up from the book she had open. She tapped the pencil against the edge of the page as she read.

"Seriously? An acronym within an acronym?" I tilted my head back to glare at the ceiling. "I'm trying to remember what IGOR means."

"Intercept Ground Optical Recorder."

Why the hell wasn't she in the astronaut corps already? I mean, besides the color of her skin. "You should be in the program."

Ida snorted, but didn't look up. Her pencil beat a faster rhythm on the pages.

"The application rules are such obvious baloney. If they could bend them for Violette and Betty, then—"

"Elma . . ." Nicole shook her head.

"Come on." All the frustration of the past months rolled out of me. "Violette barely had a hundred solo flight hours when she applied.

Ida dropped her book. "You did not just say that."

"Yeah. You want to give Dr. King some ammunition? You tell him to look into the flight records of Violette Lebourgeois and Betty Ralls. Violette's in because she's French and her husband is one of the astronauts. Married couple in space makes a nice story, right?"

Nicole closed her book. "You're not wrong. And you're not right, either."

"It's discrimination, pure and simple." It was, too. "Betty's only in because they wanted to control the publicity, and *Life* gave them a way to do so. Those two spots should have gone to the most qualified candidates."

"You think I was the best candidate they saw? You think you were?" Nicole shook her head again, her eyes glittering. "I'm good. I qualified. But my husband is also a senator, and one who's been backing the IAC since day one. Jacira was a beauty contest queen—"

"With a master's in engineering." I didn't like where she was going with this. She was undercutting the very real qualifications these women had. And . . . and I didn't want her to get to me.

From the floor, Jacira pushed up to sit and crossed her legs in front of her. "Yes. But I was not the only Brazilian woman with a pilot's license and an engineering degree. Granted, there are only four of us, but I was not the one with the most flight time."

"And I was *Mr. Wizard*'s Lady Astronaut."

"It's all about the story that the IAC wants to tell." Nicole shrugged and took a sip of her martini. "That's what politics is. Stories."

"And the story that they want to tell doesn't include black people?" I winced, realizing I'd cut Helen out of the equation. "Or Taiwanese? Just white people."

Ida shrugged and closed her book with a thump. "Same old story. Just another chapter." She stood up and stretched. "I'd better call it a night."

A chorus of yawns and agreements met her, and the party broke up. As I put on my hat and pulled on my gloves, I kept wanting to rant about the unfairness of it. But I didn't. Ida had made it pretty clear that she was done with the topic.

And then there was the other nagging thought. The thing is . . . I don't know how much of my anger was a desire to help the black cause, and how much was because I wanted to get Violette and Betty out of my way.

THIRTY-SIX

DR. KING CHARGES IAC
WITH DISCRIMINATION

Special to The National Times.

KANSAS CITY, KS, Nov. 22, 1957—Amid allegations that two of the so-called "Lady Astronauts" were not qualified for the program, a Southern Negro minister has charged the International Aerospace Coalition with discrimination. The United Nations governing committee has convened a special hearing to discuss the truth of the charges. Director Norman Clemons has stated that the two women were part of a pilot program to see if "mission specialists" could be trained for the space program without the rigid requirements of the early astronauts—something that would be necessary, he said, for the establishment of colonies.

The MASTIF is at once a joy and a bane, and not just because it's another acronym. The Multi-Axis Space-Test Inertia Facility, or gimbal rig, is a giant thing that a mad scientist designed.

I might even mean that literally.

Certainly, it would look at home as a torture device in some underground lair. At the moment, Nicole was strapped into the chair at the heart of it. The rigid plastic chair was a replica of the *Artemis* astronaut couches, except that her head was strapped in a fixed position.

Surrounding the chair were aluminum tubes that formed a three-axis gimbal rig. I say "aluminum tubes," but they were really more like cages. Each one could move independently of the others, tumbling the chair over on the roll, pitch, and yaw axes.

Right now, Nicole was rotating at a leisurely 15 rpm, but the thing could get up to 30 rpm. In theory, it gave us a sense of the sort of tumbling that might happen during a space mission, although if anyone were ever tumbling at 30 rpm, something would have gone terribly, terribly wrong.

I leaned against the wall of the control room, waiting with Jacira and Betty for our turn. An actual scientist ran the test, but our evaluation was done by one of the other astronauts, which is why Parker stood at the observation window with a stopwatch in one hand.

Betty stood next to Parker and tried to seem relaxed, but she had too much makeup on, which did nothing to mask the puffy bags under her eyes. I gathered from watercooler chatter that her testimony at the UN hearings about the discrimination charges had been rough. It was hard not to feel bad for her.

A nitrogen-gas jet hissed as Nicole tried to cancel out the rotation. It looked like she was going for pitch first. The jet popped and fired again.

A whole series of cameras chattered along with it. I'd left the Miltown at home because I couldn't risk having my reflexes slowed for this test. My stomach turned knots even before I got into the chair.

At least they'd made the reporters stop using flashes in here, though I suppose you could argue that the strobing would be good practice for being disoriented in space.

My right hand twitched, trying to anticipate the amount

of gas and the timing Nicole would need to slow the pitch down.

Jacira pulled her hair back from the nape of her neck. "Hey, boss, how much is this really like space?"

Parker shrugged. "Not much."

"So why do we have to do it?"

He shook his head, focused on the stopwatch and the window. "Come on, Wargin . . . You got this."

Moments later, the pitch evened out and Nicole started working on the roll. It was tricky, because you still had to manage the pitch, but she'd been getting faster each time.

The jets popped with fast little bursts of gas as Nicole stabilized the yaw. Parker nodded. "Good . . . See how she's doing a double tap?"

I cocked my head, listening to the jets fire as much as watching them. "Is that better than a slow sustain?"

"When you're trying to gauge how much force it will take? Yes." He shifted his weight off of his left leg and rolled his ankle a little. "The trouble with the slow sustain is that it might not be enough to make a difference, and you can bleed off a lot of fuel without realizing it."

Outside, the jets popped twice more, then gave a sustained hiss as Nicole got rid of the yaw rotation.

I watched Parker set his foot down and the way he shifted his weight, as if he were testing it. Clearing my throat, I took a step closer to him. "Should we schedule some more T-38 time?"

He almost looked away from the window, but arrested the movement and stared at Nicole spinning around and around. "Not necessary."

Since that trip to the clinic, he had only asked for one other side trip. We'd done other training, and I kept waiting for him to rat me out, but so far, he'd just been his usual condescending self—except when he taught. I almost liked him then.

"Why do we have to do it?" Betty laid a hand on Parker's arm, a disturbingly intimate gesture. "If the gimbal isn't like space?"

"It's not, sweetheart. But it's more like it than most things you'll find on Earth." He clicked the timer off. "Good. York, suit up. Wargin's been in there enough times today."

My heart ratcheted up to a higher gear. I tried to tell myself that it was excitement—well . . . I mean, it was. I liked the gimbal rig. I just didn't like having to run the gauntlet of reporters to get there.

Parker walked to the door and rested his hand on the technician's shoulder. "Good job with her. Get the logs for me?"

"Yes, sir." The tech straightened up, as if just having Parker touch him had somehow revitalized him.

"Excuse me." Betty put her hands on her hips. "This is our third time here, and I haven't had a turn yet."

Parker barely cast a glance over his shoulder. "I'm not being paid to waste time, or the government's resources. You just keep being pretty, and writing your little articles."

Juuuuust when you thought he wasn't so bad. I mean, I didn't *disagree* with him, but I wouldn't actually say that out loud.

Wait . . . no. I had said things that bad about Betty before. That's why she had to testify to Congress. I sighed and turned to her. Her cheeks had gone red, and she had pulled out her reporter's notebook.

"You okay?"

"Of course!" She smiled brightly and jotted a note. "Just need to describe what one of these tests looks like. It's easier to do that as an observer. Right?"

"Sure."

"Better get going, or Parker will have your ass."

I headed to the door, grabbing my helmet from the bench. One of the technicians was helping Nicole out of the gimbal cage, while Parker stood and talked with her. By his hand gestures, he was giving her some tips about the pitch corrections she'd made. I think his patience as a teacher was part of what blindsided me every time we clashed.

I very deliberately stopped in front of the reporters to put my helmet on. Much like the other astronaut skills I was practicing, I had been trying to desensitize myself to the reporters. Today I focused on posing without seeming to pose. Who knew that astronauts had to do so much modeling?

"Elma! What's been the most exciting task today?"

It was always tempting to say something like "Getting my nails done," except I knew that they'd print it. "Today I simmed terminal docking maneuvers and tried to fine-tune RHC inputs through an overly generous deadband."

See, learning acronyms was useful for something.

The cameras snapped and whirred as I strapped the helmet on. This was fine. They weren't a threat, and I knew what they wanted. Maybe that was the key to my anxiety in general: figuring out what people wanted from me. Although, if I kept that in mind, I would have gotten my flight suit tailored to show off my shape a little more, like I'm pretty sure Nicole had done. As she walked toward me from the gimbal rig, her waist nipped in just a little more than seemed possible in these boxy overalls.

Parker followed her, smiling at the reporters. His limp didn't seem so bad today, just a slight favoring of the left leg, and only if you were looking for it.

"Colonel Parker! How are the ladies doing?"

"They're a credit to their nations." He gave that shit-eating grin of his. "We're all very proud of them."

I headed for the gimbal rig, eager to see if I could drop my time from my last run.

"Any truth to the rumor that you're being replaced on the moon landing?"

The room went silent. Even the hum of the generators seemed to pause in mid-oscillation. Parker went pale, but his smile never faded. "I'd be curious to know your sources, but yes."

I hadn't told anyone anything. God. What had Nathaniel done?

The room snapped back into motion. All of the reporters were shouting questions at Parker now. He held his hands up and, miraculously, they responded by shushing.

"I have a lingering war injury that needs some attention, so the agency and I decided that it would be better to attend to that." He gave another smile. "I'm sure you understand that I can't make any speculation about who is going to replace me. Now, if you'll excuse me, we have some testing to do. York. Get in the chair."

Parker walked away from all of us. Instead of heading back into the observation booth, he left the room entirely.

I hadn't told. Goddamn it. I hadn't told anyone. But there wasn't a chance in hell that Parker would believe me.

Smiling at the tech, who stood by to strap me into the rig, I gave a little shrug. "I need to run to the ladies' room. Back in a flash."

I hurried across the lab and out the door that Parker had used. As the door swung open, I caught him straightening from the wall, as if he'd been leaning against it, and only the sound of the door had brought him upright. He looked over his shoulder with an easy smile.

It fell from his face when he saw me. "I told you to get in the chair."

"I didn't tell anyone." Besides Nathaniel, of course. But he'd said he would tell me before he took any action.

Parker's face stayed blank, but he looked at the floor. "I did."

I was still about ten feet away from him, but that stopped me in my tracks. "But—"

"I have bone spurs in my neck, likely from ejections during my test pilot days. They're pressing on my spinal column." He shrugged, as if that was somehow no big deal. "I know what you think of me, but believe it or not, I care more about the program than I do about my place in it. I would have been a danger."

"I'm—" What do you say to that? "Are you going to be okay?"

"Surgery. Tomorrow, actually."

"Is there . . . is there anything I can do?"

"Yeah. Get in the fucking chair. Like I told you to." He raised his head and took a step closer. "And don't insult either of us by pretending you care."

"Wow . . . You really do practice being offensive."

The side of Parker's mouth curled. "Go. When I come back, you'd damn well better have mastered that thing."

"Yes, sir." For a moment there, he'd seemed human. I forgot who I was dealing with.

"Just so we're clear, you still need to keep your head down and do as you're told. So long as you aren't a threat to the program, my lips remain sealed." He took another step. "You earned that much, but the moment I think you're a danger, you're out. Are we clear?"

Swallowing, I nodded. Ironically, I wished that I hadn't left the Miltown at home.

The rumor mill said that if Parker hadn't done the bone spur surgery, he'd risk paralyzation, which made the whole "I care more about the program" thing complete bunk. Of course, the rumor mill also said that aliens had implanted probes in him.

The Monday-morning staff meeting started with Clemons and his usual cloud of cigar smoke. "So. The first thing is to let you all know that Colonel Parker has come through his surgery just fine. No complications, and we should see him back here in a month or so."

I have to admit that my first thought was of intense relief that Parker would be gone for a month. That got me farther away from my last doctor's appointment, and maybe even if he told someone about the Miltown, it wouldn't look like it was a problem. No one had to know that I still had pills, which I was hoarding for an emergency.

"What? He had already the surgery?" Lebourgeois raised his brows in surprise. "I have only just heard that he was ill."

Clemons nodded, puffing on his cigar. "He'd set up the appointment some time ago, but didn't want anyone to know because he thought it would distract you. Good man."

I may have rolled my eyes at that version of history.

"Who's going up instead?" Betty, ever the journalist, leaned forward across the table. "To the moon, I mean?"

"His shadow was Malouf, so he'll step forward." Clemons pulled his agenda toward him. "That's jumping ahead on today's schedule a bit, but . . . We'll need to pull Malouf from the next *Lunetta* flight so he can concentrate on training for the lunar mission. Benkoski and Terrazas are already up on the station. All of this has made us realize that we need more manpower."

Manpower. Of course. Why use any of the women who were qualified and sitting right here when you could bring some more men in?

"Now, I want to be clear that this isn't a PR decision. It has nothing to do with the UN hearings. We'd always planned on expanding the program as things got settled, and Colonel Parker's injury just accelerated that timetable a little."

Sure it did. I glanced at Nicole, who had her mouth twisted in a little moue of displeasure.

"It'll take a while to get them hired and up to speed, so I'll need your patience and help with that. Meanwhile . . . I think it's time to deploy one of the ladies."

Sabiha scooted her chair forward and stared at Clemons intently. You could see the same thought bubble over her head as was no doubt appearing over all of ours. *Me. Let it be me. Please let it be me.*

I sat calmly, with my hands folded on my lap, the way my mother had taught me. Beneath my shirt, my heart was leaping out and waving its metaphorical hands. *Pick me. Pick me . . .*

"Parker's suggestion, and I concur, is that we send up Jacira Paz-Viveiros." He lowered his cigar. "Congratulations."

Finally! A woman was finally going into space. Normally duty assignments were quiet, professional affairs, but even the men were visibly thrilled for Jacira. I congratulated her, grinning so hard my face hurt.

And I meant it, too.

But . . . I was feeling such a weird mix of emotions. Jacira deserved the flight. I was thrilled for her that she was going to be the first woman in space. I was relieved that it wasn't Betty or Violette, who clearly would have just been picked for publicity. Jacira was a real pilot. I was also weirdly relieved that it wasn't me, because as the first woman in space, she would be subjected to a level of scrutiny that would break me. Especially without resorting to Miltown.

But beneath all of those thoughts, I was afraid, because there was a part of my brain that wondered if Parker really *had* managed to ground me.

THIRTY-SEVEN

WOMEN ARE READY FOR SPACE

By ROBERT REINHOLD

KANSAS CITY, KS, Dec. 16, 1957—Next week—if all goes as planned—a new milestone in space history will be reached when Jacira Paz-Viveiros is lofted into space for nearly six days to become the first woman there. The decision by the International Aerospace Coalition to send the 32-year-old beauty queen into space along with two male crewmen has been made despite long doubts, and what some might call prejudices, about the abilities of women to withstand the physical and psychological rigors of such an ordeal.

Sitting at the CAPCOM desk, I began to understand why Parker always had that damn tennis ball to throw. Mind you, I wasn't actually the CAPCOM yet—Cleary had that pleasure. I was just shadowing him while Benkoski and Malouf wrapped up their space walk.

Cleary occupied himself by doodling, and had filled a page with circles attached to circles attached to circles and then a sudden jagged line. "Shit."

He sat up in his chair and turned the microphone on while simultaneously patching the capsule through to the loudspeakers. "What sort of problem?"

Benkoski's voice crackled through the room, and the

quiet murmur of idle conversation stopped. "We can't get the hatch closed."

Everyone started to move at once. Nathaniel grabbed his headset and the phone at the same time. I spun in my chair and reached for the library that spanned the shelves immediately behind the CAPCOM. The IAC had an entire volume dedicated to hatches and their closures.

"Copy that. Describe the malfunction?" Cleary's voice gave no indication of the quiet energy that filled Mission Control. His job was to be the sole voice that the astronauts had to deal with while everyone else ran through all the possibilities.

"It gets within one centimeter of closure and then stops. We've looked for obstructions, but nothing is obvious." His breath echoed through Mission Control.

I winced. The capsules didn't have airlocks, just a hatch on the side. For the space walks, both astronauts were in pressure suits. If they couldn't get the door closed, they couldn't repressurize, and they also couldn't reenter the Earth's atmosphere.

"Is it aligned correctly?"

"Yes. It is not an alignment issue." Behind his voice was the steady hiss of oxygen flowing into his helmet.

Nathaniel walked over carrying a schematic. "Tell him to open the hatch all the way. There's a stop that keeps it from swinging all the way open, but if he pulls it, then they can open it fully and get a better view."

Cleary nodded and repeated all of that to Benkoski.

"Confirmed door release. Working on it now."

Through the speakers, we could hear his conversation with Malouf as they worked on the problem. Or, rather, we could hear Malouf working on it. The capsule was so small that, when suited, only one of them could be near the hatch at a time.

While they worked, Nathaniel conferred with the mechanical team. At some point, Clemons came stalking into the room, still shrugging into his coat. He demanded a status report.

I just tried to stay out of the way.

"Kansas, we see the problem." Malouf's voice broke through the chatter. "A loose washer is jammed in the seal near the hinge. We are attempting to pry it out."

"Glad to hear it." Cleary's shoulders relaxed a little.

Mine too. The worst part was not knowing what the problem was. Now all we could do was wait while they dealt with it.

Nathaniel leaned over the CAPCOM desk and asked Cleary, a little too casually, "Any word on how Colonel Parker is doing?"

"Very well. Although he has to wear the most amusing collar around his neck." He grinned. "He does not find it amusing, of course. I think he called it the fu—ah . . . the fun collar."

"The 'fun' collar." I looked at him. "Really."

I don't know if he blushed, but he suddenly became very interested in his circles again. Nathaniel exchanged a glance with me, and mouthed, "Fun collar," with an accompanying masturbatory hand gesture.

Clearing my throat was probably not the most subtle way of masking a laugh. "Any idea when he'll be able to, ah, launch again? I'm sure that's high on his mind."

"Yes." Nathaniel nodded, suppressing a smirk. "Launches are very important."

Thank God Cleary missed all of that. "I believe it will be another year for the bones to fuse together. Though he will be back at work much sooner."

Too bad. A year free of Parker would have been a joy.

"Kansas, we cannot get the washer out. The gloves are

too bulky to grab it. Malouf wants to try to use a screwdriver to pry it out. Will this compromise the seal? Please advise."

My husband faded away, and Dr. Nathaniel York snapped into focus. "How much oxygen do they have left?"

Cleary frowned at him. "They are asking about the—" He shook his head. "What are your oxygen levels in the suits?"

"Forty-five minutes, plus or minus five." Benkoski's voice had that disconcerting pilot calm, as if he weren't discussing possible death.

Nathaniel rubbed his mouth. "Here's the call we have to make. If they rip the seal, they can't pressurize."

"If they can't shut the door, they also can't pressurize."

Nathaniel turned to the computers. "Basira—what's the current state vector of the *Lunetta* platform?"

She grabbed a sheet of paper and rattled off all seven parts of the vector: three for position, three for velocity, and one for time. It was in a higher orbit than the spacecraft, which, thanks to orbital mechanics, meant it was going slower. They might be able to catch it.

Clemons nodded, seeing where Nathaniel was going with that question. "Can they get to the space station before their air runs out?"

"In theory. Maybe." He called across the room again to the computers. "Basira, I need a trajectory and burn rates for a station rendezvous. Get the station's MC on the line. They may need to transfer to a lower orbit to meet them."

My legs itched with the urge to go to Basira and Myrtle's table, look at the numbers, and just do the math. But there were competent people there, and my job was here. To shadow. To sit, and learn, and do nothing unless asked.

Clemons said, "Here's my thinking . . . Can we have Benkoski pilot toward the station while Malouf continues to work on the hatch? If he gets it, well and good. If not, they're closer to the station."

Nathaniel shook his head. "If they fire the rockets with the hatch open, there's a high probability the kick will torque the hinge out of true. I think they'll either have to lash it open while Malouf works or just go for digging it out." He glanced at Cleary. "Check me on any practical considerations, since you've spent time in the capsule. "

Cleary squinted, moving his hands as if he were trying things out. "Lashing it in those gloves . . . that's going to take some time."

Time. It would take them ten minutes to dock, at best, which only gave them half an hour to do the rendezvous. "They have to do the burn now."

Everyone stared at me as if a potted plant had spoken. Except Nathaniel. His vivid blue eyes locked on mine like a tracking laser. Without turning from me, he raised his voice. "Basira, I need the state vectors on both craft. Now."

She didn't blink, just grabbed the right page on the first go. Across from her, Myrtle circled numbers from the Teletype and handed them to her.

She was a good mathematician, and methodical, but I was faster. I'm not sure where the pencil came from, but as Basira called out numbers, I jotted them down for reference across the page of Cleary's circles.

While we worked, Nathaniel turned to Cleary. "Tell the crew to dig the washer out."

"What about the seal?"

"Even if the capsule is leaking, that's going to give them a better shot at docking than having it wide open. At this point, we're assuming no reentry."

Clemons nodded. "Tell them that we're sending up a burn attitude and targets, and they should maneuver as soon as they get them, and load the targets."

There are times when numbers paint pictures in my head. They intersected with my pilot's brain and I could see the arc of the ship and the controls in my hand. I double-checked my numbers anyway. Malouf and Benkoski had one chance.

"Kansas, we have the washer out. The seal did tear. Two centimeters. Should we attempt to repressurize?"

Back at his desk, Nathaniel said, "Negative. We may need to redirect oxygen to their suits."

The atmosphere in the firing room crackled with such intense focus. Somewhere in the support room, an engineering team was jumping into motion to figure out how to do that. And yet we all sounded as if we were discussing weather.

Cleary might have been offering them lemonade. "Confirmed seal breach. Do not, repeat, do not attempt repressurization. We'll have the burn attitude and targets for you shortly."

"Confirmed, Kansas. We'll stay in our suits."

Still writing, I glanced at the clock and my insides clenched. 12:32. This was so close. "Expect a forty-three-second burn, starting at 12:35—"

Someone cursed as they saw the margins snap into place.

"Final approach to *Lunetta* station commences . . . ten minutes—one zero minutes—after the burn." I lifted my pencil. "Also contact station and have them maneuver to docking attitude, perform attitude hold, and feather the arrays." If they didn't do that, the solar arrays would be in the way.

Nathaniel took a step closer to me. He inhaled, as if he were about to ask if I was sure and then nodded. He looked at the clock. 12:33. "Do it."

Cleary looked to Clemons, who hesitated for a fraction

of a second, and then nodded. "GC. Give us a ten-minute countdown on the clock."

The ground controller set one of the mission clocks to count down from ten. While he did that, as matter-of-fact as a janitor, Cleary relayed my numbers to the capsule.

From the calm of Cleary's voice, you'd think we'd just pulled this out of the library. We had hundreds of volumes of calculations for things that might go wrong en route to the moon. But needing to make a rendezvous in forty minutes with a leaking hatch? Nothing we had took that into account.

Benkoski responded with a calm to match Cleary's. "Copy, Kansas. Commencing burn."

The next half-hour dragged and raced at the same time. It felt like forever, listening to them and being able to do nothing except adjust numbers as they got closer. And then time would jump ahead, eating up the amount of oxygen they had left.

At some point I moved over to the computers' table and joined Myrtle and Basira in tracking the two spacecraft.

Engineering managed to buy them fifteen more minutes by having Benkoski bleed oxygen from one of the fuel cells, but it reduced the amount of power that they had available. If they took any more, none of the electrical systems in the capsule would work.

The station came online. "We can see the shape of their vehicle now."

They were still miles away from the station. If they got the approach wrong, they could whiz past and lose time trying to correct.

"Zero point seven miles out. Closing at 31 feet per second."

This was all up to Benkoski now. He wasn't talking,

because the flight surgeon had instructed them to remain silent to conserve oxygen.

"2,724 feet. 19.7 feet per second."

So close. Please let them be okay.

"1,370, 9.8 feet per second."

"Kansas. *Lunetta.* We're braking." Benkoski's voice had a wheeze to it. I traded a look with Cleary.

"Fifty feet. And holding steady."

In the control room, no one was breathing, as if we were all trying to conserve air for Benkoski and Malouf.

"Kansas. We have them."

Around me, the room erupted in cheers and prayers while I slumped forward to rest my face on the desk. That had been terrifyingly close.

And if it had happened at the moon, with no space station to retreat to, we would be listening to them dying right now.

The moment we were through the apartment door, Nathaniel dropped his briefcase and kicked the door shut with his foot. His arms slid around my waist and pulled me back against him where his . . . attention was quite apparent.

His breath warmed my neck as he kissed it. "You are a miracle."

"I'm a computer."

"And a pilot." He kissed a spot higher on my neck. "And an astronaut."

"In training."

Nathaniel nipped my neck.

"Hey!" I laughed and turned in his arms to face him. The apartment was dark save for the street lamps shining through the window in a sodium glaze. "Someone else would have realized the burn issue."

"But not fast enough." One hand came up to draw a line across my forehead. His fingers were cool and rough against my skin. "We've been damn lucky. And you, today, were part of that luck, by your convergence of experience and your extraordinary, captivating, exquisite mind. So let me call you a miracle."

"I don't know . . . that sounds entirely too holy." I found the buckle of his belt.

Nathaniel twisted his hips away and spun me so my back was against the wall. Running his hands down my sides, my husband sank to his knees in front of me. "Then let me worship you."

His hands ran up the inside of my legs, under my skirt, until I gasped. "Confirmed, worship is Go."

A month after we heard about Parker's surgery, I walked into the Monday-morning meeting and he was sitting there. A stiff neck brace held his head rigidly in place. He was thinner, and he'd been trim to begin with. He had shadows under his eyes, and I hadn't seen that even during the worst of the leg problems.

But if you just looked at his demeanor, none of his troubles were apparent. Laughing, he leaned back in his chair, using the angle of it to look up at the folks surrounding him. ". . . So I said that if they were trying to save weight, they'd have to get the astronettes to leave their purses at home."

The guys laughed. Nicole lifted her cup of coffee and said, "But if we did that, where would you keep your balls?"

I loved her so much.

"All right, people. Let's get to work." Clemons strode into the room, trailing smoke like a badly tuned engine. "Parker. Good to have you back."

I grabbed a cup of coffee and settled into my seat next to Nicole. Leaning over, I whispered, "You are my hero."

"You'd think it was a war wound, the way everyone is carrying on over him." She opened her binder, pretending to pay attention to Clemons. "I hear that the reason he had to have surgery was to reduce the size of the rod up his ass."

"Then it failed."

"So true."

The meeting fell into its familiar rhythms as we worked through the plans for the week. Each of us had an area to report. While Parker had been away, I'd begun to feel like the women were integrated into the department more. I'm sure that would change now that he was back.

"Paz-Viveiros and Cleary, you'll be happy to know that the simulator has been repaired, so you can resume your mission prep." Clemons peered at his agenda. "Malouf, you did a good job with the issue with the hatch seal, but it revealed some problem areas with the mission, and I want to do some reassignments. I'm reassigning you from the CM on this lunar mission to commanding the second one."

I winced for him. That had to be tough, but with Parker back, I guess they were assuming he'd be fit enough for launch. Parker's brows went up and he sat forward, head held at a rigid angle. "Sir, I'm not going to be ready for flight for another year."

"I know." Clemons waved his cigar at him. "York's the new CM."

Air roared past my ears as if I were suddenly feeling all 1,040 miles per hour of the Earth's rotation. I shook my head, trying to clear it. The CM. The command module. That wasn't just being a computer—that was also piloting the craft that would orbit the moon while the lander went to the surface.

Someone said my name. More than one person. Pressure and sound came back into focus as Nicole squeezed me into a hug. Malouf came up from behind and wrapped his long arms around me. He said something kind. I don't know what.

Across the table, Parker smoldered. He put his hand flat on the table. "May I ask a question."

No. No—I hadn't said anything. I gripped my hands into fists until the nails bit into my palms, then forced myself to breathe. My stomach had knotted into a ball so tight it hurt.

3.1415 . . .

"Go ahead."

"Why York?"

"It has been made abundantly clear to me that the moon mission isn't going to succeed without a computer on board. The CM will be out of contact with the Earth every time it flies into the moon's dark side." Clemons slid a sheet of paper toward me. "This is a list of the computers that work for the IAC. I want you to go through it and identify anyone that can be trained as a pilot."

I didn't need the list to know whose name belonged at the top. "Helen Liu. Already a pilot, and has jet experience." But I took the list. "I'll work on the rest."

"I'd like to help York with that." Parker gave an earnest smile.

He wanted to help? Help *me*? "What kind of pain medicine are you on?"

"You'd like some, wouldn't you?" His smile was casual— all joking between colleagues, but I could see the threat that lay underneath it. Toe the line, he'd said. And he had to see me getting the first lunar landing instead of him as jumping the line. "It's important to think about the temperament of the candidate as well. York's got the expertise to talk about the computing side, and I trust her as a pilot, but space is a different thing and she hasn't been up there. Besides, I'd like to feel like I'm of some use."

He sounded so reasonable. He'd even slipped a compliment in there. But I'd seen him use that earnest smile as a weapon before. The paper with the computers' names rattled in my grip.

Clemons nodded along. "Good. Good. I'm going to use you as CAPCOM on a couple of missions, but this shouldn't interfere."

"Actually, maybe we should take advantage of having some of the other ladies here to talk through what attributes we're looking for in a candidate, since the computers are all women." He held up his hand. "But I don't want to mess with your agenda on my first day back. I'm just so eager to get back to work."

I swallowed my fear and tried to take control of the conversation. "That's a great idea, Parker. Why don't you and I come up with an initial list, and then we can vet it with the group later. That'll give the director time to get it on the agenda."

"Absolutely." There was his shit-eating grin. "And there are some easy points that we can establish right up front. For instance, the candidates need to be emotionally stable. So it would be an obvious black mark if any of them were, say, taking Miltown."

1, 3, 5, 7, 9, 11—

Nicole gave her debutante laugh. "Don't be foolish. That would disqualify half of the United States."

Oh. No. Nicole, don't. Don't sacrifice your own chance in space . . .

. . . 13, 17, 23 . . . I somehow managed to match her laugh. "Right. I mean, for heaven's sake. I take it."

Parker's brows went up so fast that you might almost

have thought I'd surprised him. "Is that—oh. Is that what's been affecting your reaction times in testing?"

Malouf snorted. "If this is York when she's thinking slowly, then I'd be terrified of her at full speed."

Next to him, Cleary nodded. "She had the trajectory calculated, in her head, in less than ten minutes, then ran it again on paper for safety." He held up his hands and shook his head. "I've never seen anything like it."

Parker couldn't join the nodding because of his neck brace, but he leaned forward in his chair. "And thank God for that." There was that earnest shrug of his. "I just worry what she'll do in space if she's in a high-pressure situation and can't get the Miltown."

I kept trying to find words to stop him, but my tongue latched itself down, as if it wanted to prove him right.

And then Benkoski cleared his throat.

He steepled his fingers and gave Parker a solemn stare. "Look. We all know that you don't like her. And we all know why. And we also know what would have happened to Malouf and me if she hadn't been on duty that night." He jabbed a finger at Parker, and I ground my teeth into the inside of my cheek to keep from bursting into tears. "You're telling me that saving our lives wasn't a high-pressure situation?"

"All I'm saying is that the floor of Mission Control is completely different from space."

Terrazas spoke up from his place near the rear of the room. "Just as point of data, the flight surgeon offered me Miltown when we came back to Earth. I turned him down, because I was worried it would get me grounded. So, I would like to volunteer my services to review the right 'temperament' to be an astronaut. But I'll tell you this: York has it."

Parker drew breath, and Clemons held up his hand, cutting him off. "You weren't there, Parker. I've got no questions about York's fitness, and that's not the topic of discussion. All we're concerned with is which computers to add to the list."

"Of course." Parker gave a little shrug and glanced at Betty for just a bare moment. "I'd be happy to work with York on that."

Drawing a line through something on the agenda, Clemons said, "Terrazas, you help York with sorting the list. You'll be working together on moon prep anyway."

By all that was holy . . . I was going to the moon. Parker had tried to ground me and failed. I was going to the goddamned moon.

Nathaniel and I were going to have *such* a good rocket launch.

THIRTY-EIGHT

ENGINEER'S PLAN FOR TRIP TO MARS

Jan. 8, 1958—In a book entitled *Das Marsprojekt,* published in Germany, Dr. Wernher von Braun has developed a plan for a journey to Mars, which he has presented frequently in lectures and in popular magazines of large circulation here. He is convinced that it is technically possible to organize and send out an expedition of seventy to Mars.

As soon as the Monday-morning meeting let out, Nicole grabbed my arm and pulled me into the ladies' room. A moment later, Jacira and Sabiha followed us in. Sabiha leaned against the door, as if any of the male astronauts would be caught dead in the ladies' room.

Or, maybe it wasn't to keep the men out. Betty and Violette weren't here. Nicole leaned me against the sink as if I were a delicate flower that needed to be propped up. She glanced at Sabiha and Jacira. "Did you see the way Parker was looking at Betty?"

My heart, which had begun to slow down, ramped back up again. "I did."

Jacira nodded as well. "I think she's going to run the Miltown story straight to *Life*."

Thank God Nicole had given me the sink to lean against, because my knees might have buckled right then. In her drive to advance her career, Betty had already tossed me to the reporters once. That was not nearly as juicy a story as this. If the fact that one of the lady astronauts needed to take a tranquilizer hit the paper, that would make things more difficult for all of us, so I needed to tell Clemons that I couldn't go, and get him to pick someone else. Helen— Helen had the same math skills I did, and—

A tiny rational part of my brain screamed from way down deep inside: *You are panicking.*

I gripped the edge of the sink until the Formica bit into the flesh of my fingers. *1, 2, 3, 5, 7 . . .* Nicole's, Sabiha's, and Jacira's voices came at me through a vat of tar. *11, 13, 17, 19 . . .* There had to be something I—we—could do. This wasn't something I could face on my own. It would affect Nicole as well, if anyone started really digging into our medical records. I turned my head to them and clawed my throat open. "Betty."

"What?" Nicole broke off in mid-sentence and turned to face me.

"I need to talk to Betty. Parker won't go to the press on his own, because if it ever got out that he'd leaked the news, that would tarnish his reputation." If I knew nothing else about Stetson Parker at this point, it was that he valued the idea of his own legacy. He also, I think, genuinely cared about the space program. I didn't like the way that manifested, but it was real. "If I can convince Betty not to run it . . ."

Sabiha shoved off from her place by the door. "Be right back."

"You'll want backup." Jacira followed her out of the bathroom, ponytail swinging in an arc with her turn.

By my side, Nicole pulled some paper towels from the wall dispenser and wet them. "You okay?"

My head dropped forward so that my chin rested on my chest. "Yes?"

"Wash your face." She handed me the wad of damp towels. "You'll feel better."

"You sound like my mother." But I took the towels, because Mama had always been right about that. The cool paper blotted some of the heat from my cheeks and forehead. "How did we get here?"

"By being good."

"No—I mean, I used to be friends with Betty, and now . . ." I shrugged. "I shouldn't have gotten so mad with her about the Girl Scout thing."

Nicole snorted. "Please. She made that bed."

"I helped."

"Maybe, but—"

The door to the bathroom opened. Jacira pulled Betty in, with Sabiha close on her heels. She let Betty go and positioned herself with Sabiha by the door, arms crossed over her chest. Betty glanced over her shoulder and then back at me.

"Well . . . I feel like I'm back in high school again." Her lips curled in a sardonic smile. "Going to accuse me of being a slut?"

I still had the damp towel in my hand and set it down on the counter. "I was going to apologize."

"Was."

"Am. I'm sorry for being so angry about the Girl Scout thing. I've treated you badly." I took a breath and wiped my hands on my trousers. "And I wanted to ask for a favor."

"It's not really an apology if it comes with a price tag."

"True. Fair."

"But then, I wouldn't expect a Jew to give something away for free."

Through the white heat of my rage, I saw Nicole push off from the sink. "I find that offensive."

"Oh. Are you a Jewess now?"

"I don't have to be to recognize offensive language." She crossed the room and glared at Betty. "You were a WASP. Have you forgotten why we fought the war?"

"It's okay." It wasn't, but I needed to pretend it was, so I stepped away from the sink. Our intervention wasn't helping and might even make things worse. "Betty, I'm sorry. May I . . . I just wanted to talk to you. May we?"

She pursed her lips for a moment, then gave a cursory nod. "Go ahead."

"Could you—could you not tell *Life* that I take Miltown?" Tension locked my ribs into a knot. "Please."

She shook her head slowly. "Look . . . I'm sorry. This is my career."

"Ours too." I gestured to the five of us crowded into the bathroom. "Women in the space program are already on shaky ground. How do you think it will look if one of them is on tranquilizers?"

"If you don't get to go into space, you can go back to the computer department. You have a husband who's in the program. It *is* a colony effort, so it will just be a matter of time before they let you go up, even if I run the article tomorrow. Me . . . they're never going to let me go. I don't have another career. All I've got is this job with *Life* magazine." Betty rested her hands on her hips and stared at the floor. "I'm sorry. I really am."

Jacira cocked her head. "Do even you *want* to go into space?"

"Yes!" Betty's voice cracked, and she balled her hands into fists. "Jesus. Why does everyone think that I don't care? Parker keeps saying I'm not a pilot, but I *am*, and— forget it."

"I'll teach you math." The offer came out before my brain caught up with me.

"What?"

"I used to tutor at university. Not just arithmetic, but the higher-level stuff." This was like Parker offering to certify me on the T-38 if I didn't tell anyone about the weakness in his left leg. Had he felt this gripping desperation wrapping itself around his middle when he'd been talking to me? I sighed, letting my ego out so I could keep going. "They want more computers. I can teach you to be one."

"And if I say no?"

Behind me, Nicole shifted and sighed. "Then we go back to high school. I know about Parker. And I know about his wife."

Betty's face went pale. I'd thought that she might be sleeping with Parker, but whatever was going on with his wife was outside my awareness. And it didn't matter. I wasn't Parker.

"No." I turned to face Nicole. "We're not going to play that game. If Betty doesn't want to help us, then that's her call. We'll respect that, and I'll figure out something else."

Nicole's jaw set, as if she were about to argue with me. In the mirror over the sink I could see Betty, brows drawn together, leaning back on her heels as if she would flee if she could. Behind her, Jacira and Sabiha guarded the door. All of them watched me.

And in the mirror, I could see who I could become. I could become Parker, pushing with everything I had to get into space.

I let my breath out, counting through a Fibonacci sequence. "I'm sorry, Betty. I'm sorry I've treated you badly. And I'm sorry I tried to bully you into changing your story." Turning, I rubbed my forehead. "The offer to tutor you in math still stands."

She blinked at me and then, surprising everyone—including herself, I think—Betty burst into tears. For a moment, we all stood there, shocked. I don't know who moved first. Maybe Nicole. Maybe Jacira. Maybe me. But in a moment, we all had her surrounded and held.

And that—that was when I knew that we really had something. We were Lady Astronauts. All of us. And, god-damn it, we were all going to go into space.

I was not the first woman in space. Nor would I be the first woman on the moon. My role was to fly the command module while my male colleagues went to the surface.

The night before we all went into isolation—it wouldn't do to get ill during the eight days we were in space—Nathaniel and I threw a party. Nicole let us borrow her house, since our apartment was too tiny.

It is a strange thing, knowing that, in a little over a week, you will be strapped to a four-megaton bomb and hurled into airless space. Every time I spoke to someone, I couldn't help but think, *This might be the last time.*

But I'd been given a second chance with Aunt Esther, hadn't I? She sat next to me on the sofa in Nicole's living room with a rum and Coke perched on her knee. The party might have been in my honor, but she was the life of it.

"The worst of it was that I'd lost Mama's union card under the roller coaster! There I was, on the horns of a dilemma . . ."

Eugene Lindholm knelt on one knee to listen to Aunt Esther, while Myrtle perched on the arm of the sofa. He seemed to find my aunt endlessly charming. "What did you do, ma'am?"

I'd been a little concerned when I introduced her to the Lindholms. What would this old Southern woman think about our black friends? I needn't have worried.

She laid her hand on Eugene's arm. "Well, I'm glad you asked. I knew that if I didn't find the card, Mama would know that I'd snuck out to the carnival, and worse, she wouldn't be able to work . . . so Rose and I snuck behind the roller coaster, then I hitched my skirt up to my thighs and crawled under it. If Mama had known how much leg I was exposing, she would have been more upset by that than the loss of her card! But I got it back. Yes I did."

Hershel sat in the chair to my right, his crutches propped against its side. He leaned over to me and gestured to Aunt Esther. "It's like this at home. If we can get her telling stories from when she was a kid, there's no end to them. What she had for breakfast? Not so much."

"But it's working out?"

He smiled. "It's perfect. Well, all right, not perfect, but the kids love her, and she's able to help Doris with cooking, so it's pretty good. Speaking of kids . . . Tommy!"

"Now, I've been talking so much I haven't had a drop to drink. Why don't you tell me about yourself, young man?" Aunt Esther took a sip of her rum and Coke, bright eyes shining at Eugene.

I had to admire how skillfully Aunt Esther dodged the fact that she couldn't remember Eugene's name. I made a note to try that line next time I was "in the barrel" on a press junket.

Tommy arrived at his father's side. "Yes, sir?"

"Go get the present we brought Aunt Elma."

He nodded and ran off again, all long legs. I shook my head. "I swear he's a foot taller than last year."

"We can't keep him in clothes."

"—heading in for astronaut testing."

I swiveled to Eugene. "What? When were you going to tell me? Congratulations!"

"They just sent the letters out." Eugene shrugged, looking surprisingly sheepish. "You've been a little busy."

"Which is understandable." Myrtle rested a hand on his shoulder with proprietary pride. "He passed the tests before, so hopefully this time they'll have the sense the good Lord gave them, and accept him."

"Well, Parker likes you, which will help enormously." I left alone our continuing animosity. At times it seemed as if it had vanished, but he never let me forget about the Miltown. "You said the letters just went out . . . ? Excuse me."

I stood and went in search of Helen. She, Ida, and Imogene stood near the punch bowl, giggling with Betty. ". . . still can't belie—Shush!"

"Shush?" I stopped next to them and arched a brow. "So, you've either just spiked the punch, or you got a letter that *none of you told me about.*"

Helen bounced on her toes, face splitting into a grin that looked like it must hurt. "I get to take the tests!"

"Us too!" Ida clinked her glass against Imogene's and Helen's. All three of the women looked as giddy as kids starting summer vacation.

Betty grinned at me. "I'm going to walk them through the physical tests."

"And I'll keep up the math coaching while you're in space." Helen punched me in the shoulder. "I never get tired of saying that."

Nathaniel came up behind me and draped an arm over my shoulder. "I can tell these are your friends, because they're excited about taking tests." He kissed my cheek and raised his glass. "Congratulations, ladies. Here's to the stars."

Laughing, I clinked my glass against my friends'. "Better yet: Here's to the Lady Astronaut Club."

THIRTY-NINE

TWO ASTRONAUTS AND AN ASTRONETTE
PREPARE FOR THE MOON

KANSAS CITY, KS, July 20, 1958—The two men who will be the first to tread the moon early on Monday may find that walking is not the best way to get around. The answer may be a "kangaroo hop." While they are exploring the surface, lady astronaut Dr. Elma York will be keeping the home fires burning in the capsule orbiting the moon, waiting for their return.

Today, I am going into space.

Everything about today is vivid in ways that nothing else in life can equal. My wedding to Nathaniel has been reduced by time to a series of snapshots and captured moments packed in a haze of joy.

But today, the light gleaming atop the egg yolk in my breakfast contains the most vibrant yellow-orange. This is the last meal I will eat before going into space. Lebourgeois and Terrazas are sitting across from me and we are talking through the last details before the flight. There is a photographer in the room—screened for health by the IAC—but he does not matter.

We are going into space today.

This is Terrazas's fifth flight and Lebourgeois's seventh. I am the only rookie here. I am the only woman.

A tall, broad-shouldered man with gray hair and jowls comes into the room, and for a moment, I don't recognize him as Clemons. He does not have his cigar. The smell of it still lingers, though, in a heavy musk.

"All packed?"

I nod, pushing my chair back from the table. "My post-flight things are in my room. There's . . . there's a note."

"I'll hold on to it." Clemons nods and shoves his hands into his pockets, as if he can't figure out what to do with them without the cigar.

We walk down the hall—it might be the last time I walk down this hall—to the dressing rooms. The photographer follows us, but splits off to go with the men. I am grateful, for the first time, that I am the only woman on the flight.

That changes when I enter the dressing room, because the other two astronauts have each other for company while they are getting suited. I know the team here, of course—part of my training included dry runs of this moment—but I find that I have no words in me but the single phrase *I am going to space today.*

In relative silence, I strip and pull on the long underwear that will be next to my skin for most of the flight. I will wear this into space today.

They've dressed other astronauts, so they don't force me to talk. Thank God for professionals. It takes all three of us to wrestle me into the pressure suit. It is designed to be snug and protect me from the elements—or the lack thereof—in space. Where I am going today.

Settling into the chair, I stare straight ahead at the concrete wall as they lower the helmet over my head. These are the last breaths of the Earth's atmosphere that I will take for the next eight days. Someone is wearing *White Shoulders* bath powder. I recognize the fragrance because Grandma used it.

The helmet clicks into place, changing the sound of the room. It does not muffle the way a jet flight helmet does. It reflects the sounds of my own body back and the metallic stink of canned oxygen hisses around me. I inhale, slowly and carefully. Then I lift both stiff arms of the suit to give them a thumbs up. All good. They nod and give me the okay sign.

The outside world sits at a distance. I won't be able to hear it until I am patched into the ship's system. Now I have to wait for the nitrogen to work its way out of my bloodstream. If I didn't, I could wind up with the bends when we went into space. The Earth's atmosphere is 14.7 psi, but the capsule is only pressurized to 5.5 psi.

There is a cluster of imperfections on the cinder-block wall that looks like a dragon's head. I wonder what the psychologists at our initial tests would have made of that. Awkward in the suit, I turn and wave to catch one of the dressers' attention. When she looks at me, I mime opening a book.

She smiles and reaches into the cabinet for the reading material that I selected for this wait. It is the gift my brother gave me at my going-to-space party.

Superman #11. The prize of his comic book collection.

Weeping would be an unfortunate choice. I am an astronaut. I am inside a space suit. And I am going into space today.

The elevator down from the astronaut's isolation suite is only three stories, but it is slow. The portable oxygen unit I'm carrying is heavy, but when someone offered to carry it for me, I declined. If the men can do this, so can I. Still,

I am beginning to regret the choice by the time the elevator finally reaches the bottom.

Two elevator repairmen ride down with us, just in case. It would be an inauspicious start if we all got stuck in an elevator on the way to the moon. Lebourgeois is shifting from foot to foot. I have never seen him nervous before.

The doors open, and a crowd of reporters is waiting for us. They told us to expect that, so when we get outside, the three of us pause for a minute to let them take pictures. I take a deep breath of the canned oxygen and smile.

My heart has been trotting along, faster than usual, but my space suit protects me from their questions. What will people think, seeing these photos, of three astronauts in their tinfoil suits?

Inside the building, my brother, his family, and Aunt Esther are waiting for the launch. They will be in the observation room looking over Mission Control right now. Nathaniel will be on the floor, standing at his desk instead of sitting like a normal human being.

We walk away from the reporters and get into the van that will drive us to the rocket. It stands like a vast monolith, a testament to the persistence of mankind. That. I am going to ride that.

There is, of course, the possibility that we won't go today. Launches get scrubbed all the time. A faulty wire. The weather. A man with a bomb . . . We might have to go through all of this again tomorrow. I'd been in Mission Control often enough when we had to scrub.

When we get out of the van, there are technicians waiting for us by the bottom of the elevator leading up the gantry. Terrazas stops me with a hand on my arm and points up.

I lean back, the only way to look up in the suit. The sound of my gasp echoes against the sides of my helmet. The *Artemis 9* steams in the morning sun like a living beast.

Intellectually, I know it's because of the super-chilled oxygen, but . . . my God, she is beautiful.

When I look back down, Terrazas is still looking up, and so is Lebourgeois. Both men are grinning when we finally finish gawking like tourists, and walk into the elevator. It rattles and shakes as we ride up, and the vast prairies of Kansas spread out at our feet.

Without being told, I stop on the gantry before I climb into the capsule. We all do. Inside, the windows face straight up. This will be my last view of Earth until I am in space.

The high, clear silver of the sky lays over the Earth like a blanket. In the distance, a pair of T-38s circle the perimeter of the IAC to keep our flight path clear. We'd once had to delay a launch because some tourist decided to fly in to watch the launch from the air.

The grasslands have just begun to turn green after a too-short winter with barely any snow. A patch of pink shifts in the breeze as early wildflowers greet the dawn.

I inhale, as if I could breathe in the fragrance of the Earth one last time, but all I get is more canned oxygen. I turn to face our craft, one glove against its side. Terrazas gets to his knees and crawls inside.

I give the crew time to get him settled, and then it is my turn. I'll be in the center bench for the ride up. Lebourgeois will have the left, as is traditional for the commander of a mission. The seat cradles me, with my legs up in the air. The crew tightens down the straps that will hold me firmly in place as we launch, and switches my oxygen over to the ship's source.

It is still metallic, but less tinny than the little portable pack. That might be my imagination, though.

Lebourgeois is settled, and then sound comes back into my world as our comms are patched in.

Lebourgeois says, "Kansas, *Artemis 9*. We are in position."

Parker's voice crackles into my ear from his seat at CAP-COM. "Position confirmed. Welcome aboard."

The hatch closes, taking away the last view of Earth. All I can see now is the silver sky above us. All of us have checklists to run through, and I do, making sure that all the gauges and switches that I am responsible for are in the correct position. For the trip up, I will have very little to do. I am a passenger, while Lebourgeois is the pilot. Even that is mostly in name, because he will only need to take the controls before we are in space if something goes wrong.

And even then, the list of survivable errors is short. When we get into orbit, we have only two hours to prep for the transition to the translunar insertion. In theory. Everything we can do now to prepare for the TLI will buy us time, which is why we practiced this until we can do the checklist by rote.

There is something about having your legs over your head that makes you need to pee. This makes it into none of the press releases, but every single astronaut talks about it.

The men have complicated condoms and catch pouches. I have a diaper.

Two hours into our three-hour wait, I use it, sure that the urine will overflow its confines and spread up the back of my suit. It does not, but I am once again enthralled by the glamour of being an astronaut.

And then, somehow, we are in the last six minutes before launch. I have gone through my checklist four or five times, certain that I've missed something. Outside our tiny capsule, my family is being led to the roof of the IAC to watch the launch.

Before I was assigned to a mission, I thought that this was a kindness, to give them a spectacular view. I thought that, right up until I was asked to pick an escort for my family from among the astronauts. Benkoski's wife once made a joke about her "escort to widowhood." Our families were on the roof, isolated from the press, so if something went wrong . . .

So if we died during launch, the IAC would have control over them. The media would get no pictures of the moment grief set in.

We projected the appearance of triumph.

Parker's voice crackles in my ear. "York. The engineering desk says to remind you of prime numbers."

The engineering desk. He can't say "your husband," or just give Nathaniel a moment with the comm? On the other hand, Nathaniel should be able to hear me at this point. "Please thank engineering, and say that I'll continue work on my theorem regarding divisibility when we return. Pending a successful rocket launch."

"Message confirmed." And without a pause, he returns to the technical jargon. "Engine test is Go."

The ship shudders and lurches against its bolts. Beneath us, the two massive Sirius engines swivel, to test their range of motion. We'd been told to expect this, but they couldn't get the simulator to mimic the moment when the engines first got power.

"T-minus sixty seconds and counting. We have passed T-minus sixty. Fifty-five seconds and counting."

Lebourgeois says, "Thank you, Mission Control, for the smooth countdown."

"Confirmed thanks. We've passed the fifty-second mark. Power transfer is complete."

The last of our gauges leaps to life, needles spiking like my heart.

Lebourgeois nods, watching the gauges. "Confirmed internal power."

"Forty seconds away from the *Artemis 9* liftoff. All the first-stage tanks now pressurized."

"Confirmed pressurization." Lebourgeois is the French priest in our tiny chapel, reciting the litany of space.

"Thirty-five seconds and counting. We are still Go with *Artemis 9*. Thirty seconds and counting."

"Everything is very good here."

"Twenty seconds and counting. T-minus fifteen seconds, guidance is internal."

"Confirmed internal guidance." Lebourgeois lifts his hand to rest it over the clock, waiting.

I clench the arms of my couch, counting with them in my head.

"Twelve, eleven, ten, nine. Ignition sequence starts . . ."

The engine roars to life beneath us and the entire rocket shakes like a cabin in an earthquake. It's always been quiet at Mission Control during this moment, but now, sitting atop the rocket, there is no delay between ignition and the sound.

"Five, four, three, two, one—zero. All engines running. LIFTOFF."

The rocket thunders beneath us and pushes me deep into my couch. The acceleration pulls me back, as if the Earth is trying to keep us from leaving.

Lebourgeois pushes the clock start. "Roger. Clock."

"Tower cleared."

"Roger. We have the roll program."

Clouds spin past the windows as we roll into the right attitude for our orbit.

"Confirmed roll program."

We rip clear of the clouds into startling blue.

Abruptly the ride smoothes out as we push through the sound barrier, and the thunder of the rocket falls away behind us faster than we are traveling. We're on our own now. There's nothing that Mission Control can do until we are in orbit.

"*Artemis 9,* this is Kansas. You are Go for staging."

Now Lebourgeois's voice sounds strained by the G-forces pressing us into our seats. "Inboard cutoff."

"We confirm inboard cutoff."

The blue of the sky grows deeper, into a rich velvet, then darkens to black. It is so dark that it is not a color but an absence. Ink. Velvet. Dark. None of these give the sense of the depth of space.

"Staging." His hands move over the controls, flipping switches.

The G-load vanishes and I fly up against my restraints. Past our windows, the dark sky flares red and gold. Pieces of housing whip past, trailing sparks.

"And ignition."

And then silence.

Beneath us, the smaller engine pushes us higher, out of the Earth's influence. But without an atmosphere it is largely silent, letting us know its presence only through the vibrations of the ship. We are technically in space, but if Lebourgeois and Mission Control don't get us into the right orbit, we'll fall back to Earth.

A loose end of my harness floats up in front of me. Up.

I turn my attention from that and watch the gauges, doing the first task of the navigation that will be my job for the next eight days. "SECO. We are showing 101.4 by 103.6."

Parker replies with the same calm he has for everyone. He's probably tossing his tennis ball in the air. "Roger. Shutdown. We copy 101.4 by 103.6."

The capsule is silent, save for the sound of my breath and the hiss of the oxygen fans. One hundred and one miles below us, the tracking stations are following our flight path and sending numbers through the Teletype to a table in Kansas City. Two computers are there, Basira and Helen, who will convert those numbers into elegant equations.

"*Artemis 9,* this is Kansas. You are confirmed Go for orbit."

Lebourgeois turns his head and grins at me through his helmet. "Congratulations. You are officially an astronaut."

My face hurts. I'm smiling so hard that my cheeks are tight balls of joy. "We have work to do, right?"

"No shortage of it. But, wait—" Terrazas puts a hand on my arm and then gestures to the windows. "Look."

There is nothing to see but that vast blackness. Intellectually, I know that we've passed into the dark side of the Earth. We slide into her shadow and then magic fills the sky. The stars come out. Millions of them in crisp, vivid splendor.

These are not the stars that I remember from before the Meteor. These are clear and steady, without an atmosphere to make them twinkle.

Do you remember the first time you saw the stars again?

I am sitting in a capsule, on my way to the moon.

ACKNOWLEDGMENTS

This book is filled with the power of other people's brains. Let me tell you about some of them.

Very early on, Brandon Sanderson talked me through plot problems when I realized that I had not one book, but two. Stetson Parker's existence is directly his fault.

Liz Gorinsky, my editor, and Jennifer Jackson, my agent, both rolled with it when I came to them and said, "Um . . . two books?"

Many thanks to Diana Rowland. She and I were both on tight deadlines and she's an amazing cheerleader.

My father-in-law, Glenn Kowal, was a Vietnam-era fighter pilot and also a test pilot during the Apollo days. Thanks to him for the spectacular bird strike details and the snow landing.

Derek "Wizard" Benkoski—yes, that Benkoski. In real life, he is an actual Air Force pilot and also knows his aviation history. He helped me with a lot of the pilot jargon, and by "helped" I mean actually wrote some of it. It's like playing Mad Libs. I would have square brackets like, "[More pilot jargon here]" and he would turn them into, "Wright-Patterson Tower, this is Cessna Four One Six Baker at eight thousand five hundred, direct to the field."

Speaking of Mad Libs, I had two actual astronauts filling in the blanks for me as well. Because, seriously, NASA jargon is . . . really jargony.

Kjell Lindgren, astronaut, flight surgeon, CAPCOM, and a willing beta reader. Not only did he supply lines like,

"Today I 'simmed' terminal docking maneuvers and tried to fine-tune RHC inputs through an overly generous deadband." He read the whole thing and saved me from having shuttle-era acronyms in an Apollo-era story. He also took me to Ellison Airfield and let me see the T-38s and let me try on some of his flight gear. I wound up rewriting stuff because of that visit and added a ton of sensory details.

Another astronaut, Cady Coleman, was also amazing about filling in my blanks. She saved me from ginormous errors during the spacewalk-gone-wrong scene, when the hatch wouldn't shut. That scene got totally rewritten because of her input. Whew.

Stephen Granade, rocket scientist, was just amazing. He read the entire novel and supplied pretty much every calculation that Elma spews. I understand none of them.

Jessica Marquez supplied me with a ton of resources about human spaceflight and was a very smart beta reader.

Stacey Berg is another writer and also a medical researcher. Having her on the team was fantastic.

Sheyna Gifford, flight surgeon and virtual Martian, helped me with some of the medical stuff here, but you'll really see her shine in the next book. All I'll say about that is *mwahahaha!*

Andrew Chaikin—read his book *A Man on the Moon*—came in as a last-minute pinch hitter and helped me rework some of that shuttle-era stuff.

Chanie Beckman guided me on the Judaism aspects of Elma's life, helped by David Wohlreich, who is from a Charleston family. More on that in the historical section.

Lucianne Walkowicz is an astronomer at Adler Planetarium and is the one who turned the disaster into a water strike, when she explained how very bad that would be. Without coffee with her, the runaway greenhouse effect would not be part of this novel. Many thanks to Vicky

Hsu and Yung-Chiu Wang, who helped me with various Taiwanese expressions. I just have to trust that they haven't snuck a dirty joke in. Yung-Chiu and I met at NASA social when we roomed together for a launch at the Kennedy Space Center. She was very patient about listening to me gush about sensory details.

My assistants, Beth Pratt and Alyshondra Meacham, kept me sane and my calendar clear so I could work on this.

Then there are my wonderful beta readers, with specific thanks to those who stuck it out to the end of the novel: Chanie Beckman, Hilary Brenum, Nicholas Conte, Peter Hentges, Amy Padgett, Julia Rios, Branson Roskelly, and Eva VonAllmen.

And of course, my family, but I need to call out two of them: My husband, Rob, is very good about letting me ramble about the story at random moments; and my brother, Stephen K. Harrison, who is a historian and helped me with the way the world altered after the Meteor.

Thank them for the stuff that is right in the book. Email me about the stuff that is wrong: anachronisms@maryrob inettekowal.com.

BUT before you do . . . read the Historical Note section, because there are some places where I know I cheated.

HISTORICAL NOTE

Shall we talk about the changes in this timeline? They begin, obviously, before the books start, with the defeat of Truman by Dewey. I did this because I needed a president in office who would be more likely to start the space program a little sooner.

This is because I had boxed myself in on timelines with the novelette "The Lady Astronaut of Mars," to which this is a prequel. I have three other short stories in my "punch-card punk" universe, the first of which, "We Interrupt This Broadcast," is about the asteroid strike. Being short stories, I skimmed the research and didn't think about the fact that in 1952, we were still five years from getting anything into orbit.

As I began researching the novel, I realized that the technology existed to have launched satellites earlier if I made a couple of very small tweaks in the timeline. For instance, in the real world, when Wernher von Braun and his team were brought to the United States, they were held for a couple of years before being allowed to begin work in rocketry. During that time von Braun wrote *Mars: A Technical Novel*, in which he proposed a manned mission to Mars.

The novel is . . . technical. It has charts. It has a table of equations in the back. It demonstrates that von Braun was a brilliant scientist and was incredibly useful for research details. Did I mention the graphs?

The point being that if people had thrown money at him in 1945, von Braun had a plan to get people to Mars. So I put a president in power who would throw money at him, and then I dropped an asteroid on D.C.

For more information about the early days of rocketry, I highly recommend Amy Shira Teitel's *Breaking the Chains of Gravity*, which is a look at spaceflight pre-NASA.

Most of the headlines and articles in this novel are real and are taken from *The New York Times*. I tweaked some of them for historical continuity, but most of them are unchanged.

One that is particularly worth pointing out is the headline about the women taking the astronaut trials. This is a thing that really happened. There were twelve to thirteen of them, depending on how you count it. They were invited to take the tests as a way of gathering data and then political machinations put a stop to it. Before it did, though, the tests were showing that the women could handle higher G-forces and tended to score higher on stress testing. Since one of the women had eight children, I rather imagine that the stress tests seemed relaxing.

Check out *Promised the Moon* by Stephanie Nolen. Several of the women who were in the testing scene were pilots from the real-world tests. In particular, learn more about Jackie Cochran and Jerrie Cobb. When you do? You'll think I modeled Nicole and Elma on them. I didn't, when I created the characters, but once I realized the parallels, I absolutely milked it.

Speaking of Jackie Cochran . . . she created the WASPs and was a founding member of the 99s. Without her, women would have had an even more difficult road to becoming commercial pilots. She was a remarkable and complicated woman.

The WASPs themselves were skilled pilots, and all of the statistics I cited about them are completely true. Including the fact that the only black woman pilot to apply was asked to withdraw her application.

During this time, black air clubs and air shows were extremely popular. I make a nod to Bessie Coleman, who couldn't get her pilot's license in the U.S., due to discrimination laws. So she taught herself and went to Paris to get her license. For more on Miss Coleman, and other African-American aviators and astronauts, check out *Black Wings* by Von Hardesty.

And what about the computers? I have three books you need to read. *Rise of the Rocket Girls* by Nathalia Holt, *Hidden Figures* by Margot Lee Shetterly, and *The Glass Universe* by Dava Sobel. All three of these books focus on the women mathematicians—the "computers"—who powered astronomy and rocketry. They were doing these calculations by hand, with pencil and slide rule, long before mechanical computers were a thing. Could we have gone to the moon without mechanical computers? Women were doing these calculations before the machines were around. The machines were faster—once they started working—but they couldn't design the equations. Those were still all written by hand in the early days. Even if you've seen the film *Hidden Figures,* just go buy the book. It is exhaustive in the details of what these women actually did. Likewise, *Rise of the Rocket Girls* demonstrates women's involvement at the Jet Propulsion Laboratory from day one. They actually had a policy not to hire men for the computer department.

I wrote the novel in 2016, before *Hidden Figures* was published, and when I saw the trailer for the film I bounced around the room with delight, because these were the women I was writing about. I was also so relieved because the stickiest "willing suspension of disbelief" point with my beta readers was the inclusion of women of color in the computer department. These women were there. Helen, in fact, is very loosely based on Helen Yee Chow Ling. Ida Peaks's career path takes some inspiration from Janez Lawson. So

I was relieved when *Hidden Figures* came out, because it was a step toward putting these women back into the histories they were erased from.

In the 1950s a man with an advanced degree in mathematics was an engineer. A woman was a computer. There was a huge discrepancy in the pay rates for those two job titles, even though the women were the ones designing the algorithms that drove much of the space industry. Likewise, white workers were paid more for the same work. I wish that these historical battles did not still have to be fought, but neither of these two statistics has changed.

So could we have gone to the moon without mechanical computers? Maybe. Here is where I'm taking the most liberty. In the real world, most of the early LEOs (low-Earth orbits) were calculated by hand. There were vast teams of human computers working together to do the calculations required for every aspect of the space program.

Once the mechanical computers were reliable, they were faster and—more importantly—did not require the same quantity of skilled labor that the human computing departments did. The mechanical computers also allowed binary transmission of visual images. The Apollo capsules used UNIVAC to track the spacecraft and to decode the signals coming back to Earth.

Honestly, the Lady Astronaut timeline does have mechanical computers, although more limited than in the real world. Could we have gone to the moon with *only* a human computer? Maaaaybe. But we wouldn't have been able to track them, and might not even have been able to communicate with them en route.

Other than that, I tried to play fair with the science in this book.

Some real-world incidents that I "borrowed" and adjusted for the book:

Mr. Wizard really was a pilot in WWII. While he never had a Lady Astronaut on, when I watched episodes of his show I was struck by the fact that the little girls did the same type of science as the boys. He didn't gender it and treated them with intellectual respect. I extrapolated from that to come up with the Lady Astronaut episodes.

The rocket that exploded and came down on the Williams' farm is based on *Mariner 1,* although in that case the range safety officer did his job and blew the rocket up. But the details about the missing hyphen caused by a transcription error are completely true. And in the real world, the fellow who made the mistake got a promotion.

Michael Collins, who was in the command module during *Apollo 11* and was supposed to be on *Apollo 8,* had bone spurs in his neck. The process and recovery that he went through is documented in his excellent autobiography *Carrying the Fire.* I totally stole that and gave it to Stetson Parker.

He also tells of difficulty getting the hatch latched on a capsule after a spacewalk. I took it further, but the inspiration came from him.

Space is really amazing. We tend to focus on the astronauts, but there are thousands of people who are dedicated to the exploration of space. When I visit NASA, I'm always struck by the fact that each person I meet believes that they have the best job and that they are doing something important. And they are. Our timeline hasn't had a disaster to push the space program into high gear, but exploring space is still important. So many aspects of your everyday life come directly from research for the space industry. Computers, satellites, GPS, cordless drills, cell phone calls . . . all of these things were sparked by the people at NASA and the other space programs around the world. We see the astronauts, but they are just the tip of the rocket.

BIBLIOGRAPHY

Chaikin, Andrew. *A Man on the Moon: The Voyages of the Apollo Astronauts*. Penguin Books, 2007.

Collins, Michael. *Carrying the Fire: An Astronaut's Journeys*. Farrar, Straus and Giroux, 2009.

Hadfield, Chris. *An Astronaut's Guide to Life on Earth: What Going to Space Taught Me About Ingenuity, Determination, and Being Prepared for Anything*. Back Bay Books, 2015.

Hardesty, Von. *Black Wings: Courageous Stories of African Americans in Aviation and Space History*. Smithsonian, 2008.

Holt, Nathalia. *Rise of the Rocket Girls: The Women Who Propelled Us, from Missiles to the Moon to Mars*. Back Bay Books, 2017.

Nolen, Stephanie. *Promised the Moon: The Untold Story of the First Women in the Space Race*. Basic Books, 2004.

Roach, Mary. *Packing for Mars: The Curious Science of Life in the Void*. W. W. Norton & Company, 2010.

Scott, David Meerman and Jurek, Richard. *Marketing the Moon: The Selling of the Apollo Lunar Program*. The MIT Press, 2014.

Shetterly, Margot Lee. *Hidden Figures: The American Dream and the Untold Story of the Black Women Mathe-

maticians Who Helped Win the Space Race. William Morrow Paperbacks, 2016.

Sobel, Dava. *The Glass Universe: How the Ladies of the Harvard Observatory Took the Measure of the Stars.* Penguin Books, 2017.

Teitel, Amy Shira. *Breaking the Chains of Gravity: The Story of Spaceflight before NASA.* Bloomsbury Sigma, 2016.

von Braun, Dr. Wernher. *Project MARS: A Technical Tale.* Collector's Guide Publishing, Inc., 2006.